SCARED MONEY

ALSO BY JAMES HIME

The Night of the Dance

SCARED MONEY

JAMES HIME

ST. MARTIN'S MINOTAUR ⚞ NEW YORK

www.minotaurbooks.com

Library of Congress Cataloging-in-Publication Data

Hime, James L.
    Scared money / James Hime.—1st ed.
      p. cm.
    Sequel to: The night of the dance.
    ISBN 0-312-33136-3
    EAN 978-0312-33136-8
    1. Washington County (Tex.)—Fiction. 2. Ex-police officers—Fiction. 3. Missing persons—Fiction. 4. Embezzlement—Fiction. 5. Drug traffic—Fiction. 6. Sheriffs—Fiction. 7. Retirees—Fiction. I. Title.

PS3608.I47S27 2004
813'.6—dc22

2004048179

First Edition: October 2004

10 9 8 7 6 5 4 3 2 1

For my mom and dad, and for Paulette's, too.
It is from you that we learned how to parent.

Mexican Drug Dealers Turning U.S. Towns into Major Depots

—Headline, Front Page, the *New York Times*,
November 16, 2002

. . . the weight of his heart had begun to lift and he repeated what his father had once told him, that scared money cant win and a worried man cant love.

—Cormac McCarthy, *All the Pretty Horses*

One never knows when the blow may fall.

—Graham Greene, *The Third Man*

SCARED MONEY

1

"NOW, DIEDRE, I DON'T WANT YOU MESSIN' AROUND WITH THAT LAMONT Stubbs. Ain't nuthin' but bad can come uh that. You listenin' to yo' mama, chil'?"

Diedre Brown grips the portable telephone to her ear with her shoulder, using her left hand to apply to the nails on her right hand a polish the color of ripe mango, a totally exotic color, makes her feel like she could be a tribal princess on a South Sea Island, going around in a grass skirt, flower lei, nothing else. She holds out her hand so as to admire the color better. It's elegant and it's sexy and her mama wouldn't have sat still for it one minute if she knew about it. But Mama is stuck in the ancestral shotgun house over in Austin County, forced to phone in to town when she wants to burden Diedre with her warnings and her scolds.

"Oh, Mama."

"Don't you 'oh, Mama' me. I want you to *hear* what I'm sayin' to you."

Diedre plunges the little brush back in its bottle, takes the phone in her left hand, starts flicking her right hand like she's shooing flies, the motion sending the bangle bracelets on her right wrist up and down her arm, clacking against one another.

"Yes, Mama, I hear you."

"I mean it, chil'. I may be way out here in Bleiblerville, but I hears things. Peoples talk, is what they do. I knows about the likes of Lamont Stubbs."

Diedre glances at the clock, sees the man is late by a half hour as usual. "What do y'all hear down yonder?"

"I hear he makes his livin' on the wrong side of the law, sellin' drugs to kids." Diedre's mama has that country way of talking, makes the word "kids" sound multisyllabic. *Kee-uds.*

Diedre says, "Oh, Mama, that's just silly. Lamont has him a regular job, down at Mr. Sparkles. You know, the car wash place."

Diedre is smarter than that herself, of course. No way a man can afford to style around like Lamont does, with the jewelry and the clothes and that fine 1999 Lexus ES 300, if all he's got is shammy-cloth jockey pay.

Word among the children is Lamont paid cash for his ride. Walked into the dealership with a briefcase, opened it up, pulled stacks of Benjamins out of it until he got to the man's number. Car salesman stood there with his mouth hanging open.

Diedre knows Lamont's economic activities go well beyond his Mr. Sparkles gig and embrace certain entirely illegitimate pursuits. But it's this very *badness* that attracts her to him. It's that forbidden fruit thing, old as time.

Now her mama is saying, "Well, folks tell me that car wash job ain't all he's got."

I swear, sometimes it's like she's readin' my mind.

A car horn blows out front. Diedre looks through the blinds, sees Lamont's Lexus at the curb. "Listen, Mama," she says. "I need to run. Y'all gon' be around tomorrow?"

"Yes, baby."

"I might come out there, then. Spend the afternoon. Would that be alright?"

"Oh, yes, baby. Yo' daddy would love to see you."

"Okay, then. Good night, Mama."

"Good night, baby. And you stay away from that Lamont Stubbs."

Diedre grabs her purse, heads for the front door, still flipping her hand in the air, bracelets going *clack clack clack*.

Soon as she opens her front door she can hear the bass line coming from the music in Lamont's ride. Lamont's got his favorite CD cranked way up, Notorious B.I.G.'s *Born Again* reverberating off the walls of her little place. *That's another thing mama wouldn't approve of. Biggie's lyrics are way too hot for Bleiblerville.*

When she gets to the curb Lamont leans over, pushes the door open for her. She slides into the bucket seat, gives Lamont a peck on the cheek, says, "How you doin', baby?" Having to speak at about the same decibel level you would use to get somebody's attention across a ten-acre parking lot.

Lamont's got his black hair pulled back in a ponytail, diamond stud in his left earlobe, gold lamé vest covering a black T-shirt, gold chains hanging down, leather pants on. He has a thin beard that runs around his oval jaw, two strips of hair connecting it to a mustache trimmed close. His eyes are close set, hidden behind three-hundred-dollar Maui Jim's.

"I'se doin' good, real good," he shouts back. "You lookin' mighty nice tonight, Diedre. You ready to go to town, have ourselves some fun?"

Diedre can feel Biggie's bass line in her rib cage. The backup singers are singing, *"Notorious! No, No, No, Notorious!"*

"I been lookin' forward to it all week."

"That's what I'm talkin' about."

Lamont pulls away from the curb, slips his hand onto Diedre's thigh, jacking up her heart rate, giving her little electric charges up and down her spine. Then he goes to the sound system, changes the tracks a couple times.

He hollers, "Before we leave town though, I got a little bidness to take care of."

"What's that, baby?"

"There's this dude, see, from up Dallas way, wants a moment of my time. I tol' him I'd check with him this evenin', see if we can't get some shit sorted out."

"We goin' to yo' office then?"

"Baby, I ain't got no office. What I got is more like a street corner."

Lamont steers the Lexus up Main Street through the town square, quiet and dark this time of the evening for the most part, no illumination coming from the stores on account of they close by six o'clock, just a couple lights burning over where the courthouse used to be.

Diedre is thinking how little passes for excitement around this little bitty old town of Brenham, Texas, which is what makes it such a burdensome place to live, nothing interesting ever going down. In a place like this, rich in boredom and poor in everything else, a girl would be insane not to yield to the charms of a fast-living man like Lamont Stubbs. A man with plenty of ready cash, a nice ride, exotic tastes in clothes and music.

Lamont takes a left onto Martin Luther King Avenue, proceeds down it a ways, pulls over into a vacant lot next to a convenience store. Parks beside a black Cadillac Escalade with gold trim. He looks over at Diedre, says, "Won't take but a minute. I'll leave the engine runnin' so's you can listen to the music."

"Lamont. You so thoughtful."

"Yeah."

She watches as he crosses in front of the car, his vest shining in the headlights, then he's out of them, becoming a shadow against the convenience store wall where two other shadows have emerged, a tall one and a short one, their faces obscured, sweatshirt hoods pulled up over baseball caps.

Biggie's singing, *"Check it out, here comes another one."* Looks like the shadows are talking now, with some body motions thrown in, gestures, shoulder shrugs, arm waving, fingers pointed into chests. Then Lamont's shadow turns around, headed back.

Several things happen all at once. The two shadows in sweatshirts make some kind of movement in concert. Two lights split the darkness, one on the right side that's like a pulsing orange flame. The other, on the left, quick, elliptical blips. Lamont's shadow twists, falls to the ground.

The two lights go out. The shadows start walking her way.

"Oh, my God," she says. She reaches over to the door frame, fumbling for the switch, throws the locks. Scrambles to get behind the wheel, trying to lift a leg over the gearshift but her skirt restricts her movement. She jerks her skirt up as high as it will go, throws her leg over the gearshift, grabs the steering wheel for leverage. On the CD player, the backup singers are singing, *"Would you get high with me?"*

She tries to swing her other leg over the gearshift. The dashboard catches her foot. Outside, the shadows are beside the car.

They're singing, *"Would you die for me?"*

Then the windows explode.

At that moment, across town, a man in a business suit is parking a rental car in one of the few empty spots in the parking lot at a high school football stadium. He opens the door, shifts something under his coat, steps into the parking lot. Starts toward the lights, the sounds of band music and cheering.

He is here to talk to a man named Jeremiah Spur.

2

NO ONE WEARS A BUSINESS SUIT TO A HIGH SCHOOL FOOTBALL GAME IN Brenham. Boots, jeans, western shirt, cowboy hat—that's the proper attire. As soon as the man in the suit walks out from under the stands, everybody who sees him knows he isn't from these parts. He looks as out of place as a bird dog at a cotillion.

Among the first to see him is a weathered rancher with mostly gray hair, a jaw like a plow, honest eyes corralled by crows' feet. A man who's spent better than half his life looking for things that don't belong. While the Brenham High offense huddles, Jeremiah Spur watches the man as he stares up at the stands, searching the crowd.

The huddle breaks and the Cubs jog to the line of scrimmage. Jeremiah returns his attention to the football game, the two teams of youngsters facing off over the striped grass, the scene brightly lit by the towers that stand behind the bleachers. The darkness beyond is so complete, it is as though all the light there is has been concentrated here, as though nothing taking place anywhere else in the universe is so worthy of illumination as the exertions of the Brenham Cubbies against their ancient rivals from Brazoswood.

Jeremiah can't think of a better way to top off a week of punching cattle. Brenham is ranked number two in the state, Division 4-A. They run the ball well and pass it even better and the defense is big and fast. Jeremiah fully expects them to pull the little arms and legs off the Brazoswood team, have the Cubbies' scrubs playing before the third quarter is over.

The quarterback takes the snap from center, fakes a handoff to the fullback, and runs down the line, with the tailback trailing behind. Option play. The quarterback flips the ball to the tailback who gains the corner, picks up eight before a Brazoswood cornerback can run him out of bounds. Across the way the band cranks up the Brenham fight song.

A norther had blown in earlier in the week. For an entire day it had rained like a cow pissing on a flat rock, then it had faired off and cooler weather had set in. The breeze still blows out of the north as light and fresh as a child's memory. Jeremiah wears a blue windbreaker over his usual getup, rancher's khakis and boots. His cream-colored Stetson is perched back on his head.

The Cubs break their huddle, spread out along the line of scrimmage, their green and white uniforms opposite the Brazoswood gold and black. The tailback goes in motion, linebackers shift and stunt. Jeremiah shakes his head at how nuanced, how sophisticated the game has gotten at the high school level.

The man in the suit must have found who he was looking for. He's climbing the stairs toward Jeremiah. He's a big guy, in his thirties, fit looking. Hair cut short, military style. Erect posture, serious face. He looks like a repo man come to claim somebody's pickup.

The Cubs' quarterback takes the snap and fakes a handoff to the full-back, rolls to his right just out of reach of a couple of blitzing lineback-ers and throws on the run. The ball rides the north wind downfield. The crowd is on its feet by the time the wide receiver gathers it in and goes racing all the way down the sideline for six points. There's roaring all around. Ten minutes into the game and the Cubbies have scored first.

"Captain Spur?"

Jeremiah looks away from the field into eyes so dark and hard they could be in the head of somebody doing twenty-to-life in Huntsville. "That's right."

Hard Eyes hands him a leather case, the kind people carry business cards in. Jeremiah flips it open as he and the stranger sit down. Inside is an ID card. Says Frederick Wilson Kirby, Office of the Deputy Director of Operations, Central Intelligence Agency. Has Hard Eyes' picture on it.

Jeremiah flips the case closed, hands it back to the suit. Out on the field the Brenham kicker sends the ball through the goalposts.

Watching the teams headed to the sidelines Jeremiah says, "I worked a case once. Gunrunner out of El Paso who was still passing himself off as CIA even though the Company had previously off-loaded him. Had an ID badge he had fashioned for himself with the help of a copy shop. Looked about as good as the one you got there, Mr. Kirby."

"You worked with Spencer Tillman in the Inspector General's Office. The gunrunner's name was Paco Chavez and we had used him from time to time in Central America before he went nutso."

"You can always tell a fed."

"Yeah?"

"But you can't tell him much. I'm watchin' a football game here."

"Spencer sends his regards, by the way. He's only got a couple years to go before he hits the rocking chair."

"Be sure and howdy him for me, next time y'all run into one another."

"Your country needs a minute or two of your time. It won't take long."

Jeremiah looks at the Agency man. "Alright, then. You talk and I'll listen while I watch the Cubbies, see if they can hold on to their lead. Maybe even pad it some."

"Not here, sir. Out in the parking lot, if you don't mind." Fred Kirby's got an accent that's Back Bay Boston, like he's rehearsing to play JFK in a TV movie, makes the word "parking" sound like "packing."

Jeremiah hesitates, then shrugs. They stand up, walk down the bleacher steps, Jeremiah watching over the Company man's head as the Brazoswood fullback dives into the line for maybe a yard, stifled by the middle linebacker, Rudy Schoppe's kid, the one that spends his summers pitching hay bales around for fun. Under the bleachers they walk through the crowd, mostly kids chasing one another, people standing in line at the one concession stand, folks queued up to get into the facilities.

Jeremiah's boots crunch across the parking lot gravel until he gets to his pickup. Out here away from the lights he can see a star or two in the sky.

He turns, says, "This alright? Or would you rather sit in the vehicle?"

Fred Kirby's eyes have disappeared into the shadows cast by his forehead. "This will do."

"Alright then. Speak your piece."

"Okay. A few years back, when our people were . . . active in Eastern Europe, there was this guy. He was indigenous to the area. We had him do jobs for us, jobs that were particularly difficult or dangerous or—"

"You're sayin' y'all used him to cap folks."

"Yeah. And he was good at it. Really good. It was like he had a special gift for it, or just enjoyed it in some unnatural way. Maybe it was in his blood. He's Hungarian by origin and they can be a particularly violent people. So this guy—"

"He have a name?"

"His name is Farkas. Benjamin Farkas. The deal we made with him back then—more or less at his insistence—was that once we didn't need him anymore we would bring him to the U.S., set him up in business, let him live out the rest of his life in peace. So in the late 1980s he moved to Dallas, started a few businesses—"

"Like what he was in back home?"

"No. These were legit. Real estate development, brokerage, that kind of thing. We got him started like we promised and then we cut our ties. We sort of hoped we had heard the last from him, to be honest. And that was the way it was for over ten years. Then last week, he called. He wanted something from us."

Jeremiah reaches into his pocket for a piece of nicotine gum and pops it into his mouth. "Go on. I'm listenin'."

"Mr. Farkas told us one of his key people had gone missing, along with some money. A very considerable amount of money. He wanted help finding his missing employee. That put us in kind of a bind, you see, because—"

"Because y'all can't operate domestically and you ain't about to go to the FBI, own up to having invited some Hungarian button man to live here, ask them to help find some hired hand who had vamoosed on the guy."

"I had heard you don't mince words, Captain Spur. We told him no can do. He understood our difficulty and had an idea of his own. Somebody else he could call on for help. Somebody outside the government."

"I'm his idea?"

"That's right."

"How come him to pick me?"

"He didn't say and we didn't ask. Although I suppose we could guess. Anyway, we kind of liked his suggestion. I mean, you're retired from law enforcement, so there aren't any delicate cross-jurisdictional issues. We've worked with you and know how good you are. You could have been one of us if you had wanted. I mean that as a compliment."

Jeremiah grunts and works the gum in his jaw.

"So we told Mr. Farkas we would come to you on his behalf."

Over in the stadium a roar builds and the band fires up the fight song.

"Listen to that," says Jeremiah. "You done made me miss a touchdown."

"We would like for you to speak with Mr. Farkas, Captain Spur."

"And I'd like you to go to hell."

"He said you would say that. He told us when you did, we should tell you he knew your father."

"Now I know one of two things is true. Either he's lyin'. Or you are."

"Captain Spur, he's not lying. My agency knows this to be true."

"Prove it."

"I can't. You'll have to take me at my word."

Jeremiah Spur chews his nicotine gum. "You're startin' to work my patience."

"Mr. Farkas is sending his private jet to pick you up at the Washington County airport tomorrow morning at ten o'clock. I'd pack a bag for a few days if I were you."

"I got a herd to attend to."

"We'll send around a couple guys to take care of that for you. They'll be at your place first thing tomorrow. You'll have plenty of time to show them the ropes before you leave."

"Y'all done thought of everything, huh?"

"The United States government appreciates your help, Captain Spur."

Kirby holds out a hand. Jeremiah's stays by his side. The man drops his hand. "I'll let you get back to your football game now."

Jeremiah watches him walk to a car and get in it and drive off.

That wind out of the north suddenly doesn't seem so light and fresh. Jeremiah turns up his jacket collar up and stares at the ground.

3

WASHINGTON COUNTY DISTRICT ATTORNEY SONYA NICHOLS STARTS THE water running in her oversized tub, tosses in some of the seaweed-based muscle soak she got for Christmas last year from her gentleman friend, Deputy Clyde Thomas. She flips a switch and the water commences to churn, a thick layer of greenish bubbles building up.

She peels out of her workout gear and slides in. The hot water feels good after an hour of driveway one-on-one basketball.

Directly here comes Clyde, fresh beer in each hand, nothing on, looking like a big black exclamation point against the bathroom's white theme, a smaller black exclamation point cranking itself up between his legs. *This does not qualify as news.*

Clyde hands her a beer, slides into the water. "Yo! This mother be hot!"

"The better to loosen your muscles with, my dear. You seem to have one muscle that's getting tighter, though. Maybe we should add some more hot water."

Clyde leans back and leers. "Oh, baby, I can think of a much better way to loosen it, you know what I'm sayin'?"

"How about we just relax for a while, okay?" She closes her eyes, feels the water jets working, easing the lactic acid buildup. But now there's a toe poking around down below the bubbles somewhere causing her to crack open a critical eye. "Just where do you think you're going with that foot, Junior?"

"I'se just tryin' to stretch out, you know, get relaxed, like you was sayin' not thirty seconds ago. Man, you suspicious."

"Yeah. Right."

They're quiet for a while. Then Clyde says, "Sonya, honey?"

"Uh-huh."

"Lately I kind of been thinkin'."

"About what?"

" 'Bout how to advance my law enforcement career past the rut it's done dropped itself into here in Cow Turd, Texas, where there ain't nothin' ever goin' on."

"You mean nothing going on other than white racists blowing up the courthouse?"

"Man, that was months ago. Now we back to the same ol' shit, ain't had so much as a B and E all summer. It's so quiet a mouse fart sound like a sonic boom."

"So you're getting restless."

"That's right. I been goin' through my options and I come up with one."

"Which would be what?"

"Maybe I ought to be checkin' out the Department of Public Safety, see if I can get on with them."

Sonya opens her eyes, sits up, looks straight at Clyde. He has his big hands resting on the rim of the tub, the water glistening on his upper body, highlighting the muscles in his arms and shoulders. His face is indecipherable. "What, highway patrol?"

"Uh-huh. They's s'posed to be needin' some good black talent."

"But, Clyde, you hire on with them, they could post you anywhere. Down in Brownsville, up in Pampa, out in Midland–Odessa, anywhere in between."

"That's what I know."

"You're saying you're prepared to leave Brenham?"

"May not have much choice if I wants to keep growin' my career. I got like all kinds of untapped potential. What's happenin' is, it's goin' to waste 'round here."

"But exactly where would that leave us?"

"Shit if I know. I ain't worked it all out in my head just yet."

Why, you big jerk. I ought to run your thoughtless ass out of this tub. Out of this house. Out of this life.

She's thinking what a fool she is for loving this moody shithead with his Bad Nigger attitude, his selfishness, all the other fleas that come with this particular dog. Now there's a thought. "What about the attitude, Clyde?"

"What about it?"

"Look, the Highway Patrol is not the Washington County Sheriff's Department. You would have to get a real grip or those guys would bounce you like you had Spalding written on your side."

"Hey, I been workin' on learnin' how to be all sweet and shit. I ain't lost my temper since I don't know when."

"Okay, great. But showing respect full time to authority, even when maybe it's a white man who's not as smart as you? You'd have to commit to a major long-term personality change, strong as a fundamentalist commits to the Ten Commandments."

"What? You think I ain't up to it?"

Damn if he's not serious. Sonya looks around, her redone bathroom as beautiful as she had imagined it would be when she was designing it, planning it, working on it with Team Stereotype—her mental nickname for her church-mouse-poor architect, gay interior designer, contractor in bib overalls. She has made the place such that it's ready for its own *Southern Living* spread. But it's still just a house, just walls and paint and paper and furniture, and it's got an emptiness to it.

After all these years of living by herself, Sonya is ready for some full-time company, somebody to come home to in the evenings, even somebody to fight with from time to time. Even if there's no fighting to be done or hoops to be shot or love to be made and basically there's nothing to do but stare at the walls she has made so pretty, she'd like to have someone else in this house to do that with.

She says, "I have a better idea for you."

"What do that be?"

"Why don't you move in here with me for a while—"

"Now, baby, why you wanna go and—"

Sonya holds up her hand. "Wait. Stop. Hold it a minute. Don't start getting all defensive. Just hear me out. Move in here just long enough to get your bearings, sort out your future, make sure you've thought your options all the way through. Then, if you decide the best way to advance your career is by hiring on with the DPS, it won't have been out of impulse. You'll have made an intelligent choice."

Clyde swallows some beer, slides a little farther down. "Yeah, but I ain't sure movin' in here with you is such a good idea. I'm like old Mr. Lion in the jungle, I needs my room, you know, to run and hunt, like that."

"What exactly is it you want to hunt?"

"Come on, baby. You know what I mean."

"Yeah, I bet I do. Only too well." Sonya sips her beer. "Look, why don't you think it over, Mr. Lion? You'll still have lots of running room, operating out of here as your base. Come on, give it a try. You know, it could be a lot of fun."

She leans forward, hands under the water, grabs him.

His eyes widen. "Oh, baby." He reaches for her, starts stroking her with his fingertips. Her breath is getting shorter, her heart pounding. She slides closer to him.

He kisses her hard, his tongue deep inside her mouth, his fingers still working her, then moving down her body. He starts shifting his body.

She whispers, "Maybe we ought to dry off, go to the bedroom."

"Yeah. That's a good idea."

From across the room where Clyde had dropped his jeans, a cell phone commences to ring. Clyde rolls his eyes.

Sonya whispers, "Let voice mail get it."

He shakes his head, stands up in the bathtub, water and soap suds running down his body. "I can't. That's Bobby Crowner's ring."

"His ring?"

"I programmed it in special. Told him not to use it, 'less he had an on-duty 'mergency. Maybe I can just call him back."

He towels himself off while he walks across the room, grabs the cell phone. Sonya slides down farther into the water.

"Yo, Bobby, what's up, man? . . . What? . . . When did this go down? . . . Was a girl, too? . . . Okay, where you at now? . . . Alright. Why don't you see if you can get the DPS to send a crime scene search team 'round. I'm gon' come on over there myself. Don't touch nothin' 'til I get there, you know what I'm sayin? And keep all the civilians away. . . . Yeah. See you shortly."

Sonya sits up, soapy water running off her breasts. "What's going on?"

Clyde starts dressing. "You remember Lamont Stubbs?"

"The pusher?"

"That'd be him. Couple stiffs done turned up over in the 'hood, and Bobby thinks Lamont might be one of 'em. Looks like somebody might of popped a box of caps in that nigger's bucket of extra crispy. Some girl caught it, too. Bobby says he wants some help with the ID, but I think it's more like he's in over his head. He's a good fertilizer salesman, but he ain't much of a cop."

Sonya gets out of the tub, starts drying off. "Mind if I join you?"

Clyde shrugs. "Why would I mind?"

4

His most unforgettable childhood memory is from that night in 1956. He can still see them in his mind's eye, those legs kicking helplessly in midair, silhouetted against the yellow wash of the Budapest streetlight. On the sidewalks and in the street below where the man hung jerking, a crowd stood and cheered.

He had watched from the window of his family's fourth-floor flat as the crowd surged down the Nagykörút, carrying torches and weapons. Pushing before them a man, his hands bound behind his back. Someone tossed a rope over a lamppost. All their heads turned up as the man was hoisted by his neck. They cheered as though their team had scored a goal at a football match. He had stood transfixed by the sight.

His father had come into the room and walked to the window and pulled the blinds closed with a jerk and leaned down in his face. He smelled of onions and tobacco. "You must stay away from the windows."

"But, Father, that man—"

"That was an AVH man. Stay away from the windows."

An AVH man, he thought. If they are hanging the secret police, then the uprising must be succeeding.

Long into that night, even after he had gone to bed, he could still hear the crowds in the street. Cheering as though another goal had been scored. And another. And yet another.

5

THE NEAR NORTH SIDE IS WORLDS APART FROM SONYA'S NEAT LITTLE
neighborhood of clean yards and fancy homes and water oaks that grace
the median of her wide boulevard. She glimpses these precincts in frag-
ments like still photographs through the window of Clyde's cruiser—
vacant lots conquered and occupied by the forces of decay and neglect,
broken bottles, fast food wrappers, God only knows what else lurking close
to the ground in the darkness. Shotgun houses leaning this way and that,
abandoned vehicles, hurricane fences with gaps in them. Potholes like a
pox on the streets. In this neighborhood razor wire is an amenity. She
wonders if the people who first lived here had hopes for something better.

Clyde parks in front of a convenience store next to another couple
of units from the Sheriff's Department and ambulance, their lights going
on top. Two deputies, white guys named Jake Goodman and Bobby
Crowner, are standing next to a vacant lot with yellow crime scene tape
strung around it. A handful of onlookers, all of them black, mill around
visiting with one another like shoppers who had showed up early for a sale
at a five-and-dime and were waiting for the doors to open. Inside the
marked-off area, a late model sedan idles, headlights on, rap music blaring.

"Yo, Jake," Clyde says, "you wanna go shut off that bullshit music so
we can hear ourselves think?"

The deputy with the handlebar mustache and the cleft chin says, "Happy
to. Them lyrics is vile." He ducks under the crime scene tape. Directly, the
music stops.

Clyde hollers, "Thanks, man." He turns to Bobby. "Where'd ol' Jake
learn a word like 'vile'?"

"Sunday School, prob'ly. I don't know how he can even understand
them danged lyrics. Just sounded like a lotta noise to me."

"So what y'all got, man?"

Bobby points back in the direction of the lot. "Two bodies over yon-
der, male on the ground, female in the car, shell casings all over Creation.
Looks to be multiple gunshot wounds on both. We make the male to be
Lamont, but you should have a look for yourself."

"You called the medical examiner yet?"

"Paged him. He's probably over at the Cubs game. We also put a call into the DPS, like you wanted. They done dispatched over a Crime Scene Investigation Vehicle. We got lucky on account of it was already in Smithville, just through processin' a scene. Oughta be here any time now."

"Let's go check out them bodies, then."

This is why Sonya had wanted to come out here. To see that rarest of rare things in Brenham, a violent crime scene, and to see it fresh, as it was being investigated. To face the death that is here. Sudden, violent, messy death.

She has some familiarity with it, but not much. She knows it's impor-tant to her ability to do her job, to be able to walk where death has been, coolly, professionally, without nervousness, fear. Nausea. She had little in her life to prepare her for it.

As Bobby leads them under the crime scene tape, her heart begins to pound. She follows Clyde and Bobby through the trash and weeds, Bobby showing the way with his flashlight. When they get to the car, Bobby points the beam through a shattered window. Sonya's insides start to get active. A young black woman lies sprawled across the bucket seats, her legs tangled in the gearshift. Glass and blood cover everything, her body, the upholstery, the floor. They can see wounds in her legs, torso, and head.

"God damn," Clyde says.

Sonya's hand goes to her nose. "You know her?" Her voice comes out squeaky.

"With half her face blowed off, it's kinda hard to say for sure, but I don't think so. But I know this whip. Belongs to Lamont." Clyde turns, points deeper into the vacant lot. "The other vic over thataway?"

"Yeah."

They follow Bobby over to what looks like a pile of wet clothes heaped up on the ground. Clyde takes the flashlight, leans down, shines it into the face of a dead black man, eyes open, staring.

Clyde straightens up, shines the flashlight up and down the length of the body. "That's Lamont, alright. What else you got, man? Any wit-nesses?"

"Just one so far. Guy that minds the counter at that store. He called it in."

"What do the dude say?"

"Says he seen a black Escalade with gold trim driving away from the scene. Says it was really skinnin' it back."

"Don't suppose the man got a look at the tags."

"Nope. Didn't see no tags and didn't see no people, neither."

"You gonna talk to any these other folks that's hangin' around?"

"Yep. Jake's over there doin' that now."

They look toward the street, see Jake collecting blank looks and head-shakes and shoulder shrugs.

Clyde says, "Looks like y'all got control of it 'til the DPS gets here. If y'all don't need nothin' else from me this evenin', I think I'll bounce on outta here on account of this ain't how I planned to spend my Friday night, you know what I'm sayin'?"

"Fair enough. 'Preciate you comin' over and all, helpin' with the vic ID."

"I'll check with y'all tomorrow." He says to Sonya, "C'mon, let's go on home."

As they head over to Clyde's cruiser, a vehicle having the body style of an ambulance, "DPS Crime Scene Investigation Vehicle" written on the side, pulls up and parks in front of the convenience store. The passenger's-side door swings open, and a woman of about thirty, wearing jeans and a leather jacket over a T-shirt, steps out. She has skin the color of roasted almonds, eyes like sparklers, hair worked into beaded braids, nails painted Smith & Wesson silver. Her body would set off a riot in a monastary.

Clyde stops in his tracks. "Oh, shit."

Sonya says, "What?"

The other doors to the CSIV open and four guys get out. Two start unloading gear, the other two head toward the Lexus. But the black lady makes straight for Clyde.

"How you doin', sweetie?" she says, flashing white teeth. "Long time no see. I heard you split from Big D, somehow landed in this little nothin' town, with a deputy gig. Hard to believe it, but here you are. Tragic, you ask me." She stops in front of Clyde.

He says, "How y'all are, Yolanda?"

She gives Clyde a big hug, stands back, holding him at arm's length, says, "Fine, sugar, now I got my eyes on you again." She looks him up and down. "Word is you took up with a white woman." She looks over at Sonya, then back at Clyde. Jerks her head in Sonya's direction. "This ain't her, is it, baby?"

The look on Sonya's face would stop a charging rhinoceros.

Yolanda lets go of Clyde, says, "Don't I get an introduction, baby?"

Clyde does a little throat clearing. "Yeah, man. Yolanda Banks, this is my, uh, lady friend. Sonya Nichols. She's the DA."

Yolanda sticks out her hand. Sonya takes it like she would the hand of disease itself.

"District attorney, huh?" says Yolanda. "That's big stuff."

"Pleased to meet you," Sonya says unconvincingly.

Yolanda turns back to Clyde. "You got my message, right? One I left about a month ago, sayin' I'd got on with the DPS? How come you didn't return my call, baby?"

Somebody calls "Yolanda!" from over near the Lexus.

She hollers back, "Alright! I'm comin'!" She turns back to Clyde. "We can talk later." She nods at Sonya, gives her a big smile, walks off.

Sonya says, "So, Clyde. *Baby*. Yolanda?"

Clyde watches Yolanda walk off toward the crime scene, made bright now by spotlights running off a generator in the CSIV. The medical examiner, who had just pulled up in his sedan, is walking behind her. Clyde looks back at Sonya. "We acquaintances from way back. Went to college together. That's all."

"That's the whole story?"

"Pretty much."

"Pretty much. But she apparently likes to phone you now and then to keep you posted on her life, I guess."

"That was bullshit, man. I ain't never got no voice mails from her."

"Uh-huh. And I guess along with buying that I'm supposed to believe it's just a coincidence she works for the DPS. The same DPS you've been thinking about hiring on with, Old Mr. Lion."

Clyde clears his throat, runs a hand across his shaved head. "That's exactly right. A coincidence is just what it is. Besides, she's crime scene search. I'se thinkin' 'bout highway patrol. So don't go actin' like they's dots to be connected or some shit."

Sonya's eyes harden. "You know what? I feel like the monkey who was humping the skunk."

"Say what?"

"I've enjoyed about as much of this as I can stand. Come on. Let's go home."

Clyde looks off in the direction of the vacant lot. "On second thought, I'm thinkin' I ought to hang here awhile."

"Excuse me?"

"You know, help out with the crime scene processin' and all. I mean, we don't get all that many homicides, 'round here, and tonight we got ourselves a double. No tellin' what the DPS might need, you know, by way of local color."

"You're local color all of a sudden?"

"Maybe I can get Bobby to run you home."

Sonya folds her arms in front of her, gives Clyde some posture, then turns on her heel, marches off to find Deputy Crowner.

Watching her walk off like that, Clyde's body is saying, *Man, I can still feel her hand on that thing of ours. What'd you want to let her go off like that for?*

Then he looks over where Yolanda is, backlit by spotlights like she was Mary J. Blige or somebody, talking with a guy from the forensics team. *Yeah, but this one over here, remember what that's like? Maybe we ought to go check it out, just for variety.*

That part about them being "just acquaintances" back in college? Bullshit, plain and simple. Yolanda had arrived at Prairie View, fresh from the home of the most Pentecostal people in Lufkin, Texas—folks who talked in tongues, handled snakes, thought the Pope was the Antichrist. Released at last from her East Texas mind jail, she made it clear on arrival she thought college was intended to be one extended post–high school coming-out party, a four-year fuckathon.

It seems to Clyde that happens a lot, the kids of the super-strict storing up all their wildness in some special locker God had the sense to equip them with, a locker which blows open as soon as they and their folks no longer share the same zip code.

Clyde was a junior criminology major when Hurricane Yolanda hit campus. They met on a blind date and then she spent three months using his bed for a trampoline before dropping him like he had body parasites and taking up with a player on the college basketball team, a swing man from Enid, Oklahoma. By then Clyde had been so used up, his grades suffered so much, he was almost glad Yolanda had found some other post to scratch.

But the memory of those days is sweet standing here, watching her backside twitch as she walks around under the klieg lights. Old Mr. Lion saunters off in that direction. He can hear Yolanda giving orders, telling this one to dust the Lexus for prints, that one to take photographs, make sketches, the other two to do the grid search.

When she's done barking at the others, Clyde says, "How can I help y'all out?"

Yolanda looks at him a moment, says, "Staying out of the way would be a good start, baby." She walks over to talk to Doc Hutcheson, who's leaning over what's left of Lamont Stubbs.

Clyde approaches the dude who's lifting prints off the Lexus. The man is down on one knee next to the passenger's-side door.

"Yo," he says. "I'm Clyde Thomas. I'm a deputy sheriff here in Brenham."

The guy is dusting powder lightly on the side of the door. He glances up at Clyde, then goes back to what he's doing. "Is that a fact?" he says.

"Yeah. I know Yolanda, too, from back when we was at Prairie View together."

"Was she a hard-ass back then, too?" The guy asks this without looking up.

"She always been kinda feisty."

"Feisty, huh?" The guy leaves off brushing, looks up at Clyde, pushes his eyeglasses back up on his nose. "You want to see feisty, you just keep bothering me while I'm trying to lift prints off this vehicle, or do anything else to mess up this crime scene."

"Hey, man, I'm a cop. I got every right to be here, and you can't do shit about it."

"I ain't talkin' about me. I'm talkin' about her." He points off in Yolanda's direction with his brush, then goes back to work on the car. "You get in her way and she'll rip you an off-brand asshole."

Clyde shrugs, walks over to the convenience store, looking for a comfortable spot on the wall to lean against, watch the DPS from a safe distance.

For three hours they process the scene, taking pictures, making sketches and notes, bagging and tagging evidence, lifting prints, all under the bright lights set up by the CSIV team. Yolanda moves around giving orders, correcting little things here and there, now and then bending down to look at something up close. About halfway through the process, the bodies are hauled off by ambulance.

When the DPS is done and the rest of the team is busy collecting their gear, Yolanda goes to the back of the CSIV, starts looking at the sketches and photographs. Clyde walks over to see what she's up to.

"Lookee here, baby," she says to him. She holds out a sketch of the scene, points with a silver painted nail. "Looks like the two of them parked here, the dude probably at the wheel. He gets out, leaves the engine running, which says to me he must not have expected to be here long. Walks back yonder to visit with somebody. Whoever he was meetin' opened up on him. The girl watches all this goin' down, see, tries to get over into the driver's seat, bounce on outta here. But she gets hung up on the gearshift and buys it on the console. From the looks of the brass, how it was patterned on the ground, we make two shooters."

Yolanda picks up a plastic baggie with a driver's license in it. "You know this Diedre Brown?"

"Naw, man. Ain't never heard of her." He takes it, looks at the address.

"Not your style, huh, baby? When'd you decide to switch to white meat?"

"You'd like Sonya if you got to know her, you know what I'm sayin'?" He hands the driver's license back. "I got the address memorized. I'll check her out. The Brown girl, I mean."

"I didn't think you meant the white girl, baby."

"I knew the dude, though. Lamont Stubbs. Big fish in the local drug scene."

"Who would want to cancel his library card?"

"Ain't got no idea just at the moment. Gonna need to nose around some before I can say. What else we got?"

"Not much other than their brass. Something like thirty-five casings. They must've emptied a couple clips apiece. Look to be nine milli. I'm guessin' two different guns, machine pistol and semiautomatic, somethin' like that. We'll take 'em back to Austin, run 'em through ballistics, check 'em out on DRUGFIRE."

"That's like that computerized ballistics deal, right?"

"Yeah, baby. It's a networked database of ballistics evidence collected by police departments, ATF, the FBI, from all around the country. If these weapons been used in another killing anywhere in the last few years, and slugs or casings from that other scene have been processed and scanned in, we'll know about it."

"When you think you'll have some kinda report?"

Yolanda cogitates some. "We're s'pposed to do things first in, first out. Which means we ought to work this case after we finish that shotgun killin' we did earlier today over in Smithville. But since it's you, baby, we'll start with this one first thing tomorrow. By the time we done processin' everything we got, I'd guess Sunday evening."

"Alright. I'll be seein' if I can figure out what ol' Lamont was up to. You gonna call me when y'all get done up yonder?"

Yolanda flashes a smile at him. "I got a better idea."

"What?"

"Why don't you come on up to Austin Sunday afternoon? We can sit down, go over it together, then maybe get some dinner. Talk about old times."

Clyde starts to say something, then hesitates.

Yolanda puts on a fake frown. "What? Your boss lady won't let you leave town without her permission?"

"Same ol' Yolanda. Can't see your way clear to play fair. What time?"

Yolanda is smiling again. "How 'bout four o'clock. That'll give us a couple hours. Then we can catch dinner and the sunset at the Oasis over on Lake Travis."

"You on. Where you wanna meet?"

"Out at the crime lab. You know where Camp Mabry is?"

"Yeah, sure."

She closes the back door to the CSIV. "See you then, darlin'. Wear somethin' nice too. The Oasis ain't no Prairie View dive."

As Clyde heads back to his car, he's thinking how he hasn't seen this woman a single time in better than ten years and now inside of one evening she has come along and rearranged all his mental furniture, not to mention getting him crosswise with Sonya. What he would really like to know is, had she done it on purpose or was it just Yolanda being Yolanda, only older since he last saw her and that much more dangerous?

And he'd also like to know just how much misery he has signed up for.

6

SATURDAY MORNING, STRAIGHT UP TEN O'CLOCK. FROM BEHIND THE WHEEL of his pickup Jeremiah Spur watches the little red-and-white jet land at the Washington County airport, smoke kicking up under its tires, engines roaring in reverse thrust. He considers his reservations about this affair, how they're growing at some power inversely proportional to the time he has left to board that aircraft. Pretty soon they'll be nigh unto infinity.

The jet taxis toward a shack that has a sign above it reading Brenham Flight Base Operations. Jeremiah gets out of his pickup and heads toward the Brenham FBO.

The pilot of the Falcon 50 turns in his seat and leans Jeremiah's way and says, "We'll be landing in about fifteen minutes, sir."

Jeremiah says, "Much obliged." He looks around at the mahogany trim, cream-colored leather seats, entertainment system with DVD player, fully stocked bar, all so high tech it makes a man who punches cattle for a living feel as anachronistic as a barrage balloon. He wishes Martha were here so he could show it off to her. Then he thinks about why he's here and decides he's glad she's completely unaware of it.

He thinks of the letter that came yesterday. The first thing that caught his eye was the return address embossed on the stationery. Silver Lakes, Bethel, Connecticut. No indication of what Silver Lakes is. Could be a resort or a spa for all anybody knew. One of the keys to getting Martha to go had been their show of how discrete they are. Bless her heart, she was more afraid of being talked about than she was of the devil himself.

He had read it so often now he had just about memorized it. She had written of the trip up yonder, the check-in process, what her room was like, her first dinner with the other "inmates" as she'd called them, the coming week's treatment schedule. How she had hated that it had come to this, but now that she was there, she was glad to be doing something about her drinking problem instead of just letting it continue to fester in her as it had for lo these many years.

He takes a swallow of the bottled water that sits in the cup holder at his elbow, looks down at the earth far below. Works the nicotine gum in his jaw. His love for her is like what the physicists say about the speed of light. It's constant in all frames of reference. The moment she had disappeared down the jetway over at Houston Intercontinental, boarding her flight back east, he felt as though the wind of life had left, as though his soul were at sea in the horse latitudes.

And if Martha hadn't finally agreed to go up yonder for thirty days of treatment he more than likely wouldn't be sitting here right now, on his way to Dallas to meet this paid killer turned real estate tycoon. Why would a man want to absent himself from the company of the woman he loves if he didn't have to?

Sure, from time to time he misses the action. Jeremiah had been retired from law enforcement almost a year and but for that sorry Sissy Fletcher business last spring had pretty much stayed clear of it. He had stuck to his ranching, tended to the beef cattle business. And to the business of trying to help his wife get over their own daughter dying from leukemia. Tended to the business of trying to get over that himself.

As though he ever could.

They're descending toward Dallas now, streets full of Saturday morning traffic, residential neighborhoods, shopping centers, and, off in the distance, the tall buildings downtown. He listens to the flaps extend and the landing gear deploy.

The young man who meets him as he deplanes is so well turned out it makes Jeremiah's ass hurt. No older than thirty, every blond hair on his head blown perfectly into place, cobalt blue eyes, flawless teeth beaming a smile so bright it looks like it could cause skin cancer. He's dressed in chinos and a golf shirt.

The kid steps forward and sticks out a hand and flashes the high beams in his mouth and says, "Captain Spur? Bruce Snyder. I work for Mr. Farkas. Welcome to Dallas, sir. How was your flight?"

Jeremiah shakes the kid's hand. "Fine, I reckon."

"Great. Come on. I have a vehicle waiting in the parking lot."

Directly Bruce is using his teeth to try to blind Jeremiah from behind the wheel of a Ford Explorer as he drives away from Love Field. "First time in Dallas, sir?"

Jeremiah fetches his dark glasses out his shirt pocket, pops them on his head. "Nope. Was born here. So where is it we're goin'?"

Bruce uses a manicured index finger as a pointer. "Over to catch the

Tollway, take it out to LBJ, to the Dallas Galleria area. That's where our offices are."

Jeremiah chews his nicotine gum, examines the scenery. Convenience stores, strip clubs, hamburger joints. Listens to this young feller having himself some small talk. *Maybe I ought to engage him some, ask about Farkas, find out what this boy does for him, how long he's been in the man's employ.*

But then, of a sudden, he's not interested in visiting. He's preoccupied instead with a memory from forty-five years ago, a memory of the day when he left his Dallas boyhood behind. He was riding in the backseat of his grandparents' car, with the two of them up front, his grandmother still crying some over her daughter's sudden passing. He had watched as Dallas slipped away, wondered what his new life on a Texas cattle ranch just outside the town of Brenham was going to be like.

Had wondered what it was going to be like, growing up an orphan.

7

It was, he knew, exceedingly contrary to align himself with the French and against his own people. But his father had banished him to his bedroom, cutting off his access to the picture window overlooking the Nagykörút and the glorious history being made there. Banishment and deprivation always made him feel contrary.

In his windowless little room a twin bed was shoved against one wall and his desk sat at right angles to it with a lamp on top that provided the only light. A bookshelf ran along the wall above his bed, and there he kept his histories, his copies of Tolstoy, Petőfi, Hesse. And, of course, the Englishman. Mr. Greene. Someday he wanted to write like Mr. Greene.

The two armies faced off over a square meter of worn blue throw rug, Napoleon to the left, the Allies to the right. The Battle of Austerlitz in miniature, ready to be played out through the hands of a fifteen-year-old god. He had not made his bedroom floor into a battlefield in many years, but there was little else to do. The events in the streets had him too agitated to read.

Soon the Allies made their key error, weakening their defense of the Pranzen Heights—represented by a copy of Tolstoy, the cover of which was coming loose—in an effort to turn Napoleon's right flank. Napoleon ordered Soult's corps to take the Heights. There the battle raged, while on the left Lannes overcame and isolated Bagration's 13,700 men. Soon the battle was in its final stages, the Allied army split into three separate retreating units, with General Doctorov's broken troops running for their lives across the frozen lakes and marshlands to the south.

Napoleon was just turning his artillery toward Saschon Pond when the fifteen-year-old god heard the phone ringing. He got up, slipped to his bedroom door, opened it a crack. Down the hall, he could see his father, dressed in a sweater, gray trousers, slippers, holding a newspaper, lifting the handset, speaking for a few minutes, then replacing it. His father turned his direction, and he ducked behind the door.

"You are not going to do this, László," he heard his mother say. The anxiety in her voice raised it an octave, and his heartbeat quickened.

"My dear, I must."

"But, please, tell me why. Tell me why you must leave us and—" Voice faltering, almost in tears now. He heard them pass down the hall.

His father's voice in reply was soft, too soft for him to hear all the words, just "Nagy himself," "engage the West," "have to try."

Then he heard his mother's footsteps as she ran down the hall toward the front of the apartment. In the background, her muffled sobs. Five minutes later, the sound of his father's street shoes moving down the hall, the opening and closing of the front door.

He waited awhile longer, listening. Then he slipped out of his bedroom and walked quietly through the apartment to the kitchen. He found his mother sitting at the kitchen table, crying, tearing at her hair, hair already almost entirely gray even though she was not yet forty. She did not look up, and he did not know what to do.

So he returned to his room where on his order Napoleon's artillery dispatched two thousand Russian soldiers to their deaths at the bottom of Saschon Pond.

8

IT'S AROUND TEN IN THE MORNING WHEN CLYDE WALKS OUT THE FRONT door of the little farmhouse, closing the screen door behind him as quietly as he can so it won't make a loud and disrespectful racket. Wincing even as he eases it home at the way the spring screeches.

Diedre Brown's mama and daddy are inside, perched in staring and woeful disbelief above that hole that had opened up in their lives with no warning, there now for so long as they draw breath. As he practically tiptoes across the front porch Clyde can hear Mrs. Brown sobbing in the front room.

Clyde had wanted to handle next-of-kin notification, figuring Diedre's folks would rather hear the worst from one of their own kind, knowing that would have been the case if it had been him. But that hadn't made it any easier to come way out here to Bleiblerville, sit on their tattered old couch with his Stetson in his hands, tell these simple folks their daughter had died the way folks sometimes do, they get that taste for the fast life and set out after it.

Diedre's mama said the last time she talked to her daughter she had warned her not to hang around Lamont Stubbs, had been afraid something like this might happen. Not that she had any idea who might have wanted Lamont or her Diedre dead.

"There's certain things a mama just knows," she had said, between sobs that shook her entire body.

Diedre's daddy, a big man with heavy shoulders and gray hair, wearing overalls but no T-shirt and work boots that looked to be older than Clyde, had just sat in his rocker, his elbows resting on his knees, staring down at the floor like there was some redemption to be found in the faded yellow-and-white linoleum. When Clyde would ask him a question, he'd look up, his eyes flat and unfocused, as though behind them his mind was engaging God in some conversation too important to be interrupted, in some belated negotiation. He would grunt, shake his head, go back to his floor staring.

Clyde chucks his Stetson on the passenger's seat of his cruiser, cranks the engine. Mrs. Brown's crying echoes inside his head.

It's a melancholy start to a bluebird day. The morning sky is cloudless, and there is a wind blowing like a benediction from the northwest. It's the beginning of the end of the Texas sauna season, its limits set by God's most important laws. Laws nowhere to be found in holy writ, beyond the ken of any pope or imam. Ordinarily Clyde's heart would be as light as this breeze, but not this morning. Not this morning.

He's pulling on to the County Road headed back into town when his cell phone chirps. He puts it to his ear. "Deputy Thomas."

"Good morning," Sonya says to him.

"Yo. I was gonna give you a call in a little while. How you doin' today?"

"Fine, thanks. I would have slept better, though, with a roommate."

"Yeah. Sorry about that. We was at the scene kinda late."

"When did you finish?"

" 'Bout midnight."

"You still could have come by."

Clyde pulls up to the stop sign where the County Road meets the by-pass, looks for a chance to merge into the traffic that's howling past. Some of the drivers tap their brakes when they see his cruiser. He flips the switch on the radar, aiming to give their fuzzbusters a jolt even if he's too busy to pull any of the speeding sumbitches over.

Sonya says, "Come on, Clyde. Don't make me beg for it."

"Say what?"

"I just want to know what you would want to know if you were me."

Clyde sees an opening in the traffic, hits the accelerator. Sprays gravel out from under his back tires. "You know what? I ain't got no idea what you're talkin' about."

"I'm talking about what I might have missed by going home last night. Anything of an after-hours nature between you and the comely Ms. Banks."

"Yo, man. You best leash up that imagination of yours."

"I wasn't imagining the way she looked at you."

"Yeah, well, we just old friends is all. They wasn't no after-hours shit goin' down, you know what I'm sayin'? Why you so insecure all of a sudden, huh? That ain't like you."

"I'm given to self-confidence, alright. But blinded by it, I'm not."

"What the fuck is that supposed to mean?"

"Come on, do I really have to paint you a picture? I find out you're thinking about putting in for the DPS the same evening you turn down what I would have *thought* was a reasonably tempting offer to move in with me. And then along comes your old friend, Ms. Halle Berry Body Double, and gee, guess what? She's with the DPS *too*. I'm faced with all that and I get to wondering what's up between the two of you."

"Yeah, well, you too suspicious, is all. I ain't done shit, and you go and make me sound like I been cattin' around."

"If the paw fits, Mr. Lion."

"Listen, I ain't had nothin' to do with Yolanda since college."

He hears her exhale. "I'm not just talking about what you've done. I'm talking about what you may have been thinking about doing."

"Girl, you don't know shit 'bout what I been thinkin'."

"You got that right, Junior."

The tips of Clyde's ears are getting hot. "Watch it with the names."

"Sorry. I forgot. You prefer 'Mr. Lion.'"

Clyde steers the cruiser off the bypass, headed to Brenham's north side. "You know what? I'se way too busy to be dealin' with this bullshit jus' at the moment."

"Fine."

Click. Dial tone.

Clyde spikes the cell phone off the floorboard of the cruiser. "Goddamn it, you don't own me! Bitch!"

He clutches the steering wheel, trying to find some place to put his anger, some cage to lock it up in before it runs wild on him and causes him to fetch his cell phone up, call her back, share with her what he thinks of getting his chops busted for something she thinks he might have been thinking about doing.

So what if I was thinkin' somethin' along them lines last night when I seen Yolanda? That was just spur-of-the-moment shit right there. Didn't have nothin' to do with no career moves—that's somethin' different altogether, havin' to do with my self-respect and advancement. Besides, I done tol' Sonya I never got no voice mail from Yolanda. Ain't heard from her in years. That was just some punk-ass garbage she was runnin', tryin' to get Sonya all exercised, get her panties all twisted up. Worked, too.

God DAMN it. Whatever happened to the benefit of the fuckin' doubt?

By the time he gets to Lamont's crib he's calmed down some. He gets out of the cruiser, leaves his cell phone lying on the floorboard as though waiting to be rescued by some long-tempered new owner, someone not given to bouncing it off automobile interiors.

Clyde stretches himself to his full six foot three, sets his Stetson on his head. He had been over here to Lamont's once before, back in the spring-time, when he was looking to brace Lamont about what he knew of a liquor store robbery. Lamont had been of some modest assistance then, but only after Clyde had worked him over some.

Clyde had decided Lamont's house was the best place to start figuring out who had punched the dude's body full of more holes than a hurricane fence. Clyde looks up and down the dusty street, lined on both sides with shacks like this one, little kids playing out in front, crooked porches with rockers on them, black folks sitting in them. The air is thick with the smell of bacon frying and biscuits baking.

He can feel hooded eyes on him from all directions. Word would have gotten around by now about Lamont getting eighty-sixed. He reckons he'll need to talk to Lamont's neighbors, not that they're likely to say much to the law. Most of them would rather peel and eat a skunk than truck with cops.

Clyde walks through the yard, all weeds and fire ant hills, up to the front porch, wondering if the same woman who answered the door last time is still in Lamont's house. It hadn't been Diedre Brown. Diedre had been nice-looking, healthy, judging from her driver's license photo. No, that other woman was a junkie, near as Clyde could tell.

At the front door he squares his shoulders, ready to deal with another scene of grief, someone else trying to reset their lives to deal with that hole that's opened up. He pulls the screen door back, knocks gently on the wood door behind it. The door creaks open a few inches from the force of his knock. He pushes the door a little farther open, peers inside the house.

He steps inside the room. "Th' fuck?" He grabs his Glock, chambers a round.

He remembers from last time that Lamont wasn't a neatnik by a long shot, had litter scattered around the place, fast food wrappers, whiskey bottles. But what he's looking at now is something else altogether.

Drawers had been pulled out of bureaus, their contents dumped on the floor. Couch cushions slashed, insides pulled out, chairs overturned. Pictures jerked off the walls. Floorboards pulled up.

Clyde hollers, "Yo! Washington County Sheriff's Department! Anybody home?"

No response. He moves carefully through the debris, gun held in front in both hands, index finger lightly touching the trigger. He makes his way to the hall, checks all the rooms one by one. Everywhere the same thing, mattresses slashed, wallpaper stripped from the walls. The last room he checks is the kitchen. The floor is littered with utensils, pots and pans, broken crockery. Cabinet doors yawn open. The pantry floor is covered with flour, canned goods.

Clyde holsters his Glock, walks out the house to his cruiser. He grabs the mike on the two-way. "Yo, Sammy."

"Come in, Clyde."

"Listen, I'se over here at Lamont Stubbs's crib. Somebody done tossed it from one end to the other. I needs to process it, but I'm gon' need me some help."

"That's a roger, Clyde. Let me see if I can round up Jake, send him over there."

"Yeah. 'Preciate it." Clyde gives the address, signs off, tries to decide what to do while he waits for Jake to show.

9

During the time before the tanks came his mother was as silent, as beautiful, as existentially alone as the morning star. It had turned cold toward the end of October, and she floated about their apartment like a ghost, a shawl around her shoulders, the knuckles on her hands white and sharp, her eyes not quite in focus. She hardly spoke.

He spent days in his room with his books and his toy soldiers. School had been suspended until the streets could be made safe. For long hours he proved geometry theorems and wondered where his father was, what he was doing.

They waited for phone calls that never came. The phone in the front room sat stubbornly, arrogantly silent.

At night they would huddle around the radio with the lights turned low. The programming tended toward orchestral music interspersed with the Nagy government's pronouncements. "Hungary announced today that it is withdrawing from the Warsaw Pact. Now we shall play a recording of a symphony from Mozart."

Or a speech by the prime minister, appealing to the West for help. Preceded by the Hungarian National Anthem. Followed by Beethoven's Fifth Concerto.

On that occasion he had turned to his mother, who was staring out their front window at the shapes moving along the Nagykörút in the darkness, at the new corpses suspended from the lampposts. "America is led by the great hero Eisenhower, is it not, Mama? Won't he come to help us?"

For a long time she said nothing. Then, without turning from the window, she said, "I thought when he came back to me after the war that I would not . . ." She never finished the thought.

Around midnight on November 3 he awoke to the sound of diesel engines in the streets. Then automatic weapons, firing in long bursts, single shots in answer. The sound of shells exploding.

He slipped from his bed, pulled his robe over his pajamas, eased down the hall to the front room. His mother sat by the window, dressed in her nightgown, watching the Nagykörút, clutching a handkerchief. She was shaking, but not from the cold.

As he hugged her, the Soviet tanks rolled slowly down the avenue, their turrets turning this way and that. And as he watched them clank over the cobblestones, he felt that they did crush under their treads every precept and requirement of his world as if dispatched by some malign power for that very purpose.

10

THE ELEVATOR CARRIES JEREMIAH AND HIS YOUNG GUIDE TO A FORTIETH-floor lobby clad in pink granite. A sign on one wall says "Benjamin Farkas Interests" in raised gold lettering. The floor is covered with a thick Oriental rug. A table sits in the middle of the rug, a vase of fresh flowers resting on top.

Jeremiah follows Bruce through double glass doors. A reception desk sits off to the left, but no one's behind it. Jeremiah says, "Don't look like anybody's home."

"The office is usually closed on Saturdays."

In here, Oriental rugs are laid over marble flooring. The walls are covered with a gray fabric. Silk, from the looks of it. Large posters, photographs of high-rise buildings, hang in expensive-looking frames. On display in the middle of the reception area, a six-foot-tall architectural model of what looks to be an office tower in a glass case.

Jeremiah eyes the model. "Looks like a trophy somebody might win for doin' somethin' special."

"As a matter of fact, they're called trophy office buildings. Mr. Farkas builds them all over the world. That one is Transpacific Resources Center. He developed it in downtown Seattle last year."

Bruce leads Jeremiah down a corridor past offices that sit weekend empty, lights off, computer screens dark, chairs just as their occupants had left them when they sprinted to the elevators. They reach a closed door where Jeremiah's guide knocks gently. Inside, a woman's voice. "Come in."

Bruce opens the door and steps aside. Jeremiah enters a large, sunlit corner office with unobstructed views to the south and east. It smells of perfume and cigarette smoke. The door closes behind him. Bruce and his alabaster choppers stay outside.

A woman stands behind a desk in the corner. The desktop is clean save for a letter opener and a couple of paperweights. The woman is in her early thirties, close to six feet tall, wearing a tangerine blouse and dark leather pants. Her blond hair is pulled back in a French twist. Her facial features are symmetrical, her cheek bones pronounced, her makeup lightly applied.

Although he's been faithfully married for more than thirty years to the same woman, it registers on Jeremiah that this blonde is both beautiful and fetchingly top-heavy. She's so good-looking she could be a Dallas Cowboys cheerleader so long as she didn't let her self-respect become an obstacle.

"You must be the legendary Captain Spur. I was told you are retired. I suppose I was expecting someone a bit older." He can hear the British Isles in her voice.

"Sorry to disappoint you. And I ain't so sure about legendary. I'm here to meet Mr. Farkas."

The woman gestures to a couch sitting against a wall beneath a large painting, some pretentiousness of modern art, a couple of large black dots against a white background. "Please, do have a seat."

"I said I'm s'pposed to meet Mr. Farkas. Where's he at?"

She takes a chair next to the couch, crosses her legs. "I'm afraid Mr. Farkas won't be joining us. You see, he recently had hip replacement surgery, and the doctors bollixed it up. His hip became infected and two days ago they were obliged to remove the new joint until they can cure the infection. He is rather bedridden at the moment."

"Maybe I ought to come back when he ain't stove up."

"I'm afraid this cannot wait, Captain Spur. Mr. Farkas asked me to proceed without him. Please." She pats the couch next to her.

Jeremiah walks over, drops on to the couch as far from her as he can get, sets his Stetson down between them. Before him sits a glass-topped coffee table, a couple of architectural books on it, an ashtray, a package of cigarettes.

The woman holds out her hand. "I'm Leslie Whitten. I'm Mr. Farkas's CFO."

Jeremiah leans over, and they shake. "CFO?"

"Chief financial officer. I look after Mr. Farkas's money. Which is why the disappearance of our treasurer, along with close to ten million of the dollars I am charged with looking after is, well, a problem I am very keen to have solved. Would you mind terribly if I smoked?"

Since Jeremiah swore off cigarettes only last May so as to honor his dying daughter's request, he would rather she pounded him over the head with a claw hammer. "Go ahead on. But I ain't sure why I ought to make your problem my problem."

She lights a cigarette, blows smoke. "First, let me tell you a bit more about what you so rightly refer to as 'my problem.'"

"Fair enough."

"Our treasurer has been with us about seven years. We hired him from our outside auditing firm."

"He got a name?"

"Edwin Nelson. Although no one ever calls him that. His preferred nickname is Dusty, but that gets precious little use either, at least, here in the office."

"What do you call him, then?"

She smiles, taps ash, leans forward with her arms on her knees. "Dusty is an accountant, and therefore is capable of being a very boring little chap. But he can also, on occasion, create quite a stir. Just such an occasion occurred awhile back, when he made bold to deny another employee, one Lester Scurlock, a rather expensive country club membership Lester deemed crucial to his success at business development."

The cigarette smoke she keeps blowing has Jeremiah's nerves twanging like banjo strings.

She says, "Now, in fairness I should probably mention that once one has been exposed to Lester a bit one comes to understand that, improbable though it may seem, there are people here in America whose manners are even more wretched than the most vulgar Turkish soccer hooligan. In the event, when Lester learned he wouldn't be getting his precious country club membership, he went storming about the office, calling Dusty a Little Green-Eyeshade Fuck who never added value, or some such poetry. Since then Dusty has been known around the office as 'Little Fuck.'"

"B'lieve I'll stick to Dusty."

"Yes. Well. Just to bring you up to date on our current predicament, about three weeks ago I was reviewing the disbursement schedule with respect to an office building we are developing down in Houston, and I noticed some rather odd payments to a firm I did not recognize. They added up to quite a tidy sum—something around seven hundred thousand dollars. Since Little Fuck cuts the checks for all such jobs, I asked him to please come by my office for a chat concerning these amounts. Left him a voice mail, actually, since it was rather late and he had already gone home.

"The next morning, when he didn't present himself bright and early, I went in search of him. He was not in his office. His secretary had not heard from him. I had her call him at home. No answer. I drove around to his apartment building and got the manager to let me in his flat—it's in one of our buildings, you see. No Little Fuck. He had dropped from sight.

"I spent the next two days locked in here, looking through the disbursements for all the jobs he had handled. On each job he had created dummy subcontractors, and had written them checks. I called in our auditors and they confirmed that Little Fuck had been stealing from us rather regularly for some time now. Money on the order of nine point eight million dollars has gone missing on us, Captain Spur, along with our Little Fuck."

"Mr. Farkas can't have been too happy 'bout that."

She leans forward, stubs out her cigarette. "Indeed. I had to be the one to tell him and it was a distinctly unpleasant experience. Ten million dollars is a meaningful amount of money, even to a man of Mr. Farkas's considerable fortune. He was, shall we say, quite put out that a sum of such magnitude had been nicked by one of our own people, and really very adamant that I recover it, since had I been doing my job better in the first instance, the theft never would have occurred. That, at least, is his perspective, and his is the only one that matters, I'm afraid. What's more, most of the money seems to have been pinched from our working capital line. We haven't quite gotten around to advising the lending bank of this little cock-up, but it shan't be long before they're privy to it."

"What will happen then, you reckon?"

"The bank will be looking to us to make good the missing millions. Under the circumstances, that might be a bit difficult."

"You're sayin' Farkas ain't good for it? From the looks of this place I would of thought he had enough money to burn a wet mule."

She smiles. "Fascinating mental image, that. The problem is not one of wealth, but rather of liquidity. You see, in these rather robust times, we have been growing our franchise most rapidly, tapping our credit lines as we go. We are stretched rather thin, which makes it somewhat imperative that we get our hands back on those ten millions."

She tosses her hair. "Toward that end, Mr. Farkas has called in some chaps, friends of his, who know a thing or two about tracing cross-border money transfers."

"Friends from the Agency?"

She sighs. "I do not know and I wasn't about to ask. All Mr. Farkas said was that they are jolly good at tracking sums being moved about. Perhaps we shall presently know what's become of our money. Perhaps we shall never know."

She drops her head, looks at the floor. Her shoulders sag. Jeremiah watches her. He can't shake the feeling that there's something wrong about her, that she is somehow misplaced here. Something about her is too . . . exactly what, he's not sure. Maybe "refined" is the word. Too refined to be the chief bookkeeper for a real estate business owned by an Eastern European button man.

Right this minute, though, the main thing he can see about her is she's having trouble keeping her very British upper lip properly stiff. He can see she is afraid. He says, "And if you don't?"

When she looks back up, her eyes are glistening but her voice is steady. "We are at somewhat of a crossroads around here, and I shan't allow myself to think about failing. Although Mr. Farkas certainly did not make things any easier by instructing me that I was not to involve the police."

"You got any idea why?"

She shakes her head. "In a private company like this, the owner is not obliged to provide the help with his reasons. He said we should find someone competent, someone retired from law enforcement who could lend us a hand. He concluded that you are that someone. Yesterday he called, informed me that you and I would meet late this morning, here in the office." She leans forward. "Please, Captain Spur. We very much need the help here."

Jeremiah's thinking, *Farkas don't want the police brought in, huh? If this ain't a setup, then I'm a Japanese aviator. I wonder if this young lady is the mark. And if so, I wonder why.*

Jeremiah had tried not to let it, but her story has gotten to him some. *This could've been my own daughter, right here, with an ox in the ditch, needin' some total stranger's help. Maybe that's the way to look at it. What harm can it do, to check around some? It's not like there's anything pressin' at the ranch just at the moment. Martha ain't even there. And maybe I can get me a handle on ever-what kind of sharp dealing is going on here. Keep this young lady from gettin' mixed up in it.*

He stands up. "Why don't we have ourselves a look at Dusty's office?"

She smiles, stands up, too. "Thank you so much, Captain Spur."

11

CLYDE AND JAKE WALK OUT THE FRONT DOOR OF LAMONT STUBBS'S HOUSE, stripping off latex gloves as they go. Clyde says, "All that work and we didn't find shit."

"What was you expectin' to find, bud?"

"I don't know, man. A roach clip. A dime bag. A crack pipe. A wad of bills. Somethin'. Man, the dude sold drugs."

"That's what I know."

"You'd expect some kinda evidence."

"Maybe they took it."

"Who they?"

"Ever-who tossed the man's place."

"Yeah, maybe." Clyde looks across the street at a dozen black kids who are playing touch football in an empty lot. He starts walking that direction.

Jake says, "Where you off to, bud?"

"Gonna go talk to them kids yonder. See what they might know."

"You need me anymore?"

"Naw, man. Seal off Lamont's crib, then you can bounce."

Clyde crosses the street. The kids stop their game, stand around in a tight knot watching him. They all wear hundred-dollar sneakers, loose T-shirts, shorts hanging down low. Some got their heads shaved, some got dreadlocks working.

Clyde says, "Y'all mind if I ask y'all some questions?"

"You Clyde Thomas, ain't you."

"Folks calls you 'the Judge.'"

"You the one capped that dude in the deer blind awhile back. Dude that hung with that fool motherfucker, blew the courthouse."

Clyde looks at the one that just spoke. Kid can't be more than twelve years old. He says, "Yo mama know you use that kinda language?"

Kid says, "I hear tell you fuck a white woman. What's that like? She any good?"

The other kids snicker, say, "Yeah, man," "That's what I'm talkin' about."

Clyde says, "I ain't here to answer your impertinent-ass questions."

"Yeah, man," the kid says. "You here because Lamont got offed last night."

"That's right. Any of y'all know anything about that?"

They all shake their heads, mumble "No, suh."

Clyde says, "Let me ask you this, then. Back in the springtime, I come by to see Lamont about a holdup over at Uncle Freddie's. Was a woman livin' here then, but she ain't around no more. Any of y'all know her?"

"That was Laurice. Lamont's sister."

"Where she at now?"

"She move in with Gutter Ball Jones, 'bout two months ago."

"Who is Gutter Ball Jones?"

"Man works down at the bowlin' alley. Maintains the 'quipment."

"Why he messin' around with Lamont's sister? She looked like a junkie to me."

"Word is, she come into the bowlin' alley last summer, lookin' for a handout, or maybe just a cool place outta the heat. The white dude own the place, he run her ass back outside. Gutter Ball seen him do it, took his pity to her. Offered to take her home, clean her up, help her get straightened out."

"Where's Gutter Ball's house at?"

"He live behind the Moon Lounge in a pink brick house with a fence around it."

"Thanks." Clyde turns to walk away.

"Hey, Judge."

Clyde turns back, sees the twelve-year-old with the too-grown-up mouth on him, trying to look tough. He's got dreadlocks, wears an LA Lakers T-shirt, number 5 on the front. Clyde knows it says Horry on the back.

"Laurice knows Lamont bought it already."

"What's yo name?"

"Klingon Stottlemeyer."

"Klingon? What kinda name is that?"

"My mama got it off that TV show, *Star Trek*. She love that show."

"Ain't the Klingons the bad guys?"

"My mama say, black men is like the Klingons of America."

"What's that supposed to mean?"

The kid shrugs. "Fuck if I know. I don't watch that shit. I watch MTV."

"Yeah, well, you got a mouth on you, Klingon, that's for sure."

Another kid says, "We all call him 'Rocket.'"

Clyde says, "Uh-huh. You got a daddy at home, Rocket?"

Clyde can see the kid flush, can see that old anger, born of abandonment, building in the kid's chest, swelling him up. The kid says, "There's a dude my mama lets come around sometime. Sorry motherfucker, thinks it's cool to beat up on kids. Wished I was older, man. I'd smoke that motherfucker's ass."

Clyde says, "You ain't smokin' nobody. Not now and not ever. Get that through yo' head."

"Yeah, Judge. Shit."

"Alright, y'all, now listen up. I needs me some help out here on these streets. Some eyes and ears, you know what I'm sayin'?"

They all look at him. A couple nod.

"Alright then. Y'all be watchin' for a black Slade with gold trim that don't belong in this little dinky-ass town. Anybody see one, y'all is to let me know. We think might have been folks in that kinda ride, made meat loaf outta Lamont. Rocket?"

"Yeah." The kid is focused on the dirt he's working over with an Air Jordan toe.

"Can you get these brothers organized or what?"

"Say what?" He looks up at Clyde.

"I said I need you to captain this thing for me. You up for it?"

"You the man, Judge." His grin is like a spotlight, and it makes him look like the twelve-year-old he needs to try to be.

"Alright then. Y'all see that Slade, you let Rocket and me know. Rocket, you check in regular-like. Keep me in tune with the children."

Somebody says, "How we reach you, Judge?"

"Dial nine one one, man. Ask for the Judge." He walks back across the street.

As Clyde pulls the cruiser to the curb, he sees a man getting up from a porch swing, walking through the yard to come meet him. He's a tall gray-headed African American with tired eyes and a thin mustache, wears dark slacks, a white shirt, red cardigan sweater, black Kangol hat, smokes a pipe. Looks more like a small-town college professor than a bowling alley mechanic.

Clyde gets out the cruiser. They meet at the gate. Clyde says, "You Mr. Jones?"

The man looks him in the eye, puffs on his pipe.

Clyde says, "I'm Deputy Clyde Thomas."

The man takes his pipe out his mouth, moistens his lips. "I know who you are."

"I'd like to talk to Laurice, 'bout her brother Lamont. Y'all done heard, huh?"

"We got a call, little before midnight. You ain't talkin' to Laurice, though."

"Why not?"

He points his pipe back toward the house. "She's asleep. She needs her rest."

"What, she gon' sleep the day away? It's almost noon now."

"She was up 'til dawn cryin' over her brother. She's an addict in recovery, see. So she can't take nothin' to calm her down, no tranquilizers, nothin' like that. I just had to let her cry 'til she was too wore out to go on anymore."

"Maybe you could have her call me when she's up and about then."

"I'd be surprised if she's gonna want to talk to you even then, Deputy Thomas. Like she said last night, if y'all was any good at what you do, y'all would have got Lamont off the streets. He'd be alive now."

"So it's our fault he's dead instead of locked up in Huntsville, is that it?"

Gutter Ball puts the pipe back in his mouth, puffs a time or two. Shrugs.

"How we supposed to find the dudes whacked him, she won't talk to us 'bout what she knows?"

"What she knows is, her brother's gone. Don't make her no never mind whether you catch who done it. I 'spect that's the way she sees it, anyhow."

"Yeah, well, I got a job to do, you know what I'm sayin'?"

"Have a nice day, Deputy." Gutter Ball turns his back, starts walking away.

Clyde says, "I'll be back later. Don't you be thinkin' I won't."

He gets back in the car, pulls away from the curb, leaving rubber. He thinks about giving Yolanda a call, make sure they're still on for tomorrow. That gets him to thinking about Sonya and their fight earlier. He can't help but feel bad about it even though it was her that was to blame. He unclips his cell phone from his belt, finds her number in his address book. Punches send. Gets the machine at home.

Tries her office. Gets the machine there, too.

Decides to swing by her house, see if maybe she's out working in the yard, it being such a pretty day and all. But as he glides down Price

Boulevard in his cruiser, he can tell her yard is empty and her car is missing from the driveway.

So that's how it's gonna be, huh?

He shrugs, points the cruiser toward the office, steps on the gas.

12

LESLIE WHITTEN OPENS THE DOOR AND SWITCHES THE LIGHTS ON. "HERE IT is, then. You may look until your heart's content, but I rather doubt you will find much. Little Fuck appears to have left what you Texans are wont to call a cold trail."

Jeremiah steps into the room, another three-hundred-square-foot shrine to orderliness and contemporary furniture. Same desk and coffee table, mahogany credenza behind the desk, a few books between bookends shaped like Rodin's "The Thinker." There's a black computer monitor but no actual computer Jeremiah can see. On the desk, nothing but a telephone. No papers in sight anywhere.

"Don't y'all use papers in y'all's business?"

"Mr. Farkas is rather intolerant of clutter. He is also something of a fiend for efficiency. He says the key to success in business is to handle each paper that crosses one's desk once only. Either respond to it, forward it, file it, or toss it in the rubbish."

"What about the mail that's come in for Dusty since he's been missin'?"

"Wait here a moment." She steps outside and then comes back with a thick accordion file that she sets down on the desk.

"Where's Dusty's computer at? Don't ever-body use a computer these days?"

"Little Fuck used a laptop. It plugged into this docking station here." She crosses to the credenza, indicates a short piece of metal with wires attached to it. "It seems he must have taken the computer with him when he last left the office. It also seems rather likely that he had no intention of returning."

"How come you to say that?"

"Because the practice in this office is to back one's hard drive up to the network at the end of each day. Not only did Little Fuck not do that, he apparently spent a good many hours deleting files from our server, probably by accessing it from off site. All that activity occurred after the time I left him my voice mail, according to our IT people, who can find nothing of his remaining there."

Jeremiah opens a drawer in the credenza. "Y'all been through these files?"

"Nothing to be found."

"What about his calendar?"

"Kept it on his computer, I'm afraid."

"His address book, too?"

"So it would seem."

"He left this place clean as a hound's tooth, didn't he?"

"Little Fuck must have had his escape plotted for some time."

"Or somebody else cleaned up after him."

"I beg your pardon."

"Has Farkas had access to this office?"

"Yes, of course. But are you suggesting—"

"I ain't suggestin' nothin' just yet. Can you get me the records of all the phone calls that was made from here?"

"Of course. But we've been through those, and most of them seem pretty routine."

"Most of them?"

"There were a few calls we couldn't quite puzzle out. To phone numbers in Mexico City, of all places."

"Y'all don't have no business in Mexico?"

"No. We rang the numbers ourselves and found them to have been various public telephones. That bit was rather dodgy, but nothing else out of the ordinary."

"What about his automobile?"

"His silver 966 is still parked in its assigned spot, at his flat."

Jeremiah takes a seat at Dusty's desk chair, pulls the accordion file toward him, starts sorting through it. Leslie crosses the room, sits on the couch, looks pensive.

After ten minutes, Leslie says, "Finding anything?"

"Mostly junk, fliers for accounting conferences, office supply catalogs, couple of business magazines." He holds up an envelope. "What's the Rusk Fitness Club?"

"It's a health club, downtown. Little Fuck apparently worked out there. Had a personal trainer or some such nonsense."

Jeremiah squints at the envelope. "This must be his monthly dues statement. Mind if I keep it?"

"Of course not."

"Okay. What else? What about family?"

"None that we are aware of, although we did make an effort to find some. We checked the beneficiary designation on Little Fuck's group life insurance form. The primary beneficiary was a Mabel Nelson, of West Orange, New Jersey. No secondary beneficiary. Gave a telephone number, and I personally rang it up. Proved to be a bloody old folks home. They told me Mrs. Nelson had passed on a couple of years back. I asked them to check their files for living relatives. They called back, said there appear to be none. They claimed not to have a record of Little Fuck being her son, which is what I must assume he was."

"How did Dusty make his way from New Jersey all the way down here?"

"Moved out here to go to university, apparently decided he liked it. Stayed on to pursue his business career."

Jeremiah leans back in the desk chair, pushes his Stetson back on his head so he can scratch his hairline. "How'd he come to hire on with Farkas?"

"Mr. Farkas's son, Jonathon, knew him from school and recommended him."

"Maybe we ought to talk to Jonathon then."

"I'm afraid that is quite impossible."

"How come?"

"Jonathon passed away last spring. After a short illness."

"Real sorry to hear that."

"Yes. It was most tragic. He was Mr. Farkas's only child, you see. Mr. Farkas expected he would someday run the business. Quite a shock to us all when he died."

Jeremiah starts to say something about his daughter Elizabeth passing away last spring too, then decides against it. His instinct is nagging him, though, prodding him to learn more about this entirely too beautiful, too elegant real estate CFO, if that's what she is. "What about you?"

Her face goes blank. "What about me?"

"With that accent of yours, you ain't from around here. How'd you get to be the CFO of this outfit?"

"I joined Mr. Farkas's London office six years ago. He took a liking to my work, asked me to relocate here three years ago and assume my current position."

"What do you think of Texas?"

"Too bloody hot in the summer. Rather a lot of insects."

"You and Dusty—did y'all work together the entire three years?"

"Yes. But we were never close. Little Fuck was not the kind of person one wanted to spend much time with outside of the office environment. Or in the office environment, for that matter. He was, in fact, such an unpleasant little man that had he not been a personal friend of the founder's son, I should think he would have been dismissed long ago. By me, if not by someone else."

"Don't sound like you miss him much."

"I could not possibly miss him less. It is the almost ten million dollars he embezzled that I miss."

"Do you recollect if he had any friends other than Mr. Farkas's son?"

"I'm sorry, but I honestly don't know."

Jeremiah stands up. "Well, we ain't gonna learn nothin' about the man in here. Can you get me into his apartment?"

She stands up, too. "Of course. Your driver will take you there. I shall call ahead and clear it with the property manager." She walks over to Jeremiah, holds out her hand. "I cannot tell you how grateful we are for your help, Captain Spur."

He shakes her hand. "I wouldn't go thankin' me just yet. I got a hunch your man ain't gonna be all that easy to find."

She sighs. "My fears exactly." She straightens her shoulders, looks him in the eye. "Nevertheless, it is kind of you to try. Moreover we intend to see you properly compensated. In addition to covering your out-of-pockets, Mr. Farkas proposes that, should you find Little Fuck and recover our lost funds, we pay you ten percent of the amount recovered."

"Yeah, well, we'll see. But you know what I would do if I was y'all?"

She smiles. She's so good-looking Jeremiah wonders why she isn't married. Or if she is, why she doesn't wear her wedding band. "Call in the police, I'd wager."

"You'd wager right."

She shakes her head slowly. "Not an option, I'm afraid. Mr. Farkas has been very clear about that. Very clear indeed."

Jeremiah feels a mild jolt of irritation at the arbitrariness of the rich. *That's their great luxury—gettin' to make the rules other folks have to live by. That's what they really like about havin' money, the power it gives them over folks. That's better than all their jets and mansions and jewelry, all that fancy stuff. Seeing their rule-making in action, it's enough to peeve a man.*

And this particular rich man is up to somethin' with these rules he's laid down, I guaran-damn-tee you that.

His irritation has an edge made jagged by his craving for a smoke, but he's not about to give up his pledge. He pops a piece of nicotine gum into his mouth. "Would be a lot easier for regular law enforcement. They can get search warrants, check airline manifests, talk to Immigration, see if Dusty has left the country, cover a lot more territory by way of witnesses and what have you. They'll know right off if a John Doe checks in down at the county morgue. Any county morgue, across the entire state of Texas."

"I seriously doubt that our Little Fuck plans to pop into a morgue anytime soon."

"There's all kinds of other things they can do. Maybe even mobilize the newspeople, get them to help."

"Ah, yes. The press. The very kiss of death."

"Still and all, regular law enforcement can access all kinds of information a private citizen like myself can't get at. Your odds go way up, you bring them in."

"I am entirely in agreement with you. But we are where we are, I'm afraid. Don't you see?" She spreads her hands in a gesture of futility.

Jeremiah grinds away at his nicotine gum. "God O-mighty. You know, this don't make a lick of sense."

"Unfortunately, Captain Spur, you and I do not get to make that judgment. Now, Bruce will be waiting for you in the lobby. His instructions are to take you wherever you would like to go, to be available to you twenty-four seven. Tell me, do you have a mobile phone, by any chance?"

"Can't say as I do."

"Bruce will take care of that as well. He has one in his vehicle that he can lend you, with my telephone numbers programmed into it. He will show you how to operate it. That way you can stay in touch."

"Fair enough."

Jeremiah walks out of Dusty's office, headed for the elevators.

13

In the gray prewinter days just after the Russians came, there were occasional moments of hope. It was whispered that Imre Nagy and his advisers had been granted asylum in the Yugoslavian embassy, were negotiating for their lives with the new regime, led by the puppet Janos Kadar.

Then word that Kadar had promised Nagy safe passage to the West. This they heard directly from Benjamin's father. He telephoned one night, told his mother to pack a bag for each of them, that he would come fetch them soon. Then the connection was cut.

They never heard from him again. The criminal Kadar announced the arrests of Nagy, Farkas, and the others three days later. After the news came over the radio, his mother ran sobbing from the room. She did not come out of her bedroom for two days.

The short, mocking season of hope was over. It only served to make what followed seem worse. For months he felt as though he were trapped in a Russian novel, suffering long periods of despair, broken only occasionally by moments of tragedy. Their friends from before avoided them. Now and then the telephone would ring, but there was never anyone on the other end of the line. He knew, because he was the one who answered it.

His mother bought black bread and Polish vodka with their savings. She sat at the kitchen table in a housedress, drinking vodka and smoking cigarettes. That's where she was when he left for school each morning, and where he would find her once he returned home from classes. There, or passed out on the couch in the living room.

But the worst part was never knowing what had become of his father.

In February he came home from school and found his mother sitting on the curb in front of their building surrounded by luggage. The government had evicted them.

They had nowhere else to go, so they moved in with his mother's half brother, a dark, violent man with a mousy wife who, his mother had once said, was barren. They lived in a one-bedroom walk-up off a dirty street in Pest. His uncle worked in a slaughterhouse. At the end of each day he came home drunk, smelling of sausage.

Benjamin and his mother slept on the living room floor. And in that room, late one May night, his uncle assaulted his mother.

Benjamin did what he could. He jumped his uncle. Fought to get him off her. Hit the big man with his fists. His uncle threw him across the room as though he were one of the frayed pillows that lined the couch. He landed hard on the floor, the breath knocked from him. He lay there gasping. Once he caught his breath he pulled himself to a sitting position. Pushed himself across the rug. Cowered in the corner, tried to shut his ears to his mother's cries of fear and pain, cries muffled by her brother's rough hand.

When it was over, she lay in the dark whimpering, and he did not know what to do to comfort her.

14

WHEN CLYDE PULLS UP IN THE CRUISER, THE REVEREND DOCTOR EBENEZER Flatley is out in the yard in front of the Bethel Baptist Church trailing along behind a Lawn Boy, the sweat stains on his T-shirt dark under his armpits, around his neck. Dr. Flatley kills the lawnmower, pulls a big red-checked handkerchief from his hip pocket, sets to wiping his face as he walks Clyde's direction.

Not only is Dr. Flatley the best preacher Clyde has ever heard, he's also the foremost authority on the daily goings-on among the black folks of Brenham. If anything goes down in the black community, trivial or profound, word of it usually makes its way back to him. He's a one-man switching station for the black grapevine.

"Good day to you, Deputy Thomas," he says in his great baritone.

"How y'all are, Dr. Flatley?"

They meet halfway between the cruiser and the lawn mower, shake hands.

"Fine, fine, sir. Couldn't ask the Lord for a better day, could we now?"

"It's a nice day, alright, but there's better ways to spend it than bein' your own yard man. Can't you get no one else to do the mowin'? Like some kids from Sunday school or somethin'?"

The preacher shakes his head, chuckles. "The good Lord prizes nothing higher than honest, physical labor, Judge."

"Don't the church say, we saved by grace, not by works?"

"Very good, my boy, very good. But you can wait all day on grace and the yard'll still need mowin'. Besides, I like doing the yard myself, making it look good for the flock the next day. Gets me out in the fresh air and the sunshine, where I can think about what I'm going to preach on in the mornin'."

"Yeah, well, I never been able to generate much enthusiasm for yard work myself. Listen, I need to ask you somethin', you don't mind."

"By all means."

"What do you know about a brother, name of Gutter Ball Jones?"

The preacher looks off in the distance. "I know he isn't a churchgoing man. Other than that, just scraps of gossip."

"Don't suppose I could talk you into sharin' some of them scraps with me."

"Bet I could guess why you're asking."

"You heard 'bout Lamont Stubbs, huh."

The preacher shakes his head. "Mighty bad business. Mighty bad indeed. Since the victims were black, I assume the sheriff has you working the case." He shakes his head some more. "This town."

"I been checkin' around, tryin' to find out who it was would've wanted to let the air out of Lamont's balloon. Word is his sister took up with this Gutter Ball dude. I go around just now to his place, see about askin' Lamont's sister what she might know, and he won't let me see her, nor talk to her, neither. So I get to thinkin', what's up with him? I figger anybody around here knows, would be you."

"Gutter Ball Jones," the preacher says. "Seems to me he came to Brenham about five years ago. Rumor was, prior to his arrival here he spent a number of years in the custody of the state of Texas."

"Huntsville?"

"Sugarland, if memory serves. After he showed up here, he got himself a job over at the bowling alley. Bought himself a house."

"I seen his house this morning. Pretty nice for an ex-con works at a bowling alley. You know what he was sent up for?"

"No, sir."

"That's alright. I can find that out."

The preacher nods. "And as you've already learned, he has taken up with Laurice Stubbs. The way I hear it, Lamont didn't care much for that. He seems to have felt, since Laurice was his sister, he had the higher claim on her. He depended on her to look after his domestic affairs. Took umbrage when she left his house, moved in with Mr. Jones, whose actual Christian name, I believe, is Melvin."

"Lamont try to do anything about it?"

"Went over yonder, tried to get her to come back home. Mr. Jones and he had words, as I understand it. The argument escalated to the point where Mr. Jones is said to have pulled a weapon."

"A gun?"

"I'm not sure if it was a gun or what. Whatever it was, it ended the argument. Lamont got out of there, but he said they ought to plan on him coming back. Better equipped next time, according to the gossip."

"Any chance you could recollect where you heard this?"

Dr. Flatley knits his brow. "I want to say that I heard it from Mrs. Lawrence, who's our organist, and who uses the same hairdresser as Lamont's cousin Wilhelmina. But I might be wrong."

Clyde walks into the Sheriff's Department offices over at the First State Bank of Brenham. The place is empty except for Sammy the dispatcher sitting behind a glass partition in the back. Clyde waves his sack of fast food at her.

Before the Sheriff's Department took this space over, it had been home to an insurance agency. The former occupant had left behind motivational posters that are the only wall decorations in the bullpen where the deputies have their desks. In their quieter moments the deputies can sit in their chairs and contemplate such profundities as "There is no 'I' in 'team,'" and "You never get a second chance to make a first impression."

Clyde boots up his computer, and as the machine clicks and hums and struggles to come to life, he unwraps his cheeseburger and checks voice mail. Got a message from Yolanda saying she ought to have something for him when he shows up tomorrow, reminding him to dress nice. Another message from Sheriff Dewey Sharpe, asking him to take the lead on the Stubbs shooting.

"Way ahead of you, man," Clyde says, through a mouthful of cheeseburger.

Nothing from Sonya.

Clyde sets his burger to one side and bends over the keyboard. He launches the Web browser, navigates to the Web site of the DPS Crime Records Service, logs into the Conviction Database, runs a search for "Melvin Jones." Gets fifteen hits.

His man is hit number four. Gutter Ball had been convicted in Harris County in 1986 of three counts of possession of cocaine with intent to distribute. It was his first fall. Got fifteen in Sugarland, paroled out after eight. Clyde prints a couple of pages, rolls his sandwich wrapper into a paper ball, takes aim at a trash can halfway across the room.

"Mr. Gutter Ball," he says, "you in yo' fancy sweater and Kangol hat and shit? You ain't nothin' but a lowlife." He launches his shot at the trash can, then goes to pick it up when it bounces off the rim. He slam-dunks it, then collects his Gutter Ball printout.

15

JEREMIAH'S THINKING, *REMINDS ME OF THAT COUNTRY SONG THAT GOES A little bit is better than nada but in this case not much better.*

Jeremiah and Bruce are driving away from Dusty's apartment building with just about nada to show for their two hours there. The property manager had promised to get Jeremiah a list of all the people who had cleared the front desk on their way to call on Dusty over the last couple years. And at Jeremiah's suggestion Bruce had helped himself to a photograph of Dusty that was sitting on a bookshelf. There had been a message on the answering machine from somebody named Paul asking Dusty to call him back at some club that Jeremiah's guessing is the Rusk Fitness Club. And Jeremiah found a matchbook from another establishment, JR's Bar & Grill, over on Cedar Springs. Jeremiah had spoken to the people in the other units on that same floor. Noboby knew anything that they would own up to concerning Dusty or his whereabouts.

Jeremiah works his jaw as he watches the scenery on the Tollway flash past. *I reckon I found what I was intended to find. Farkas owns the building, and like as not he policed that place, too.*

Lunch is burger baskets at Chip's over on Lovers Lane. They sit at a table drinking iced tea and waiting for their number to be called. The place is crawling with yuppies plowing through their Saturday repast. Jeremiah had noticed the BMWs and Lexuses congregated outside, probably a million dollars' worth of vehicles.

Bruce produces a cell phone, takes Jeremiah through its fundamentals.

Jeremiah pockets it and says, "How long you worked for Farkas?"

"Just two months. I got my MBA from Wharton last spring, then spent three months traveling."

Jeremiah's not acquainted with Wharton, and he's not sure how a man spends three whole months traveling unless he's running from the law. "Did you know Dusty?"

"We went to lunch once, right after I joined the firm, and all we did was talk shop. After that, I haven't seen him except to say hi in the halls now and then. He's too senior to have much to do with me." Bruce squints at his receipt. "I think they just called our number." He leaves the table.

Later, as they're working their way through their burgers, Jeremiah says, "What is it makes you partial to the real estate business?"

Bruce wipes his mouth with a napkin. "I'm attracted to the challenge of putting together a project—say, an office building—that will succeed both aesthetically and financially. Not to mention the fact that many of the great American fortunes were made in real estate. I'd be lying if I said that wasn't a motivation, since I think getting rich doing real estate is still possible today. It's funny, you know? If he were here, old Dusty probably would have taken issue with that."

"What? That there's money to be made in real estate?"

Bruce nods. "That one time we had lunch? He sorta shocked me with his attitude toward the business. He said it was backward, low-tech, more a craft than an industry, whatever that's supposed to mean. He said there's no operating margin in real estate, so it's never going to allow for tremendous value creation. He said he wished he was in a high-margin business, like technology or the Internet. He's very much a New Economy guy, likes to go around saying that real estate guys 'don't get it.' "

"Was he maybe thinkin' about leavin' you to get in one of them high-margin businesses?"

Bruce leans forward with his elbows on the table. "I don't know. But I don't think so. He said Mr. Farkas had in the past been in other lines of business, some of them pretty high margin, and he was kinda hoping he might transfer into one of them."

"Such as?"

"He didn't say."

"You got any idea your own self what he coulda meant by that?"

Bruce hesitates. "It would just be speculation."

"Well, then, speculate."

"I'd really rather not."

Jeremiah says, "Fine. I'll ask Leslie."

"Look, I'd appreciate it if you didn't, you know, let on . . . I mean, that I was the one who said Mr. Farkas had been engaged in . . ."

"In what?"

Now Bruce is beginning to look miserable. "Just leave me out of it, okay?"

"I ain't entirely sure what it is you're askin' me to leave you out of." Jeremiah gathers his trash up and stands. "Time to get high and behind it."

"Yes, sir."

16

"JUDGE THOMAS! HOW IN THE WORLD ARE YOU DOING? COME ON IN THIS house."

Gutter Ball's parole officer, Francine Andersen, throws open the door to let Clyde into her home in Briar Grove, a new subdivision where most of the middle-class Washington County black folks now live. Clyde wedges in between her and the door. Francine weighs in at a number usually associated with livestock, and her entry hall is so small, the two of them are almost belly to belly. Clyde stands with his back pressed into the Sheetrock behind him trying his best not to make contact.

Clyde says, "Sorry to be droppin' in like this, without callin' or nothin'. I just needed to talk to you a few minutes 'bout Gutter Ball Jones."

She gives a little headshake, swats at the air, says, "Oh, don't worry about that. Come on into the sitting room and we'll visit. Can I fix you something to drink? You want a cup of coffee or a soda water?"

"No, ma'am."

"Alright then."

She shows him into a simply furnished little room, done in light greens and yellows, with a couch, a couple of chairs arranged around a coffee table. There are windows on two sides. Sheers pulled back to let in the sunlight.

"Nice place you got here, Francine," Clyde says, taking an armchair.

Francine positions herself in front of the couch, lowers herself a bit at the knees, then falls the rest of the way, her feet lifting off the floor a little as she bottoms out. The couch goes *whufff*. "Thank you, Judge. We've been here almost a year now. We're real happy with it. Just a few little things wrong with it I'd like to get fixed."

"Like what?"

"Well, for one thing, the toilet's too low."

"How can the toilet be too low?"

She leans forward, drops her voice. "When Albert sits on the toilet, his thing hangs in the water."

"I hate when that happens," Clyde says uncertainly.

"So, you interested in Gutter Ball? He doesn't care to be called that, you know."

"What's he want to be called then? Melvin?"

She shakes her head. "He doesn't want to be called that, neither. See, he says he come outta prison a changed man."

"He find Jesus down at Sugarland?"

"Allah. He wants to be called Mustafa X. Nobody around here gonna pay him any mind though. Nigger going around with an A-rab's name. Lord have mercy." The thought sets her to chuckling.

"Tell me what you know 'bout him."

"This about what happened to Lamont Stubbs and the Brown girl from over in Bleiblerville?"

"Yep. You probably know Lamont's sister took up with Gutter Ball awhile back. Word is, Lamont and Gutter Ball was crossways over it."

"You sayin' you like Gutter Ball for what happened to Lamont?"

Clyde shrugs. "Lamont sold drugs. Gutter Ball got sent up for possession with intent to distribute. Maybe Gutter Ball was thinkin' 'bout gettin' back in the business, decided to thin out the competition. Or maybe it was about Lamont's sister."

"You talked to her yet?"

"Tried to. He wasn't havin' none of it though."

Francine shakes her head. "I'd be surprised if he was to go back to the life. Seemed to me like he really wanted to stay straight. It wasn't like he was all that dirty to begin with."

"How's that?"

She folds her big arms across her chest. "Gutter Ball used to own a bowling alley down in Houston, in the Fifth Ward. One day a couple of guys, guys connected to the Cantú drug gang down in Mexico, showed up. Told Gutter Ball they needed him to place an order, every month, for some bowlin' pins from a plant down in Guadalajara. And to call a phone number when them pins arrived. They told him every time a shipment of pins came in, they would come collect 'em and pay him $15,000."

Clyde runs his hand along his smooth scalp. "Man. That's some serious money."

"Yeah, but Gutter Ball knew what they were up to, see. And he didn't want the slightest part of it. They didn't give him any choice, though. Well, I guess that ain't exactly right. They let him choose between doing like they asked or waking up some mornin' to find his bowlin' alley burned to the ground."

"So Gutter Ball played ball, so to speak."

"That he did. Worked for a while, too, maybe six months. Then some customs officer got suspicious about all those bowlin' pins coming in every month at the Port of Houston. They checked a shipment with one of those drug-sniffin' dogs, and he lit up like Las Vegas. They waited until Gutter Ball signed for the delivery and raided his place. Bowlin' pins had been hollowed out and filled with cocaine."

"So Gutter Ball got sent up. Why he come here when he paroled out?"

"Claimed he didn't want to go back to Houston. Wanted to start a new life. Got a job working for the white man over at the bowlin' alley. Goes to work, prays five times a day in A-rab, doesn't touch liquor. Thinks Louis Farrakhan is the Messiah."

"He been in any trouble?"

"Not so much as a speeding ticket."

"What you reckon is up with him and Laurice Stubbs?"

"Could be he took her in outta pity. She was a junkie, you know."

"Yeah."

"He says, under Islam, we are all supposed to take care of one another. Especially our fellow black man, who's been oppressed by the white devil all his life. To hear him tell it, all the black folks got to reach out to one another. Only way to keep the white man at bay. That's probably how come him to reach out to Laurice Stubbs. Give her a chance at a better life." She shakes her head some. "I don't think it was him shot Lamont and that poor girl. Doesn't seem like his style to me, Judge."

"You know, it ain't unheard of fo' a man to change his style." He stands. "I best be runnin' along. I really appreciate yo' help, Francine.

She thrusts her upper body forward, then pushes herself off the couch. Gives him a smile. "Come on, I'll show you out the door."

17

Within the space of a week he lost both parents.

They announced his father's death over the radio. Nagy, Farkas, and the others had been tried, convicted, executed. Hanged from the gallows in some prison. Helpless, kicking legs.

That night his mother disappeared from his uncle's flat. Her body was found three days later, floating in the Danube, downstream from Budapest.

The shock of that week would be with him all his days.

A couple of months later, his uncle came for him. It was dark, he was quick— he awoke at the sound of his uncle stepping into the room—and his uncle was clumsy. Had it been otherwise, he could not say how his life would have turned out. Some inner voice counseled him to expect it, an inner voice he would learn to heed as he grew older. He had been sleeping in his clothes ever since the night his mother was first attacked.

He ran out of the apartment and down the stairs. He wandered Budapest for two days before stumbling into a gypsy camp at the edge of town, a collection of disreputable-looking people, tents and smoky campfires, a few dogs and donkeys, some broken-down vehicles and wagons, wash hanging on lines.

He sagged to the ground beside a fire. Ate the goulash and bread brought to him by an old woman who was like something from a fairy tale. Simple dress, shawl, kerchief. All but toothless. She watched him as he ate, then laid a blanket on the ground for him. He undressed, lay down, and slept well into the morning of the next day.

When he awoke, his clothes were gone and other clothes, rough pants, a shirt, a jacket, a funny hat, had been laid out. The old woman brought him tea.

"What is your name, my child?"

"Benjamin Farkas."

"Strange. You don't look much like a wolf." Then she smiled. No teeth, but warm enough.

Benjamin watched her. He tucked his knees beneath his chin and began to rock.

"You must have a story. All little wolves have stories. Tell me yours."

He rocked back and forth. It came out of him a bit at a time, but toward the end sadness and despair and the pain of it caused him to rush it through. He sat and rocked, and she watched him for a while before she arose.

"Come with me."

"Where are we going?"

"To see Gitch."

"Who is Gitch?"

She smiled her toothless smile. "He is a magician. He is a trainer of little wolves."

18

HIS ENTIRE LIFE HE HAD TRAINED HIMSELF IN TOUGH-MINDEDNESS. GIVEN neither to giddiness nor despair. Never a prisoner of his moods. But his tough-mindedness went out the window when his daughter Elizabeth died of cancer. Even though he had had months to prepare for it. What he learned was, this business of losing a daughter wasn't something a man could prepare for.

For weeks after she passed away he couldn't get his brain to work. Instead of doing its job, it seemed to be eating itself. It felt like a mess of pebbles just taking up room in his head. He would sit down in his thinking position, leaned forward, elbows on knees, reading glasses twirling between his fingers, to puzzle through some problem, then straighten back up after a spell, not sure how long he'd been sitting there, not even sure what problem he had set out to solve.

The world became a fractured mirror reflecting at every turn some facet of his grief. Everything he saw reminded him of his daughter—the stump out back where she practiced her roping, the county fairgrounds where she barrel-raced, the filling station where he took her to meet the Greyhound when she left home.

He found himself brooding on his own mortality, on what he felt was a major flaw in the Creator's design, the mindless loss at death of all the things a person worked hard over his life to accumulate, wisdom, knowledge, experience, memories. How to cast a fly, the names of the starting cornerbacks on the 1996 Texas A&M football team, the equation that describes force, lyrics from Emmylou Harris songs. All the things a man had grown to be in the long-as-a-whore's-dream years of his life, gone once he was gone. Wasteful was what it was.

It would have been more comforting to him if he could have allowed himself to believe that once he died his spirit would roam the universe like it was just a big ranch with no fencing. Humming "One of These Days" to itself.

At times he looked at himself, saw his own arm, all blue veins and sinews and skin like wallet leather, and thought, *This, all this, will someday be buried in a box. Along with everything it's ever done or was capable of doing.* Times like that he would saddle his horse Redbo, ride his land, try to find a spot in the sun so hot it would melt those thoughts that froze his marrow.

Over time he began to reclaim his bearings, began to feel like his brain was back in working order, his mind was toughening up. But he still had moments when memories washed over him like a fever, moments like this one right here.

He and his towheaded doppelgänger walk into JR's Bar and Grill. The main room is a big square, this side occupied by the bar itself, a long oval patrons could approach from any angle. Beyond that is a dance floor. To their right, men shoot pool on an elevated platform. The wall opposite has a dozen video monitors set in it, all showing the same music video, a lean young man wearing white butterfly wings on his shirtless back, undulating to music so loud it causes the fillings in Jeremiah's molars to hum.

A couple of dozen people are hanging around the place, washed-out looking young men in tight T-shirts, their arms blued over with ambiguous tattoos, middle-aged men with paunches. What catches Jeremiah's eye when they walk into the place, though, what sends his mind spinning back to Elizabeth, are the two women holding hands with one another at the bar.

Just like Elizabeth used to do with Amanda.

He looks around the room, takes in the folks, people alive on a sunny October day, drinking and laughing, not a furrowed brow among them. Oblivious to the grave.

They, too, will end up someday buried in a box in the ground. Lord, I wish I could have been there when she breathed her last. Instead, he had learned of it when he picked the phone up in his kitchen and heard his wife sobbing.

He says to Bruce, "Let's go talk to one of them bartenders."

Jeremiah leads the way, fully aware of the eyes watching them from all around. He hopes all the attention they're attracting means they look as out of place as he feels. Folks move aside, make room for them at the bar.

The bartender that's nearest at hand is a big woman with her hair cropped close to her scalp. She looks like a member of the Bulgarian women's Olympic shotputting team. She says, "What can I get y'all?"

Jeremiah hesitates, decides it would be impolite not to order something. "Coke."

Bruce reaches for his wallet. "Shiner Bock."

All this commerce is conducted by shouting on account of the music that throbs in the place.

While the bartender fetches the drinks, Jeremiah says to Bruce, "You bring a photograph like I told you?"

"Yes, sir." Bruce hands it over.

"Which one is Dusty?"

"The one on the far left."

Jeremiah squints at the picture. It shows Dusty and two other men in black tie seated at a table. "Who are them other two?"

"All I know is, they don't work for Farkas."

When the bartender returns, Jeremiah says, "Mind if I ask you a question?"

The bartender leans with one elbow on the bar. She has a tattoo on her forearm. Minnie Mouse riding a chopper. She says, "Okay."

Jeremiah hands over the photograph, indicating Dusty's picture with a weathered forefinger. "You recognize this feller?"

The minute I heard Martha cryin' into the phone, that's when I knew. I should've been down yonder with her.

She says, "That's Dusty Nelson."

"You seen him lately?"

"He's been scarce. Been at least a month since he was in here last. How come?"

Jeremiah sets down his Coke. "He up and disappeared a couple weeks back. I been hired to find him." He coughs. The constant shouting is stressing his throat.

The bartender shakes her head. "Sorry. I couldn't tell you where to find him. But he could." She hands the picture back, points at the man sitting next to Dusty. "His name is Paul Lipper. They came in here a lot together. They were good friends, maybe even seeing one another."

Jeremiah takes the picture back, studies it. Paul Lipper looks to be blond, square-shouldered, very fit. "Where you reckon I could find him?"

She gives the very answer he expects. "He works at that fitness club downtown."

Directly they're back outside, the Saturday afternoon traffic noise almost gentle compared to the rock music inside the bar. They get inside Bruce's vehicle. Bruce cranks the engine, backs out of the parking spot, looks at Jeremiah. "Shall we go check out the Rusk Club?"

Jeremiah nods. He's thinking, *The message on the machine back at the apartment, all the leads to this health club or whatever it is. I'm bein' pointed in the direction of this Lipper kid. Wonder where he fits into all this foolishness.*

A few minutes later, Bruce starts snickering.

Jeremiah says, "What's so funny?"

"I knew old Dusty was an odd duck, but I never made him for a faggot."

He glances over at Jeremiah and the look he gets almost causes him to jump a curb. "What'd I say?"

Jeremiah turns, stares out the windshield. "You know," he says, "that ain't a very polite term."

He had been fixing to leave for the hospital when the kitchen phone rang and he heard his wife crying into it from the other end. *That's when I knew she was gone. Lord, I wished I had been down yonder.*

19

AS CLYDE PULLS AWAY FROM FRANCINE'S HOUSE HIS TWO-WAY SQUAWKS.

Clyde grabs the mike. "Yo, Sammy. What it is."

"Lamar Jackson called. Doin' a story for Monday's *Gazette* on last night's doubleheader. Wants an interview. This afternoon, if possible."

"Department policy is, the man's got to get the sheriff's okay first."

"Dewey called in, said it was fine with him."

Clyde's mike hand drops to his lap. He's wondering what's up with the sheriff. It's not like him to pass on a chance to get some ink, not with him looking at a contested primary next May. Dewey likes to keep his name in front of the voters, let them know he's Mr. Tough-on-Crime.

Maybe it's on account of the vics was black, and Dewey's done relapsed into his racist ol' motherfuckin' ways, don't want the white folks thinkin' he's extendin' the county's resources just 'cause a couple children got capped. This be his subtle-ass way of sayin', 'I lets the niggers take care of the niggers.'

Clyde says out loud, "Shit. I bet that's it." Clyde and Dewey had a pretty good relationship going back last spring but here lately Dewey's been acting more like his old, shifty, flatulent self.

The radio squawks, "You there, Clyde?"

Clyde lifts the mike. "Yeah. Where's the dude at?"

"Said he'd be in his office all afternoon."

"Call him, ask him if he wants to meet over at the Farm-to-Market Café."

"Sure thing, Clyde. And you had another call, but I don't much know what to make of it. From some kid, said his name was Rocket."

"What'd he want?"

"Didn't say. Didn't leave a number where he could be reached, neither. Was whisperin' so I could barely hear him. Said he'd call you back later."

"Look, when the kid call back, patch him through to my cell, okay?"

"Sure thing, Clyde."

"Thanks. Over and out."

Lamar Jackson is sixty years old, completely hairless, and so skinny that if he stood sideways and stuck out his tongue he'd call to mind a zipper. He goes around looking like he's been mainlining Paxil. It's fraudulent, though, his apparent relaxed dimness, just as fraudulent as the bib overalls he wears half the time, as if he spends his days behind a plow instead of being the publisher, editor, and chief reporter of the only newspaper in town. It's all part of an act Lamar has polished over the years, made necessary because in a little Texas town like Brenham everybody tight-holes everybody else and anybody even remotely connected to journalism gets tight-holed worst of all.

They're all tickled shitless to share with Lamar their births and graduations, their promotions and retirements, their chili recipes and rhyming tributes to the Birthplace of Texas. But real news? They'd volunteer for root canal surgery without the benefit of anesthesia before they'd tell Lamar anything of the sort. Lamar knows he has a better chance of sneaking up on the news in these parts if it doesn't see him coming. That's why he goes around disguised as a lobotomized field hand.

Most people who have known Lamar any length of time are wise to it, of course, this little deception he practices. But as he walks into the Farm-to-Market Café, Clyde Thomas is about to meet Lamar Jackson the Reporter, acting in his professional capacity, for the first time.

Clyde steps inside the front door, sees Rose Emory, owner of both the café and the sweetest disposition in Central Texas. She gives him her seven-trillion-dollar smile from behind the cash register.

Clyde doffs his Stetson. "How y'all are, Rose?"

"Never better, Deputy Thomas, nice to see you again. How about yourself?"

"Doin' good. You seen Lamar Jackson? I'm supposed to meet him here."

She points down the long plateglass wall to the far booth. "He's waiting for you down yonder. How about a cup of coffee?"

"That'd be mighty kind, ma'am."

Half a dozen steps carry him to Lamar's booth, where the man is getting up to greet him. Clyde waves him off with his Stetson. "Keep yo' seat, man." He offers up a hand. "Clyde Thomas," he says.

The editor gives him the grip. "Pleased to meet you. Thanks for coming."

"Don't mention it." Clyde slides into the booth, sets his Stetson on the seat next to him, nods his thanks at Rose for the cup of coffee she delivers. Clyde takes a package of sugar and starts flicking it with his middle finger.

Lamar plucks a notepad and a stub of a pencil from his overalls, looks at Clyde with his dreamy eyes. "Okay if I ask you 'bout last night's shooting?"

"Shootings, man. Plural. Was two folks bought it."

"First, your full name is—"

"Deputy C. Livermore Thomas. Folks call me Clyde."

"How long you been workin' for Washington County?"

"Goin' on six years."

Lamar makes notes. "So last night—"

Clyde nods, shows the man he knows his cue. "Yeah. I was called to the scene by a couple other deputies. They was two bodies. Been shot to death. Man by the name of Lamont Stubbs and his lady friend, Diedre Brown."

"Any witnesses?"

Clyde slurps his coffee. "We got one guy seen a black Escalade with gold trim in the vicinity. But he didn't see the actual shooting go down."

"Who's leading the investigation?"

"That would be me, man."

"This Lamont Stubbs. Any truth to the rumors we hear, he might have been involved in certain illegalities?"

"The man dealt. We knowed it, but couldn't never catch him dirty."

Lamar scratches on his pad, looks across the street, forehead creased. "We don't get much murder in Washington County and when we do, it's almost always someone who knew the victim what did it. You think that might be the case here, too?"

Clyde shrugs. "Maybe. Lamont's got a sister, shacks up with an ex-con named Gutter Ball Jones. We gon' talk to them, see what they might know."

"Could one of them be a suspect?"

"Can't rule nothin' out this early on, man." Clyde watches Lamar scratch something down on his notepad, says, "Hey, don't be writin' that down. That's just off the record shit, man, you know what I'm sayin'?"

Lamar looks up, smiles a spaced-out smile, just as Clyde's cell phone chirps.

Clyde puts the phone to his ear. "Yo. Deputy Thomas speakin'."

"Clyde, it's Sammy. I got that Rocket kid on the line. You want to talk at him?"

"Yeah. Patch him through." Clyde hears the line click. "Yo, Rocket."

"That you, Judge?"

"Yeah, man. You got a Slade sightin' fo' me?"

"No, but I got somethin' else. Somethin' I think you be likin'."

"Let's have it then."

"Not over the phone. Hang on a sec."

Clyde hears a hand go over the mouthpiece, muffled voices in the background. He looks up, sees Lamar Jackson's sleepy eyes checking him out. "Sorry 'bout this."

"No problem."

Rocket comes back on the line. "Judge?"

"Yeah."

"Could you maybe meet me back of the Golden Cue, in 'bout half a hour?"

"Sure, man. See you there."

The line goes dead. Clyde puts his phone away, takes a sip of coffee, pulls out a dollar, drops it on the table. "What else can I do you for, man?"

"Seems like we're 'bout done here."

"When you gon' run yo' story?"

"Monday morning paper."

"Alright, then. I be lookin' for it. But keep that off the record shit out, you know what I'm sayin'?"

All he gets back as he lets himself out the booth is a dreamy smile.

Clyde has been sitting in his squad car behind the Golden Cue for twenty minutes, wondering if Rocket is going to show, half inclined to believe the little reprobate was jiving him. The alley behind the Cue is empty, except for a Dumpster, some litter on the ground. There's some parking back here, and Clyde has pulled the cruiser in nose first, so he's looking at the back of the pool hall building.

He's about to roll on out of there when there's a tapping at the passenger side window. He looks over, sees Rocket. He hits the switch to slide the window down. "Yo, man," he says. "You late. Didn't yo' mama teach yo' punk ass no punctuality?"

"Had to make sure I wasn't bein' followed, Judge."

"Who would want to follow you around? You jus' a little bit o' nuthin'."

The kid shrugs. "No tellin'. But I can't be havin' the brothers think I'se a snitch. They think that, they poun' me into the ground."

"So, you talk to a cop, you automatically a snitch? That how it is?"

"It wasn't that way when you was a kid?"

Clyde ignores the question. "What you got fo' me if you ain't got no Slade?"

Rocket looks around, leans in a little closer. "I got the name of the dude done took over Lamont's trade. How 'bout that shit?"

Clyde frowns a skeptical frown. "Where'd a kid like you come up with that?"

"Word gets around, Judge."

"Who is it, then?"

"You ain't gon' rat me out for bein' a snitch?"

"Cops don't rat out confidential informants. Ain't you never watched no cop shows on TV?"

"Shows I watch, cops pay a man to dime a dealer. You got any money on you?"

Clyde sighs, shakes his head. "Ain't it enough to be a good citizen, man?"

The kid holds his hand inside the cruiser, rubs his fingers and thumb together in the universal sign that says "Let's see the whip-out."

Clyde pulls out his money clip, peels off a five, holds it up.

Rocket grins. "They say, you wanna get high now the Lamont sto' done gone outta business, you aks fo' a pachuco from over in Caldwell. Name spelled like Jesus but them Mexicans say it 'Hey-Suss.'"

"Jesus, huh? From Caldwell. You sho' 'bout this?"

Rocket nods.

"Alright then." Clyde hands over the five dollars. Rocket snatches it. "And I still needs you to find me that Slade."

"That'll cost you twenty." He grins, pulls his head out of the cruiser, runs off.

Clyde hollers after him, "Go home and do some homework or somethin'!" Clyde slips the cruiser into gear, heads over to the crime scene, still got a few doors to knock on yet. His cell phone commences to chirp. He checks the display, sees it's Sonya.

"That's what I'm talkin' about." He answers the phone. "Yo."

"Hey. What are you up to?"

She sounds a lot less agitated than when they talked earlier. *Maybe she's commenced to chill some, spent some time this afternoon giving her old suspicious mind a talkin' to. Maybe she's got an apology all teed up.*

"Workin' the Stubbs case," he says. "What you been doin'?"

"Went to Houston. Bought some new court shoes. How about a rematch?"

Now this is way *more like it.* "You on. What time?"

"Six o'clock work for you?"

"See you then." Clyde ends the call, starts planning the evening in his head. Some hoops, another turn in that big tub of hers. Finish what they started last night. *That's what I'm talkin' about.*

20

They found Gitch near the river, standing at an old delivery truck that listed to one side, hood open. He was wiping engine parts with a red grease rag. He was tall, lean, pale, shirtless, in his early thirties. He wore his dirty blond hair long, combed back, a few days growth of beard. His dungarees covered the heels of his pointed-toe boots.

The old woman introduced Benjamin, told his tale for him, speaking rapidly, using many hand gestures. Gitch leaned against the truck and listened.

When she finished, he said, "You think he can be taught?" He was speaking to the old woman, but his eyes studied Benjamin.

"You can see how smart he is."

"Perhaps."

She said, "He must learn what he can. Otherwise—"

Gitch looked up at the sun, then back down at Benjamin. "Come back in two hours' time." He picked up the grease rag and turned his back on them.

A week later, five o'clock in the afternoon in the great hall of the Nyugati Pályaudvar, the west Budapest train station, designed by the Eiffel firm, built in the 1870s, all glass and iron. A place thick this evening with traveling folk. The hall echoed with their voices, with their footsteps as they crossed the marble floors.

Benjamin stood near one wall, hidden behind a great column. He watched Gitch as he moved through the crowd. Benjamin was wearing the same dirty clothes he had worn when he arrived in the gypsies' camp, but Gitch had been transformed. His hair was washed and combed, his face shaved. He wore a gray three-piece suit and tie that looked reasonably new. Black lace-up shoes. He carried a smart-looking attaché case.

Gitch closed to within a few feet of a goateed man in an expensive charcoal gray overcoat and a Homburg, then shifted his attaché case from his right hand to his left. That was the signal.

Benjamin moved across the train hall until he was standing beside the man in the Homburg. He grabbed the man's coat. "Please, sir. Can you spare some change?"

The man looked down at him as if from a great height. He tugged his coat out *of Benjamin's grasp. "Go away, you little beggar," he said, in German-accented Magyar.*

Benjamin grabbed his coat again, tugged harder. "Please, sir. If only a coin."

"Go away, I said." Louder this time.

Then, a hand on Benjamin's shoulder, spinning him around. He looked up into Gitch's frowning face. "See here, boy," Gitch said in a voice so refined Benjamin would not have thought him capable of it. "Leave the gentleman be."

Benjamin swung his fist at Gitch's stomach. As the punch landed Gitch crumpled and dropped the attaché case. It popped open on contact. Papers scattered everywhere, causing passersby to slip and stumble, the paper on marble turning the footing tricky.

Benjamin ran for the main doors. He looked behind him only once before he gained the safety of the anonymous streets. He saw people picking up the papers Gitch had dropped.

He saw the man in the Homburg helping Gitch to his feet.

21

THE HEALTH CLUB MANAGER TURNS OUT TO BE AN IMPOSSIBLY FIT-LOOKING young woman named Denise who wears her blond hair in a ponytail, gym shorts over a leotard stretched across small breasts and an abdominal wall that's set at a right angle to the floor. Once she hears what Jeremiah wants, she invites him and Bruce back to her office, which sits just inside a glass door leading to the weight room, where men the size of Kodiak bears wearing tiny shorts and singlets strain at lifting bars that look to weigh as much as a subcompact automobile. Her office walls are covered with diet and exercise posters. Denise takes one of the two chairs. Jeremiah and Bruce stand.

"So," she says, "you're looking for Paul Lipper."

Jeremiah says, "We need to ask him 'bout a client of his what's gone missin'."

She sets her jaw. "I'd like to talk to him, too. To tell him he's fired."

"On account of how come?"

"He walked out of here during the middle of the day about two weeks ago. Didn't say a word to me or anyone else. Stood up about a half-dozen clients. I tried to reach him by phone to find out what was going on. Called both his apartment and his cell phone. Nothing."

Jeremiah's thinking, *First Nelson disappears and then his boyfriend, all inside of the same week.*

"And you ain't heard from him since?"

"Not a peep."

"What about this client of his? Man calls hisself Dusty Nelson. You seen him around lately?"

"He quit coming around about the same time Paul dropped out of sight."

"What do you make of it? The two of them disappearin' all of a sudden like?"

"Beats me. Maybe they eloped."

That prompts a short laugh from Bruce, but he dummies up at a glance from Jeremiah. Jeremiah can hear noises coming from the weight room.

Judging by the sound of it, one of the Kodiak bears had just given birth.

Denise says, "In all seriousness, personal trainers tend to be an unstable bunch. They come and go. I'm used to it. Comes with the territory. But I would have appreciated the two weeks' notice I was entitled to. As it is, I've had to reschedule all of Paul's clients with other trainers, and we're struggling to keep up."

"How long had he been with y'all?"

She pulls a file from her desk and refers to its contents. "About three years."

"That his personnel jacket?"

"Yes."

"Mind if I take a look?"

She hesitates a moment, then hands it over.

Jeremiah says, "You know much about this man Nelson?"

"Just that he was Paul's client, and they had some kind of relationship. I discouraged that, of course. I told Paul it was very unprofessional. But what are you going to do?"

Jeremiah leafs through the file, wondering what it would be like to have to spend your life wrangling personal trainers. Not much here other than work records, a couple of thank-you notes, an employment application. He looks the employment application over. Paul Lipper was born in 1967. Went to high school here in Dallas, then got a degree in physical therapy from a state college. Worked a few years as a therapist with orthopedic patients at a local hospital, then came over here.

Jeremiah flips to his emergency contact information. A Winston Lipper up in Richardson. Says here the man is Paul's father. Jeremiah pulls out a notepad, jots down Paul's address, his father's phone number, sticks the employment application back in the file, hands it to Denise.

"'Preciate your help. If you was to hear from either of these two rascals, would you mind givin' me a call?"

She says she'd be happy to, jots down the cell phone number Bruce gives her.

Ten minutes later Jeremiah and Bruce are pushing their way through the door of the property management office at Paul Lipper's apartment complex. A middle-aged man in a sports jacket gets up from behind a desk to greet them. He had been making notes in some kind of book, and he shifts his ballpoint pen from his right hand to his left so he can offer up a shake.

"I'm Lawrence Chambers," he says, smiling wide. "How can I help you gentlemen?"

Jeremiah says, "Name's Spur. This here's Bruce. We're lookin' for a man, name of Paul Lipper. We're given to understand he rents number three twenty-two."

The guy switches his smile off so fast you'd have thought Jeremiah was peddling religion. "He did until recently. And if you all are looking for him, that would make three of us."

"Meanin' what?"

"Meaning we discovered him gone about ten days ago, and he left quite the mess behind. I have a substantial bone to pick with that gentleman, and I intend to get it well and truly picked before he regains custody of his furniture and other personal effects."

"What, is he late on his rent or somethin'?"

"Would that it were something that simple, not to mention hygienic. A little while back we got a call from his next-door neighbor, complaining about a distinctly unpleasant smell coming, she thought, from Mr. Lipper's apartment. When we couldn't get him on the telephone either at home or his place of employment, our maintenance people let themselves into his unit. What they found was—and you cannot imagine how utterly awful this was—what they found was the body of a dog that appeared to have been shot. It had been dead for several days. What's more, the place was turned completely upside down. Drawers pulled out of cabinets, cushions slashed, cupboards empty. It took a cleaning crew the better part of a week to restore order and move Mr. Lipper's belongings into storage pending his resurfacing, if he ever bothers to resurface."

"You think it was him shot the dog?"

The man shakes his head. "Heavens, no. He loved that animal."

"Must of been ever-who tossed his place then. Anybody see who might of gone into his apartment?"

"No one has come forward if they did. To be honest, I doubt it. Mostly professional people live here, and they pretty much keep to themselves."

"He have any friends here that might know where he vamoosed off to?"

"Couldn't honestly say."

Jeremiah pushes his Stetson back on his head a bit so he can scratch at a spot in his hairline. "You mind if I ask around some, talk to a few of the folks what live here?"

The man hesitates. "Is he in some kind of trouble?"

"Nothin' I would know about. I just need to talk to him, 'bout a friend of his."

The man bites his lip. "Are you by any chance with the police, Mr. Spur?"

"Used to be a Texas Ranger. I took retirement, 'bout a year ago."

"I see. Look, I'd like to be helpful, but we have fairly strict policies against soliciting inside the—"

"I ain't sellin' a thing, Mr. Chambers, not a blessed thing. I just need to ask folks what they know about Lipper and about what happened in his apartment. That's all."

"I'll need to talk to my boss."

"When can you do that?"

"He's traveling. It won't be until sometime next week, I'm afraid."

"Alright, then. You got a card?"

The man reaches into his desk, pulls out a business card, hands it to Jeremiah.

Back outside, Jeremiah says to Bruce, "You see why Leslie ought to sic the police on this here thing? A cop wouldn't even have had to ask that guy back yonder for permission. Would've just started knockin' on doors."

"But Mr. Farkas—"

"Yeah, I know. I'm just sayin'." Jeremiah reaches in his pocket, pulls out the cell phone Bruce had given him. "Let's see if I can figger out how to work this gizmo."

He punches a button and it beeps to life. He pulls out his notepad, keys in the phone number for Winston Lipper. A man answers on the second ring.

"Hello?"

"Mr. Lipper?"

"Yes. Who's calling?"

"Mr. Lipper, we don't know one another, and I'm sorry to bother you on a Saturday afternoon. My name is Jeremiah Spur, and I'm a retired Texas Ranger. I'm lookin' for your son, Paul. You got any idea where I might could find him?"

There's a moment of silence on the other end of the line. Then the man says, "I don't have a son named Paul." With that, the line goes dead.

22

Benjamin was asleep on the ground outside Gitch's little shack made of scrap wood hammered together at drunken angles when he felt a pointed toe digging into his back. He awoke, looked up at Gitch standing above him, smoking one of his Turkish cigarettes.

Inside his shack, Gitch lit a candle. He was still wearing his suit, but he had removed his tie and unbuttoned the vest. He sat cross-legged on his bedroll. Benjamin sat down across from him. Gitch reached inside his coat pocket, produced a wallet. Calfskin, very fancy design. Gitch stubbed out his cigarette, flicked the butt outside.

He sorted through the wallet. Several thousand forints in cash. Gitch peeled off one hundred forints, handed them to Benjamin, set the rest aside. Benjamin whispered his thanks and gripped the money in his hands.

Gitch pulled a passport from the wallet. Austrian. He opened it. The picture was of the fat man in the Homburg. He set it on the ground.

Gitch began to turn the wallet around in his hands, looking at it from every angle in the candlelight, working its leather with his fingers. Then he grunted again, reached in his pocket for a knife. He cut the lining away from the inside of the wallet. Pulled out two more passports. One Hungarian. One East German. He set aside the three passports and the wallet and stood up and began peeling off his clothes.

Benjamin reached over, picked up the passports, opened them. They all showed the fat man, but with different names and nationalities. Benjamin looked up at Gitch. "Are you going to sell these on the black market?"

Gitch was pulling off his trousers. He had not been wearing underpants. Benjamin was staring at Gitch's recumbent, uncircumcised penis. He dropped his eyes while Gitch pulled on his dungarees.

"They have been purchased already, those passports."

Benjamin stared at the ground. "By whom?"

"By the man who loaned me these fine clothes, little wolf." Once Gitch was dressed, he left the shack, carrying the suit, the wallet, the rest of the money, and the passports.

Benjamin stayed behind, counting and recounting his money by candlelight.

23

BEHIND THE OLD OAKS THAT RUN THE LENGTH OF PRICE BOULEVARD SIT THE homes of the Brenham elite, the lawyers, the bankers, the merchants, the entrepreneurs, the small-town affluent. This is Sonya Nichols's street. She lives in an eighty-year-old white Victorian with forest green trim, white wicker furniture on porches that wrap clear around, ferns hanging in baskets, ceiling fans turning. Sonya's yardman has her half acre looking like it's ready for a Monet acolyte to drop by with his easel—green St. Augustine grass, impatiens in every color you can think of, lots of mums in deference to the season.

Sonya comes through her back door hauling grocery bags. In a little while Mr. Punctuality will be here. After she stores her purchases, she heads up to her bedroom, taking the stairs by twos, unbuttoning as she goes. She changes into her workout gear and fixes her hair in a ponytail.

She fishes under the bed for an exercise pad, begins her stretches, her mind busy with her newly minted Clyde problem. When she had asked him to move in, she had been half expecting a turndown. What she hadn't reckoned on was him looking to hire on with the DPS, maybe leave Brenham altogether.

Then along came that Yolanda, completely mooting Sonya's roommate plans, making it seem like the imperative thing was just to keep Clyde in Brenham, away from the DPS and that café au lait hussy. That, together with the gyrations of an imagination that had long been dormant where Clyde was concerned, set off a chain reaction—fitful night's sleep, foul mood this morning, telephone confrontation with Clyde.

It was probably a mistake, out-and-out challenging his motives, really leaning on him. Mistake to call at all when she was too cranky to exercise choice-of-word care. She turns over on her back to do her iliotibial band stretches. *That's the problem right there, huh? All this tiptoeing around you have to do.*

On their first date he had told her about his family, him growing up one of six kids, living with a single mother in a shotgun house in Oak Cliff, up in Dallas. Had a brother doing life down in Sugarland for first-degree murder. A crack addict sister. Two brothers had been gunned down in the street, including Leon, Clyde's favorite. Another sister was over in Louisiana, studying to be a nurse. That one and Clyde were the only two of the bunch who were able to fight their way out. He had seen the rest destroyed by the world into which they were born, and it had planted this nucleus in him, anger and fear fused into a hard ball, welded inside his chest. That's what makes him the way he is. That's the part of him you always have to be careful about, the part she hadn't been careful enough about this morning on the phone.

She heads downstairs, out the door, collects her basketball from the garage. Shoots jumpers at the hoop she had hung above her driveway. Thinks about this recent turn of events, the whole DPS-Yolanda thing. She had tried hard all day to look at the situation from another angle, tried for once being honest with herself about her relationship with C. Livermore "Clyde" Thomas. Asked herself, where's it all going, really? Does she honest-to-God want him for her life companion, maybe all the way to marriage, put them, not to mention their kids, through what she had seen other interracial families go through?

Is she really going to be happy spending the rest of her life easing around Clyde's ego, his racial sensitivity, his deep-as-the-ocean-floor insecurity? His alienation from both races? Is she just settling for him because that's the best bargain there is here in Washington County and, imperfect as it is, it beats being alone?

Yeah, she had told herself, but the sex is disco and he can be sweet and funny, when he's not pouting or skyrocketing around, and the work gives them a lot in common.

She had spent the better part of the day piling up her little stacks of pros and cons, like it was an everyday decision, using the same syllogistic logic she would use if she were trying to settle on which food processor to buy.

She knows she should have had the presence of mind to think all this through before she invited Clyde to move in, knows she probably belongs in the Flighty Hall of Fame, going from "Let's live together" to rethinking their entire relationship inside of twenty-four hours.

But, hey, he hadn't gone for her offer anyway. And then there had been his flirtation with this DPS notion, not to mention Miss Yolanda's surprise appearance, jumping out of that crime scene vehicle like a centerfold leaping out of a cake at some horny old goat's birthday party. This was all breaking news to Sonya, and she had it to thank for finally facing up to her subconscious, which had been growling at her for a while now about all this.

Clyde's gold Z-28 pulls up at six o'clock on the money. Sonya stands on her driveway, basketball on her hip, wondering as she watches her gentleman friend get out of his car whether the time hasn't come to share some of her questions with him.

Ever since Sonya had called him, Clyde had been thinking how he had some contrition coming, some acknowledgment from his prideful woman that she had wronged him, engaged in stereotypical thinking, hauled off and suspected him when she had no cause to. He even said it out loud to himself, while he was driving over to her house in the rich white part of town. "That's what I needs. I needs me some contrition."

He gets out of his ride, sees her standing on the driveway, basketball on her hip. *Ain't much contrition in that posture. If any.*

"Here comes da Judge," Sonya says, her tone of voice ambiguous.

He feels the needle on his racism meter go *bump. That can't be right. We talkin' 'bout Sonya here. She can be a bitch sometimes, but she ain't no racist. Maybe it's just this game of one-on-one we fixin' to have, gettin' her talkin' trash.*

"That's right," he says. "The Judge is fixin' to show you how the game's played. Gimme the ball, woman."

"Don't you want to warm up first?"

"No, man. I'm ready. The spot is five."

"The spot is seven."

"Seven! That ain't right."

"Yeah, it is. And I'm bringing it in."

"Shit. That's fucked up."

"Deal with it." Dribbling now, Sonya turns, faces the hoop. Clyde's on defense, body crouched, feet spread, hands up.

"Hey, wait a minute," he says, straightening back up, pointing. "Them flowers been moved back." Two pots of geraniums, his three-point line, are closer to the street than they were yesterday.

"You got it. They should have been back there all along. Your percentage from three-point land is way too high, so I moved 'em back to make things more competitive."

"More competitive, huh?"

"Yeah." She dribbles the ball, looks at him hard. "Like they're sure to be if you hitch up with the DPS. It'll take more than just showing up to be the star with those guys. A lot more competitive than the Sheriff's Department."

"You know what? That shit don't have nothin' to do with you."

"Whatever." Sonya shoulder fakes, switches hands, drives, hits the layup.

"Nine–zip," she says.

Clyde dribbles back to half-court, a long crack in the driveway. Sonya clears her hair out of her face, leans forward with her hands on her knees. "So how'd you do with the Stubbs case today?"

"Fine, I reckon. Did the next-of-kin on the girl, then went by Lamont's crib." Clyde drives to his left, pulls up, shoots the jumper. It clangs off the iron. Sonya shags it. "God damn! Shoulda warmed up first. Hold up, let me shoot a little, get my stroke down."

"Sorry, Junior. You had your chance."

"You feelin' mean today, huh."

"Did you find anything at Lamont's place?"

"Somebody tossed it before we got there. No tellin' who. Then come to find out, Lamont has a sister, livin' with an ex-con name of Gutter Ball Jones. I go to see him and he give me all kinda attitude. I'm wonderin' if it was him that done it, or hired it out to be done."

Sonya drives to her left, Clyde slides over, seals her off. She dribbles, ball just out of his reach.

Clyde says, "On top uh that, word on the street is, some Mexican from up in Caldwell's already moved in on his action."

Sonya pivots, tries the fadeaway. Clyde gets the block and the ball, sprints back for a three-pointer, drains it. "That's what I'm talkin' about. There's my stroke. Just had to get the geometry down in my mind, you know what I'm sayin'?"

"I should have moved those pots further back. So what's your next move?"

She fakes a drive to the basket, pulls up, shoots from her three-point line, a good ways in from Clyde's, watches the ball slip through the net. "Twelve–three."

"I'se goin' to Caldwell tomorrow, see about checkin' out this Jesus cat who's supposed to be the new man on the drug scene, then I'm gon' go on up to Austin, see what the forensics look like." Clyde dribbles back, drives in, pulls up, nails it over Sonya's outstretched hand. "Twelve–five."

The pace they're going at now has them working too hard to talk. Back and forth they go, sweat flying, breathing hard, scrambling for rebounds, looking for the open shot. Clyde soaks his T-shirt through. He strips it, tosses it on the lawn.

Sonya can sort of keep up on account of her ballhandling, honed in college, playing guard for Texas Christian. Clyde hasn't played organized ball since high school. But he's quick, has a thirty-inch vertical leap, sticks close on defense, long arms and big hands closing off a lot of sky.

It's eighteen–fifteen when Clyde blocks a couple of shots, hits two back-to-back from downtown. Sonya grabs the basketball, spikes it hard, sends it shooting off into the azaleas. "Damn it!"

"Call my agent! I'se ready for prime time! You want another shot at the title?"

She wipes her face with the tail of her singlet. "No. Not tonight. Why don't you pretend you're a gentleman and go grab us a couple of beers? I'll meet you on the porch."

A few minutes later they're sitting next to one another on the swing, drinking their beer, looking out across the lawn, Clyde quiet for a change, wondering if they're going to go back to arguing about him and Yolanda and all that.

Sonya turns to him. "I've done a lot of thinking today."

" 'Bout what?"

"C'mon, Clyde. About us."

"What, the move-in offer done expired?"

"You want to accept?"

He looks off across the lawn. "No. We done been through that."

"Then what did you bring it up for?"

"You was pretty pissed off this mornin'. I figgered you changed yo' mind, which you is free to do. But you ain't free to be 'cusin' me of playin' 'round with Yolanda. I ain't laid eyes on her nor talked to her neither since Prairie View."

"Look, I am sorry about that. You're right. I overreacted."

Clyde thinks, *That's more like it.* He knows better than to say it out loud, though.

"But," she says, "I have to be honest with you. The last twenty-four hours do have me thinking."

"Thinkin', huh."

"Yeah. About how differently we see things."

"Girl, I ain't got no idea what you talkin' about."

"Take our conversation while we were playing one-on-one. You said something about how your joining the DPS doesn't have anything to do with me. That's not how I see it, particularly if it takes you away from Brenham."

"I s'pose that's right."

She stands up, walks across the porch, turns back to look at Clyde. Leans against the porch railing. She's about to say something. If Clyde didn't know her better, he would think she was trying to be dramatic.

She says, "Has it ever occurred to you how mismatched we are?"

"Say what?"

"Think about it. What do we have in common, really? Other than law enforcement?"

"Where is this comin' from all of a sudden?"

"Like I said, the last twenty-four hours have me thinking. About the real fundamentals underpinning our relationship. Whether it's sustainable long term."

Clyde drains his beer, sets the bottle down. "What you want to go gettin' into all that fo'? Seem like a lot of unnecessary bullshit to me."

"It's not unnecessary. See, that statement there sort of makes my point for me."

Her circumlocutions are beginning to make Clyde testy. "I wish you would make yo' damn point."

"My point is, I'm not sure we're going to be able to make this work long term. You know, we come from such totally different places, have different backgrounds, look at the world so very differently—"

Clyde is on his feet now. *"Have different skin colors?"* The needle on his racism meter has whanged hard over to the right now, is completely pegged out. His blood is a jackhammer inside his head.

She sighs. "Come on, Clyde, you know me better than that."

He all but shouts, *"No,* I don't think I *do."*

"You're accusing me, of all people, of being a racist? Don't you think the fact that we've been lovers for the last three years sort of precludes that?"

"White folks in this country happy to sleep with black folks, long as they own 'em. Been true a lotta years, you know what I'm sayin'? Just look at Thomas Jefferson."

Her hands go to her hips. "That is complete and utter bullshit."

In two steps he's across the porch, standing right in front of her, staring down into her eyes. "Let me ask you somethin'. If I was white, would we be havin' this conversation?"

She just hesitates a moment, but that's all it takes.

"Thought so," he says. "See you around, bitch."

Ten seconds later he's collected his T-shirt from her front yard and left rubber on the pavement in front of her house.

24

THE SUN HAS NEARLY SLIPPED BELOW THE HORIZON WHEN THE YOUNG LADY who had checked him in—her name tag reads "Irene"—shows Jeremiah into the hotel room Leslie had reserved for him.

It's not just a room. It's a suite. There's a sitting area with a desk, a blue couch with thick cushions, a coffee table with chairs on either side. The couch faces an oak armoire containing a television set, CD player. The coffee table has magazines on top, along with a plate of fruit, a knife, a cloth napkin, an envelope with "Mr. Jeremiah Spur" written in a flowery hand.

To the left is the bedroom. Jeremiah walks in there. The bed is so big you could land a helicopter on it. Next to the bed a radio plays classical music, just loud enough to hear from the door. Jeremiah chucks his grip on the bed.

Irene shows him around the room like she thinks maybe since he's from the country he's dimwitted, needs instruction in big-city hotel room ways. Here's how you work the television set, here's how you adjust the room temperature.

Then she shows him around the bathroom, which looks like it was designed for some sultan, what with its pink marble, gold fixtures, glass shower separate from the bath, little bars of soap, bottles of shampoo, towels big enough to wipe down Redbo, enough floor space in here to hold a square dance.

When Irene has finished her routine, she asks him if he needs anything.

He looks around at all the finery, thinking what he needs is a surface so plain he'd feel at liberty to sit on it. "No, ma'am. But in all honesty, I have to say, this here is about the finest hotel room I ever did see."

Her smile widens such that if it got any bigger, Jeremiah is sure it would be painful. "The Crescent is regularly voted among the best hotels in the world."

Jeremiah wonders who votes on such things. Certainly nobody he's ever met. Probably nobody who's ever even been to Washington County.

After she leaves, he unpacks his grip, takes his shaving kit and sets it on the marble counter in the sultan's bathroom. He walks back into the sitting room, pulls from his pocket the envelope that had been waiting for him at the front desk. He starts to open it, then decides not to just yet. He sets it down on the desk.

He walks to the window, looks out at the trees and rooftops of the suburb of Highland Park to the north, the sun's rays casting long shadows across the land. He glances at his watch. An hour before Leslie is supposed to carry him to dinner at some restaurant Bruce had said was one of the best in town.

Staring out the window as dusk gathers, Jeremiah thinks over all that's happened. *How's a man like Farkas let his chief bean counter make off with ten million dollars of his money? Don't most businesses have procedures in place to prevent just such a thing? And why am I bein' sent down a rabbit trail after this Lipper? 'Cause that's what's happenin'—I'm bein' sent down it just as sure as the world.*

Farkas is the key here. The man is up to something which is without a doubt why he ain't showed himself yet. What he is showin' is his hand. One card at a time.

As he turns away from the window Jeremiah decides he needs to lean on Leslie, get her to set up a meeting for him with her boss.

And then there's this preposterous business of Farkas claiming to know Jeremiah's father. "Shoot," Jeremiah says out loud. "I never even knew him."

Jeremiah doesn't remember exactly how old he was when he noticed his family was different, that it was short a parent.

When he was a boy, he and his mother lived north of downtown Dallas in a section of little houses built mostly in the twenties called the M Streets. They rented a red brick number with a tiny living room and dining room up front and a hallway that ran down the middle toward the back, with two bedrooms on the left and a kitchen and family room on the right. A tree in the backyard with a tire swing hanging from it. The windows were covered with pull-down shades and the walls with fading paint. The floors were linoleum in the kitchen and hardwood everywhere else. The house was built on pier and beam and in his head Jeremiah can still hear the *kuh-lunk, kuh-lunk, kuh-lunk* of his mother's footsteps when she came down the hall to check on him at night, a sound like syncopated echoes of distant hammer blows.

Jeremiah glances out his hotel room window toward the northeast, wonders if the old house is still there. Thinks how simple it was, the polar opposite of this hotel room. The furniture had either been bought new from Sears, Roebuck or, more likely, secondhand from some neighbor or friend.

He still has some reliable scraps of memories about growing up there, playing barefoot and in short pants with kids from other young families, families with husbands who'd been in the war. Jeremiah's mother didn't stay home during the day like the other boys' mothers. She taught over at Bowie Elementary, walked the half mile each way to her job every school day. When she got home she graded papers, cleaned house, fixed their meals.

No daddy ever came walking through the front door swinging a brief-case or a lunch pail.

Until Jeremiah was old enough to go to school himself, his mother dropped him off with an old black lady who lived near the schoolhouse, paid her twenty-five cents an hour to look after him. Her name was Bertha, she had something wrong with the right side of her face that caused hair to grow there, and she was kindness itself. Even after Jeremiah started school and didn't need looking after in the daytime, Bertha would come sit with him nights when his mother would go out with the men who came calling.

That made them different, too. No strange men ever called on any of his friends' mothers.

They all seemed nice enough, the men who called on Fiona Spur. Usu-ally dressed in a suit and tie, driving a late-model sedan. His mother would kiss him good-bye, then leave him to play board games with Bertha until bedtime.

Sometimes he would wake up at the sound of her coming back home from her night out. He would lie in bed, listen to those hammer-blow echoes, *kuh-lunk, kuh-lunk, kuh-lunk,* her coming down the hall, pausing at his door to check on him before she went to bed. She always came home alone. There was never a second set of hammer blows moving around the house late at night. Just the one lonely set.

At some point the question appeared in his brain, lurked there, a tres-passer on his peace of mind. The natural thing would have been to go to his mother, ask her. But, he told himself, if she had thought it was impor-tant for him to know what had become of his daddy, wouldn't she have brought it up? He thought about that a lot, finally decided she had her reasons for not talking about it. Her silence on the subject is what kept him from asking, how come him to grab that trespasser by the neck, lock him away in a cage he built in his mind, rather than run the risk he'd open up a topic his mama found somehow inappropriate. Or painful.

Jeremiah shakes his head, tries to get the memories to scatter. He goes to the desk, picks up the envelope they had handed him when he checked in, opens it. It contains the list of people who had signed in to visit Dusty at his apartment building. The information is organized in columns down the page. A column each for the date and time of sign-in, then the name of the visitor.

He scans the first couple pages. Paul Lipper's name appears numerous times, as do others he doesn't recognize. On page three he sees the name Jonathon Farkas. He stops, checks the date. He sets the list down, decides he'll just have to see what Miss Leslie has to say about that when they have dinner here directly.

He stands up, stretches, walks over to the coffee table, opens the hand-addressed envelope next to the fruit plate. He pulls out a card. It has a paragraph of text written on it. That's it. No salutation, no date, no signature.

He says out loud, "Now we're gettin' somewheres."

The paragraph says: "You will never find Dusty Nelson, Captain Spur. Go back to your ranch where you belong. Farkas is taking you for a ride."

25

FROM BEHIND THE STEERING WHEEL LESLIE IS SAYING, "RENTS NORTH OF Market Street are above sixty dollars net, and since there's no bloody vacancy, we think tenants who plump for the best space, with the smashing views of the Bay and all that, will pay close to a hundred dollars before this cycle cools off, which is why we're offering nearly two hundred an FAR foot for the poxy land. I'd rather give it a miss myself, but not Mr. Farkas. He's always wanted to develop a project in Ambrose Bierce's adopted hometown. Bloody foolish."

"Who's Ambrose Bierce?"

"Minor American writer Mr. Farkas fancies to the point he's collected all the chap's works, first editions each and every one, plus rather a lot of his correspondence. That's one of Mr. Farkas's passions, you see. Collecting books. He also has the entire Graham Greene canon. All first editions as well. At least Greene was a decent writer, and an Englishman. Mr. Farkas can be forgiven a passion for him."

Jeremiah would just as lief she spared him the primer on San Francisco office development and the book-collecting predilections of her employer and pay more attention to her driving since he can't much follow her jargon anyway and meanwhile they're bombing through Dallas at what feels like a hundred miles an hour with their butts six inches above the pavement.

The woman drives like she enjoys a personal exemption from the speed limit, talking as fast as she drives, arms waving in the air, babbling on about this development site in San Francisco her boss has taken a shine to, most of it unintelligible to Jeremiah, who has to restrain himself mightily not to interrupt her with various admonitions about motor vehicle safety. She whips back and forth in traffic, cuts off other cars, changes lanes without a signal, rolls through stop signs, tailgates. Were he not biting his tongue plum through, he would be pointing out that today is not so far as he knows National Drive-Like-an-Asshole Day. He's got mental images of the automobile accidents he's seen over the years, all that needless carnage.

Directly she's tailgating a Ford Excursion, nose of the sports car practically up its tailpipe, the Ford's rear tag above eye level. Jeremiah's toe digs into the floorboard, his braking reflex too powerful to overcome. She whips the Ferrari to the left, directly into the path of an oncoming refuse truck. One spiked heel jams the clutch to the floor, then releases it as she works the gearshift and the other spiked heel hits the accelerator. She cuts in front of the Excursion, gets serenaded by stereophonic horn blasts.

"God O-mighty damn."

She glances in the rearview mirror. "A bit close, that."

"If I still carried handcuffs for the state of Texas, you'd be wearin' 'em right now."

She glances his way. "It's a bloody Ferrari, Captain Spur. One jolly well can't resist the temptation to let it do its thing from time to time."

"One can if one don't want to end up in County, if not on a slab down at the morgue."

She laughs at that. But she also eases off the accelerator some. Jeremiah doesn't exhale fully until she stops to have her six figures' worth of car valet-parked in front of an unassuming restaurant named Sebastian's. He unfolds himself from the front seat a body part at a time.

There's a crowd waiting inside the front door. Leslie weaves her way to the maitre d', who calls her by name and leads them to a corner table in the front room. Jeremiah's thinking, *There's so many folks in here you couldn't stir 'em with a stick.*

On the way to the table, Jeremiah gets his first good look at his dinner companion. She's wearing a tight-fitting black dress with a neckline that runs down past her topheaviness and a hemline that's a few inches north of her knees. Her hair is combed back behind her ears, where diamond studs sparkle, so big they must be worth at least a couple of dozen heifers apiece. Jeremiah can't help but wonder why this woman isn't out tonight with her husband or boyfriend, instead of squiring him around. The only answer he can come up with is that Farkas has ordered it that way.

Jeremiah had changed into a fresh white shirt, clean pair of khakis, same Western-cut sports jacket he had been wearing all day. Not knowing what to expect when he was packing his grip for this adventure, he had thrown in a bolo tie, a turquoise stone encased in silver, that Elizabeth had given him one Christmas. He had slipped that on tonight. His buff-colored Stetson completes his rig. He knows he looks country compared to all these duded-up Dallasites, but that's who he is.

They take their seats. "What do you think?" Leslie says, gesturing at the room.

Jeremiah looks around. To his right there's an oversized armoire that's been converted to a wine rack. On the other side of the room bas relief goddesses painted earth tones lean against a brick wall. One has the sun on its head, the other the moon. To their right a mounted blue marlin floats in a sea of cigarette smoke. The pressed tin ceiling is held up by carved wooden pillars. Fern baskets hang from the ceiling beams.

Jeremiah says, "It's a lot fancier than anything we got back home."

"The owner moved up here ten or twelve years ago from Mexico. He's making a bloody fortune. Ah, here comes Rafael."

An older waiter dressed in dark slacks and a short-sleeved white shirt and bow tie approaches their table. He's a short man, with gray hair he combs straight back. Jeremiah can see something is wrong with his left arm. It's scarred and shriveled and wounded altogether. Leslie half stands to accept a kiss on the cheek.

"*Buenas noches,* Miss Whitten," Rafael says. "Good to see you again."

"Thanks, Rafael. You'll take good care of us tonight, won't you?"

The waiter makes the okay sign with his right hand.

"Brilliant. Why don't you start us out with a couple of margaritas while we parse the menu and the wine list."

"Regular or top shelf?"

"Rafael, dear man. When have I *ever* ordered *regular* tequila?"

"*Muy bien,* Miss Whitten." The waiter disappears without asking Jeremiah how he wants the margarita he hadn't ordered, didn't want, and probably wouldn't drink. On the rocks? With salt? *Maybe they only come one way in this place,* he thinks.

Leslie opens her menu. "Everything is good here, but I personally recommend the Filet Cantiflas." They study their menus until the waiter brings them their drinks, takes their orders, disappears.

Leslie looks at Jeremiah, smiles brightly, says, "So, making progress, are we?"

"You mean your boy Bruce ain't reported in?"

She shakes her head no. "Haven't heard a peep."

Jeremiah's progress is precious short in the telling. He finishes about the time they polish off their tortilla soup. She orders a second margarita. His sits just where the waiter had set it, as untouched as a spinster. Tequila is apt to make him sleepy and cause him to belch like a bloated mule.

Jeremiah says, "So it all seems to point to this Lipper feller. Almost like I'm bein' steered in that direction. You got any idea why that would be?"

"Haven't the foggiest, I'm afraid."

"Let me ask you this, then," he says, as the waiter sets their entrees down. Jeremiah notices how well the man handles the tray and plates despite his infirmity. Jeremiah had ordered the filet Leslie had recommended, a cut of beef with cheese inside, served with refried beans and rice. *I bet I have them barbecue dreams tonight.* "You say Nelson was introduced to y'all by Farkas's son?"

"Excuse me," the waiter says, "but will there be anything else?"

Leslie gives him a smile. "Not at the moment, thanks." He shuffles off.

She redirects her attention at Jeremiah. "Yes, it was Jonathon that first brought Little Fuck around."

"And you say Jonathon passed away last spring?"

"Quite so. Fell ill and died. Cancer, alas."

"Do you recall when it was he passed away exactly?"

She chews a bite of red snapper thoughtfully, dabs at her mouth with her napkin. "That would have been sometime in April, I should think."

Jeremiah reaches in his pocket, pulls out the papers that had been delivered to him at the hotel, hands them across the table to her. Goes back to attacking his steak.

"That," he says, using his fork as a pointing instrument, "is the log of folks who visited Dusty at his apartment over the last two years. Flip it over to page three, look at the entries for April."

She does as he asks, then looks up. "Well?"

"You see Jonathon Farkas's name there?"

"Yes, of course."

He sets his knife and fork down. "I lost a daughter to cancer in May of this year."

"I'm so sorry."

He waves her off. "I ain't bringin' it up to get sympathy. I'm bringin' it up because for the last two months of her life she was so sick she couldn't've left her hospital room for love nor money. But that says Jonathon Farkas was callin' on Dusty at his apartment the month he died."

Leslie stares at the paper in her hands. Jeremiah can tell, she doesn't have an answer for him. He says, "Somethin' ain't right here. And I need to talk to Farkas so as to figger out what it is."

26

His diploma from the School of Gitch was a knife. An Italian switchblade with black horn handles and nickel bolsters, tucked into his bedroll, waiting for him when he returned one morning. He had been working with Gitch for almost two years, had returned at dawn to the camp from a night of freelancing, lifting wallets, letting himself into the odd apartment to look for things worth having while the occupants slept. One of the rare nights when Gitch left him entirely free, had no set task for him to perform, nothing planned to advance Gitch's own obscure purposes.

Later that day he went looking for Gitch, finding him once more bent under the hood of his truck. He said to Gitch, "It is time."

Gitch straightened up. He grabbed a grease rag, wiped his hands. "When?"

"Tomorrow night."

Gitch looked down at the truck's engine. Thought a minute. "No. In two nights' time. The truck will not be ready before."

"Two nights' time, then." He walked away, his hand in his pocket, fingers wrapped around the switchblade.

27

CLYDE'S BOWELS ARE STILL IN AN UPROAR WHEN HE GETS BACK TO HIS apartment. He goes into his tiny bathroom with the cracked linoleum and plain porcelain fixtures, so unlike Sonya's fancy digs, all he can afford on the pissant amount of money he makes keeping the peace in Washington County. He kicks off his Air Jordans, strips, turns the shower on full blast, steps into the tub, stands there letting the shower rake him. Tries to get a grip on his anger, his hurt, his sudden profound loneliness.

He cuts the shower off, goes to toweling. He recollects he'll see Yolanda tomorrow night, tries focusing on that. Some of the memories of old times come back, and his business starts to stir. *Least I won't be feelin' guilty 'bout nothin' that happens.*

He pulls on a knit shirt, jeans, loafers but no socks, goes into his kitchen. Decides to heat up soup out of a can, sit in front of the television, see what the cable man has to offer. Fifteen minutes later he's been through his soup and a hundred cable channels without finding anything satisfactory. He cuts the television off, checks his watch.

"Fuck this," he says.

The Paradise Alleys bowling establishment sits back from the bypass over on the south side of town. The place looks to be pretty active. The only parking spot Clyde can find for his Z-28 is way on the other side of the lot from the front door.

The bowling alley is packed. Clyde has never seen so many white people sporting mullets and beer guts and tattoos and NASCAR T-shirts in his life. And that's just the women. A large banner hangs from the ceiling of the place, says, "Welcome Central Texas Hot Wheels Association."

In the back, where the actual alleys are, people are bowling away, most of them in mullets and NASCAR T-shirts, too, chugging their love handles a few steps across the floor, then heaving a bowling ball. Clyde can see them standing with their hands on their knees, big butts hanging behind, while they watch the ball go careering down the lane toward the pins, then turning around to do elephantine end zone dances.

The front of the place has been converted into a miniature car souk. Folks are buying, selling, trading toy cars, operating from card tables and out of suitcases, going this way and that with dollies loaded with boxes of the things. What with the sound of balls rolling and crashing into pins in the back, and the feverish mercantilism of the tiny car people in the front, Paradise Alleys throbs with noise.

Off to one side, a man in a green smock stands behind a counter in front of shelves crammed with bowling shoes. Clyde picks his way through the crowd of car traders until he's waiting in the line of customers. When he gets to the head of the line, the man looks down at Clyde's feet. "Size thirteen. Am I right?"

"I don't need no shoes, man. I'm lookin' for the man."

"The who?"

"The man. The owner. The pro-pri-e-tor. He around tonight?"

The shoe man points across the room. "In the office upstairs."

Clyde turns, sees a glassed-in room up a set of stairs on the other side of the bowling alley. "Thanks, man. Say, what's with all the Maury Povich finalists?"

"Regional Hot Wheels convention. They have one every year. Washington County's turn to host."

Clyde picks his way through the throng, climbs the stairs. He can hear someone working a keypunch machine on the other side of a closed door, and he raps on the door.

Voice inside says, "It's open."

Clyde lets himself in. A man sits at a metal desk set against the far wall, metal filing cabinets to his right, a window overlooking the bowling alley to his left. The man turns in his chair. He's a little guy with a bald head, bad teeth, and a worried expression. He's clutching a yellow pencil, teeth marks running up and down it.

" 'Scuse me," Clyde says. "You the owner?"

"Yes. What can I do for you?"

"I'm Deputy Clyde Thomas, from the Washington County Sheriff's Department and I was wonderin', Mr., uh—"

"Cicco. Simon Cicco's my name. Have a seat, Deputy."

"Thanks." He settles into a wooden armchair. "I was wonderin' if I might could ask you a question or two 'bout one of yo' employees."

Simon Cicco's expression dials up from Considerable Anxiety to Deep Concern. "How come? One of my people in trouble?"

"I wouldn't go so far as to say that just yet. I been workin' a case, couple people shot to death last night here in town, and the name of Gutter Ball Jones come up."

"Gutter Ball Jones?"

"Yeah. Folks also call him Melvin. I hear tell since he got outta the joint he goes around calling himself Mustafa X."

Simon's expression shifts from Deep Concern to Profoundly Troubled. "The joint? Mustafa was in prison once?"

Clyde nods. "That's right. You sayin' you didn't know?"

The man shakes his head. "I'm don't think I would've hired him if I had. I'm pretty sure it wasn't on his employment application. Although, in fairness, he's terrific at keeping the machines working. That's critical in this business. You get a couple, three, lanes down for a few days because of some cockamamie malfunction of the pinsetter or the ball return and you can lose an entire week's margin."

Watching the look on Cicco's face as he contemplates his hypothetical loss of a week's margin, Clyde can almost feel the duodenal ulcer forming inside the man. "Well, I hate to be the one to tell y'all, but ol' Mustafa Melvin Gutter Ball done a stretch down in Sugarland."

"What for?"

"Smugglin' cocaine."

"Lord have mercy." Simon's facial expression seems to have reached the limits of its capacity to convey distress, so he starts swiveling back and forth in his chair to compensate. The chair makes a noise like a finishing nail scratching on a chalkboard. "Now you tell me he might be a suspect in a murder."

"I didn't say that. I'se just doin' some checkin' around and his name come up. Seems he lives with a sister of one of the victims."

"I wouldn't know anything about that."

"How long he worked here?"

"Four or five years."

"He ever give you any kind of trouble?"

"No. Keeps to himself pretty much. No tardiness or absenteeism or drinking, even comes in late some nights when we have a problem with a machine."

"How much money he make?"

"Depends on how much he works. We pay him twenty dollars an hour and he probably works, on average, twenty hours a week."

"So maybe sixteen hundred bucks a month."

"Yeah. I'd say about that."

Clyde is thinking about Gutter Ball's nice crib, better than Clyde's dinky little place, wondering how he gets by, no more money than that coming in, less even than Clyde takes home. Wondering if he's getting a supplement somewhere along the way from his old friends the drug smugglers.

"Anybody ever come 'round to see him?"

"Not as a regular matter."

"Whatta you mean, 'not as a regular matter.'"

The man stops squeaking his chair so he can concentrate on his recollection. "I mean, I don't recall him ever having a visitor on the job, but I saw him talking to someone out in the parking lot as he was leaving one evening."

"What was they talkin' about?"

He shakes his head. "I don't know. I was on my way home myself, just saw Mustafa out where he parks his truck, talking to somebody."

"What did the person he was talking to look like?"

"I don't know," he says again.

"How can you not know?"

"Because he was sitting in a car. Looked to me like he had seen Mustafa while he was driving by or something, pulled into the parking lot, stopped and rolled his window down so they could visit with one another. Their visit didn't last very long, because before I could get in my own vehicle, the man in the car drove off. Really peeled out, too."

"You happen to remember when this was?"

The guy frowns. His chair goes *squeak, squeak*. "Maybe two months ago?"

"What about the car? You remember what kind it was?"

He shakes his head. "I'm not sure. It was black, late model. Seems to me like it was one of those foreign luxury autos. An Infinity, maybe."

"Or a Lexus?"

"Could be."

"You remember anything else?"

"Only that as the driver pulled away, Mustafa was shouting at him."

"What did he say?"

"He was too far off for me to understand the words. I just heard him hollering, saw him waving his arms some."

Clyde is thinking, *I bet that was Lamont and they was arguin' 'bout Laurice or Lamont's dealin' or some shit.* He says, "Okay. Anything else I oughta know?"

"Not that I can think of."

"Anything come to mind, you give me a call over at the Sheriff's office."

The man's expression downshifts to Considerable Anxiety. "Sure thing, Deputy."

Clyde leaves the office, weaves through the minature car people, walks out the front door side by side with a tall skinny young man wearing greasy hair over his ears and a Stone Cold Steve Austin T-shirt. They stop on the sidewalk as an old beat-up sedan pulls along the curb, slows to a stop.

Clyde's trying to decide where to go next, what to do with the rest of the evening he had freed up by calling his girlfriend a bitch to her face. He looks at the rattletrap idling at the curb. *Man, just look at this piece-of-shit car with the dented fenders and the bumpers hangin' loose. These low-rent motherfuckers still be arrivin'. Hot Wheels party probably just now heatin' up. Shit. Better to be descended from slaves than to be one of these inbred crackers with teeth growin' out the roofs of their mouths.*

The dude in the Stone Cold T-shirt says, "Are you Deputy Clyde Thomas?"

Clyde turns, looks at him. "What's it to you?"

The young man reaches into his jeans, pulls out a badge, flashes it at Clyde. "DEA. We'd like a moment of your time, Deputy." He jerks his head in the direction of the beat-up sedan.

Clyde says, "Lemme see that badge."

The guy hands it over. "Let's go before somebody sees us. You can get yourself comfortable with the credentials in the car."

Clyde follows the guy into the backseat of the vehicle.

28

LESLIE WHITTEN SHAKES HER HEAD. "I'M AFRAID THAT'S QUITE IMPOSSIBLE, Captain Spur. Blimey, I thought we had been *through* this."

"Why? Because the man is laid up?"

"Well, he does have this bloody hip."

Jeremiah holds up a weathered hand. "But that don't make it impossible. Your boy Bruce could carry me to see him tomorrow, ever-where he's at."

"Believe me, his physical condition is quite beside the point." She sighs, looks around the room. She has eaten maybe half her meal but has laid the cutlery aside like she's ready to be shed of what's left. She catches the waiter's eye, then turns back to Jeremiah. "Mr. Farkas has long said that the one thing he cannot afford to get wrong is the management of his own time. Every day there will be a hundred things that need doing, and should he try to do them all himself, he wouldn't get very far, now would he?"

Jeremiah works his jaw. He's running a little low on patience for lectures about Mr. Farkas's management philosophy.

The waiter with the withered arm appears, places an ashtray and a new margarita on the table in front of Leslie. She pulls her cigarettes from her purse, lights one. "In the event, a man like that must be frightfully good at delegating problems to the people he has hired for their ability to solve them. In this case, he has delegated to me the task of finding this dodgy Little Fuck and the missing ten million. And if I prove not to be up to it for some reason, then he will have to reevaluate my usefulness to him."

"That what he said to you?"

She blows smoke, shakes her head. "He didn't have to."

Jeremiah pushes his plate away. "Well, you can't expect me to find Nelson unless I know everything I need to know what might be relevant."

"Such as?"

"Such as how Farkas's son died. You say them two was friends. Now one ain't nowhere to be found and the other's dead. And I don't think he died of cancer. Did he?"

She sits back, crosses her legs. "No."

"What was it then?"

"I assure you, it is irrelevant to the matter at hand."

Jeremiah leans forward across the table. "I need to see Farkas."

She leans forward to meet him, her perfume in his nostrils. She reaches out, puts a hand on top of his. "No. What you need is to get to know me better."

Jeremiah knows he ought to sit back in his chair, reestablish a decent separation. He's conscious of being in full view in a public place, the cool palm of a woman not his wife resting on his hand. But for a short moment, half a dozen heartbeats at most, he feels something he hasn't felt in a good many months of Sundays, a kind of warmth that starts inside his rib cage and runs down to his boots. Then he thinks, *God O-mighty damn, Jeremiah. What do you think you're doin'? Where's your tough-mindedness?*

He retrieves his hand, sits back, crosses his legs, grabs his knee with both hands so they'll be safely in his territory. "I don't know what you're sayin'."

She stubs out her smoke, sits back, too, smiles. "Tell me, Captain Spur, how did you find your hotel room?"

"Your boy Bruce carried me over there."

She laughs. "That's not what I'm asking, dear man. I'm asking if you liked it. Did you find it suitable?"

"It's way too nice to be suitable for a simple rancher."

The waiter reappears. "Would anyone care for coffee?"

"I might have me a cup."

"And an espresso, Rafael. *Grazie.*" She turns back to Jeremiah. "Maybe when I take you back to your hotel I should park, come upstairs. You could favor me with a tour of your hotel room, Captain Spur. I've heard the beds at the Crescent Court are the biggest in Dallas. That someone could get lost in one. You know, sleeping alone."

The tips of Jeremiah's ears feel like someone is holding a match to them. He clears his throat, goes to his pocket for a cigarette. Realizes he quit smoking. Wishes like the dickens he hadn't. "I don't b'lieve that would be proper."

"Why not?"

"If you don't know yourself, I ain't for sure I can 'splain it to you."

She leans back to let the waiter serve the coffee. "You are quite old-fashioned, aren't you?"

Jeremiah takes a sip his of coffee. "A thing can only be what it is."

She laughs again. Jeremiah has to admit, he likes her laugh. "What a quaint and completely ludicrous notion."

"Beg your pardon?"

"This pronouncement you just made. 'A thing can only be what it is.' You cannot possible believe that."

"I've believed it all my life."

"Oh, Captain Spur, come now. The quantum physicists long ago established the duality of things, how they can be both what they are and what they are not."

"Never got past classical physics myself."

She sips her tiny cup of coffee. "Wave-particle duality, Captain Spur. One need look no farther. We think of light as a wave, but place a beam splitter in its path and straightaway it acts like a particle. So a thing can be both what it is and what it is not."

"I don't think of light as a thing."

"The same could be said of an electron, then. It has the characteristics of both a wave and a particle. Duality, see. It is literally what makes the world go 'round."

Jeremiah knows he doesn't have the learning to play this game, but he doesn't aim to quit without a fight. "Didn't Einstein say all this quantum mechanical stuff was hogwash?"

"A blot on an otherwise enormous legacy, I fear. He famously said God doesn't play dice with the universe or words to that effect. Another demonstrably false proposition, just like your little aphorism."

"How's that?"

"Einstein obviously was saying that God's laws, such as the laws of physics, did not leave room for chance occurrence. God, being omnipotent, had no need to gamble with how His creation would turn out at the end of the day. But one look around this room, where God's greatest creation is on vivid display, proves otherwise."

"You talkin' 'bout folks?"

"Yes, of course." The waiter arrives with the check and she reaches for her pocketbook. She stops a minute to figure the tip, signs the charge slip. "God said He made us in His own image. But at the end of the day, what in fact was He doing other than gambling on how we would turn out? God was the Great Cosmic Punter, blowing on the dice that were man's DNA, hoping that having made us in His image we would turn out to His satisfaction."

She stands to leave. He plants his Stetson on his head, stands with her.

As she walks past him toward the parking lot, she says, "And as luck would have it, Captain Spur, God rolled boxcars. Pity, that."

He follows her out the restaurant, conscious of the eyes that watch them move through the crowd, for his part prayerful that no one's looking on who might have stumbled in here from Washington County.

Her Ferrari's already waiting when they reach the parking lot. Jeremiah starts to say something to her about the margaritas she'd packed away, maybe offer to do the driving back to the hotel, but before he can put the words in a sentence that won't sound too judgmental, she's behind the wheel and he has lowered himself like a load of pea gravel into the passenger's seat.

Their way is blocked by a late-model Cadillac, a big white car idling in front of them in the alley that runs beside the restaurant, only two people in it. The Cadillac sits there like it's got nowhere to go.

"Bloody hell," Leslie says. She hits the car horn, really leans into it.

"Easy."

The driver's-side door of the Cadillac opens, a man steps out, walks slowly their way. Jeremiah realizes all the valets seem to have disappeared. There's no one in the parking lot but the two in the Cadillac and them. He looks behind them. Another car is parked there, it's engine off, no one inside. He tries the door handle. It's locked.

"Unlock the door," he says.

She looks his way. "I'm sorry?"

"Unlock the door!"

She turns away from him at the sound of a ring knocking against her window and hits the button to lower it. As the man at the window leans down, Jeremiah's cursing himself for leaving home without his Sig Sauer.

29

Dusk. The streets were almost deserted. A few pedestrians, one or two cyclists, a truck parked a couple of blocks down. He stood in a doorway smoking a cigarette. He wore an old sweatshirt, dungarees, soft-soled shoes. His uncle walked past him without a glance, then turned off the street into his building. He stubbed out his cigarette, flicked the butt into the gutter, slid to the ground and sat.

A little before midnight and the street was completely empty except for the truck, still parked where it had been all evening. He got up, stretched, walked down the street. Let himself into his uncle's building. Climbed the stairs to the flat. At the door he took a ski mask from his pocket, pulled it over his head.

The lock was no challenge, and he eased the door shut behind him. The apartment was completely dark. He stopped to let his eyes adjust.

Snoring. Coming from the direction of the living room. He had gotten lucky. He pulled the switchblade from his pocket and crept forward, one gloved hand lightly touching the wall as a guide. The living room was the first door down the hall to the left. When he reached the door, he looked around it.

There was a bit of light coming through a window. He saw his uncle, facing the door, asleep in his chair, a newspaper on his lap. An empty bottle turned on its side on the floor. He eased around behind his uncle. He was so close he could smell the man's breath.

He pressed the button on the switchblade just as he clamped his other hand over his uncle's mouth. The blade deployed with a click. His uncle grunted, stirred.

He plunged the knife into the left side of the man's neck, jerked hard across his throat. His uncle thrashed as blood geysered down his front. Then he was still. The room filled with stench, blood, and shit. He wiped the knife on his uncle's shirt, folded the blade, pocketed it.

He heard a gasp, looked up, saw a small figure standing at the hall door. His aunt. He watched as she crumpled to the floor.

Moving quickly, he walked past where she lay, out the apartment, down the stairs. In the alley next to his uncle's building, he pulled off his mask, his gloves, his sweatshirt. Stuffed them into a rubbish bin. He walked into the street, turning toward the lone truck parked against the curb.

The truck's engine started. It pulled up next to him and stopped. He got in. Gitch looked at him from behind the steering wheel.

Benjamin said, "Let's go."

The drive to the Austrian border took four hours. He slept most of the way, awakening only when the truck left the pavement for a rough country road that ran along a forested hillside fifteen kilometers west of Magyarovar.

He sat up, rubbed his eyes, tried to see out the windshield. Gitch was driving with the headlights off, hunched over the steering wheel, his face made green by the dashboard lights, taut with concentration.

He said, "How can you see where you are going?"

Gitch ignored him.

Fifteen minutes later, Gitch pulled off the road. They got out, went to the rear of the truck. Gitch reached under a tarp, pulled out a rucksack, handed it to him. "It is five kilometers that way to the border." His pointing arm was a shadow against a moonless sky littered with stars. "From there, it is about fifty kilometers to Vienna. You have an hour and a half until daylight. You must be across the border by then. If they catch you crossing, they will shoot you."

He shrugged on the rucksack. "I know this."

"Do you remember what you are to do when you get there?"

"Go to the Café Central, in the old city. Find a waiter named Kraus."

"There is a letter in your rucksack. Good luck."

"Thank you."

A minute later he was walking up the hillside, listening to the receding sound of Gitch's truck as it drove away.

30

CLYDE SHIFTS AROUND ON THE VINYL UPHOLSTERY, PEERS AT THE ID IN HIS hand, sees the man's name is Cummings. Hands it back. "What about these two?"

The guy riding shotgun turns around, says, "I'm Agent Ramirez. Agent Fischer is driving."

"What's DEA doin' out here in Buffalo Butt, Texas?"

Ramirez says, "That's just what we want to talk to you about."

"Yo. Y'all got some kind of operation goin' down in our jurisdiction, ain't we s'pposed to get a heads-up?"

Cummings says, "Consider this your heads-up."

"That ain't right. You s'pposed to go directly to the sheriff with this shit."

The car pulls into a church parking lot and stops under a streetlight. The driver kills the engine and the two agents in front turn around. Ramirez looks like he belongs at the wheel of a low-rider, driving around the barrio with that Mexican music blaring out the speakers. He's got a black T-shirt on, black greasy hair combed back.

Fischer looks more like a banker on his way to a golf tournament, knit shirt, hair cut junior vice president style. He's the oldest of the three, Clyde's guessing thirty-five or thereabouts. He says, "My impression is, your sheriff is eat up with the dumb ass."

"You got that right. Wasn't for me, his entire department would be broke dick."

"You're saying it's not?"

These federal assholes are starting to try Clyde's patience for real. "What, you haul me all the way over here just to disrespect me?"

Fischer says, "What were you doing back there in that bowling alley?"

"Lookin' at little cars, man. That shit gives me a hard-on. You ought to try it sometime, 'stead of that Viagra you old white folks gots to do."

"You were doing the same thing you were doing when you went by Melvin Jones's house this morning. You were checking up on Melvin."

"Yo. If you knew the answer already, why'd you ask?"

Fischer glances at Ramirez, then looks back at Clyde. "We need you to steer wide of Melvin Jones."

"Yeah, well, fuck what you need, man. I got a job to do. His name come up in a case I'm workin'."

"As in who whacked Lamont Stubbs."

"Or had him whacked."

This time it's Ramirez that speaks. "You can forget about Melvin Jones, *cabrón.*" He's looking at Clyde with his mean little eyes.

Clyde's jaw tightens. "Watch it, man. I know what that word means."

Fischer waves at Ramirez to back off. "We don't make Melvin for that."

"Why not? Seems he might've had a motive."

"And that would be?"

"He took Lamont's junkie sister in off the streets, cleaned her up. Word is, Lamont didn't much care for that. The two of them was headed for a collision."

Fischer is shaking his head. "Look, maybe Melvin is up to something, alright? But bringing a shooter in from out of town to wax Stubbs is not part of his program. If anything, it would be counterproductive."

"You mind tellin' me what his program is?" He looks at all three of them. "Assumin' y'all not just jivin' me."

Fischer says, "Could be Melvin is laying in the plumbing for some old friends of his who want to expand their operation out of its current south-of-the-border base. Expand it right into these parts."

"You talkin' 'bout drugs?"

"I'm talking about the Cantú drug cartel."

"Wasn't it them who got Gutter Ball to order up bowlin' pins full uh blow?"

"That's right."

"But I heard Gutter Ball wasn't nothin' but a chump in that deal."

Ramirez says, "Who told you that?"

"His PO."

That gets a laugh from all three of them. Ramirez shakes his head, says, "*Chingo,* Washington County's finest."

"Watch it, motherfucker."

Fischer waves at Ramirez again. "Look, we hear the Cantús have big ambitions for this area. Maybe not right here in Brenham, but maybe so. Or over in Giddings or up in Caldwell. And this is how they got it scoped. They can recruit unemployed Mexicans, or Mexicans who still have family down south, to hump Colombian product across the border in small loads for redistribution from here, rather than bulk-ship it to Houston. Cuts down on their risk, makes it harder for us to interdict the stuff. And they can set up crystal meth labs in little out-of-the-way places like this, produce it cheaper, then undersell the Nigerians and the Dominicans in the cities."

"But why here, man? What's so magical about this cracker-ass town?"

"Like I said already, maybe it's not here, but it's somewhere like here. Somewhere reasonably close to the major population centers. Houston, Dallas, Austin, San Antonio. Some place with no Hispanics on the police force. I'll bet there's no one in Washington County law enforcement that speaks Spanish. Right?"

"Ain't nobody speaks Chinese, neither."

"So when they communicate in their own language, it's like having a code."

"Gutter Ball don't speak Spanish."

"How would you know?"

Clyde shrugs. "Anyway, just sounds to me like another reason ol' Gutter Ball would of canceled Lamont's shit. He's a brother, not some Frito bandito." Ramirez's nostrils flare, a vein goes to standing out on the man's temple.

Fischer shakes his head. "Don't think so. Stubbs dealt for the Cantús. They're happy to use the in-place infrastructure so long as it's reasonably efficient."

Clyde says, "Let me ask y'all this. Word is, man wants to score these days, he needs to see a beaner up in Caldwell name of Jesus."

Ramirez says, "Now *you* better watch it, bro."

Fischer says, "Yeah, we're not sure about him. Could be he works for the Cantús."

"So maybe the Cantús ain't into diversity so much. Maybe they retired Lamont's cornrows to the graveyard so they be vertically integrated with folks, look and smell like yo' man Ramirez. Folks that talk that Mexican shit."

"Maybe. Or it could be someone else making a play."

"What you talkin' 'bout, someone else?"

"You remember, a couple years back, that paper out west ran a series of articles said the CIA set up a network of Nicaraguan expats to distribute crack cocaine to the inner cities as a way of financing the contras?"

"Yeah, man. The children was all up in arms and shit. But the government said it looked into it, said it was bogus."

"Right. They conducted this big internal investigation, announced the Company wasn't connected. But, you see, they were on our turf, and we knew more about what was going on than they thought we did."

"Like what?"

"Like the only reason they could claim to be clean with a straight face was they ran the entire operation through a cutout, an asset they used to manage in Europe, then resettled over here. We never knew much about him other than they called him 'the Wolf.' Never could track him down though, Lord knows, we tried. Langley dealt only with the Wolf, and he dealt with the Nicaraguans. That gave 'em what they like to call 'plausible deniability.'"

"So the children was right to be steamed."

"That's the way we see it."

"What's that got to do with the here and now?"

"After that operation was shut down, the Wolf dropped out of the life. He's been dormant for at least ten years. But this past summer, we started hearing the Wolf might be back. Just street talk, all very vague and hard to pin down. But there's something there. He could be working with the Cantús—he did back in the eighties. Or he might be going into competition with them."

"So?"

"Jesús Salinas, that whack job up in Caldwell?"

"Yeah?"

"Used to be one of the Wolf's. He's been strictly small time since the Wolf hung 'em up. But now . . ." Fischer shrugs.

Ramirez leans over the seat. "As you can see, Deputy Thomas, this thing runs a little too deep for Washington County law enforcement to be trickin' with it. So you need you to go back to writing speeding tickets and clearing livestock off the right-of-way until the real cops can sort this out. You dig, man?"

Fischer says, "Which means keeping your distance from Melvin Jones, Jesús Salinas, and the rest of this scene."

Clyde clenches and unclenches his fists, tries to think what to say. Finally, "Y'all made y'all's punk-ass point. Now why don't you fire up this piece uh shit federal hoopdee uh yours, carry me back to my ride, so I can get on 'bout my bidness."

31

AS THE WINDOW SLIDES DOWN, THE MAN LEANS JUST FAR ENOUGH FORWARD
for Jeremiah to see the bottom of his face. Stubble beard, thick mustache.
He speaks with a heavy Mexican accent. "We understand, your business is
your business. One nigger, more or less? Is possible, no one cares. But you
must watch how far you push us, *comprende*?"

Then he turns, walks back to the Cadillac, gets in. As it pulls away, Jeremiah relaxes out of his clinch, makes a mental note of the license plate
number and the sticker on the bumper, "Jesús es el Señor."

Leslie looks at Jeremiah, her face the color of typing paper. "Bloody
hell."

"Let's get this buggy back over to the hotel."

She nods, lets the clutch out. She drives back to the hotel like she's au-
ditioning for the lead role in a defensive driving video. As she rolls up the
hotel's cobblestone drive, Jeremiah says, "Happy to see your reckless drivin' and your margarita consumption are inversely related."

She brakes to a stop. The color is back in her cheeks. "I like fast cars
and I like fast driving. I find it exciting. But I must say, I do believe I've
had quite enough excitement for one evening, Captain Spur, thank you
very much."

"Good. If that's the case, why don't you step inside with me?" The
look on her face prompts him to say, "You ain't followin' me upstairs. But
there is somethin' I want to show you, and we got a thing or two still in
need of sortin' out."

They walk into the two-story marble lobby with the glass chandelier
and fancy furnishings and Oriental rugs and fresh flowers all around. Leslie
says, "I think I shall powder my nose, then find a quiet table in the bar."

"Be there in a minute."

Directly they're seated across from one another at a marble-topped
table. The lights in here are turned so low Jeremiah is having trouble dis-
tinguishing the patrons from the furnishings. Other than the light coming through the door to the lobby, what light there is comes from votives

flickering on the tables and on the shelves along the far wall, a wall done in squares of beveled mirrors. Black-suited waitresses glide along the terra cotta floor. Some kind of dance music is coming from the ceiling.

Jeremiah sips a cup of black. Leslie's got cognac in a snifter, no ice. Lying on the table between them is the note that had been left for him in his room. Leslie had had to hold it next to a votive candle to read it.

Leslie says, "It's very dodgy, this leaving of anonymous notes lying about."

Jeremiah stuffs the note in his pocket. "I got me a strong feelin' that ever-who left it connects up somehow with that restaurant parkin' lot business."

She sips her drink. "Perhaps. I find it all a bit bewildering."

"That Mexican seemed pretty sure you would know what he was talkin' about."

"Yes. Peculiar, that. I'm rather of a mind to conclude it was a simple mistake."

"A mistake?"

"Of course. His message made not the slightest sense. It therefore must have been intended for someone else."

"Some other blonde in a red Ferrari. Dallas must be crawlin' with 'em."

"I'm really not sure what you're implying."

"There's somethin' goin' on here either you or your boss ain't owned up to."

"Captain Spur, I assure you, I have told you everything I know that could possibly be relevant to your search for Little Fuck."

"Okay, let's suppose you have. What about Farkas? What's he know we don't?"

"About what, pray tell?"

"About Dusty, for starters."

"Can't say as I follow you there, old man. As I think I have made abundantly clear, Little Fuck cleaned out the cash drawer and vamoosed, as you Texans are wont to say. He simply needs finding."

"He won't be. Farkas has seen to that."

"Really, Captain Spur. That is the most preposterous—"

"How much do you know about Farkas's background?"

"Not all that much, really. That he emigrated to the United States from Europe in the 1980s and commenced real estate development."

"Know anything about what he did for a living before he come over here?"

"No."

"Your boy Bruce told me Dusty was hankerin' to get into some kind of activity that had higher margins than the real estate business."

She shrugs, examines her manicure. "Matters of the bedroom aside, greed was always Little Fuck's favorite amongst the seven deadly sins."

"And he said Dusty told him Farkas had been in some high-margin businesses in the past."

"Rumor and gossip. How could Little Fuck possibly have known what—"

"From his buddy Jonathon, way I got it figgered. Jonathon is the one who would've known the most about his old man's past. And if you was to sit down and try to think of all the high-margin businesses a man could pursue, you'd come up with some that ain't on the up-and-up."

She arches an eyebrow, reaches for her cigarettes. Lights up. "Captain Spur. Please don't tell me you subscribe to that old nonsense from Balzac. That behind every great fortune is a crime."

"Does Farkas know y'all's liquidity is tight?"

"Of course. He owns the firm."

"Got him feelin' some pressure, has it?"

"All of us on the finance side of the business—"

"Right. Now, this money that was stolen. You say it came from a bank line. Can y'all borrow against that line for anything you see fit or only for certain purposes?"

She blows smoke. "That line can only be used for our real estate development and acquisition activities."

"And who is it that deals with the banks for y'all?"

"That is the CFO's responsibility."

Jeremiah nods. "And that would be you. Alright, you ready to hear my theory?"

She sips her drink and nods.

He says, "Farkas has hatched some scheme to shore up y'all's liquidity using the bank's money, and he's recruited Nelson for it. He knows where both Nelson and the money are. He had to make it look like Nelson stole the ten million and disappeared, otherwise the banks wouldn't let y'all draw it down because what they're workin' on don't fit with what the bank'll let you do. It ain't real estate, and it may not even be legal. And he put you up to hirin' me so that he'd have a cover story for you—"

"Captain Spur, I mean really—"

Jeremiah holds up a hand. "Yes, ma'am. He's usin' me to pull the wool over your eyes, but by not goin' to regular law enforcement with all this, he's set it up for me to fail and he knows it. Neither Nelson nor the money gets found. I ain't for certain what they're up to, but I got an idea or two, and whatever it is, it's for sure stirred up that Mexican in the Caddie and ever-who left this note for me to find."

She is shaking her head. "I could not possibly disagree with you more."

"Fair enough. But you have to let me talk to Farkas. That's the only way we'll know for sure if I'm pissin' up a rope."

"I'll be sure to ask him for you."

Jeremiah works his jaw. "That ain't what I said. I want a meeting with the man."

"And what, pray tell, happens if it isn't forthcoming?"

"Then y'all can get yourself another boy."

She blows smoke, levels a look. "Let me make sure I understand what you just said. You are threatening to leave your task unfinished unless I arrange an audience for you with Mr. Farkas, to discuss with him your largely unsubstantiated theory that he has stolen money from his own firm to advance together with that loathsome Little Fuck some obscure plan that you can at best speculate about."

"That and one other thing."

"And that would be?"

"That's between me and him. But he'll know what I got on my mind."

"My, but you are a stubborn man, Captain Spur."

"A thing can only be what it is."

She crushes her cigarette butt, takes her hair down, shakes it loose. "Still not convinced of my theories on duality, I see."

"Not hardly."

"Very well." She leans in. "I shall convey your . . . *request* to Mr. Farkas. I doubt that he will be inclined to entertain it, since he is not a man much given to yielding under threat."

"He may make the rules where y'all are concerned. He don't make 'em for me."

"I shan't be able to arrange it before Wednesday, I'm afraid."

"Wednesday? On account of how come?"

"On account, Captain Spur, of the fact that this is, after all, my poxy little project, at least so far as my employer is concerned, and he will insist that I attend your little tête-à-tête. And as it happens, I am leaving"—she checks her watch—"in a few hours for the West Coast, where it is my rather wretched fate to spend the next three days entertaining a most disgusting man who has invested great gobs of money with us."

"Entertaining?"

"Yes. At golf, as it happens."

"Tell you what. Why don't you see if Mr. Farkas can spare me a few minutes even while you're away. That might save us all a lot of time."

"I shall see what I can do." She picks up her purse, stands up. "Now, if you don't mind, I really must be going. You still have that mobile Bruce gave you?"

Jeremiah pulls the cell phone from a pocket, holds it up for her to see.

"Jolly good. I shall ring you once I've spoken to Mr. Farkas. In the meantime, please do me the favor of pushing on, seeing what you can learn about Little Fuck."

"Happy to spend another day goin' through the motions. Bruce available to ride me around tomorrow?"

"Of course. He's standing by."

" 'Preciate it."

"Well, cheers, then."

She leans over, pecks him on the cheek, strides out of the bar. Against his better judgment he watches her every step of the way, silently working his jaw at the sight of her backlit against the door to the lobby. When she's gone, he stares out toward the lobby, brightly lit beyond arched doorways. A pier glass separates the doorways, catching his shadowy image, throwing it back at him. Beckoning him to watch his own struggle. He looks down at the guttered candle stub on his table, clears his throat, signals for his waitress.

"Yes, sir," she says when she arrives. "Freshen that coffee up for you?"

"Much obliged." He hesitates, struggles some more, gives up. "Who's a man need to see in this place to get a pack of cigarettes?"

"I can bring you some, sir."

"Camels. Two packs. And a book of matches."

"Right away."

When his lungs are full of smoke again for the first time in nearly five months, his mind fills with words. *Elizabeth, honey, don't be put out with me. I know I swore I'd quit, and I still aim to, soon as I get back to the ranch and get your mama home*—he thinks of Martha, back East fighting her own addiction, and a guilty feeling jumps him like a bandit—*but I need a respite from quittin' until I can get shed of this pickle I've landed in, what with all these strangers and their ways.*

He smokes and puzzles on all that has happened. Thinks about Farkas and Nelson, what they might be up to. He lights his second cigarette from his first, chain-smoking for the first time since he was in his forties. The thought of Leslie Whitten drives him to it. He tries to set aside her . . .

whatever it was she'd tossed his way. Maybe she was being forward, or maybe she was just playing with him. Or testing him.

He figures she's got to be mighty confused right now, maybe even a little frightened. About her boss, her job. About that Mexican back in the parking lot. Even about Jeremiah himself. What with ten million dollars supposedly down a rathole and Farkas's breath on the back of her neck, she's got to be playing with museum-quality scared money despite her tough Englishwoman act. *Scared money can't win.*

He puffs his cigarette a few more times, stubs it out.

The one person he doesn't figure is playing scared money at this point is Farkas himself. That's what makes it imperative that he sit down with the man. Among other things.

He signs the tab, takes a notepad from his pocket, jots down the license number of the car from the restaurant parking lot. He's reluctant to trust it to memory overnight. Tomorrow he'll get someone to run it through a DPS computer. Not that he expects to learn anything from it, but cop work is all about running to the end of every trail, even if it's a gut cinch to lead into a box canyon.

He gathers his packs of cigarettes, wondering as he heads upstairs to bed whether he ought to try one of those nicotine patches on the next go-round.

That night he would at first sleep but little and then wake up after an hour or so feeling like he was suffocating with no fresh air coming in and he would get up and go to the sliding door that led outside and open it. He would breathe in hard. He would go back to bed then, and listen to a sound he finally made to be a lanyard slapping against a flagpole.

At length he would fall asleep and dream of nothing at all.

32

In those days Vienna was beginning to prosper, for the first time since the war looking like the city it once was. But under the surface still the tense knowledge that Vienna was the front lines and would certainly feel it fully should the cold war explode into something that would look a lot like the end of time.

Gitch's friend Kraus had gotten him on at the Hotel Imperial, working the four o'clock to noon shift as a bellhop, wearing a dark green tunic and pillbox hat with gold trim. He was tipped with cash peeled off money clips or plucked from wallets by men who barely looked at him. Occasionally the opportunity to steal a little something presented itself, but he was careful about that.

At the end of his shift he would go to the Café Central, drink tea, eat sausages, read the German and English newspapers they had hanging on wooden rods, practicing his language skills. He had discovered he had a natural ear for languages, and after a year in Vienna, his German was reliable, and he could get by on his English. Kraus let him sit there for hours reading the papers, not thinking of the future. At dusk he would leave the café, trudge home to his dingy apartment across the river, a fifth-floor cold-water walk-up.

One autumn afternoon a man wearing a business suit and an overcoat walked by his table at the café. The man stopped, bent down, straightened up, said in German, "Excuse me. I believe you dropped this on the floor." He handed Benjamin a folded piece of paper and left the restaurant.

Benjamin tucked the paper in his pocket. He finished reading an article in the International Herald-Tribune about the upcoming United States presidential election, a contest between the incumbent vice president and his challenger, a senator from Massachusetts, a young, Catholic war hero named Kennedy.

He paid the bill, nodded at Kraus, walked outside the café two blocks down to the covered sidewalk outside the Lipizzaner Museum, took the note from his pocket. On it was typed, in Magyar: "Be on a bench inside the hedges at the foot of the Belvedere Palace at five o'clock this afternoon." There was no signature.

He jammed the note in his pocket, walked over to the Ringstrasse, bought a package of cigarettes from a street vendor. He lit one and strolled back toward St. Stephan's Cathedral, stopping there in the plaza. He leaned against a wall and smoked and stared up at the great cathedral, its walls stained black by the dirty city air.

A little before five o'clock he walked through the gates of Belvedere. At the top of the hill, past the landscaped gardens, he could see the great palace itself, reflecting the light from the afternoon sun. Down here, four lines of fir trees formed a square. Inside the square, concrete benches backed up against each line of trees. He chose a bench and settled in to wait.

The man appeared from behind the fir trees right at five o'clock. He was a big man, with blue eyes, a square jaw, and a touch of gray at his temples. He sat on the bench next to Benjamin, produced a pack of American cigarettes. Benjamin took one. They both lit up.

"Sprechen Sie Deutsch?" he said. His accent was American.

"Ja."

"Sehr gut," the man said, continuing in German. "That will make it easier, since my Magyar is a little rusty. You frequent the Café Central. I have seen you there often. Did you know Lenin did as well, when he lived in Vienna?"

"No."

The man took a drag, tipped ash onto the ground. "It's true. I'm sure you must see the irony. Since your father was murdered by the Communists."

Benjamin said nothing.

"You are Benjamin Farkas, son of László Farkas, whom the Communists hanged for sedition in connection with the 1956 uprising. You spent two years with a friend of ours in Budapest where you learned a few useful things. Then you cut your uncle's throat and escaped here. You are fond of the works of Graham Greene and must be very happy to be in the Third Man's Vienna, instead of back in Budapest."

He puffed on his cigarette. "The question I have for you, Benjamin, is whether you have any desire to see your father truly avenged."

Benjamin flicked his cigarette butt to the ground. "You seem to know a lot about me. Yet I know nothing about you. Not even your name."

The man smiled for the first time. "You can call me John."

33

"WE PREPARE THE WELCOME CARDS THE NIGHT BEFORE A GUEST ARRIVES, then housekeeping delivers them the next day along with the fruit plates. Mr. Spur, I have spoken to everyone who is a link in this chain, and nobody has any idea how that note got in your room."

The hotel manager is named Derek Spreckle. He is a little man with greasy hair parted down the middle, a thin mustache, and too large ears that stand out from the side of his head like direct broadcast satellite dishes. Put a top hat and a black frock coat on him and he'd look like the villain in an old-timey movie.

They're sitting in the man's office, a tastefully appointed little oak-paneled affair on the hotel's second floor, with a view of the front drive. Out the window Jeremiah can see cars pulling up, discharging passengers headed for Sunday brunch—Jaguars, Mercedes, BMWs.

Jeremiah pops the cigarette package in the palm of his left hand. "Who owns this hotel?"

"A private manager of ultraluxury hotels."

"Benjamin Farkas got anything to do with it?"

The man shakes his head. Jeremiah fancies he can feel the breeze from his ears. "Not to my knowledge."

"Anybody on your staff got a criminal record?"

"Of course not."

"I might want to have me a look at your employee roster."

"I'll leave a copy at the front desk for you."

Jeremiah stands to leave. "Alright then. 'Preciate it."

Jeremiah finds Bruce sitting in the lobby, reading the sports section of the Sunday *Dallas Morning News*. Jeremiah head jerks him in the direction of the front door. Out front they wait for the valet to deliver up the Explorer. The wind has shifted out of the south and moisture rides it. Clouds are working the edges of the sky, but it doesn't feel like rain to Jeremiah. Directly the vehicle arrives, and they climb inside.

"Where to?" says Bruce.

"Highway 80, headed east."

Bruce gives him a confused look. "What's out that way?"

Jeremiah lights a cigarette, opens the dashboard ashtray. "Just do like I asked."

They take 80 past the city limits and exit at Collins. From there, Bruce follows Jeremiah's monosyllabic commands until he pulls into the parking lot at the Long Creek Baptist Church. He looks at Jeremiah, says, "We going to services?"

"*We* ain't goin' nowheres. You sit here until I get back."

Jeremiah walks past the cars parked in the lot. From inside the church he can hear hymn singing. "The Old Rugged Cross." The church looks much as it did back when he and his mama went here, except for an addition that looks like it might date from the seventies. Around back now, he walks through the graves in the old cemetery. Stops at a headstone: Fiona Schmidt Spur. 1926–1956. Got lilies etched on it.

He places his Stetson over his heart. Whoever looks after this little graveyard keeps it tidy. The land slopes up from the church to the cemetery, neat rows of graves, most marked by stones, some by crosses. No fencing around it but an oak at each of the four corners, to mark off the land dedicated to the dead.

He remembers waking up to the sound of Bertha saying his name softly in his ear. He opened his eyes, saw her kneeling next to his bed. The room lights were still off and she was backlit by hall lights and her voice was strange and then he heard something catch in it when she said his name and he sat up and said, "Where's Mama?"

He was ten years old.

Two days later he had stood right here, watched them lower the coffin into the ground, too numbed by events to cry. The preacher had said words lost to him now through the years and the first shovelful of earth thunked on top of that box and he felt his granddaddy's hand tighten on his shoulder at the sound.

All he could think of as he stood here that day was how he wanted to go back in time and fix events so that she wasn't gone. Rearrange matters so that she went to a different restaurant in some other part of town for dinner. Or left a little sooner, or stayed a little longer. Just a minute either way would have done. Then she wouldn't have stepped off the curb into the path of that vehicle that ran her down and kept going.

It took them a week to pack up the house. They gave away her clothes, reduced all there was of his life with her so that it fit into the trunk of a 1954 Ford sedan, and then they got into it themselves for the long ride south to Washington County. Around dusk they pulled off the county road on to the dirt drive, his granddaddy parking the Ford behind the house. While his granny went inside to make supper, he helped unload the vehicle.

The last thing to come out of the trunk was a shoe box he'd never seen before. He took it from the vehicle, looked inside it, carried it to the porch where his granddaddy had gone to sit and smoke. By then it was full dark, the porch lit by a yellow bulb set on the wall. Cicadas were beginning to saw, and out in the fields he heard a calf bawl.

He said, "Granddaddy?"

"What is it, Jeremiah?"

"What is this here?"

His granddaddy was a big man, well over six feet, with white hair and coppered skin. He stuck his cigarette between his lips, leaned forward, took the shoe box, peered inside. Jeremiah can still remember the cigarette smoke drifting up into his eyes, causing him to squint as he studied what lay in there.

He handed the box to Jeremiah, leaned forward with his elbows on his knees. "Them's things your mama kept to remember your daddy by."

"Can I have them?"

"I reckon. Your mama ever tell you anything 'bout your daddy?"

"No, sir."

"No, I 'spect not." He crushed the cigarette butt against the floor and flicked it out into the yard. "Your daddy was a mighty brave man. But he thought it was more important to go off and fight com-nism in some durn place than to be home with his own family. That's how come him and your mama to fall out."

"Where's he at now?"

He shrugged, leaned back in his rocker. "Ain't nobody got no idea. Don't s'ppose it matters much nohow. Now get on inside, wash up for supper."

The cell phone ringing in his pocket jerks Jeremiah back to the present. He sets his Stetson back on his head, fetches out the phone. "Jeremiah Spur."

A voice says, "I hear you want to talk to me."

"Who is this?"

"This is Paul Lipper."

Jeremiah turns from his mother's grave, starts walking back toward the Explorer. "How did you get this phone number?"

"My mother. She said somebody claiming to be a retired Texas Ranger called the house from this number. She got it off caller ID."

Jeremiah starts to say something about the conversation he'd had with Lipper's father, where the man said he didn't have a son, decides if they don't get along it's none of his affair. He says, "Look, I'd like to get together. There somewhere we could meet?"

"Why do you want to meet?"

"I'm lookin' for Dusty Nelson. I was kinda hopin' you could help me find him."

A pause on the other end of the line. "Sorry. Can't help you there. Haven't seen him in a couple weeks. Haven't heard from him, either."

"I'd still like to visit with you 'bout him, his possible whereabouts and all."

"Why are you looking for Dusty?"

Jeremiah reaches the Explorer and leans against it. "I was hired to do it."

"Who are you working for?"

Jeremiah hesitates. "I ain't at liberty to say."

"We got nothing to discuss then."

"If I tell you who hired me on, could we get together then?"

"That depends on who it was."

Jeremiah decides he doesn't have much choice but to own up to his employer. "I'm working for Benjamin Farkas."

Jeremiah hears a sound at the other end of the line. Could be a sharp intake of breath. Then, "Do you know what 'Farkas' means in Magyar, Mr. Spur?"

"I ain't got no—"

"It means 'wolf.' Good-bye, Mr. Spur. You won't be hearing from me again." The line goes dead.

He tucks the phone back in his pocket as Bruce rolls down the passenger's-side window. "Who was that?"

Jeremiah gets in the vehicle, pulls the door closed behind him. "Paul Lipper."

"Terrific. Did you find out where he is?"

"No. When I told him I was workin' for your boss, he hung up on me." Jeremiah reaches for his cigarettes. Lights up.

Bruce waves his hand in front of his face, trying to chase off the cigarette smoke. "Dang. That's too bad. Where to now?"

Jeremiah looks at Bruce from under his hat. "Devonshire."

Bruce fires up the Explorer, heads back the way they came.

"Land it over yonder," Jeremiah says, using his cigarette hand as a pointer. Bruce pulls the Explorer to a stop along the curb on Caruth Street.

Jeremiah reaches in his coat pocket, fetches out the cell phone. "This thing keep a record of incoming calls?"

"Sure."

"Show me."

Bruce takes it, pushes buttons. Hands it back.

Jeremiah peers at it, says, "You stay here." He goes to open the door.

Bruce says, "Maybe you ought to leave the phone with me."

"On account of how come?"

Bruce points at the display. "You don't have much battery life left. I can charge it for you."

Jeremiah hesitates, shrugs, pulls out a pencil and a notepad, jots some numbers down off the cell phone display, hands the phone to Bruce. He gets out of the vehicle, walks up to the front door of a one-story house, sand-colored brick and black trim, boxwoods lining the front. A 1994 Chevy Impala SS sits in the driveway, a four hundred horsepower muscle car. Jeremiah rings the bell, doffs his hat.

A middle-aged woman with long blond hair opens the door and smiles him a smile that's warm as lamb's wool. "Lord have mercy," she says, "Jeremiah Spur."

"Howdy, Linda."

She comes across the threshold, gives him a hug, steps back. "I swear. I do believe retirement agrees with you. You look ten years younger than last time I saw you."

"Well. I am only fifty-four."

"And young looking for your age, too. I heard about Elizabeth. I'm so sorry, Jeremiah."

" 'Preciate it."

"Now, get in this house this minute." Then she hollers over her shoulder, "Trey! Guess who's here." She pulls him inside and closes the door.

34

Its official name was the Armed Forces Experimental Training Activity Center at Camp Peary, ten thousand acres in the Virginia Tidewater. But at the Company they called it the Farm.

He trained there for five months. He arrived on a military transport plane that landed at Newport News late one January night after sixteen bone-jarring hours over the Atlantic. He walked stiffly down the movable stairs onto the tarmac carrying only a paper sack containing some toiletries. He got into the backseat of an unmarked sedan. He was in his dormitory room at the Farm two hours later.

His days there were full. He studied languages—German, English, Russian. He completed the Basic Operations Course, moved up to advanced weapons and explosives training, forgery, driving techniques, disguises, cover stories, field surveillance, infiltration, exfiltration, electronics. He practiced clandestine communication methods—brush passes, servicing dead drops—in nearby Williamsburg, having to focus at times to keep himself from gawking at these Americans, so rich and happy and well fed and free, surrounded by cars, television sets, so many wonderful things.

He turned twenty years old there. He was five feet seven inches tall, weighed one hundred thirty pounds, had bright eyes, a long nose, rather longish brown hair that he combed back over his head.

He watched the American movies they showed on weekends in the cafeteria, with Cary Grant and Doris Day and the indescribable Marilyn Monroe. And then one night, a miracle. The Third Man, with Orson Welles and Joseph Cotton, from the story by the incomparable Greene. He was enthralled.

He ate cheeseburgers and drank chocolate malts. He smoked Marlboros, kept the pack rolled up in the sleeve of his T-shirt. He listened to their music. Elvis Presley, Chuck Berry, Buddy Holly.

He fell in love with America.

He returned to Vienna in the spring of 1961. Pan Am from New York to London to Hamburg, then by train to Vienna. His taxi dropped him off on the south side of the old city, and he walked to his new flat down a side street a few blocks from St. Stephan's.

He carried a weathered grip containing a couple changes of clothes, some art supplies, papers that said he was Dieter Bruner, an art student from Hamburg, in Vienna for a one-year work-study program. If you were to ask him, for instance, how to get from the Hamburg Intercontinental Hotel to the Reeperbahn, he could not only give you directions, he could tell you which cabarets featured what sex shows—topless dancing, live sex, S&M—and which brothels had the cleanest girls.

He climbed the two flights of stairs, unlocked the door to his apartment. The window across the room was open and the slanting light caught dust motes in the air and the smoke from John's cigarette.

"Welcome home," John said, as he stood up from the couch to shake his hand.

"Thank you." A manila folder that lay on the coffee table caught his eye.

John followed his glance, picked up the folder, handed it to him.

He opened it, looked at the grainy black-and-white photograph that lay on top. He said, "I see you already have work for me."

"We want to realize on our investment. Tell me, what did you think of America?"

"Actually," he said as he closed the manila folder, "I'm glad you asked."

35

BREAKFAST FOR RASHAD FLEECE IS A COUPLE CHILI DOGS AND A BUDWEISER. He is enjoying his repast to the accompaniment of Dr. Dre on the boom box, volume turned up such that it's all but moving the Venetian blinds back and forth. He's in the living room of the crib he shares with his cousin Marcus, who's across the room smoking a joint, sprawled out on a beat-up couch they'd picked up off the side of the road one day.

Rashad eats his dogs, slurps his beer, thinks about the better days that are coming, pretty soon now, too, when he can move out of this shithole into someplace nice, someplace where the cockroaches aren't so big they carry sidearms.

His hand moves to the right front pocket of his jeans, feels the ticket from the ATM crammed in there. He had taken the little white paper from the machine on Friday, stared at it like it was a winning Lotto ticket. The dude had done just what he had said he would. Twenty-five. Rashad is expecting another twenty-five after.

Rashad had picked up some jack along the way, dealing some, more often putting down motherfuckers who got seriously behind, then tried to duck the badasses over on Dixon Avenue who would then call on Rashad's services. He averages a job a month, strong-arm shit mostly, the occasional hit. It pays, but not too well.

Not like this gig. This was serious money coming in, what with all them zeroes. When this one's done, he plans to hire himself out for more such jobs with his new rep, jobs that would support an improved lifestyle. No more Kmart discount shit for the Dixon badasses.

Rashad tosses the hot dog wrappers on the floor, shouts at Marcus, "Gimme a hit uh that, man."

Marcus unfolds himself, slouches over, hands over the joint. Rashad pulls on it, hands it back while he holds the smoke in his lungs. Marcus takes it back to his couch, shouts, "You want to go shoot some pool or somethin' 'til the Cowboys come on?"

Rashad shakes his head, exhales the smoke. "I got to hang close."

"You expectin' a call?"

Rashad nods. Then, just like that, the phone rings. *Funny how it works like that sometimes.* He points to the boom box. "Turn that shit down." Marcus cuts the volume.

Rashad reaches over, picks up the phone. "Yo. This is Rashad."

"Yew know who this is?"

"Yeah, man. I recognize that cracker talk you like to fake."

"It ain't fake."

"Yeah, right, whatever. We got another job needs doin' or what? 'Cause I can't be waitin' 'round this phone forever." Rashad likes to make like he's got other accounts need servicing, so the notion doesn't take root in the dude to change the deal maybe.

"That's why I'm a-callin', see. I'm gon' come by and git you, four-thirty this evenin'. We got ourselves 'nother long ride, 'fore we git where we're goin'."

"Alright man, see you at four-thirty." He hangs up, sees Marcus watching him. "What?"

Marcus shrugs, his eyes half-lidded, smoke wreathing his head. "Nothin'."

"That look wasn't nothin'. You got somethin' to say, then out with it."

Marcus sits up a little, trying to show some spine now. "What them brothers down on Dixon gon' think, you expandin' yo' client roster and shit?"

"Fuck 'em, man. I'se a free agent. Who ask you anyway, mister work at the hi-fi sto', mister employee uh the month."

"I'se jus' sayin'."

"You's just sayin'. You don't even know the dude."

"Neither do you, man. You don't even know his name."

"I know the jack is good and it delivers right on time. So far as the dude goes, I don't got to know his name nor what he looks like, neither, he don't want me to. Him coverin' hisself all up in his sweats and gloves and shit, hood all pulled tight, shades on, not speakin' more than three words, if that, in that funny, fake-ass voice. Sound more like a bitch than a man, you ask me. But he don't like to leave witnesses and he can fuckin' *handle* a gat. That's all I got to know."

Rashad stands up, tosses the empty beer can at a trash basket halfway across the room. "Let's bounce on outta here, go shoot some hoops or somethin'. I got to be back by three o'clock, get ready."

Marcus picks himself up and they head for the door.

36

JEREMIAH FINISHES TELLING ALL THAT'S HAPPENED, THEN REACHES INTO HIS pocket for a cigarette, figuring to have himself a smoke while it sinks in on Trey.

Texas Ranger Sergeant David G. Beacon III sits frowning at something in the middle distance, as if he's looking at something he recognizes but can't name. Trey is tall, lean, strong jawed, has hair the color of single malt whiskey. He's wearing boots and jeans and a short-sleeved knit shirt. He taps the ends of his fingers together. "So all you know about Farkas is, he once did extermination work for the Agency."

"And that he come over here, went into real estate, took bad rich."

Trey taps his fingers. Directly he looks back at Jeremiah, starts to say something.

Jeremiah says, "Go ahead on. Speak your piece."

"I'm not sure I understand why you would want any part of this."

"Don't believe in signing up just until it quits suitin' me."

"But what if that woman doesn't produce Farkas?"

"That'd be different. I ain't puttin' up with no more of her humjawin' on that."

"I don't know anything about Farkas. But I could check around."

"What about the other?"

"We'll run the tag and the phone number and get someone to look into how Jonathon Farkas died. In fact"—Trey leans forward—"why don't you let us take over the whole thing? Find this guy Nelson for you?"

Jeremiah takes a drag, shakes his head. "Can't allow it. Leastwise, not yet."

"You're sure?"

"If I'm right about what's goin' on here, I've just about culled the blackfeet from the whitefeet and after that the rest should be easy. Besides, I trust the woman. Sort of."

Trey stands up. "Okay. Come on, I'll walk you out."

Outside the front door, Trey says, "It may take me a day or so to get back to you. I've got to be in court down in Navasota first thing in the morning, but I'll try to get somebody on it while I'm down yonder. How do I reach you?"

Jeremiah writes down his phone number on his notepad and tears the page off for Trey. He looks at the car sitting in Trey's driveway. "I see you still got your hot rod."

Trey grins. "Yeah. She runs like a spotted-assed ape."

"I don't know where my manners went. I ain't asked after Andy. How's he doin'?"

"Great. Gettin' ready for basketball season. Coach shifted him to forward."

"How old's he gettin' to be?"

"Just turned fifteen."

"Almost drivin' age."

Trey follows Jeremiah's gaze out toward the Impala. "Yeah."

"You still get a lot of offers for her?"

"One a week on average."

"What about your state vehicle?"

"Parked in the garage, along with Linda's. I only drive the Impala on weekends."

"Any chance I could borrow your street car for a couple days? As it is, I'm tethered to the kid drives that Explorer." He gestures toward the curb.

"No problem. I'll go get the keys."

Trey walks back in the house. Jeremiah proceeds down the sidewalk, gets to the Explorer. Bruce rolls the window down.

Jeremiah leans in. "Hand me that cell phone and the charger."

Once Bruce hands them over, Jeremiah says, "You can go on. I don't need you to carry me around no more. My buddy here's gon' lend me a vehicle."

For a moment it looks like Bruce is fixing to argue. Then he shrugs. "Okay. You know how to get in touch with me if you need me."

"'Preciate all the help. We'll be seein' you." Jeremiah backs out of the car window. Bruce ignitions the vehicle, pulls away.

Jeremiah meets Trey back out on the sidewalk. Trey hands him the keys. "Keep her as long as you like. But remember. She's a rocket."

"*Gracias.*"

They shake hands and Jeremiah walks over to the Chevy.

37

CLYDE HAD ARRANGED TO CALL ON BURLESON COUNTY SHERIFF CHESTER Gadson at his ranch on his way up to Austin. When Clyde pulls his cruiser into the driveway, the white-haired sheriff comes down off the porch to shake hands, offer him some iced tea.

Clyde says, "That'd be nice of you, man."

Clyde follows the sheriff up on the porch, grabs a chair. The porch runs the length of the house. On this side of the door, there's the rocker, a couple straight-backed chairs. A swing hangs on the other side of the door, creaking as it drifts back and forth in the breeze. An old white-faced golden retriever sleeps under the swing. He opens his eyes when he hears the men's boots on the wood flooring, bends his neck backward, blinks at Clyde a couple times. Stretches, closes his eyes again, sighs.

The sheriff comes back out on the porch, hands Clyde the glass of tea. Clyde says, " 'Preciate you lettin' me crash in here on yo' Sunday."

"Happy to oblige. What can I do you for?"

"Word down in Brenham is, man name of Jesús Salinas is the one to see these days 'bout scorin' dope. S'pposed to operate out of Caldwell."

The sheriff nods, scratches at a place under his neck. The skin under there hangs loose like a turkey's. "That's right. I had me a visit from some DEA boys couple weeks back, advised me they had an eye on him, too. Said we ought to steer wide."

"Yeah, they leaned on me 'bout that."

"You ain't steerin' wide though."

"I'm workin' a double killin'."

"I heard. Lamont Stubbs and a woman. You think it might've been Salinas?"

Clyde sips tea. "Don't know what to think just yet. But if he's makin' a play for Lamont's action twenty-four hours after the brother got capped, it would put him on the list."

"I reckon."

"So I was wonderin' if I could get y'all to work with me on this.

Bring the man in, let me brace him, since he's in your jurisdiction. You know what I'm sayin'?"

"DEA ain't gonna care for it."

"They can't tell you what to do in your own county."

The sheriff looks off across the land, down the hill toward the pastures, looks at it as would a man who has watched off that way for many years expecting to see something there, some sign or portent, and who's about decided he isn't ever going to see what he's been looking for. "It's liable to take us awhile to find him and bring him in. Can you come back tomorrow, say around eleven in the morning? You and I can talk to him together."

"I'd appreciate that."

After he left Trey Beacon's house Jeremiah went back to the Rusk Club, talked the manager into giving him a list of the names and phone numbers of Lipper's personal training clients. He had had the idea that maybe one of them might know something about what had become of Lipper or Nelson. *Maybe personal trainers are like barbers, maybe they talk a lot to their customers. Anyhow, it'll give me somethin' to do until Farkas turns over his next card.*

He had parked the Impala on the street outside the club. When he gets back to it, there's a note stuck under the windshield wiper. He takes it out. An offer to buy the car. Hispanic name and a telephone number. Jeremiah tosses the offer in the glove box, cranks the engine, heads to the hotel.

As he drives, his mind wanders back to the three items that were in the shoe box he had carried back to his room the day he went to live with his granny and granddaddy.

One was an old black-and-white picture, a wedding photo near as he could tell. It showed a tall, square-jawed young man in a business suit, wearing a fedora, standing next to his mother, looking very young, wearing a pretty dress and a nice hat, holding a bouquet of flowers. His mother was smiling. The man wasn't. He stared at that photo, trying to decipher the look on that young man's face, trying to make it for happiness or satisfaction or anticipation or hope.

He set it aside and picked up the second item, an official-looking document. It was a medal citation, for the Distinguished Service Cross. It read:

First Lieutenant FRANKLIN L. SPUR, 01278419, Infantry, 415th Infantry Regiment, 104th Infantry Division, United States Army, for extraordinary heroism in connection with military operations against the enemy.

On 28 December 1944, Lieutenant SPUR led a six-man patrol across a damaged bridge over the Roer River in Germany and encountered an enemy patrol. When two of his men were wounded by enemy rifle fire, he rendered first aid and ordered the squad to withdraw, dispatching one man to return for litter bearers. Lieutenant SPUR remained behind and, with no thought for his personal safety, alternately fired upon an advancing enemy patrol and assisted his wounded men, holding the enemy back while his men crossed the bridge. Learning that one of his men was missing, he courageously started to return to the scene of the fighting, despite the known dangers of the lurking enemy troops. As he reached the bridge, he heard the missing man call to him, saying he had reached safety by swimming the river. The devotion to duty and great leadership of Lieutenant SPUR were an inspiration to all. His extraordinary heroism and courageous actions reflect great credit upon himself and are in keeping with the highest traditions of the military service.

Entered military service from Texas.

He set that aside too and picked up the thing that gave the shoe box its heft. A first edition of Walter Prescott Webb's history of the Texas Rangers. He cracked it open and read it late into the night. When he finished that fat book some days later, he knew what he wanted to do with his life.

38

When he looks back on his life in Europe, he counts but two mistakes of consequence.

Her name was Anna. He met her by chance. She was waiting tables at the Spatenhaus in Munich. He had come in for dinner late one night, fresh in town from a job in Leipzig, looking to take a few days off in the Bavarian countryside. He sat at a table by the window where he could sip his beer, eat a pretzel, watch the crowd spilling out of the opera house across the square.

He didn't really notice her until she had cleared the dinner dishes and asked if he would like coffee. She was twenty-two, five-five, brown hair down her back, almost to her waist, freckles, roundish face. Hazel eyes.

"What is your name?" he had said.

Looking back, he knew what a mistake it had been, a few years later, not to take her seriously when she told him that if nothing changed she would take the children and leave.

39

IT HAS BEEN WORKING CLYDE ALL DAY LIKE A TOOTHACHE, HIS REGRET OVER his choice of words, tone of voice last evening, with Sonya. Sometimes his emotions are in words and airborne almost before he's started feeling them, leaving him wishing he could reach out, grab his utterances, stuff 'em back inside his mouth. He had even started to call her a couple times, take a stab at making some amends.

But the thought of seeing Yolanda tonight had stopped him every time. And now that he's pulling the cruiser under the arch over the main gate at Camp Mabry it feels like he dropped his regret off back in Bastrop. He's thinking about Yolanda, her big breasts, how smooth her skin feels, how all of her tastes. He has to switch to thinking about buzzards and roadkill and shit like that so he can get out and walk without lumpy jeans.

Camp Mabry is 375 rolling acres in northwest Austin, the third oldest active military base in the state of Texas. Seven hundred thousand square feet of built space serving the Texas National Guard and various Texas state agencies. Clyde has to cruise around some before he finds the DPS crime lab.

The door is locked so he presses the button on an intercom, says his name to the man who answers. Directly Yolanda appears, throws the deadbolt, opens the door wide. She's dressed in tight jeans, sleeveless blouse, hoop earrings, bracelets on her arms, platform soles.

She hugs him. "Welcome to Camp Mabry, sugar."

Clyde says, "You lookin' mighty fine today, Yolanda."

"Thanks, baby. Come on back."

She leads Clyde through the maze of offices and laboratories. Clyde pays no attention to how the offices are laid out. He's too busy watching her butt, mesmerized by its taunting rhythm, like two pigs fighting in a gunny sack, framed by a moving background of institutional green walls and worn gray carpet. He's always been a fool for it. Hers is bigger and rounder than Sonya's little aerobicized ass. Yolanda's is just the right size and shape for an African-American woman and his fingers are itching to reach out for it. Suddenly it stops, turns right. Causes him to stumble a little.

Clyde looks up, sees Yolanda smiling at him. "You best get your mind back on your business, baby. F and B has a report to make and you need to be all ears."

"What you talkin' 'bout, girl? I ain't nothin' *but* business."

She wags a finger at him, pushes through the door marked "Firearms and Ballistics." It opens into a long room with benches down both sides, microscopes, computers, manuals sitting on top. There's one guy in the room, a tall, lean, middle-aged white man in a lab smock, peering through a microscope. He looks up, blinks at them from behind black horn-rims. "Hey, Yolanda."

"Hey, Scott. This here's Clyde Thomas, from down Washington County way."

The man gets up, crosses the room, sticks out his hand. "Scott Zuckerman."

"Clyde Thomas. How y'all are, man?"

"On the right side of the grass. Come on over here, have a seat." They pull three chairs up to the bench next to the microscope.

Scott leans forward. "Okay. We've run checks on the brass and the slugs. There were two weapons, a semiautomatic pistol and a SMG. Let's start with the pistol."

He hands Yolanda a sheet of paper. She looks it over, hands it to Clyde. It says:

GRC Bullet Results

CARTRIDGE	MANUFACTURER	TYPE	L&G	TWIST	LWDMIN	LWDMAX	GWDMIN	GWDMAX
9MM LUGER	WALTHER	PI	6	R	0.045	0.116	0.066	0.137

Scott says, "Those are the general rifling characteristics of a Walther P99. We recovered three slugs that match this profile." He reaches over to the desk, picks up a photograph of a handgun, hands it to Clyde. "Walther began developing this pistol in 1994 at the request of the German police. It's very lightweight, made mostly of polymer, sort of the German answer to the Glock."

"Glock's a good gun. It's what I carry."

Scott nods. "You might like this one even better. It has four safeties. The Glock doesn't have but three. This one was nine-milli but it also comes in three-eighty auto. The ammo was Federals, full metal jacket."

Clyde studies the photo. "It don't look very big, man."

"It's not. It's an inch and an eighth wide, maybe five and a third inches tall, seven inches long. Fits nicely in a coat pocket or a waistband. Weighs less than a pound and a half empty. The P99 was a major improvement over their PPK model. The PPK is what 007 carries, you know."

Clyde hands the picture back. "You said the other one was a SMG?"

"Yeah. Illegal as hell. The ballistics were a challenge, too, since the GRC are consistent with several other weapons, including the Tec-9. But take a look at this."

He gestures to the microscope. Clyde stands up, peers in.

Scott says, "That's one of the shell casings. See the firing pin impression?"

"I see somethin', looks like a little rectangular dent maybe."

"That's it. It's almost identical to the firing pin impression your Glock makes."

Clyde sits back down. "Glock don't make a SMG, do it?"

"No." He hands Clyde a sheet of paper. "Here's the ballistics on this bad boy."

GRC Bullet Results

CARTRIDGE	MANUFACTURER	TYPE	L&G	TWIST	LWDMIN	LWDMAX	GWDMIN	GWDMAX
9MM LUGER	SWD INC	PI	6	R	0.043	0.080	0.098	0.140

Scott says, "It's an SWD/Cobray M-11. Lately we've been seeing a lot of these, turning up in gang shootings and what have you. Here, have a look." Scott picks up a photograph, hands it to Clyde.

Clyde says, "Man, that is mean lookin'." The brownish-gray machine pistol is lying on its side. A rectangular box with a grip, trigger, and trigger guard affixed to its bottom. Stub of a barrel protruding from one end, strap hanging just under it.

"Yeah. The folks that made this didn't go in much for aesthetics. And this particular one"—he taps the ballistics report Clyde is holding—"has a history."

Yoanda says, "You run it through DRUGFIRE already?"

"Ran 'em both through. The Walther is clean. But the SMG has seen its share of action over the years, all of it in Dallas County up 'til now."

He lifts a computer printout off the bench, hands it to Yolanda. She looks it over. "Looks like mostly gang shootings, drive-bys, like that."

Clyde says, "How long this model SMG been around?"

"Nearly twenty years. Most were produced between 1983, when the manufacturer was founded, and 1986, when Congress banned these things."

Yolanda passes the printout to Clyde. "Got a bunch of unsolveds here."

Clyde runs his eye down the list. "Man, I mean. This badass weapon been gettin' around. But it's been gettin' 'round Big D, not that little wide-spot-in-the-road dink-ass town I come from. I do believe it musta been carried there by a shooter comes from the big city."

"So what you come up with so far, baby, on your end of things?"

Clyde fills her in on his doings since Friday night.

"You make this Gutter Ball dude or the Mexican in Caldwell for it?"

"Don't know. Gonna check 'em both out. Meantime, I got DEA ridin' me 'bout doin' what I gots to do. I figger I must be gettin' close to somethin', them boys gettin' all uptight and shit."

A phone on the workbench rings. Scott reaches over, picks it up. "F and B." Pauses a few beats. "Yep. She's right here." Hands Yolanda the phone.

"Yolanda Banks. . . . Oh, hey, baby. . . . You did? That's my guy." She glances at her watch. "I'd say in about an hour. We where we can see the sun go down, baby? . . . Alright. Love you, too."

She hands the phone back to Scott, looks at Clyde. "That was Lester."

"Lester?"

"Yeah. Lester Hodges. Runnin' backs coach for the Longhorns. You heard uh him, right?"

"Yolanda, I don't pay no mind to college—"

She waves him off. "We livin' together, me and Lester."

She sees the look on Clyde's face. "What? Did I forget to mention that?"

Rashad Fleece takes a pull on the blunt, hands it to Marcus, holds the smoke in his lungs long as he can, exhales slowly. "What time you got, man?"

Marcus pulls on the joint, checks his Casio, holds up four big fingers.

"Shit. I need to be gettin' ready." Rashad pads in his stocking feet to the back room where he sleeps, the sound of the NFL game following him down the hallway.

He shucks out of his jeans and T-shirt, pulls on some hooded sweats and work boots. Leaves the laces untied. Goes to his closet, pulls out the duffel bag where he keeps his gat, extra clips, ammo. Lays three clips on the bed next to him along with the green-and-yellow box of cartridges, starts loading.

When he's done, he picks the machine pistol up, inserts a clip, fetches the two-stage suppressor out of the duffel, screws it on the end of the barrel. He holds the entire assembly up in his right hand, feeling the heft of it.

From the front of the apartment he hears Marcus holler, "Slade just pulled up."

"Comin'."

He puts the weapon back in the duffel bag, zips it up, stands, tries to think what else he needs. Reaches for some dark glasses that rest on top of his chest of drawers, pops them on his head. Slings the duffel over his shoulder, heads down the hall.

On his way out the door, Marcus says, "What time you gon' be home?"

"Fuck if I know. Don't wait up."

They had eaten most of their meal and the sun had set to applause from the crowd and Clyde had had just about all the talk about the Oklahoma game he could take from Yolanda's big, black, middle-aged lover with the close-cropped hair and the biceps about to rip open the arms of his golf shirt.

Clyde wipes his mouth with his napkin. "Y'all know what? I need to be gettin' on back home, on account of I got the early shift tomorrow. It's sure been nice seein' y'all and everything. Hearin' all about those Texas Longhorns."

Lester the football coach has a mouth so full of New York strip steak all he can do is grin and nod and wipe at the grease that's commenced to run down his chin.

Clyde stands up, and Yolanda stands up with him. "I'll walk out with you." She looks at Lester. He grins and he nods and he wipes grease.

They walk out together, Yolanda taking Clyde's elbow by the hand once they're out of the coach's line of vision.

Clyde says, "Didn't know you was into them meat-on-the-hoof types."

She squeezes his elbow. "My tastes are always evolvin', baby. They might evolve back your way. You can't never tell."

They leave the restaurant, walk over to his cruiser. He turns, looks down at her. "I know you, girl. I was just some kind of learnin' 'sperience for you. A steppin' stone or some shit. The kind you don't leave and then rotate back around to one day like some orbital moon."

She reaches up, touches his cheek. "See? Just like that, you prove my point. Lester never, ever would say somethin' like, 'orbital moon.'"

"That's right. I'm the only man you ever knew that would."

"Maybe you ought to come back for a visit next Friday night."

"Somethin' tells me coach back yonder wouldn't care for that none."

"He won't know. He'll be up in Dallas. Texas playin' Oklahoma, you know. Got to be with the team."

"I might be in Dallas, too. Lookin' for a shooter."

She says softly, "Gettin' all businesslike on me now."

"That's the way it is, Yolanda."

She looks at him a long moment. "That's alright, baby. I understand. You run along now. But let's keep in touch. It's been good seein' you after all these years."

"Yeah, man. Me, too."

She stretches up on tiptoe, pecks him on the cheek. "You watch out for yourself, you hear?"

"Yes'm."

As he opens the door of his cruiser, she walks back into the Oasis.

40

THAT EVENING AROUND NINE O'CLOCK A BEECHCRAFT TAKES TO THE SKY from Dallas's Love Field. The airplane has slightly longer wings than the usual model and certain special electronics have been installed on it. In addition to the pilot it carries a young man in the backseat who is hunched over a laptop.

The airplane climbs to its cruising altitude of fifteen thousand feet and levels off. The pilot starts turning large circles over Dallas.

The young man slips on a pair of headphones, launches three software programs on the laptop, one of which activitates the transmission of a radio signal from a transponder that is specially designed to communicate with any cell phone, even one that is switched off, so long as it is attached to a charged battery.

The young man watches the color graphics displayed on the laptop screen as the airplane turns its circles in the dark night sky.

Two hundred fifty miles to the south, a black Mercedes S500 is cruising west in the curbside lane of Houston's Westheimer Road, the neon lights from the strip clubs and fast food joints flickering off its dark windows as it hums along. Inside, the driver's cell phone rings, the sound of it barely audible over the music, Santana's *Supernatural* CD pounding out from the speakers. The driver reaches over, pushes the HANDS FREE button. The music automatically mutes. *"Cómo?"* he says.

"Joey?"

"Lupe, *hombre,* what's up, man? We still on?"

"Yeah, man, but I gotta push it back a little, see. I forgot, we asked my sister and her kids over for dinner tonight, and, you know, man, I gotta, like, take 'em home later. Can we do it at one-thirty?"

"Hey, man, no worries."

"Cool. Thanks, bro. I'll let Hector know."

The driver clicks off the cell phone and Santana cranks back up. *"Gimme your heart, make it real or else forget about it."*

No worries. He had picked that up in Aspen last month, where he went to kick back for a week. All the staff at the Little Nell said "no worries," like "forget about it," but with a meaning different from the Santana tune.

José Calderón ought to be a man with no worries, what with the '99 Mercedes, the money rolling in, all cash, no taxes. In the last ten years he had moved up in the Cantú organization, now was getting what was coming to him after all that dues paying.

But Joey has worries as he cruises the Westheimer strip looking for some action to relieve the boredom of a Houston Sunday night. He's got to come up with a new man in Brenham, since someone waxed Lamont, and his list of qualified candidates is as short as a roach's pecker. Meantime that greaseball Jesús Salinas from Caldwell was looking to juke the turf. And the Cantús were sending the word around, everybody needs to stay alert. Somebody might be trying to move in on their entire operation.

A half mile ahead the brightly lit sign above Tattletails strip club catches his eye. It occurs to him a lap dance might be in order. Might give him some stress relief. He passes the club, moves over a couple lanes, pulls up at a stoplight with a protected left turn, thinking about his management problems.

Wondering if he ought to read some of those management books he'd heard about, like the one where some *puta*'s cheese got moved.

The light changes and he swings around and turns into the strip club parking lot. What with the Carlos on the box and his head full of management issues, he takes no notice of the black Escalade that follows him in, parks off to one side.

Two o'clock in the morning. A one-bedroom apartment in Denton, Texas, just north of Dallas. A cell phone, turned off, lies on the counter in a dark kitchen. The phone detects a radio signal and responds by turning itself on. Its screen lights up. It vibrates. It beeps three times.

The man sleeping in the back of the apartment stirs in his sleep, turns over.

Three miles above, a young man sitting at a laptop says, "Gotcha." He keys in the GPS coordinates and takes off the headphones.

"Okay," he says to the pilot. "We're outta here."

———

Joey swings the S500 into the parking lot of Paco's, a Mexican food joint on Bissonnet Street, a place with a big neon sign out front, a grinning cartoon Toucan with a napkin tied around its neck. Now at past one in the morning the cartoon bird is dark, the parking lot empty save for one vehicle way in back, behind the store.

Joey slows the car. "Hand me my piece."

Lupe fishes a semiautomatic out of the glove box and hands it to Joey. Joey slips it into his waistband. He rolls the Mercedes up to the other vehicle, a BMW. The two cars face in opposite directions. The driver's-side windows slide down at the same time.

Joey sees Hector behind the wheel of the Beemer, grinning his gap-toothed grin.

"Jo-eeeey," Hector says. " 'Sup, man?"

" 'Sup is, let's get our business done, okay?"

"Sure, man."

Hector pops his trunk. Joey slides the Mercedes up so that the two vehicles are trunk-to-trunk. He pops the trunk release. He and Lupe step out of the Mercedes.

Hector Villareal is already bending in to grab the two gym bags stashed in the trunk. Hector holds the bags out. "I got it all here, man." Joey takes them from him.

They look around at the sound of squealing tires, see a black SUV making a hard left off Bissonnet, coming their way at a high rate of speed, high beams on.

Joey says, "Th' fuck?" He drops the bags, reaches for his gun, sees muzzle flashes coming from the passenger's-side window of the SUV. Lupe screams, hits the ground. Joey racks the slide on the semiautomatic, brings it up in both hands, but before he can get it leveled, he catches a slug in his upper body. The force spins him around. His legs give out and he lands face-first on the pavement, the gun clattering across the asphalt.

He rolls over, willing himself off the ground, fighting through the pain shooting down the left side of his body, an insane chant in his mind— *chingo motherfucker chingo motherfucker.* He limps over to his gun. As he bends down to get it, he hears the SUV stop a few feet away, its doors opening.

He's hit again, slammed into the parking lot, grit skinning his face. He rolls onto one side, faced now toward the SUV, watches through blurred vision as two figures in hooded sweatshirts walk his way. One of them stops, stands over Hector's body, fires a pistol toward the ground.

The other one keeps walking his way.

Chingo motherfucker chingo motherfucker.

Along with the chanting in his head Joey Calderón hears someone working the bolt on an automatic weapon.

41

IN THE ZÓCALO THE BELLS OF THE CATEDRAL METROPOLITANA RING IN THE
new day, echoing through the huge plaza, no one there to hear them but
a few vagrants sprawled on the cobblestones, pigeons pecking energeti-
cally at scraps, a lone priest in a rough frock. The priest kicks his way
through the trash left from yesterday, when the plaza was filled with
tradesmen and tourists.

The morning sun is just reaching the plaza through the Mexico City
smog as Father Vicente climbs the cathedral steps, ducks under the scaf-
folding that keeps the ancient walls from collapsing and bringing with
them the stained glass windows, the vaulted ceiling, the little niches high
in the walls with the statues of the saints, their hands outstretched, blessing
the faithful. The great building lists noticeably thanks to an underground
creek that makes the land too unstable to support a large structure.

The cathedral is the third house of worship to occupy this site. Cortés
built its predecessor with stones from the rubble of the first, the Aztecs'
most sacred building, the Templo Mayor, after he razed their city. The
present-day cathedral dates to the 1570s, when Cortés's successors decided
they needed something grand to replace Cortés's crude structural nose rub.
It took 240 years to build it. Now the earth threatens to bring it down. Just
one of the many improbable ways Montezuma has worked his revenge.

The priest enters the dark main sanctuary, passes the table of sputter-
ing votives, walks down a side aisle, softly so as not to disturb the handful
of women kneeling in the pews, shawls over their heads, praying perhaps
for the souls of those gone before, perhaps for those still trapped here.
This parish has been afflicted with three kidnappings since Easter. One, a
twelve-year-old boy. His right index finger was delivered, after he had
been missing thirty days, to his rich father. Wrapped in burlap and sealed
in a tobacco tin, together with their demand for sixteen million pesos.
The man had paid. Then the family had moved to Colorado.

So it had been for several years. Ever since the Democratic Revolu-
tionary Party mayor had, promptly after his inauguration, dismissed a third
of the police force, at one stroke creating a new armed criminal class.

As Father Vicente reaches the door leading to the clerical offices, it opens and another priest, an older man, appears. The older priest says, *"Buenos días, padre."*

"Buenos días."

"Padre, there is a penitent in the confessional."

"But it is not my morning—"

The old man cuts him off with a gnarled hand.

Vicente's own hand goes inside the pocket of his frock, fingers the envelope tucked away there. "I'll see to it."

He works his away across the cathedral, enters the confessional booth, slides the screen back. From beyond the partition, the smell of cigar smoke. He says, "Welcome, my son." Makes the sign of the cross.

The penitent says, "One's expectation of a man of your holy station is that you would arrive earlier, before dawn, for—what is it called? Vespers? It makes one wonder if perhaps you spent last night communing with Santa Tequila, eh?"

The padre leans back against the wall of the confessional booth, closes his eyes. "Vespers is an evening service."

"Ah. I fear I have forgotten much of the learning of my youth."

Vicente clears his throat, opens his eyes. "This is the place for penance and forgiveness. Perhaps you have forgotten this as well. One must prepare for it properly, by comparing one's thoughts and deeds with those required of us by the Commandments, and by our Saviour. Upon entering the confessional, the way for the penitent to commence is, 'Father, forgive me, for I have sinned.'"

"But you are not my father, Vicente. You are my brother."

"And as to the rest of the declaration, Tito?"

Cigar smoke churns through the screen. "We are all sinners, Vicente. The church teaches us this. Why dwell on it?"

"You must confess it, Tito."

From the other side of the screen, a snort.

"This is not you, Tito. You are not like the others. You are not like Father or Cousin Ray. You have a conscience. You have a God. There is goodness in you. You cannot hide it from me, little brother."

"Vicente, you are correct." The other man's voice is lower now. "Indeed, I have a god. To eat a fine meal, to fly in one's own jet, to raise fine thoroughbreds, to lie with a woman, to live one's life one's own way. That is the only god, and it is the true god of our fathers. All this you have surrounded yourself with? Pfft. Myths, prized by old women, like those who are sitting out there now, praying to nothing."

"You see how you prove my point? Father does what he does for the

love of doing it. You do it for the love of the things it brings you. Someday the thing you call god will turn its back on you. And in that hour—"

"Is this why you have summoned me all the way to Mexico City?"

Father Vicente breathes deeply, pulls the envelope from his frock. "Yesterday, after the late Mass, a man came to me. A ragged old peasant with a
withered arm. He handed me an envelope and then he walked away. He
never said a word. The envelope is addressed to you."

He slides the screen back, passes the envelope through the gap. Closes
the screen.

The tearing of paper. A pause, a curse.

He hears the confessional door open and listens as his brother's boots
echo down the hall and out the door of the cathedral, leaving the smell of
cigar smoke behind.

42

JEREMIAH'S CELL PHONE RINGS EARLY MONDAY MORNING. HE PICKS IT UP, punches the ANSWER key. "Jeremiah Spur."

"Captain Spur, this is Kim Alexander from Trey Beacon's office. Trey asked me to call you with what we have so far."

"Much obliged."

"That phone number you wanted us to trace? It's a cell phone."

"I reckon that figgers."

"Uh-huh. And the tags? They trace to a Miguel Ramos with an address over west of town, on Betty Jane Lane, off Walnut Hill Road. This Ramos has an appreciable list of priors. Two convictions for possession of cocaine, the most recent one with intent to distribute, one for agg assault, one B&E."

"I wonder why he ain't in the penitentiary doin' life under 'three strikes.'"

"That's just it, Captain Spur. He is."

"So someone else is drivin' his vehicle around while he's in stir. Who do you all work with over in DPD Narcotics?"

"Depends on which division. They're divided into street level enforcement, mid and upper level, Federal task force, airport interdiction."

"From the sound of this Ramos, I'm guessing street level."

"Oh, I get it. Let me take a look at something here a second."

Jeremiah hears rustling papers. "Here it is. Sergeant Terri Hinojosa."

He writes down the telephone number she reads to him. "Did Trey ask you to look into the death of a man, name of Jonathon Farkas?"

"Yes, sir, but we don't have anything just yet. Could take us a few more hours."

"Alright then. I appreciate it." He cuts the connection and keys in the phone number for Sergeant Hinojosa.

All it was, was a four-foot putt. Dewey Sharpe, sheriff of Washington County, has sunk hundreds of those in his twenty-five-year golfing career. But this particular four-foot putt would have tied him for the lead in the Brenham Country Club championship, and he had stood over it with about as much cool as a man undergoing an anal probe.

Dewey noses his cruiser into a parking spot in front of the First State Bank of Brenham. Kills the engine, puts his head down on the steering wheel, closes his eyes, grinds his teeth at the memory of it. He can see it in his mind's eye. He was supposed to play it just outside the right lip of the cup. But the ball came off the putter face headed left from the get-go, and just like that he handed Ringer Rhoot the club championship for the third year in a row.

Dewey sighs, opens his eyes. "Maybe I'll go to the pro, get me some lessons or somethin'." He heaves himself out of the automobile.

The first person he sees when he walks in his office is Billie Clifton the receptionist, double-bred white trash, descended from a line of white trash dating back to a time before there was such a phrase. She's sitting at her desk working on a wad of chewing gum, her hair teased into an enormous pile, her face painted more colors than a Chinese kite. Billie's so bucktoothed she could eat a pie through a picket fence. She side-glances him. "Morning, Sheriff."

"Hey, Billie. Anything goin' on?"

"Clyde called a little while ago? Says he'd like a minute with you this morning?"

Billie has that tonal inflection thing, makes her sentences sound like inquiries. Dewey finds it annoying. He says, "Have him come on back when he gets in."

"Sure thang, Sheriff?"

Dewey picks up this morning's issue of the *Brenham Gazette,* swings by the office coffeepot, ankles back to his office with his cup of black, shuts the door, puts his feet up on the desk. Opens the newspaper.

Few Clues in Brenham Double Murder

By Lamar Jackson

The Washington County Sheriff's Department is investigating the shooting last Friday night of local residents Lamont Stubbs and Diedre Brown, who were found dead around eight o'clock p.m. in a vacant lot in the 2700 block of Martin Luther King Avenue. Sources report that the killings were called in to authorities by the proprietor of a local convenience store. Sheriff's deputies responding to the scene found the bodies and cordoned off the area. The crime scene search was assisted by a team from the Department of Public Safety.

Deputy C. Livermore Thomas is heading the investigation for the Sheriff's Department. In an interview, Deputy Thomas said that Mr. Stubbs was known to be a drug dealer and those activities may have provided a motive for the shooting. However, there are no eyewitnesses, and the investigation is still in its early stages.

As to suspects, Deputy Thomas said that early suspicion is focused on Mr. Melvin Jones, of the 1600 block of Ninth Street, who is said to have a personal relationship with Mr. Stubbs's sister. Reached by telephone at his home Sunday morning, Mr. Jones declined to comment.

"Godammit, Clyde," Dewey says under his breath.

There's a knock at the door. Clyde walks in. "Mornin', Sheriff."

Dewey holds the newspaper out to him. "Have you seen this?" He can't keep the irritation bottled up in his head. It creeps out in his voice.

"Yo, man, what's with all the hostility? Yo' wife throw you out again?"

Clyde walks over, takes the newspaper from Dewey, stands there scanning it.

"So is this Jones guy a suspect or what?"

"Maybe."

"Maybe? Shithouse mouse, Clyde. You got his name splashed all over the newspaper and the best you can do is 'maybe'?"

Clyde throws the paper down on Dewey's desk. "Look, Sheriff. I told the motherfucker this was off the record shit, all the way."

Dewey shakes his head. "That don't cut no ice with Lamar."

" 'Parently not. Anyway, far as Gutter Ball bein'—"

"Gutter Ball?"

"The dude's street name, man. He works down at the bowlin' alley."

"You mean this"—Dewey looks down at the paper—"this here Melvin Jones?"

"That's right." Clyde takes Dewey through what he'd come up with since Friday night. "Far as likin' him for it and all, I got witnesses say he and Lamont didn't get along none too good, was in a pissin' match over Lamont's sister, who has took up with Gutter Ball. The shooters themselves, they probably come out of Dallas, 'cordin' to what DPS F and B tol' me up at Camp Mabry last evenin'. Meantime, word is someone's already moved in on Lamont's action. Hispanic from up in Caldwell, name of Jesús Salinas. I come in here to tell you all this, since I been workin' this mother all weekend."

"But you ain't sure you can make this Gutter Ball for it yet."

"Need a little mo' time, Sheriff. Got to go up to Caldwell, question this Mexican. After that I might need to get on up to Dallas, see 'bout findin' the shooters. I'm gon' be gone and like incurrin' some per diem and shit. Need you on board for an advance against it, Sheriff. Couple hundred oughta do it."

"I'll allow it."

"Thanks, man. Listen. One other thing: I had three DEA types pick me up Saturday night, start bustin' my chops 'bout checkin' up on Gutter Ball. They say they workin' somethin' 'round here. Mexican drug dealers settin' up shop or some shit. Just thought you'd like to know."

" 'Preciate it. I'll send a memo around. They give you a hard time?"

"Yeah, man. You know how the feds is. Wanted me to back off the Stubbs case."

Dewey shrugs again. "To hell with 'em." He picks the newspaper up off the desk. He says, "I wonder if I oughta give Sonya a call 'bout this. See if there's anything we need to be doin' by way of damage control. Issue a retraction or something."

There's a knock at the door.

"Come in."

Billie Clifton's beehive leans in. Her Wal-Mart toilet water rides the breeze from outside. "Clyde?"

"What is it?"

"I got a Mr. Mustafa X on the phone for you? He seems really, like, insistent?"

"I'll be right out."

Dewey says, "Mustafa X?"

"That would be Gutter Ball. He joined the Nation when he was in stir."

"The Nation?"

"Nation of Islam, man."

As Clyde leaves the room to take the call, Dewey leans forward, picks up his phone, punches in Sonya Nichols's phone number.

43

His first mistake cost him his heart. Mistake number two almost cost him every-thing else. It came in that time of life when a man is still young but begins to worry that he is not. It was the late 1970s. He had been in town for two days, af-ter a very tricky bit of business in Kabul, was drinking espresso and smoking at a sidewalk café on the Boulevard Saint-Germain, one of those places where the fur-niture is jammed together so you have to move chairs around just to get to a place to sit.

He saw her coming up the boulevard. She was tall, had dirty blond hair she wore short, in an expensive pants outfit, small bag slung over her shoulder. She strolled along, looking in shop windows, and when she turned in profile, he could see she had curves, but the main thing was her slimness and her cinema-star face. He sipped his espresso and thanked God for Paris.

She sat at the next table over, shook her hair out of her face where the May breeze had blown it, ordered a cappuccino, reached in her bag for a cigarette. Asked him if he had a light.

He said he did and asked if he could join her.

She smiled, opened her arms, palms out to the empty chairs on either side. "Mais oui." She said her name was Hélène. He introduced himself as Albert.

The affair lasted three weeks. In that time he learned she was the mistress of a high-ranking government official she never named, a man who said he would leave his wife for her but she knew that in fact he would not. She was twenty-eight, bored, restless.

They would meet in his tiny room on the fifth floor of the Prince de Condé Hotel, a simple, clean place on the Rue de Seine, just around the corner from L'Ecole des Beaux-Arts. After they made love, they would go for coffee in the Fifth Arrondissement, or walk along the river looking through the vendors' stalls at the books and postcards. They stayed always on the Left Bank because she was afraid she would be recognized on the other side of the river.

While he waited for her to come to him, he would stand in the window of his room, smoking, watching the street, wondering if he had enough luck for this to last.

That's where he was when he saw them, four men dressed like laborers, coming down the street at different times. Three of them entered the hotel. He felt their footsteps on the stairs before he heard them. By the time they reached his floor, he had his Walther PPK in his hand. They burst through the door firing machine pistols, the noise of the heavy guns deafening in the small space. He shot them from the place where he had concealed himself, behind the armoire just to the right of the door, crouched near the floor. He shot them as though they were targets in a carnival game.

He ejected the spent magazine, rammed a new one home, chambered a round. He wondered why such amateurs, such expendable men, had been sent. He went to the window to find the fourth man. The one who must have known what he was doing, since these three dead in his room were idiots who had been sent to be slaughtered.

Then he smelled the smoke.

44

JEREMIAH SITS IN AN INTERROGATION ROOM FURNISHED WITH AN OAK TABLE and four armchairs. The tabletop is empty save for his Stetson and a dead moth.

Directly a small Hispanic woman carrying a file, wearing jeans, snakeskin boots, a T-shirt that says "Cactus Grill," comes into the room. She has no more body fat on her than a hopper-grass, long black hair pulled back in a ponytail, big, soft eyes, the kind Marty Robbins must have had in mind when he wrote "El Paso." She doesn't look like any narc Jeremiah has ever seen. He thinks maybe that's the point.

"Captain Spur?"

He stands. "I reckon you're Detective Hinojosa."

They shake hands, sit down across from one another. She sets the file on the table. "I understand you're interested in Miguel Ramos."

"Yes'm. You ever run into him?"

She smiles. "Good ol' Mikey? I and a couple others took him down. We'd had our eye on him awhile, then about two years ago we got word from one of our snitches he was holding big-time. We raided his crib, found ten kilos of coke in the wall behind a refrigerator. That was his third fall, so now the state of Texas has him for the duration."

Jeremiah wonders if she's as tough as she talks. "Was he dealing for someone else or was he freelance?"

"Oh, no, Mikey had sponsorship. He was the Cantús' man for Northwest Dallas. At least that's what we think."

Jeremiah taps his index finger on the tabletop. "You mind if I smoke?"

"Feel free. Wasn't it you popped a cap in Jorge Cantú's ass when he tried to break out of Huntsville?"

He lights up a Camel. "That's right. I sent him up, too."

She shakes her head. "Seems like there's an endless supply of lowlifes available. You take one outta circulation, and the next day a new one pops up to take his place."

"Why didn't y'all try to flip Ramos, get some of the higher-ups?"

"We did. But the Cantús were into him deep. He was afraid of what they would do to him in prison, what they might do to his family. He out-and-out said as much."

"He got family up here?"

"Mexico. Look, what's up with this? Why do you care about Mikey Ramos?"

Jeremiah tells her about the encounter in the parking lot at Sebastian's, the plates tracing back to Ramos.

She says, "Well, there's no way that was Mikey you all ran into."

"Just somebody driving around in his vehicle."

"Maybe it was a company car."

"Maybe. You got any idea what he might have've been talkin' about?"

"You mean that 'one nigger, more or less' business?"

"Yep. I'm wonderin' if the Cantús lost somebody local recently."

She purses her lips, beetles her brows. "Not that I know of."

Jeremiah looks around for somewhere to tip his ash, sees a metal trash can sitting in the corner, goes to fetch it. "Let me ask you this—you ever run across the man what employs this lady I was at dinner with, this Benjamin Farkas feller?"

"Local real estate guy, right?"

"That'd be him."

"My social circles don't tend toward billionaires."

"What about a man name of Dusty Nelson?"

"No."

"Paul Lipper?"

She shakes her head. "I could check around some if you'd like."

"I'd appreciate that. I'd also like a line on any of Ramos's known associates."

She looks down at the file in front of her, fiddles with it. Then looks up. "Captain Spur?"

He takes a drag on his Camel.

She knits her brows. "I know what a great career you had as a Texas Ranger and everything, and I don't mean any disrespect, but I have to say to you—" She stops.

"You want me to know y'all have ongoing investigations what are confidential and you ain't authorized to share Ramos's KAs with a mere civilian."

"Something like that."

Jeremiah takes a last drag on his cigarette, stubs it out on the inside of the metal trash can. "Do the Cantús still have the better part of the cocaine trade in the Metroplex?"

"Along with grass and crystal meth."

"So. Assumin' the man in the parkin' lot was a Cantú soldier, why would such a guy be sendin' warnings to my dinner companion?"

"I suppose you'd have to ask her."

"Or her boss." Jeremiah gets to his feet. "Listen, I 'preciate your time." She stands too. "No problem."

They shake hands. She says, "Say, you going to be in town long?"

"No longer than I have to."

"Well, if you get bored in the evenings, I'd be open for dinner." She gives him a smile, one that says she might be open for more than that.

Jeremiah pops his Stetson on his head. "And if I weren't married better than thirty years, so would I."

Outside the building, he gets in the Impala, lights a Camel. If the Cantús are telegraphing warnings, Leslie needs to know it. Needs to know she's got to be careful. *Got me a bad feeling about this situation, about everwhat is going on. It's not just peculiar any more. It's borderline dangerous.*

He pulls out his cell phone, selects her number from the memory, punches the SEND key. A mechanical voice says, "Please leave a message."

"It's Spur. I got reason to believe that man in the restaurant parkin' lot might be connected with the Cantú drug gang. If that's so, then it's for sure somethin' ain't right about what's goin' on, and I need to talk to Farkas to get to the bottom of it. Meantime, I'm goin' home, tend to my livestock. You want me to come back to Dallas, you call me and tell me where and when I can meet your boss. I'm keepin' your cell phone so you can reach me. I ain't heard from you in a week, I'll mail it back."

He cuts the connection, ignitions the vehicle.

45

CLYDE HAS BEEN TALKING TO GUTTER BALL JONES IN HIS HEAD EVER SINCE he got off the phone with the man. *I know how you do. I know how all you motherfuckers do. You and your indignation act, like you was Jerry Falwell and you'd just been asked to grand-marshall the Gay Pride Parade.*

Now you want me to show up over at your house, so you can thump yo' fist on the table, 'bout how innocent you is. See, that right there? That's how motherfuck-ers trip up. 'Cause it don't do nothin' but invite me to say, you so innocent, let's have a look at yo' phone records. See if there's any calls to two-one-four, where Mr. SWD/Cobray be hangin' out. Then we see who's thumpin' on what.

Maybe that bib-overalled newspaper man done me a favor, done smoked ol' Gutter Ball out his hidey-hole where the Judge can collar his punk ass.

Clyde parks behind a Cadillac that hadn't been here the other day. He walks up to Gutter Ball's front door, rings the bell, squares his shoulders. Gutter Ball swings the door in.

Clyde says, "Well, here I is. Like you asked. Mr. Jones."

"The name is Mustafa X."

"Yeah, man. You look like a real Arab to me."

"Come on in. I got some folks to introduce you to."

The man steps aside to let Clyde through, shows him into a living room. The room has a couch facing the door, armchairs bracketing a cof-fee table in front of the couch. A man and a woman are sitting there, drinking coffee out of china cups, the man in the armchair, the woman on the couch. Clyde recognizes her as Laurice Stubbs even before Gutter Ball makes the introduction.

Clyde walks over, offers his hand. "How you, Miss Stubbs?"

She gives him a cold look, shifts her glance down to the hand he's of-fered up, then looks back up at him without taking it. He straightens up, drops his hand to his side.

Gutter Ball is saying, "And this is my lawyer, Craig Stephens."

Clyde turns to look at the man sitting there, blood suddenly hammer-ing in his ears, realizing this duded-up guy here accounts for the Seville out front. Wondering now if he's been set up. The lawyer nods at him from over his coffee cup, sizing him up like he was a county fair show animal. He's a smallish black man with round glasses, a goatee, flawless white teeth, dressed in a white shirt, dark suit, pocket handkerchief, bow tie. There's something vaguely familiar about him.

Clyde says, "We met somewheres before, man?"

The lawyer takes a napkin from his lap, dabs at the corner of his mouth. "I rather doubt it. I practice in Houston. Mustafa called me late yesterday, asked me to come up here this morning to consult with him and Miss Laurice."

Clyde snaps his fingers. "I got it now. I seen you on television."

Gutter Ball says, "Craig sued the state of Texas prison system on behalf of the Islamic Brotherhood awhile back. Civil rights class action."

Clyde says, "You was on TV more than Oprah."

The lawyer sets his coffee cup down on the table. "When I undertake to represent someone, I always look to advocate that client's cause in any and all available forums."

Clyde notices he uses the precise diction of the well-educated, no dropped "g's," street language. Clyde is thinking, *Pretty good act for a brother.*

The lawyer says, "Now, maybe you would like to have a seat and explain why you have seen fit to make wildly false accusations about my client in the local newspaper and in the course of doing so gravely damaged his reputation here in Brenham."

Not knowing what else to do, Clyde takes the other armchair. Gutter Ball sits on the couch next to Laurice, reaches in his pocket for his pipe and tobacco, fills the bowl, starts puffing it. Clyde tries to tell himself not to get all defensive, but the problem is, now he's got to walk a line he's not entirely sure how to walk. He says, "Look, that fool didn't have no bidness printin' that. I tol' him that was off the record shit. Besides, this whole problem might've been avoided, yo' client would've just let Laurice give me a statement when I come 'round here couple days ago. Assumin' he's clean, like you say."

"He was under no obligation to let her speak to you. And his refusal to do so does not give you license to slander him. To make matters worse, you then talked to his employer about his criminal record. My client stands in danger of losing his job."

Clyde says, "Like I said, man, all I wanted was Laurice's statement. Was just doin' my job is all, tryin' to find out who shot Lamont."

Gutter Ball says, "For your information, after you left here and she got up from her nap, I asked Laurice, did she want to talk to you? She tol' me she wasn't gonna truck with you, and for me not to truck with you, neither."

"Say what?"

Laurice says, "You broke Lamont's nose. You *po*-lice-brutalitied him."

Clyde can taste bile in the back of his throat. "What you talkin' 'bout?"

Laurice points a finger at him. "You think I forget? No, suh. I don't forget nothin'. Back last spring you come 'round the house, lookin' for Lamont. He was out new-car shoppin'. You found him, busted his nose 'gainst a steerin' wheel. You police-brutalitied him. I don't want to have nothin' to do with no police-brutality cop."

Clyde knows exactly what she's talking about. Last May, he had had to rough Lamont up some to get from the man what he knew about an armed robbery.

The lawyer says, "Deputy Thomas, I think it is only fair to advise you, we are planning legal action as respects your slander of Mustafa and your unwarranted violation of Lamont Stubbs's civil rights in the matter just mentioned by Miss Laurice here."

"But Lamont is dead, man."

The lawyer takes off his glasses, starts polishing the lenses with a handkerchief. "We will sue on behalf of the decedent's estate, of course. This is a legitmate cause of action on the estate's part. All citizens have certain rights that are not to be wantonly violated by the authorities. We believe a court will enforce those rights even in a town as, shall we say, provincial as this one. We will also be filing a multiple-count grievance against you with the Washington County Sheriff's Department." He places his glasses back on his head. The lenses distort his eyes, make them look too large for his face.

"Come on, man. This is unbelievable. Laurice, I'se just tryin' to find who it was killed yo' brother. How come y'all want to sic this here lawyer on me?"

Mustafa puffs his pipe, takes it out his mouth, shakes his head. "You ain't doin' nothin' but the white man's bidding, shacklin' us so the white man won't have to dirty his hands. You a sorry-ass excuse for a black man. You ain't authentically black."

"Bullshit, man. I'm as black as you."

Mustafa points his pipe stem at Clyde. "No man who carries the white man's water deserves to be called black. You know why we got black-on-black crime in the first place? I'll tell you why. You go into any liquor store in this part of town, you find drink so powerful the white man won't let it be sold in his part of town. He puts it in here, though, so black folks will drink it down and then turn on one another, beatin' and shootin' and rapin' and robbin' from one another. Then the media run the stories 'bout all the violence and crime that's around and the white folks get scared by it.

That makes 'em willing to pay the white man his taxes, and he uses that money for the *po*-lice and the prisons where they lock the black man up like animals. You just a part of that whole corrupt system. That's why you ain't authentically black."

Clyde's getting angry now. "Yeah, well, you know what, man? I think this is all a bullshit smoke screen." He looks back and forth among the three of them. "I think y'all just messin' with me, tryin' to knock me off my stride, 'cause I'm about to be closin' in, you know what I'm sayin'? Only reason y'all would want to do that is, y'all know somethin' 'bout what happened to Lamont and Diedre Brown." He looks directly at Gutter Ball. "Ain't that right, *Mr. Jones?*"

The lawyer gets to his feet. "That's enough. This meeting is over. My client is not answering any questions unless he is under subpoena. We invited you here out of courtesy, because you're a brother. So you could prepare yourself for the legal action that will shortly follow. So that you would not be blindsided. That having been accomplished, I believe it is time for you to go." He whips his glasses off again, commences to polish the lenses.

Clyde stands, puts on his Stetson. "You got that right, motherfucker." He turns and walks out the house.

Out on the front porch he watches a beat-up sedan driving slowly by. It looks like the same piece-of-shit ride the DEA had braced him in the other night. The windows are up on the hoopdee so Clyde can't be sure. But he could swear that Agent Ramirez is staring at him through the passenger's-side window.

4 6

THE PLAN IS FUCKED. PAUL LIPPER KNOWS THIS.

Paul pays the clerk for his cup of cappuccino, finds an empty computer terminal way in the back. He sits down to check his e-mail. He's in one of those Internet cafés that are springing up everywhere you look, where you could sip a cup of coffee or have a snack while you surf the Web. He checks his e-mail daily, looking for something from Dusty, something that says it's alright to come out now. Maybe a message to meet up somewhere. Some kind of communication. Something.

His inbox pops up and he scans it. Spam, one hundred percent. Lots of it ads for Viagra or penis enlargement. He used to joke about this stuff, about how all these Internet people think his penis is too short and too wicked soft. Paul used to tell Dusty, "Maybe I ought to have a look at your outbound e-mail, see what's starting all these rumors about my genitals."

He goes back to the top, starts over, clicks through it all more slowly, deleting the spam, looking for something that might have come from Dusty, something encrypted maybe. Dusty, the only person in the world who has this e-mail address. The only person other than his mother and the spammers, that is.

He finishes the e-mail. Nothing. Not one word in two weeks. Not by e-mail, not by phone, not by regular mail, although he knows Dusty would play hell finding him now that he had gone into hiding way up here in Denton. Paul had drawn the logical conclusion from Dusty's silence a week ago.

The plan is fucked.

Then he'd gotten that e-mail from his mother Saturday night, about this Texas Ranger who was supposed to be looking for him. She had included the man's phone number. Paul called him up yesterday morning, talked to him. The man claimed to be looking for Dusty. Claimed to be working for Farkas. What was up with that? If Dusty hadn't made contact in two weeks, wasn't the only logical conclusion that Farkas knows only too well where Dusty is?

Yesterday afternoon Paul had come over here to the Internet café, had run a Web search on this man who called himself Jeremiah Spur. Lots of articles had popped up, about the man's career with the Texas Rangers, all the crimes he had solved, bad guys he'd put behind bars. What was a dude like that doing working for Farkas? The only thing that makes sense is, it's some kind of trap, laid especially for Paul.

Or maybe it is somehow on the level, Dusty is still loose somewhere, just hasn't found a way to get in touch with Paul.

Paul has never been more confused. He's beginning to wonder if Dusty told him everything there was to know. And if it was a mistake to trust the man he loved.

For months after Jonathon died, it had seemed like the plan was working perfectly. Dusty had said Farkas didn't seem to have any idea what had really happened that night, didn't seem suspicious or angry or vengeful or anything but sad. The man had even been more open to Dusty once his grief started to wear off, had gone to some effort to get to know him better, almost as if the fact that Dusty had once been Jonathon's good friend made Dusty special somehow, connected Farkas in some way with the son he'd lost on the grimy tile of a restroom floor. There'd been no hint of blame being assessed, of hostility, of impending retribution. It was just the opposite—Farkas was showing real interest in Dusty. For the first time ever.

This is what Dusty had always wanted, to be treated more like Farkas's own son. Dusty had all but come to hate Jonathon for the differences in the way Farkas dealt with the two of them. The preferential treatment of Jonathon the Son that Farkas withheld from Dusty the Hired Hand. Paul wondered if that's what finally made Dusty do it, instead of the money. That jealous desire to be like Farkas's own son.

Yeah, it had been going real good, but then the woman had shown up, the Ice Queen, Dusty called her. He had told Paul, "You got a bottle of chardonnay you need chilled, quick like a bunny? Just set it between her legs for like maybe ten seconds."

It wasn't long before the Ice Queen started nosing around, asking a lot of questions, looking over Dusty's shoulder. Dusty had walked in one day, found her in his office, going through his stuff, rifling through his files. Dusty had been outraged, had even thought about going to Farkas to complain. At the time, Paul had thought Dusty was overreacting. His advice was for Dusty to take it easy, not blow his good relations with Farkas by getting in a pissing match with the Ice Queen. One day, not long after that, Dusty had just disappeared.

Paul drops his empty coffee cup in a trash can, leaves the store, gets in his car. Heads in the direction of what passes for home these days, seven hundred dreary square feet of paper-thin walls and stained carpet.

Thinks about that day two weeks ago. He was calling around, trying to find out why Dusty hadn't showed up for his regular training session. He was between calls when the front desk buzzed him, told him a hysterical Mexican woman was holding for him on line two. It was Esmeralda, his maid. She had just let herself into his apartment for its twice weekly cleaning. Found it turned upside down, poor Lucky shot through the head. *Oh, Señor Lipper, is so awful!* He had told her to calm down, take the day off, then he had hung up and gotten out of the club as fast as he could.

That's when he had run up here, just as he'd planned it. Paul had come up to Denton last summer, scouted out this apartment complex with its peeling paint and torn window screens. It's not the Ritz, but it's a good place to hide, and no one knows to look for him here. Not even Dusty.

He had rented the beat-up old Toyota he's driving now, had bought a new cell phone to replace the one he'd forgotten to take from his locker. He'd spent a couple hundred dollars on a few changes of clothes and another couple hundred on prepared food since he wasn't much of a cook. He plans to keep his head down awhile longer, but if Dusty doesn't surface pretty soon, he's going to have to start thinking about moving out of this area, going somewhere else altogether, getting a new job.

Paul lands the Toyota in the apartment parking lot, gets out. He takes the stairs to his second-floor unit two at a time, lets himself inside, turns on the lights. He walks down the hall toward his bedroom. He passes the bathroom on the right. The light is on in there. He stops. *I thought I turned all these lights off before I left this morning. I guess maybe not.*

He steps inside the bathroom, looks around. It's a tiny little space, sink across from the door, bathtub with the shower curtain closed to the right of the sink, toilet to the left. He reaches up, flips the light switch off.

The sound of the shower curtain being ripped back sends him jumping. "Shit!" he hollers. Three bright flashes, one right after the other, come from the direction of the bathtub, accompanied by a soft *toof, toof, toof.* Paul catches two slugs in the chest, one in the throat. He slams against the wall, his hands go to his throat, his legs quit working.

A figure wearing sweats and gloves and a ski mask steps out of the tub, stands watching the young man writhe on the floor. Then the figure raises the pistol slightly and with one more shot brings an end to what is left of Paul Lipper.

47

He moved to the door, eased past the bodies into the hallway. Half crouched, holding his Walther in front of him in both hands. The smell of smoke was strong.

He took the stairs down quickly, stopping on each landing just long enough to look for an ambush on the landing below, but at the second floor the smoke and the heat drove him back up to his room. He could hear people screaming downstairs. He eased to the window, pulled back the curtains, jerked back as a bullet shattered the windowpane close by his head.

The fourth man was shooting at him from the street.

He went to the telephone, lifted the receiver. No dial tone. So this is how it ends.

He returned to the window, careful to stay out of the line of sight of the street. The Rue de Seine was narrow, little more than a cobblestone alley, lined on both sides with apartments, hotels. Directly across the street, only five or six meters from where he stood, was an apartment building, its windows facing his room.

He stuck his Walther in his waistband, picked up a chair, hurled it against his window, breaking the glass. He grabbed an ashtray off the bedside table, shook the butts onto the floor, threw it as hard as he could out the window. It crashed through the window of the apartment across the street.

In a few seconds, a woman appeared there, looking around.

He shouted, "Madame! Madame!"

She looked up, saw him waving his arms.

"The building is on fire! Call the fire department! The building is on fire!"

He saw her look down at the street, then look back up at him. Then she disappeared, and she was gone so long he wasn't sure she was coming back. The smoke in the room was getting thicker. The screaming downstairs had stopped.

The woman appeared once more at her window. "I have called them! They are coming!"

He moved to his washbasin, wet a rag, covered his nose against the thickening smoke. Moved back to the door of his room. The smoke was building rapidly outside. He could hear the fire, roaring and crackling, coming up the stairs, seeking him. He pulled the bodies into the hall, closed the door against the smoke.

In the distance he could hear the sirens. He eased back to the window, looked down at the street. It was filling with people drawn by the spectacle of the burning hotel.

Behind him he heard a whooshing sound. He turned to see the inner wall of his room burst into flames. The fire started moving along the ceiling and the walls. It was coming for him.

On the street below, the fire trucks were working into position.

The heat inside the room had become unbearable. Carefully, he climbed out the window, braced his feet against the wall, clinging to the windowsill with only his left hand.

By the time the firefighters got their ladder high enough to collect him, the fire had been consuming his left hand and arm for minutes. He would carry with him the memory of the smell of his own flesh roasting long after they lowered him to the ground.

He would carry with him always the memory of how it felt to be burned alive.

Six weeks later a corpse was found by a farmer on a hillside outside Mougins. It was badly decomposed, and when the coroner first saw it, in the basement of the hospital where he worked, he despaired of identifying the body. Still, with a heroic shrug, he set about his task. He ascertained that the deceased was female, probably in her late twenties or early thirties, tall, lean athletic. After two hours of careful study, he sat down to prepare his report.

He wrote that the victim had been brutally murdered. Her throat had been slit from one ear to the other. And both her arms had been burned severely, as best he could tell, while she was yet alive.

48

CLYDE IGNITIONS THE CRUISER AND PULLS AWAY FROM THE BURLESON county courthouse. *Waste uh my fuckin' time, man.*

Sheriff Gadson had produced Jesús Salinas alright, but the dude had showed with lawyer bookends, a short seedy one from here in town and a taller one with white hair, wearing a three-piece suit and the obligatory affronted look, who had come over from Austin to point a bony finger at Clyde and the sheriff and tell them his client wasn't talking to the law "under any circumstances whatsoever."

I got better things to do than drive up here just to have some Billy Graham–lookin' three-hundred-dollar-an-hour suit stare down his nose at me. How come I'm such a lawyer magnet all of a sudden? Runnin' into the motherfuckers every time I turn around.

He's just crossed back into Washington County when his cell phone chirps. He unclips it from his belt, brings it up. "Clyde Thomas."

"Hey, baby. How you doin'?"

"Fine, Yolanda. Thanks for dinner last night."

"It was great seein' you. Lester says you good people. He says it's a rare man who's smarter than he thinks he is."

"I'll be sure and add that to my résumé."

"Where you at, baby? I can't hear you too good."

"Out in cow country, drivin' back to Brenham from Caldwell."

"You interview that pachuco in Caldwell?"

"Tried to. Didn't have no luck, though. Man showed up with two mouthpieces. Had his lips stapled up."

"Well, I got news for you. Your shooters been doin' that thing of theirs again."

"Where, up in Dallas?"

"Huh-uh. Houston. Triple homicide in a parkin' lot last night. HPD ran the slugs and brass through DRUGFIRE and called up here. Same SMG and Walther."

"Who caught it?"

"Dealers, Hispanics. Local Cantú boys. HPD says they're bad dudes, but they run into somebody badder."

Clyde is thinking, *Same guns, must be the same shooters. But Gutter Ball is supposed to work for the Cantús. Don't make sense, he'd have someone runnin' all over Texas whackin' their people.* He can see his Gutter Ball theory folding up like a thirty-nine-cent T-shirt. "Sounds like somebody might be makin' theyselves a play for the Cantús' turf, huh? Could be this 'wolf' motherfucker the DEA was talkin' 'bout."

"Could be. Whoever it is must have *huevos* weigh five pounds apiece. From what I've heard about the Cantús, they ain't gonna take this lying down. We could be looking at the start of some kind of gang war."

"One thing I don't get, though."

"What's that, sugar?"

"Why they would kick such a thing off in this little pissant town of mine, with somebody as small-time as Lamont Stubbs."

"Don't know, but they workin' their way up the ladder now, for sure. One of 'em that bought it last night? Ran everything between Houston and Austin. He wasn't no dime-a-dozen mule."

Clyde says, "Listen, I'm just now pullin' into town. I'll call you back, once I get to the office. Get the HPD contact info from you."

"Alright, baby. Talk to you later."

He cuts the connection, slips the cell phone into his shirt pocket. In less than a minute it's ringing again. He pulls out the phone. "Yeah, baby. You forget somethin'?"

"Clyde? This is Billie? From down at the office?"

"Yeah, Billie. What's up?"

"The sheriff is lookin' for you? Says he needs to see you? Like, right away?"

"Okay. I'll be there in five minutes."

He hears her say something to somebody, apparently Dewey. Gripes Clyde a little, Dewey's too full of himself to place his own phone calls, has to go through the brain-dead receptionist. Then she comes back on the line. "He says for you to meet him in Sonya's office?"

"Fine. Tell him I'll see him there." He ends the call. *Great. Just what I need.*

Five minutes later Sonya's secretary lets him into the DA's office where he finds the woman he'd called a bitch the last time they'd spoken huddled up with Dewey. Sonya has fixed up her temporary First State Bank digs as best she can to reflect her taste in things. She has a vase of cut flowers on her desk, a couple modern art paintings on the wall, originals, by some hippie down in Houston she had taken a shine to, making Clyde go to numerous exhibitions and galleries where he'd stand around thinking about sex and professional sports while she oohed and aahed her way through the artwork.

The furnishings include a small, round conference table and four matching armchairs with green leather seats. That's where she and Dewey are sitting when Clyde walks in the room. There are some papers, couple law books, scattered on the tabletop.

Clyde stops just inside the door. "Howdy. You lookin' for me, Sheriff?"

Dewey glances at Sonya. "Actually, we both sorta are."

Sonya says, "Have a seat, Clyde." She's not friendly and she's not hostile. She's just thought-consumed, businesslike. From the expression she's wearing you might conclude she had just been balancing her checkbook.

He takes a chair across the table from her. She hands him some kind of legal document, a court filing styled "The Estate of Lamont Stubbs, Plaintiff, v. Washington County, Texas, and C. Livermore Thomas, Defendants." He looks up. "Th' fuck?"

Sonya says, "That lawsuit was filed this morning in federal court in Houston. Alleges assault and violations of rights guaranteed to Lamont Stubbs under the Fifth and Fourteenth Amendments to the U.S. Constitution, allegedly committed last spring by you in your capacity as an officer in the Washington County Sheriff's Department."

She reaches over, picks up another document, says, "This lawsuit was filed at the same time in local state district court. The plaintiff here, a man by the name of Mustafa X, is suing the same defendants for slander. Between the two of them they're seeking twenty-five million dollars in damages."

"Say what?"

Dewey says, "Do you know anything about this, Clyde? I mean, you went over to meet with this man this morning, right?"

Clyde looks from Sonya to Dewey. "Yeah, I met him, him and his fancy-dressin' lawyer and Lamont's sister, too."

Sonya flips to the back page of the pleading. "Craig Stephens is representing both plaintiffs. Little guy with a goatee, right?"

"That's him. Fairy-lookin' motherfucker."

Sonya makes a face, but Clyde isn't sure what about. "He say anything about suing the county?"

"The dude might of said somethin' 'bout it."

Sonya says, "Why didn't you tell us, Clyde?"

"Thought the man was tryin' to bluff me off Gutter Ball's tail."

"Just to make sure we're all on the same page, Gutter Ball is—"

"Mustafa X was Gutter Ball Jones before Allah latched onto his ass in prison, made him change his name to one that's part A-rab and part letter. I been workin' a theory, Gutter Ball had Lamont and the Brown girl whacked. I ain't so sure no more, though." He tells them about the murders last night in Houston, how the same weapons were involved. "Don't see how Gutter Ball could've had much to do with that."

Sonya says, "One thing's for sure." She taps the papers with her index finger. "If this is a bluff, it's going to take a lot of the county's resources to call it."

Clyde is shaking his head from side to side. "I can't believe they done sued my ass. This is bullshit." He looks up. "We gon' be fightin' it, right?"

Sonya says, "We have twenty days to respond but I probably won't wait that long. I'll drop a general denial in the hopper, then sit down with the plaintiff's lawyer, see if we can work something out."

"'Work somethin' out?' What the fuck is that supposed to mean?"

Sonya sighs. "It means settle the case for as little as possible. My office doesn't have the resources—"

"But that'd be, like, the same as admittin' I was guilty and shit."

"Look, people settle lawsuits all the time, just to make them go away, sometimes for big money. That's the foundation of the American judicial system. It's why mass tort lawyers and the other class-action guys can afford to fly around in private jets and own professional baseball teams and buy and sell politicians like boxes of frozen vegetables."

Clyde stares down at the tabletop. "This is fucked up."

Dewey clears his throat. "There's one more thing, Clyde. Lamont's sister filed a grievance against you. For roughin' up her brother."

Sonya holds up a hand. "Allegedly roughing up her brother."

Clyde points at the tabletop. "That right there is a crock uh shit, man. It's his word against mine, and his ass is on a slab down at County. Case y'all forgot already, I just spent the entire weekend tryin' to figger out who put it there."

Dewey says, "We know that, Clyde."

"Well, his junkie sister don't."

Sonya says, "The thing is, Clyde . . ." She glances at Dewey. "After Otis Pearson turned up dead, the County adopted strict rules governing cases like this." Otis Pearson was a black man who had died while in the custody of the Sheriff's Department a few years back. As a consequence, the old sheriff had been shitcanned, and Dewey, taking his place, had hired the first black deputy since Reconstruction. A deputy by the name of Clyde Thomas.

Clyde says, "Meanin' what, exactly?"

Dewey says, "Meanin' we and the DA's office got to conduct a joint investigation into the allegations. Meanin' you got to go on ad leave 'til we can sort it out."

Clyde stares at Dewey. "You are shittin' me, right?"

"'Fraid not, Clyde. I'm gonna be needin' your badge and your gun."

"What about the case I'se workin'?"

Dewey says, "That's another thing. I got a call this mornin' from a DEA agent, name of Fischer, whinin' about how he asked you to lay off this Jones, or X or ever-what he calls hisself. He wanted you out of the way of what they got goin'."

"Fuck the DEA, man. They can't come into our county, tell us what to do."

Dewey shrugs. "Ordinarily, what they want wouldn't make me no never mind. But I can't ignore a brutality grievance, and if you're on the shelf 'til we get the prospects separated from the suspects, well, that means I'll have one less federal asshole jerkin' my chain."

Clyde looks at Sonya. "Come on, man. Help me out here. What about 'innocent 'til proven guilty'?"

She bites her lower lip, slowly shakes her head from side to side.

"Don't go bitin' yo' lip at me. You ain't Clinton."

She flushes, starts to say something, holds up a hand. "Sorry, Clyde. This is not subject to negotiation. We'll get right on it, try to get it behind us as soon as possible."

Clyde stands up, takes his gunbelt off, drops it on the conference table with a clatter. He unpins his badge, slaps it down. "The day I go lookin' to y'all two to save my ass is the day I know I'se fucked like a tied goat." He turns and walks out the door.

Dewey looks at Sonya. *"Y'all two?"*

She sighs. "Oh, yes. I suppose you haven't heard. I recently joined the Vast White People's Conspiracy to Get Clyde Thomas. Along with the DEA and the emphatically not white Mustafa X, Laurice Stubbs, and Craig Stephens."

"Lordy."

"Yes. Well, be that as it may." She reaches over, picks up Clyde's gunbelt, hands it to Dewey. Reaches for a lawbook, starts leafing through it. "Let's see what we can do about these bullshit lawsuits."

49

JEREMIAH DRIVES HOME MONDAY AFTERNOON CARRYING WITH HIM A VAGUE guilty feeling about leaving Dallas with nothing solved. But he knows he's right to require a face-to-face conversation with Farkas, and he figures going back home might be the one way he can flush Farkas out into the open. Jeremiah is more than ever convinced the man is somehow at the core of all this.

He pulls into his driveway and around behind the house. The fine clear weather of last week has vamoosed, and this evening it's warm and gray with heavy cloud cover that's bringing nightfall early and a mist that's not quite a drizzle. He parks next to his pickup, gets out, glances over at the grave where he'd buried his dog Duke. Feels the sadness and loneliness ping his heart.

Inside he hangs his Stetson on a wall peg, chucks his grip on the floor, walks around opening windows. He collects the mail from out front, sorts it into piles—bills, the local paper, a ranching magazine, junk—until he's down to an envelope addressed to him in Martha's handwriting.

He takes the letter out to the porch where he can sit in his cane-bottom rocker while he reads the news from up in Connecticut. It's only a page long. She hasn't much to report, mostly that she's homesick, is finding her sessions tolerable if not something you would mistake for fun. She says the season up yonder is one of beauty, trees lit in yellows and reds and oranges, nights chilly enough to call for a sweater.

He sets the letter in his lap, watches the mist turn to a drizzle and then rain, darkening the earth on his dog's grave out by the pumphouse. He kicks himself some for running off to Dallas to do the bidding of mysterious strangers rather than staying here at the ranch where he belongs, writing a letter to his suffering and lonely wife.

He goes inside, sits down at the kitchen table with a piece of lined paper and a ballpoint pen, undertakes to compose to her a letter. It takes him an hour and three cigarettes to produce five lines of prose. He sits for a while and stares at it. He judges it to be inadequate but the best he can do. He has been in love with this woman since the Johnson administration, but finding the right words and phrases for it had always seemed beyond him. *A thing can only be what it is.* He gets up to look for an envelope and a stamp.

Two days later the weather has faired off. He's sitting at his kitchen table early in the afternoon doing paperwork when his phone rings. He gets up, answers it.

"Jeremiah, it's Trey Beacon."

"Howdy."

"Listen, I just got off the phone with Terri Hinojosa, over at DPD narcotics. She said they found that guy you were looking for."

"Dusty Nelson?"

"No, that other one. Paul Lipper. Up in Denton. Police up that way got a call Monday from a woman who said something was dripping through her ceiling, looked like blood. They found Lipper's body in the apartment above hers. He'd been shot four times. When they got him ID'd, they connected him to a BOLO that Detective Hinojosa issued after you met with her."

Jeremiah works his jaw. "Any idea who might've shot him?"

"Not so far. Nobody in the apartment complex saw or heard anything. The ME makes the time of death late Monday morning, so most people would have been at work, I reckon. Denton PD dusted for prints and did a pretty thorough crime scene search. The shooter cleaned up his brass but the forensics team recovered a couple slugs, ran them through DRUGFIRE, got a hit. It's from a Walther P99, a gun that has been used in three separate homicides in the last week, one of which was in Brenham last Friday night."

"What?"

"That's right. Detective Hinojosa talked to the DPS crime lab down in Austin herself. There was a double homicide down yonder, a three-fer in Houston Sunday night. Both had drug connections. One of the Brenham vics was a pusher, and the three in Houston were some of the Cantús' people."

"Hang on a second." Jeremiah sets the telephone down, fetches the *Brenham Gazette* from the family room, goes back to the phone. "Sorry to keep you waitin'. I'm lookin' at the local paper. It's got a front-page story 'bout that shooting. I know the deputy who's workin' the case. Man name of Clyde Thomas. He's a good cop."

"Maybe you ought to pay him a visit."

"Reckon I should."

"Say, I got one more thing. We found out what did Farkas's kid in."

"It wasn't cancer, was it?"

"Nope. OD'd on cocaine. DOA at the Brazos County Hospital last April."

"He was supposed to be asshole buddies with Nelson, who was paired up with Lipper. Now I'm sure drugs is what links all this up somehow."

"Anything else we can do for you?"

"No, sir. I'll be gettin' your wheel rocket back to you directly."

"I'm gonna be seein' you again pretty soon, aren't I?"

Jeremiah grunts. "That'd be my guess."

The receptionist down at the sheriff's office is saying, "I don't believe Deputy Thomas is in?"

Jeremiah vaguely remembers her from the few times he's called on the sheriff. A trailer-park type who sounds doubtful about everything she says. "Is it his day off?"

"Um, I don't believe I'm at liberty to say?"

Jeremiah works his jaw. "Are you at liberty to say where I can find him, then?"

"You might try him at home? I can give you his home phone number?"

Jeremiah jots it down, thanks her, cuts the connection, punches in the phone number. It's answered on the second ring. "Yo."

"This here's Jeremiah Spur. Is this Deputy Thomas?"

"Yo, man, been awhile. How you been doin'?"

"Tolerable. Listen, you got any time for us to get together this afternoon?"

"Man, I ain't got nothin' but time."

"Good. How 'bout the Farm-to-Market Café, say, around three o'clock?"

Jeremiah is sitting in a booth in the back, mug of coffee in hand, lit cigarette in an ashtray, when Clyde walks through the front door and heads his way. They shake, then drop on the benches, either side of the table. A waitress takes Clyde's order, strolls off.

Jeremiah and Clyde had worked together some earlier in the year, on the Sissy Fletcher case and the courthouse bombing, but it's not like they really know one another. They visit about the weather and the Brenham Cubs' upcoming game with Giddings and after Clyde's Dr Pepper arrives Jeremiah gets down to business. He says, "I saw in the paper where you're workin' that double homicide from last Friday night."

Clyde's eyes drop and his face tightens. "Yeah, man. Wish I'd never hear uh the case. Sho' wish I'd never talked to that fool reporter."

"On account of how come?"

"On account of it got my ass sued twice and put on ad leave."

"Do what?"

Clyde tells Jeremiah everything that's happened since Friday night, finishing with last Monday, how he'd had to cough up his badge and sidearm to the sheriff until they could investigate the grievance allegation, how he'd been humiliated right in front of the DA herself. He finishes and says, "Look, what's it to you anyhow?"

"I been workin' a matter up in Dallas. Lookin' for a couple fellers. One of 'em has turned up dead, shot four times with the same Walther that was used here in town and down in Houston."

Clyde sits up a little straighter. "The vic another dealer?"

Jeremiah shakes his head. "Some kind of fitness coach named Paul Lipper. His best friend is the man I was asked to find, man name of Dusty Nelson."

"Don't know nobody by that name. But I reckon what you done tol' me means I can kiss 'nother theory uh mine good-bye."

Jeremiah crushes his cigarette butt. "How's that?"

"Them DEA dudes? They said somethin' 'bout some other character maybe settin' hisself up to go into competition with the Cantús. Since it was Cantú people got whacked down in Houston, I'm thinkin' maybe we got ourselves a little war goin' on between rival drug gangs."

"But how does a hit on a civilian like Paul Lipper fit in?"

"It don't. So it's, like, back to square one and shit." He shrugs. "Which is where I was Sunday morning since, after I had slept on it and all, I figered them DEA guys was just jivin' me, 'cause, you know, this character they say might be settin' up to compete with the Cantús? They say he's some kind of cloak-and-dagger man from Europe the CIA used to peddle crack to the children back in the eighties, help finance the war down Central America way. Made the man sound all mysterious and shit. Now maybe the CIA was behind the crack trade like the papers was sayin', but I ain't buyin' all this other bullshit, 'bout usin' European cutouts and what have you."

He looks over, sees the expression on Jeremiah's face. "What's up, man?"

Jeremiah clears his throat. "This European cutout. He have a name?"

"Code name. Called him 'the Wolf.'"

"I'll be damned."

Dewey Sharpe walks softly down the hall of his house, gets to the corner, ever so carefully peeks around it into the family room. He's dressed in his camouflage, has his face blacked, clutches a blowgun. He has to tilt his body some to hold his gut back, keep it from giving away his position.

He's stalking Bob.

Bob is his wife's calico cat. Lulu, the Siamese, had been in the back when Dewey got home, had seen him go into his closet and pull on his camo, had scrammed. Dewey figures to deal with her later.

Dewey scans the family room. No sign of Bob. Maybe he's hiding behind Dewey's recliner or on the other side of the couch. Dewey eases out of the hallway.

Dewey likes to come home early on Wednesdays, when Claudia works until eight o'clock down at the antique store, play his stalk-the-cats game. His weapon is a blowgun he'd bought at a gun show down in Houston one year, along with a handful of darts. Dewey had rendered the darts harmless by clipping the stingers off them with wire cutters. He has no desire to hurt Claudia's cats, actually, since it wouldn't take her long to deduce who was behind the injury and put the hurt on Dewey in the way only a woman can, ascertaining with that sixth sense they've got precisely what to do to inflict the most torment, then doing it. Without mercy.

No, Dewey's aim is just to scare the bejabbers out of the sorry little furry sons of bitches for the sheer fun of it. A cat that's been whacked on the rump by a blunt dart it didn't see coming can provide a powerful dose of amusement. It'll jump straight up in the air like an NBA player or shoot across the carpet so fast it's nothing but a blur. He figures that furnishing him with a few yucks every week or so is a fair price for them to pay to be allowed to live in his house.

He tiptoes through the family room, peeks into the kitchen. *Where is that sumbitch?* There! On the kitchen counter, back to Dewey, licking his paws. *This oughta be good.* He loads the blowgun, raises it to his lips.

"Goddamn it," he says under his breath as the doorbell sounds. He tiptoes away from the kitchen door, figuring to run off whatever vacuum cleaner salesman or Jehovah's Witness has chosen the precise wrong moment to come calling at Casa Sharpe. He gets to the front door, jerks it open.

Yonder stands Jeremiah Spur on his front porch.

The old rancher says, "It's a little early for Halloween, ain't it, Sheriff?"

Jeremiah waits in Dewey's backyard for Dewey to clean the war paint off his face, get himself into some regular attire. He watches a couple cats back toward the fence line, stepping carefully, looking his direction now and then, tails twitching in the air. Their wariness fits with the blowgun Dewey was toting when he came to the door. The sheriff emerges from the back of the house with a bottle of beer, plops down in the lawn chair next to Jeremiah. At the sight of Dewey, the cats bolt.

Dewey says, "You sure you wouldn't care for a beer?"

"No, thanks."

Dewey takes a long pull, wipes his mouth with the back of his hand. "So what can I do you for?"

"I hear you suspended Clyde Thomas."

"Had to. Standard procedure when a brutality grievance is filed."

"Well, sir, I need you to reinstate him. For a few days, leastwise."

"How come?"

Jeremiah works his jaw. Just a year ago, when he was still toting a Ranger's badge, he would have said to this ridiculous former pickup truck salesman to quit wasting his time and do like he was told. Now that Jeremiah's a civilian, though, he's obliged to explain himself to this chucklehead. Jeremiah suspects that everything Dewey knows about law enforcement would fit into a thimble, still leave room for an army of ants.

Using the fewest number of words possible, he tells the combined stories of the missing Dallas accountant and the shooting deaths of his buddy, the local pusher, the three down in Houston, all connected by ballistics. Dewey finishes his beer, sets the bottle down on the grass. It's dusk, and the light has dimmed.

At length the sheriff says, "I don't get what you need Clyde for."

"Because he's law enforcement and I ain't. I need a badge to leverage."

"You were a Texas Ranger. You must know lots of peace officers."

"Yeah, but ain't none of them already involved in an important part of the case."

"What about that lady narc in Dallas?"

"Ain't been a crime in her jurisdiction."

"Your Ranger buddy?"

"He's got other fish to fry."

"The Denton cops might—"

Jeremiah cuts him off. "Clyde's got a jump on them, too. He's the one I want."

The sheriff cogitates some. "I ain't sure I can do it. Our rules on brutality allegations is real strict."

"They ain't but departmental rules. You're the department head. You can waive 'em for good cause."

"Is that what you're askin' me to do?"

"Yep. A lot of what's going on here traces back to Dallas. I want to carry Clyde up there with me in the mornin', see what the two of us together can get done."

Dewey sighs. "And he'd be under your supervision?"

"I'd watch him like a rich man watches money."

Dewey stares at the ground for a spell, his shoulders hunched forward, the burden of decision making contorting his posture. Then he leans back. "Alright, then. Tell him to come by the office in the morning. He can collect his gear."

Jeremiah nods, spits on the grass. "'Preciate it, Sheriff."

Dewey beetles his brow. "I'm countin' on you to watch him close."

"I said 'like a rich man watches money.' Nobody ever watched anything closer."

50

JEREMIAH LEANS AGAINST THE IMPALA SMOKING A CIGARETTE, LOOKING OFF
toward the sunrise, once more getting accustomed to that light pull on his
left shoulder. His Sig Sauer P226 rides under his left armpit, concealed by
his sports coat. He had decided that for this business he'd better pack his
regular-duty sidearm instead of the Colt Commander, the intricately en-
graved model 1911 pistol the Rangers most often wear for show. In private they call the Colt their "barbecue gun."

He turns at the sound of the front door of the bank opening, sees
Clyde come out the building, back in deputy's uniform, badge and gunbelt in place.

Clyde says, "Hey, man. This your ride?"

Jeremiah drops the butt, grinds it into the pavement with the toe of his
boot, opens the driver's-side door. "I'm just borrowin' it from a man."

Clyde gets in the other side. "You think the dude might want to sell it?"

"Maybe. Since we're havin' lunch with him when we get to Dallas,
you can ask him yourself."

Clyde looks around the interior, nods. "Believe that's what I'm gonna
do, too."

Jeremiah holds up his cell phone. "You know anything about these
things?"

Clyde takes it from him. "What you wanna know?"

Jeremiah points at the display. "What's that little symbol mean?"

"Means you got voice mail, man."

"You got any idea how to fetch it?"

"Let me mess with it some while you drive." Clyde presses buttons on
the phone, holds it to his ear, while Jeremiah points the Impala toward
Dallas. It's still early, not yet seven o'clock. Traffic has yet to build.

"What's yo' password, man? I need that to, like, access this shit."

"I'm a sumbitch if I know. Phone's a loaner."

"Well, that's it, then. We ain't collectin' yo' messages without the password." Clyde cuts the connection. "This car owned by a cop, huh."

"Texas Ranger. Guy I told you 'bout yesterday."

"Uh-huh. I figgered we wasn't havin' lunch with no 'cyclopedia salesman."

Lunch is at a Highland Park Italian place jammed with trade. Young mothers gossip over salads, fuss absentmindedly with their kids. Yuppies do business with one another across the table or over cell phones.

At Jeremiah's suggestion, Trey had invited Terri Hinojosa along so their group made four. They sit off in one corner and talk small—Big XII football, high school shootings, politics, cops more than one of them knows. Their waiter arrives with the starter course, deals it, heads off to attend to someone else's table.

Jeremiah says, "Detective Hinojosa, you want to tell us 'bout the crime scene up in Denton?"

Her expression hardens, and Jeremiah can see the cop behind her smoky eyes. She recounts it for them. Paul Lipper's body on the bathroom floor. Print techs found Paul's and a bunch of anonymous latents. Shooter probably picked the front door lock. Nobody saw anyone come or go, nobody heard any gunshots.

When she's done Jeremiah says, "Okay. Clyde. Tell 'em what you got."

Clyde goes through his last few days, finishing as the waiter sweeps up their empty salad plates and starts serving their pasta.

Jeremiah follows with the *Reader's Digest* version of his Dallas weekend. "What interests me is them DEA sayin' they'd heard a former CIA hand, name of 'the Wolf,' was makin' another run at narcotics. Now, Farkas used to carry water for the Agency, and Lipper told me 'Farkas' means 'wolf' in Hungarian. So what's two and two make where y'all come from?"

Trey says, "But I don't get why that guy would go around whacking the Cantús' people. I mean, if he ever *was* in the life, he's been out a good ten years. Meantime he's made himself something like a billion dollars developing real estate."

Jeremiah nods. "Could be he's good for that much. But only his bankers and accountants would know for sure." He sets his utensils down, leans in. "But look. Leslie said somethin' about them runnin' shy of liquidity. Said their access to ready cash couldn't keep up with their growth. Now, suppose Farkas had a liquidity problem and he decided to solve it by gettin' back into narcotics. Generate himself some long green to keep growin' his real estate business. If he worked the crack trade back in the eighties, he would've known how to go about it. With some inventory and his own channels of distribution in place, he's in business."

Clyde says, "So you thinkin' the man stole from his own business? Had this Dusty dude siphonin' money off to purchase inventory with?"

"It explains the missin' ten million, don't it?"

Clyde says, "What about the missin' Dusty, man?"

Jeremiah says, "Farkas is a little long in the tooth to be doin' all this himself, plus he's just the one guy. I doubt a man his age has the time or energy to work an office full of real estate hands and still run all over creation recruiting pushers and putting the pistol to the competition. I think Farkas planned to rely on his son for a lot of that legwork. But then his kid stopped his own heart with cocaine, left Farkas with an ox in the ditch."

Trey says, "And you think Dusty was Jonathon's replacement."

"Nelson was close to the Farkas family and the Farkas money. He must've either been told or figgered out what was goin' on, and then volunteered to take Jonathon's place in all this when Jonathon went and assumed room temperature. Or maybe Farkas recruited him for it. Stacks up with what that other kid, works for Farkas, Bruce Somebody, said about Dusty hankerin' to get into a high-margin business. Business don't come much higher margin than cocaine distribution. I think Dusty dropped out of sight to put the plan into action."

Terri says, "But why would Farkas have Leslie hire you to find Dusty?"

"He had to make it look like he'd been honest-to-God embezzled from, for one thing. So they'd have some story to tell their banks. Hirin' me give 'em cover. Besides, Farkas told Leslie she couldn't call in the police, so there wasn't no way in the world I was gonna find Dusty or the money, neither, long as Farkas didn't want 'em found. He set it up for me to fail."

Clyde shakes his head. "I don't know, man. Seems like a lot of coincidence happenin', Lamont gettin' whacked by these dudes, then the woman works for Farkas hirin' you out the same town Lamont's from."

Trey says, "I'm inclined to agree with Clyde, Jeremiah."

Jeremiah says, "But it only seems coincidental if you assume Farkas decided to cap Stubbs *before* he settled on hirin' me instead of the other way around."

He pauses. "Y'all look like I just started speaking in Portuguese. Okay, in the first place, it's pretty clear Farkas told Leslie to hire me in particular, I reckon for the credibility I'd bring, and he must've done homework aplenty on me, since he knew just how to draw me into this thing."

Clyde says, "How's that, man?"

"By havin' his go-between tell me he knew my daddy. That's the very bait a man who never knew his daddy can't resist."

"I hear you, brother."

"He must've checked me from every angle, figgered out my daddy vamoosed when I was little. He knew it would get my goat but good if I thought him and Farkas had known one another. And danged if he wasn't right. Made it powerful hard for me to turn 'em down when they asked for my help. Which is what I should've done."

Clyde says, "With you, man. Still ain't seein' that ol' Lamont connection, though."

"Here it is, then, but I'll grant you, it's rank wildcat. Could be, while he was diggin' around on me, he was also lookin' at what it would take to get back in the life. Like the DEA said to you, drug gangs been movin' in on rural America here lately, instead of concentratin' on the ghettoes like they used to do. He figgers this out, then learns 'bout Brenham while he's checkin' up on me. Sees it's strategically situated, relative to major population centers and college towns and this and that. Farkas figgers Brenham to be a good place to start with his larger plan, which was takin' down the incumbent to make room for his own distribution channels."

Trey says, "Wasn't he taking a mighty big risk someone would connect the dots?"

Jeremiah says, "A man like that? He wouldn't see it that way. He probably figgers people from someplace like Brenham to be nothin' but a bunch of ignorant cedar choppers. Why should he care what kind of trail he left? He might've even been purposeful, just to carry us high."

Terri drops her head, looks out from under her eyebrows. "Carry you high?"

Trey says, "That means, make fun of somebody."

She leans back. "Oh."

They're quiet for a while. Clyde says, "So Farkas is one of the shooters then, huh."

Jeremiah says, "Not if he's only got one working hip."

"But he could've been runnin' garbage at this Leslie 'bout bein' all laid up with the hip."

Jeremiah pulls out his Camels, lights one, pulls an ashtray over. "I doubt it, but I suppose it's possible. Might explain the Walther. Not the SWD/Cobray, though."

Clyde says, "Why couldn't Farkas be usin' the SMG?"

"Because it's a cheap meat-ax weapon. Sprays ammo this way and that, no regular aim to it. With his money, if he wanted an automatic weapon, he could've bought any number of better-made models. Nope, the SWD is a street thug's gun."

Trey says, "Probably a street thug who hires out."

"Yep. I'd bet Farkas hired himself a greaseman. And I'd also wager Farkas is keepin' his own personal distance from the actual killings. He's just too old for all this action we seen here lately. Goin' from town to town, pluggin' dangerous folk. That's a young man's game."

Clyde says, "Who's the shooter with the Walther, then?"

Jeremiah blows smoke. Clears his throat. "I think it's Dusty Nelson."

"Come on, man. The dude is a CPA."

"Yep. I think Farkas is lettin' him handle the rough stuff, him and a greaseman Farkas brought in to balance Dusty bein' an amateur. That way Farkas ain't worn out by the effort, plus he would have somethin' to give the Cantús when he gets around to makin' a deal with 'em."

"What kind of deal?"

"Market-sharing arrangement. Somewhere along the way, once the bodies have stacked up like cordwood, Farkas'll go to the Cantús, tell 'em he wants control of the action in certain areas, promise 'em he'll leave the rest of their piece alone. He'll give 'em his greaseman in exchange for the people he's taken out, and if he has to he'll give 'em Dusty if the grease-man ain't enough for their blood lust. That's another reason to have Dusty do the shootings, see. Gives him something to trade with. They'll make some kind of deal, then he'll be in business, they'll be in business, everything will settle back down, him and the Cantús will stay out of one another's way. That's the only way either of 'em will make any money."

Trey says, "But you said Dusty might have been Jonathon's replacement."

"Yep."

"How could there be a deal for the shooters if Jonathon had stayed alive, done the wet work? Farkas would never give the Cantús his own son."

Jeremiah shrugs. "Don't know. Maybe Farkas had some other plan in that case. Or maybe the two of them intended for Dusty to be the shooter all along. Any way you cut it, Farkas is smart enough to know he's got to be careful not to get the Cantús so riled he can't get 'em to dance down. That's why I don't figger he himself has been doin' the killin', even if he's not stove up. He don't want them gunnin' for him in a way that's personal. And he figgers to get 'em to dance down if he gives 'em the real shooters and then promises to lay off."

Clyde says, "Wait a minute, man. What about Paul Lipper? That dude bought it with the Walther. If Dusty's doin' people with the nine-milli, why would he cap his own boyfriend?"

"Guy like Lipper is kind of a rounding error in the context of this game. Maybe Farkas told Dusty to, because he was worried Lipper knew too much. Maybe it was a loyalty test. A rounding error, all the same."

They sit in silence while the waiter clears the dishes. Jeremiah smokes and taps ash. The others stare at the tabletop or look around the room.

Terri says, "You said you told Leslie you wanted to talk to her boss. That seems more important than ever, doesn't it?"

"Yep. But I ain't holdin' my breath."

Clyde says, "So what's our next move, man?"

Jeremiah looks at Trey and Terri. "Y'all need to decide if this is somethin' you can allocate resources to, so we'll know how much help to plan on."

Terri hesitates. "I can't get clearance from my face cards for anything until I can show a City of Dallas connection."

Jeremiah says, "You forgettin' the embezzlement?"

"No complaint's been filed. Besides, if it's like you say, there wasn't any embezzlement to begin with. Not really."

Trey says, "I don't have those kinds of issues. I'm happy to run some background checks on Dusty Nelson, see if there's anything in support of what you're saying. And we can see what there is on the other people killed with the SMG."

Jeremiah nods. "Good a place to start as any."

They all stand. Trey says to Clyde and Jeremiah, "Why don't y'all come back to the office with me, then?"

Clyde looks at Trey, says, "Hey, man, I got a question for you."

"What's that?"

"You interested in sellin' yo' ride?"

51

The Parker House Hotel dining room, Boston, just past eight in the morning of February 10, 1981. He sat alone at a table, sipping coffee, soaking up America.

The dining room was large, half the footprint of the hotel. High ceilings, mahogany walls and columns, carvings of flowers and fruits set into the crown molding. Bloodred leather benches and chairs. Three enormous crystal chandeliers. He sat beneath an impressionistic painting of the Public Garden. White-jacketed waiters moved among diners who pecked at their food with heavy forks.

He had been here the better part of a month. He couldn't get over how informal these Americans were. How rich they were.

John came through the front door, shrugged off his overcoat, walked to his table, shook his hand, dropped into the chair across from him, looked around the room. He lit a cigarette, blew smoke, smiled. "Some hotel, huh?"

"Yes."

"Ho Chi Minh was a busboy here."

He didn't respond.

They ordered breakfast, steak and eggs for him, cereal and fruit for John. "Got to watch my cholesterol," John said as he handed the menu back to the waiter. "So, been getting out? Seeing the sights?"

"I went to the Old North Church. 'One if by land, two if by sea.'"

John head jerked at the rest of the room. "These people. They think they invented America, and they think it stops at the Berkshires."

"I could live here."

"Winters are too long, and the money's too old. You should go to Texas instead."

"The Wild West?"

"There hasn't been a scalping in months."

"But why Texas?"

"People aren't so hidebound. They're more open. Your opportunity is not dictated by your antecedents. That's important in a case like yours."

They smoked in silence until the waiter arrived with breakfast. Then he said, "So, then, Texas. Where?"

"One of the cities. Houston, or my old hometown, Dallas."

"I know no one there."

"We can fix you up. But there is one thing."

He looked up from his eggs to see John looking at him. "Yes?"

"We need to ask one last favor."

He listened as John went through it. When John finished, he sat silently for a few seconds. Slowly, he held up his left arm, pulled back the sleeve.

John nodded. "The cutout will need a cutout."

"Have you someone in mind?"

"No. We just started thinking about this."

He tapped his finger on the table a moment. "I know someone. Someone who is smart, capable, available. Who could be very effective, with proper training."

John's eyebrows jacked up. "What about loyalty?"

"Very much the least of your worries."

John listened while he described his idea. "It's a little out of the ordinary."

"Then you will do it."

"If that's what we have to do to get you."

He sighed. "Let us proceed on that basis, then." He pauses. "Tell me, John. Have you any kind of family?"

"I had a wife and a son once. Back in Texas."

"Where are they now?"

The man looked off in the direction of the waiter, held up his empty coffee cup, set it back down, looked at Farkas. "My wife passed away long ago. I haven't seen my son since he was little. But I've sort of kept up with him."

"What's he doing?"

John hesitated. Then, "He's in law enforcement."

After John left, he sat, smoked, thought about Texas. Images came to mind, of cattle herds and oil derricks. He couldn't imagine what a Texas city would look like. Probably many men walking around in boots and those strange hats.

He pulled a sheet of paper from an inside coat pocket. It had come to him last week, here in the hotel. He wondered how she'd tracked him down. It was from the daughter he had not seen in so many years. Telling him his ex-wife had died of a stroke. He read it once more, just a few crisp lines. He set it on the table.

He lit another cigarette and watched the American morning slip away.

52

JUST OUTSIDE THE RESTAURANT JEREMIAH'S CELL PHONE STARTS RINGING. HE stops, fetches it from his coat. "Jeremiah Spur."

"Bloody hell! Where have you *been*? I've been trying to reach you for days! Why haven't you responded to any of my messages?"

"And a good day to you, too, Miss Leslie. I went back home for a couple days, but I'm in Dallas now. And I ain't answered your messages because I never got 'em."

"What do you *mean,* you never got them? I left them at this number."

"This is your cell phone. You loaned it to me, remember? No one ever give me the whatchamacallit. The password. Had to have that to fetch the messages with."

"Bruce never gave you—"

"Nope."

"Poxy *fucking* incompetent boy."

"Sorry to interrupt your tirade, but I need to tell you, Paul Lipper is dead."

"Who?"

"Paul Lipper. Dusty's friend."

"Oh, right, right, right. Dead, you say?"

"Shot to death, up in Denton, by somebody using the same weapon was used in a couple drug-related shootings in Houston and in my hometown."

"Brilliant. That's just brilliant. Mr. Lipper won't be of much use to us, then, will he? I don't suppose you've had any luck running Little Fuck to ground, then?"

"I'm half inclined to think it's been him doin' the shootin'."

Sharp intake of breath. "Excuse me?"

"That's right. Your boy Dusty is up to somethin' that's got Farkas's handprints all over it. You speak to *el jefe* 'bout him givin' me a few minutes of his time?"

"*El* what?"

"*El jefe.* Spanish for 'the chief.'"

"As a matter of fact, I did. He hasn't called you yet?"

"Not so far as I know," Jeremiah says, thinking of the voice mail he can't retrieve.

"The only number he has is your mobile. I suggest you keep it switched on."

"Maybe Bruce could call me with that password."

"I'll find him and have him do just that. Now, the reason I've been ringing you is, our friends have had a bit of luck on the money front. They've traced twenty-five thousand dollars of Mr. Farkas's money to the Dallas bank account of a Mr. Rashad Fleece."

"Rashad Fleece?" He looks at Terri. Her eyebrows jack at the name. "You got any other details? Address, phone number, what have you?"

"*I* am not the investigator, Captain Spur."

"Okay, we'll see what we can do."

"*We?*"

Jeremiah works his jaw. "I've rounded up a little help. Couple friends from law enforcement."

An exasperated sigh. "Fine. You can just jolly well explain to Mr. Farkas that you did so in direct contravention of my instructions."

"Happy to, soon's I sit down with the man. Listen, I'd like to visit with you, too. There are certain, uh, aspects of—"

"Sorry. Not at leisure just at the moment. I've a meeting I must pop back into. Big investor, you see."

"Listen, Leslie, we really need—"

"I'm sure we do, but it can't be helped, I'm afraid. I'll be back in Dallas Friday. I'll ring you and we can chat. In the meantime, do check out this Fleece character. And expect Mr. Farkas to give you a buzz. Cheers."

"Leslie, wait." But he's talking to dead air. He slips the phone back in his pocket.

Terri's eyebrows are still elevated. "Rashad Fleece?"

"Some of Farkas's money traces back to him. You've heard of him?"

Her cell phone is already in her hand. She nods, dials, holds the phone to her ear, "That I have. Hello, Gonzo? Yeah, hombre. . . . Listen, you busy just at the moment? . . . Okay, I need something from you. I'm helping some guys out on a little cross-jurisdictional thing, drug-related shootings down in Houston and Washington County and you'll never guess whose name just came up. . . . Rashad Fleece. . . . Think you could bring C-Note in for a little chitchat? . . . Okay, meet you back at the shop. *Luego.*"

She cuts the connection. "The DPD just took an official interest in this matter."

"On account of how come?"

"On account of Rashad Fleece is a machine-pistol kind of guy."

Jeremiah and Clyde are heel-cooling in an interrogation room on the third floor of the DPD headquarters building. Trey had begged off coming, had admitted he was covered up with his own caseload, and now that DPD had stepped up, he needed to tend to his other commitments. So he had adiosed, carrying with him Clyde's phone number and a verbal offer for the Impala.

Clyde says, "I'd almost forgot what bein' a cop in a real city is like. All the office space and computers and resources and shit. Back home, we ain't got the budget for it."

Jeremiah squints at Clyde. "You mind if I ask you somethin'?"

"Fire away, man."

"What you plannin' to do 'bout the fix you're in?"

"What fix, man?"

"The ad-leave fix. The grievance."

"Fuck if I know. Hire me a lawyer, I guess. Fight that shit 'til it goes away."

"A civil rights grievance is serious business. You ought to treat it as such."

"Happens to ever-body eventually."

"No, it don't. Never happened to me."

Clyde crosses his arms. "Well, then, ain't much point in me comin' to you fo' advice then, is there? You all perfect and shit."

The door opens and Terri walks in with a fistful of files. "We got somebody running the traps on Nelson. Meantime, I pulled the jackets on all the unsolveds connected to the SMG. Gonzo just called, said he'd be here in ten minutes with C-Note."

Clyde says, "Who's C-Note, man?"

"Crawford Stuckey. We give him a hundred dollar bill a week, he gives us what's going down on the streets."

"His stuff any good?"

"Sometimes. He's one fall away from being sent away for life, and his uncle runs the best pawnshop in South Oak Cliff, so he stays dialed in to the jungle beat, who's a player, who's not, who's in the market with this or that." She holds up the files she brought in. "Thought you all might want to thumb through this stuff while I pump him." She sets the files on the table. "Anything else I can get you guys?"

Jeremiah says, "How about directions to the men's room and the cof-feepot?"

Terri finds Gonzalo Menéndez waiting for her outside an interrogation room. He's dressed for the street—jeans, leather vest over a white T-shirt, thin gold chain around his neck, three days of stubble, long hair looking like he'd slicked it back with a comb dipped in forty-weight Pennzoil.

He's the polar opposite of the former Texas Ranger she'd had lunch with, the man with the square jaw, blue eyes, funny-looking skinny tie. His simple, open, country ways. *It's a shame he's such a marital fidelity freak. His wife must be one hot mama.*

Gonzo says, "*Chingo*, baby, you lookin' nice *to*-day."

"Thanks. You look like you just sat for your Pachuco Hall of Fame bust."

He pulls a face. "You don't got to be so mean to me, man, 'specially when I went and reeled in the C-Note, just like you wanted."

She head jerks towards the closed interrogation room door. He goes for the exaggerated "after you" gesture. She pushes through the door.

C-Note sits across the table, head down, shoulders vibrating slightly, right leg jiggling up and down. He looks up when the door opens, smiles with one side of his mouth. He's in his late twenties, has cornrows, a cross hanging from one earlobe, a ragged goatee. He's wearing a flowered shirt, oversized jeans. Terri can see the crotch seam down around his knees under the table.

"De-tec-tive Hinojosa," he says. " 'Sup, girl?"

She takes a chair across the table from him. Gonzo grabs the chair to her left.

She says, "Nice of you to come in, Crawford."

"Hey, if I'd uh knowed it was you, I'd uh come a-runnin'. As it was, homeboy yonder jerked me out the Harlem Nights while I still had half a beer lef'."

Gonzo tilts back. "Too early in the day for you to be drinking anyway, hombre."

"Huh. That's what you say, man."

Terri shoots Gonzo a keep-a-lid-on-it look. "We'll make this quick, then Gonzo here'll drop you anywhere you want to go."

C-Note's smile widens. "You best go gas up that ol' hoopdee you got, then. I wants to go to Vegas, man." He starts making a sound that's half snort and half laugh.

"Crawford, you are your own best audience."

"I'se just bustin' the man's chops is all."

Terri smiles. "So, Crawford, my man. Here's what we need from you today. We are looking for a man name of Rashad Fleece."

C-Note's leg stops jiggling, his face collapses like a bankrupt's credit, his eyes search the tabletop. "Man, I don't know nothin' 'bout Rashad Fleece."

Terri leans in. "Your posture's not gonna let you get away with that, C-Note."

C-Note's leg commences to jiggle again, his head goes back and forth, back and forth. He hunches his shoulders forward, grips his hands together between his knees. "Can't be no help to you there, Detective," he says to the tabletop. "Uh-uh."

Gonzo says in Spanish, "That name has made him afraid. He will not talk now."

She flashes her eyes, says back in Spanish, "I have not started trying yet."

C-Note looks up, watches them have at one another in a foreign tongue, his eyes telling a fear that's hit some kind of glandular switch in him, caused him to odor up. Suddenly Terri's got his stench in her nostrils. She rubs her nose. "Crawford, tell me something. What is it you do with the hundred dollars of tax-free DPD cash that parks itself in your Tommy's each week, huh? Buy beers down at the Harlem Nights? Go to the movies? Invest in tech stocks so you can profit from the great bull market of 1999?"

Crawford is back to staring at the tabletop, showing them his corn-rows, swinging himself from side to side, chewing on his bottom lip.

Terri says, "Just what part of your lifestyle or stock portfolio you ready to give up, *C-Note?*"

Up comes a skinny finger. "Y'all ain't cuttin' me off, man. You know how I do. I give y'all plenty so you don't."

"Not lately. Big men upstairs, they all over Gonzo and me about what kind of return we can show for our investment in you. They say, you dry up on us, maybe we ought to dry up on you. Now that's some hard reality, C."

C-Note mumbles, "I give you that crack dealer on Madison last month."

"Uh-uh. Had that one three different ways before we heard it from you."

The snitch looks up at her, then past her to the door, like he's praying for his salvation to walk through it wearing white robes. He looks back at Terri with his yellow eyes. "Man, I snitch on Rashad, he blow my ass *up.*"

"Nobody needs to know but us, Crawford."

"Bet it won't take them brothers long to figger it out, ones watched me leave the Nights with Zorro yonder. It's like to be my ass, you dig?

That's my risk, it ain't yours. I give you what you lookin' fo', I want a raise, man. I gots to have more for my end."

Terri leans back, crosses her arms. "Mr. Wheeler-Dealer."

"Gots to go one-fifty, girl, you want me to say word one 'bout Rashad."

Terri hesitates, looks at Gonzo. "One and a quarter's what we can do. And what you give us had better be worth it."

C-Note lifts his arms out of his lap, places his hands on the table. Terri can see the veins on the back of his hand, little pipelines carrying no telling what manner of South Oak Cliff poison through his body. His nails are orange and in need of a trimming.

"I don't know where Rashad lives, alright? But I knows a dude who might."

53

It was 1984. He had lived for three years in Los Angeles, working on his final assignment. Crack cocaine was passing through South Central like the Lord passing through the land of Egypt as told in Exodus, except that crack passed through again and again instead of just the one night, and it had moved to other cities also and had begun striking down in all such cities the firstborn and more than the firstborn. Detroit, Cleveland, Houston, Washington, D.C., the South Bronx. The project had gone well but not perfectly, and there were problems particularly where his operations collided with the Colombians and their Mexican proxies. It had fallen to him to seek some accommodation.

The problem was, they never kept their word, these Mexicans. He began to think of them as an inconstant people. An inferior race.

It was on the subject of things not going perfectly that he met with John for the last time at the Huntington Gardens in San Marino, on a weekday morning.

He arrived early, got a map of the grounds, strolled through the rose garden, admiring the amazing variety of color and form. At the appointed hour he walked down to the Japanese garden. John was sitting on a bench, dressed in a charcoal gray double-breasted suit. His hair had gone from salt-and-pepper to completely white since Boston.

Farkas took a seat next to him. For a while, neither of them spoke.

Then John said, "They are giving me a retirement party next week. Too bad you can't come."

"You deserve a party. And a restful retirement."

John looked down. Farkas followed his gaze. The land sloped down to a pond where koi swam, then back up to a rise where a teahouse sat. "I suppose," John said.

"Have you thought much about what you will do in retirement?"

"Find the most peaceful place I can. And stay there."

"Somewhere like this, then. The only place in Southern California where birdsong is not in futile competition with the internal combustion engine."

"Maybe. The main thing is, I'll have the freedom to make the choice. Really, for the first time in my life. That is what I'm looking forward to. That freedom."

"That's what made that first year in Vienna the happiest time of my life."

"What did?"

"Freedom. The freedom to come and go. To do as one chooses. That is where I experienced it, that feeling, for the very first time. America is wonderful, but some-day I shall return to Vienna, to live out my days, sitting in the coffee shops, walk-ing the streets. Being part of the Europe that once was."

John glanced at him. "You sound tired."

"I am. A bit."

"I hear the Mexicans are giving you fits."

"Yes. Particularly Jorge Cantú. Every time I think I have something worked out with him, he—how do you Americans say it? He jerks me around."

That drew a smile. "He must not fully appreciate with whom he is dealing."

"It is more a case of his knowing we won't risk a war."

"I have a suggestion, then."

"Please."

"It is said he travels regularly to Texas."

"Yes. On business. Or to see his mistress in San Antonio."

"Have we any way of knowing when he plans to make a trip?"

"A couple of his sicarios have found pockets for our money."

John placed his left hand on Farkas's shoulder, turned partway to look into his eyes. He said, "Then here is my suggestion. I would consider it a personal favor, actually. There is a man, a Texas Ranger, named Jeremiah Spur."

John paused. His eyes were those of a man captured for this moment by the memory of a thing long since lost. But then the moment was gone and his eyes changed and he laid out his idea for Farkas in its entirety.

54

JEREMIAH TOSSES A FILE ON THE TABLE, GETS UP TO STRETCH. "AIN'T ENOUGH here to say grace over. Random shootings in a bad part of town is all. No pattern to 'em."

Clyde is studying a file. "No shit, it's a bad part of town. Part of town I growed up in. You took a look at this yet?"

"What?"

Clyde holds up the file. "Rashad Fleece's jacket."

"Nope. Toss it on over here when you're done."

Clyde flips the file across the table, leans back in his chair, puts his hands behind his head. "Dude first went down in 1988, grand theft auto, got sent to the juvy farm in Gainesville, wasn't but sixteen. Did eighteen months. Then nothin' 'til '93, when his ass got busted fo' conspiracy to distribute. Charges was dropped when somebody liberated the blow from the DPD property room. Then arrested in '96, first-degree murder, some punk-ass crack dealer over in Chinatown. Charges dropped again. Eyewitness had herself a memory lapse."

Jeremiah peers through the file. "Fleece has had him a run of luck. He should be looking at a lifetime of liftin' weights in the yard of some penitentiary by now."

The door opens. Terri sticks her head in. "You guys doing any good?"

Jeremiah makes a circular motion over the case files with his free hand. "Maybe there's somethin' ties all this together. I'm danged if I could tell you what it is."

"Yeah, man. Me, too."

She comes in, sits down. "How about we go for a little ride, then?"

Clyde says, "You found Fleece already?"

"No. But C-Note said if anybody knows how to find Rashad, it would be his cousin Marcus. So I wanna go lean on the guy. C-Note said he works at a consumer electronics store up north of LBJ."

Jeremiah gives his head a shake that says "bad idea."

Terri says, "What's the matter?"

"This feller sees us coming, he's gonna develop cop lockjaw, then heads-up his cousin later. If Rashad's been takin' money from Farkas to kill people, then odds are he'll go to ground."

Terris frowns. "What would you suggest?"

"Oh, I think one of us ought to talk to him alright. Just not so he'd know he was talkin' to a cop."

Clyde says, "What's that s'pposed to mean, man?"

Jeremiah looks at Clyde. "I'm talkin' about you goin' undercover, podna."

"Undercover?"

"That's right. But first we need to get you some new duds."

By five o'clock they're rolling north on the Tollway through the rush-hour traffic, Terri at the wheel of an unmarked vehicle, Jeremiah riding shotgun, Clyde in the backseat, complaining. "I look like a fool, man." Clyde's new wardrobe had been procured at a secondhand shop Terri knew of. Baggy jeans, sleeveless T, work boots, cheap gold chains around his neck, baseball cap with the bill turned sideways.

Jeremiah says to Terri, "Seems to me he looks just right for the part."

"Would've been better if we'd gotten his ears pierced, maybe some tattoos."

"Y'all crackin' my ass up back here."

They take the east exit on to LBJ, then go north on Preston, turn right into the parking lot of a shopping center, big box retail running from end to end. Place that sells bed and bath accessories sitting next to a chain bookstore, right beside a consumer electronics store. Terri parks such that they have a view of the front door, kills the engine. Jeremiah turns around. "You know what to do."

Clyde says, "My mama saw me now, she'd pinch my head off." He gets out of the car, sticks his hands in his jeans pockets, shoulder rolls toward the electronics store.

Marcus Price is standing in the television section, two long rows of TVs one on top of the other, all tuned to the Channel Eight news. Marcus is admiring that black anchorwoman they got down yonder, cool-looking light-brown bitch with the big black eyes and white, white, white, teeth. Gives him something to do here late in the day other than watch the clock like a man expecting money in the mail would watch for the postman. He gets off at eight o'clock, figures to go back to the crib, listen to some music, smoke some dope, maybe go out later with Rashad, cruise some.

Rashad had been sailing ever since he came back from that gig Sunday night, had been dancing around their crib, full-time jacked up about something. Something that had happened that night, or something he'd found out maybe. Marcus had tried talking to him about it, but that just made Rashad laugh, get all mysterious and shit.

"I knowed there was more to it than just runnin' around waxin' these motherfuckers," he'd said. "Things is fixin' to be lookin' *way* the fuck up fo' Rashad."

Marcus had said, "Come on, man. Let me in on it."

"No can do, cuz."

"Did you get paid all the way out?"

That had brought a big grin. "All but the last part of it. That's comin' in cash, later in the week. 'Long with a little somethin' extra. Kinda like a super-surprise bonus for doin' my thing, like a natural man."

"What the fuck you talkin' 'bout?"

"I'se talkin' 'bout money and pussy, all of it addin' up to some long-term quality uh life for ol' Rashad." Then he had smiled, put a long finger to his lips, said, "But that's all I can say just at the moment, cuz."

The news cuts to a commercial, some cracker in a cowboy hat standing out in acres and acres of pickups, hollering about the deals he can make folks. Marcus looks away, sees a tall, young black man with a shaved head styling his way through the car stereo section, headed back here toward the television sets.

The young man walks up to Marcus, says, "Yo' name Marcus?"

"That's right."

"Homey uh mine tol' me you sol' him a twenty-seven-inch Sony, couple months back. Made him a good deal, too."

"Could be. I sell lots of televisions to the children."

"That's good. 'Cause I'se in the market, you know what I'm sayin'?" He sticks his hand out. "Name's Clyde Thompson."

"Marcus Price." They do the shake.

Guy looks at Marcus, squints his eyes. "Yo. You ain't the Marcus Price is kin to Rashad Fleece, is you?"

"How you know Rashad?"

"We was in Gainesville together, years back. Him for grand theft auto, me for possession with intent. How is Rashad, man? You seen him lately?"

"Yeah, man. We cribbed up. He's doin' good. Workin' on somethin' big."

The guy grins. "Cool, man. You tell him I said 'yo.' Now, let's have us a look at some of these TVs."

Thirty minutes later, Clyde strolls back outside, heads over to the Impala, gets in the backseat. Jeremiah and Terri turn around. He says, "The tip checked out. Dude tol' me he and Rashad live in the same crib."

Jeremiah nods, looks at Terri. "Reckon all we need do then is wait 'til quittin' time, follow him home."

"Then what, man? What we got ain't enough probable cause to swear out no affidavit, get ourselves a search warrant."

Terri looks at Jeremiah. "I'd be inclined to agree, Captain Spur."

Jeremiah says, "What about Farkas's money?"

"Information and belief only. Nothing hard. And while Rashad is without a doubt the type that might have a SWD/Cobray lying around the house, whether he's used it for multiple killings is speculation."

Jeremiah's thinking, *Back when I was Rangerin' I wouldn't need no more than that and a friendly magistrate.* "I reckon."

Terri says, "Tell you what we could do. We could go interview him. Take his statement, see how he accounts for his whereabouts last weekend."

Clyde says, "Ain't you afraid he'll bounce?"

"Once we know where he lives, we can stake his place out, keep an eye on him, while we check his story. If it's not square, we go back with a search warrant."

Jeremiah says, "Might as well give it a shot."

Clyde says, "Yeah, man. But it's a couple hours yet 'til Marcus gets off."

"How do you know?"

"Tol' him I might come back, buy a TV from him. He said he would be there 'til closin' time. That's eight o'clock. Meantime, run me over to that Exxon." He points at a gas station across the parking lot. "I want to change outta these rags, get back into my deputy rig. I can do it in the men's room over yonder."

Terri says, "You got it." She turns around and starts the car.

55

IT'S FULL DARK BY THE TIME MARCUS WALKS OUT OF HIS PLACE OF EMPLOY-
ment, gets behind the wheel of his blue 1994 Bonneville with the dented
right fender. He's got to crank the engine a couple times to get it to turn
over, and he commences to worry that the battery is fixing to die on him
and then what's he gonna do, since there's no battery replacement money
in his budget. *Maybe Rashad be lendin' it to me. He's all flush and shit.*

The engine finally catches, and he rolls out of the parking lot. He
doesn't notice the Ford Taurus following him as he goes. He takes
LBJ east to the North Central Expressway, heads south to the Routh
Street exit. He hangs a left at Florence, goes a ways, pulls into his driveway. He notices the lights are off, wonders if Rashad went out already.
Feels a little annoyed the dude couldn't at least wait until he'd gotten
home.

*But where would he have gone off to? His ride be sittin' right here in the drive-
way. Maybe he walked over to one of them bars on Elm.*

He gets out of his vehicle, leaves it unlocked, since anybody with
enough smack to steal it wouldn't have any trouble breaking into it, too.
He crosses the yard to the front porch, notices the screen door is closed
but the door behind it is standing wide open.

"God damn, Rashad," he says under his breath. "Too much trouble for
you, take a key to the lock befo' you leave the house?" He walks inside.
As he closes the door, a couple blocks down the street, a car pulls up next
to the curb. Its headlights go dark.

He hits a light switch, walks through the front room to the kitchen,
fetches a couple slices of bologna and a beer out the fridge, heads back to
the front room, starts to punch on the TV, catch some play-off baseball.
Then he sees something that stops him cold.

Rashad's money clip and his car keys, sitting on the end table. Rashad
never goes out without his clip.

Behind him he hears movement. A footstep. He turns around, sees a
figure in dark sweat clothes, hood pulled up and over, dark shades on.

"Th' fuck?" he says.

The figure raises a weapon, pulls the trigger three times. *Toof, toof, toof.* Marcus and his snack hit the floor.

Jeremiah, Clyde, and Terri watch Marcus go inside the house. Lights shine on behind the window shades in front.

Clyde has shucked his undercover costume, is back now in his Washington County deputy's uniform. Makes him feel better, being dressed like a professional again instead of some street hustler. He says, "House was dark when the dude got here. You reckon Rashad ain't home?"

Jeremiah says, "Maybe. But there's two cars in the driveway. Says to me more than one person is home."

Terri says, "Could be he's in a back room. Taking a nap or something."

Jeremiah says, "Let's just sit and watch a spell."

"How long's a spell, man?"

"Be still and you'll find out directly."

Five minutes slide by. A couple cars pass on the street. In the distance they can hear traffic roaring on the North Central Expressway. Jeremiah checks his watch. "I reckon there ain't much to be lost by anklin' on up yonder, checkin' it out."

"How you want to do it, then?"

Jeremiah turns and looks at Clyde. "You two are the active-duty law enforcement. I'm just a rancher. Why don't y'all go knock on the door, see if Fleece is home and available to answer a few questions? Meantime, I'll walk the driveway, get the license number off that other car, then keep an eye on the backyard, in case Fleece decides he'd rather not visit with y'all."

Terri says, "That's a roger."

"Okay, man. Let's do it."

They get out of the car, walk down the street. Jeremiah swings around the side of the house, stops to make a note of the tag number on the forward vehicle, eases around to the backyard. He leans up against the wall of the garage, positions himself so he can see the back door but not be seen too easily from inside the house.

Terri and Clyde walk up to the front door. Terri opens the screen door, knocks on the wooden door behind it. No answer. A minute goes by, and she tries again.

Clyde moves down the porch, tries to see in the window. The shade is pulled down, but he can see part of a room through a crack between the shade and the windowsill. He squints. "Motherfucker." He pulls his Glock from its holster.

"What?"

"Come here."

She walks down the porch. Clyde indicates the window as he backs away holding his gun in two hands, looking around. Terri takes a look. Inside, on the floor, a black arm stretched out, one hand open partway.

Terri reaches for her pistol. They walk softly back to the front door. She opens the screen door slowly, wincing at the noise made by the spring stretching, holds it open.

Clyde moves in, gently turns the knob on the inner door. It isn't locked. He pushes the door open, goes through it into the house, crouching low, Glock held in front of him. The door opens into a center hall. A doorway on the right leads to a sitting room. It's part of that room they could see through the window. On the left a line of closed doors runs down the hall. The house smells of marijuana resin and dirty socks.

Terri follows Clyde through the front door, staying close to the wall.

Clyde points to himself, then head-jerks toward the sitting room. She nods. He moves fast and low to the doorway on the right, covering the room with his Glock, turning this way and that. He sees Marcus Price lying all twisted up on the floor, eyes wide in a death stare, shirtfront covered with blood. Some kind of liquid puddled up—beer from the smell of it—mixing with Marcus's blood. The floor is awash in litter—old jerk-off magazines, beer bottles, soda cans, fast food containers, cigarette residue. *Man, a cockroach walk in here, he'd think he'd died and gone to heaven.*

This side of the house is lit. Clyde can see all the way into the kitchen. *Might be a pantry, some place back yonder for some sumbitch to hide.* He slips his index finger inside the trigger guard.

He moves through the sitting room and into the kitchen. No one there. Sees a back door, thinks about going out that way to warn Jeremiah, decides to check the rest of the house first. He eases back to the front door, shakes his head when he sees Terri.

They move down the hall together, opening each door carefully, then going through it low, as a team, watching each other's back, their weapons covering the room. They find nothing until they reach the back bedroom.

As soon as they open the door and turn on the lights they see the body of another black man sprawled on the bed, naked except for a pair of socks on his feet. A splash of blood and brains on the wall above the bed. Clyde checks the closet to the left and Terri goes to get a look at the body, sees that most of the man's head is gone.

Satisfied no one is lurking in the closet, Clyde comes over to join Terri. She's holstering her weapon, reaching for her cell phone.

Clyde says, "This Rashad?"

She nods.

He reaches down, touches the dead man's arm. "He already gettin' cold. Been dead longer than that'n up front." Clyde walks back down the hall while Terri's on the phone, turns into the sitting room, squats down next to Marcus Price. The man's still wearing the shirt he had on at the consumer electronics store, got the name of the store stitched in blue on the left side of his chest. Blood from three entry wounds has turned most of the shirt from its original yellow to a dark red. *You was sellin' TVs jus' an hour ago, now look at you. Can happen just that fast, too.*

Clyde stands up, walks out of the house to find Jeremiah.

A while later Jeremiah and Clyde are standing in the front yard watching the DPD forensics team unload gear from the back of an SUV and walk it into the house. Terri is off to one side talking to two detectives from Homicide. Jeremiah lights a cigarette. "He had to've gone out the back. I can't have missed him by more than a minute or two."

"Yeah, man."

"And you say Fleece had been dead longer than the other one?"

"I ain't no medical zaminer, but judgin' by the body temperature, had to've been. So the shooter must've took Rashad out, then waited on Marcus. How come him to shoot the cousin, you figger?"

"Worried Fleece had talked, I reckon."

"You figure it was this Dusty Nelson?"

Jeremiah nods.

"Yeah, me, too. But why would he whack his own greaseman?"

"Cleanin' up loose ends. Probably figgered we'd be on to Fleece sooner or later. Take him down and flip him. Or maybe Farkas is already into cuttin' his deal with the Cantús, and Fleece was part of it."

Clyde rubs his jaw. "That dude be, like, the deadliest accountant ever."

Jeremiah taps ash on to the ground. "Man, I mean."

A forensics guy appears at the front door, hollers for Terri. She walks into the house followed by the two Homicide dicks. Directly she's back outside and headed over toward Jeremiah and Clyde, nodding her head as she goes.

Clyde says, "Whussup?"

She jerks a thumb back over her shoulder. "They found an SWD/ Cobray. We won't know until they're finished with it at the lab, but looks like Rashad was our boy."

"The Cap'n here thinks Nelson whacked him. Man be tying up loose ends."

She nods. "That's what I was thinking, too. We're putting out an APB on him."

Jeremiah's cell phone commences to ring. He fetches it out, holds it to his ear. "Jeremiah Spur."

A soft voice with a vaguely Continental accent says, "Ah. Success at last."

"Who is this?"

"This is Benjamin Farkas, Captain Spur. I understand you wish to speak to me."

"Yes, sir. I do. 'Preciate your callin'."

"I've tried several times, you know. Kept getting voice mail, unfortunately. Didn't you get any of my messages?"

"'Fraid not."

"That's a pity. When would you like to try to get together?"

"No time like the present."

"I was rather hoping you'd say that. You know, I've been so busy this evening, I haven't taken time for dinner. How about you?"

"Nope."

"Shall I suggest meeting for a late bite to eat? There's a very dependable Mexican place here in town, Sebastian's—"

"I know the place. I went there last weekend with Leslie."

"Ah, good. Say half an hour, then? I'm still finishing up, so don't worry if I'm running a few minutes late."

"See you there."

"Excellent. Good-bye."

"Adios."

Jeremiah puts the cell phone away. "Farkas. Wants to meet for supper."

Clyde says, "Where at?"

"Mexican joint called Sebastian's."

Terri says, "Public place. He can check it out before he commits himself, will know if cops are watching the doors."

Jeremiah nods. "If he smells an ambush, he might not show. Y'all ought to be nearby, but out of sight. I can call you if need be. And if things start gettin' lively, well—" He pats the Sig that's hanging under his sports coat.

56

TERRI SLIDES THE UNMARKED CAR INTO A SPOT IN THE DARKEST CORNER OF a parking lot. Sebastian's is a couple blocks down, but from here they can see the front door without being noticed. She turns to Jeremiah. "Give me your cell phone." He hands it to her. She keys in a number, pushes the SEND button. Her cell phone commences to ring. She cuts the connection, hands the phone back to Jeremiah.

"Okay," she says. "To call me just hit SEND twice. Meantime, I have your number stored in mine in case I need to contact you."

From the backseat Clyde says, "Technology's some shit, ain't it?"

Jeremiah gets out, walks toward the restaurant. Inside he scans the front room. Half the tables are empty. He had noticed on the way in, the place keeps late hours for a Mexican food establishment. Eleven o'clock on weekdays, two in the morning weekends. At least the kitchen would still be open and he could get something to eat. Been hours since lunch. He's hungry enough to eat the ass end out of a rag doll.

The maitre d' squints at him in the low lighting. "One for dinner?"

"My name is Jeremiah Spur. I'm here to meet Benjamin Farkas."

"Ah, yes. Right this way." The man leads Jeremiah to the same table he had dinner at with Leslie. He sits down, lays his Stetson on an empty chair. Tries to bring some order to the questions rattling around inside his head.

From his place just beyond the door to the left of the bar he watches the maitre d' lead the tall Ranger to the table. Marvels once again at how closely he resembles John. Father and son, undeniably.

His father was a better dresser though, *he thinks. The Ranger's wearing dark slacks, a white shirt, thin, out-of-style tie, sports coat with too-wide lapels. The coat almost conceals the gun hanging under his left shoulder. The only thing about his outfit that looks new or the least bit expensive is the man's off-white Stetson hat.*

He straightens up, clears his throat. He thinks, Now my Hispanic accent will get a true test. *He approaches the table where the Ranger sits, watching the front door and says, "Good evening, señor. Welcome to Sebastian's."*

The Ranger looks up at him, at his name tag and ruined left arm. "You're the same feller waited on me and that young lady the other night. Ain't that right?"

He smiles. "Yes, sir. Are you expecting someone else for dinner?"

"Yep."

"Would you like a cocktail while you wait? A margarita perhaps?"

"Just a glass of iced tea. You think anybody'd mind if I smoked?"

"No problemo, señor."

While the man reaches for his cigarette, Benjamin Farkas turns and goes to get him a glass of iced tea.

57

THE THIRD TIME THE MAITRE D' CAME BY TO TELL HIM FARKAS HAD CALLED
to say how very sorry he was to be running so late Jeremiah liked to have
told him to call the man back, tell him to forget it, the evening was at its
shank, the victuals but a memory, and they could try again some other time.
But he had just ordered a cup of coffee, thought he might as well enjoy that
before vamoosing to whatever motel he could find to rack in for the night.

It's nearly eleven o'clock and the place is pretty much deserted. Just him
at his lonely table and a few waiters here and there, barkeep behind the bar
wiping down glasses. He pulls out his cell phone. Terri answers on the first
ring.

He says, "I think we got ourselves a duster."

"A duster?"

"A dry hole. The man's toyin' with us. For what purpose, I couldn't
tell you."

"Are you ready to pack it in?"

"I'm gonna give it another fifteen minutes." He nods his thanks as the
waiter with the bad left wing serves his coffee.

Terri says, "Fine with us. It's your call."

Jeremiah cuts the connection, reaches over for his cup of black.

Terri and Clyde sit in the car with the windows rolled down. The night
air feels fresh, cool. The streets are quiet. As Terri finishes her conversation with Jeremiah, a black Escalade with gold trim drives by. Clyde leans
forward.

Terri says, "What's up?"

"We got a wit, says the dudes shot Lamont Stubbs drove a black Slade
with gold trim. Yonder goes one now." The SUV rolls a couple blocks
past the restaurant, takes a left, disappears behind a building.

"You got any idea how many black Escalades there are in Dallas?"

"I know. They probably common as pig shit. There a back way into
that place?"

"I don't know."

"Think I'll go check." He gets out, walks toward the restaurant.

Terri leans out the window, says in a stage whisper, "Be careful you don't get yourself spotted." He waves at her without turning around.

The Escalade makes the corner, pulls over to a curb. The driver kills the engine, gets out of the vehicle, crosses the street. Disappears through a gate that leads to the courtyard of an apartment complex.

Inside the restaurant the front room has emptied out entirely save for Jeremiah nursing his coffee. His waiter appears with a little black portfolio, the kind they use for check delivery in a fancy place like this. *Guy's probably ready for me to leave, so he can get on back to the house.*

The waiter says, "Will there be anything else, sir?"

Jeremiah shakes his head, reaches for his wallet. The waiter sets the portfolio on the table. Jeremiah pulls it toward him, opens it. It's empty.

He looks up at the waiter, who tilts his head, smiles, sits in a chair across the table from Jeremiah. "You know," the waiter says in a voice having no trace of a Mexican accent, "the first time I ever saw you, you were on television, being interviewed."

"You're Farkas?"

The man nods, reaches into his shirt pocket for a European cigarette, sets fire to it.

Jeremiah says, "Waitin' tables. I thought you was rich as OPEC."

He smiles. "Not quite that rich. The man who owned this place"—he sweeps the room with his undamaged hand—"he and I have been friends ever since we both arrived in Dallas. This restaurant was one of my first development projects. He and I designed it together, you see, and we have worked on it over the years, to expand it. We became quite good friends after a while. He's gone now—"

"Dead?"

"Disappeared, actually. Somewhat mysteriously. I hope he returns someday. He is a fine fellow. In the meantime, his staff still lets me do . . . little stunts. Like acting as a waiter when there is someone I would like to observe closely without his being aware. Harmless, really."

"You should've just sat down the other evenin'. Had supper with Leslie and me. You'd've been more than welcome."

"Not by her."

"I asked her if we could get together. She told me you was stove up."

The man shrugs, taps ash. "I suppose such a fabrication shouldn't surprise me. She was insistent, from the day Dusty disappeared, that it was up to her to find him, and that I must keep my distance. She refused to involve me in any way other than to accept my suggestion that she retain your services. She was simply adamant. She was always willful, even when she was small."

"You knew her when she was little?"

Farkas smiles. "Of course. She's my daughter." He sees the look on Jeremiah's face. "Do you mean to tell me you did not know this?"

"She told me you had just the one child. A son, who'd passed away."

Jeremiah can see the grief in the man's eyes instantly, mixed with something else. Guilt, maybe. "Ah, yes, Jonathon. You know, Captain Spur, it is said that the greatest gift a man can give his children is to love their mother. We know not what damage we do when we withhold that gift. And, I fear, at least in part for that reason, there was always an air of impending tragedy about Jonathon. I sensed it, Leslie sensed it. She loved him the more for it and was, perhaps, more affected by Jonathon's passing than anyone else. They were exceedingly close. She misses him terribly."

"She sure led me down the primrose path. About you, herself, her brother."

"This is the singular danger of beautiful women, you see. One so wants to trust them. And the strain she has been under is such that, well, one can understand her taking some liberties with the truth. Perhaps I should give her some time off." He looks off in the middle distance, then smiles slightly. "Now, really, you must let me finish my story, about the first time I saw you. I think you will find it amusing."

"Go ahead on."

Farkas taps ash. "As I was saying, it was a televised press conference, the day after you shot Jorge Cantú when he was trying to escape from prison with those poor hostages. I was just starting my real estate business here and the hostage-taking had been front-page headlines for a week. Of course, I found it all the more interesting since I had known Jorge, had had certain, ah, dealings with him a few years earlier."

"When you was sellin' crack cocaine to inner-city kids."

"I was doing a service for our country. A service requested of me by a man you so resemble, he must have been your father, even though I never knew him by a name other than John. That, you see, was precisely my thought when I saw you on camera. John once told me he had a son in law enforcement in Texas. I take it you never knew your father."

"You want to know the truth of it, I got my substantial doubts you did."

"Why would I lie about something like that?"

Jeremiah lights a Camel, drops the spent match in the ashtray, squints at Farkas. "I spent most of my life chasin' your kind. Still and all, can't claim to have ever understood entirely what makes y'all tick."

"You misjudge me, Captain Spur. I am an honest businessman. Nothing more."

Jeremiah works his jaw. "I may hail from some little county you never heard of, but I didn't just ride in here on a head of lettuce."

"Meaning?"

"Meanin' I ain't buyin' that 'honest businessman' stuff. I been shot from behind that rock before. And I got a pretty good idea what you been up to. You and your boy, Dusty."

"Ah, yes. Dusty. Have you by any chance tracked him down? Him and the money he pilfered from our firm?"

"You know good and well I ain't. He's been runnin' all over Texas, doin' your bidding. Cappin' the Cantús' folks, so you can get back into the drug business."

Farkas examines the end of his cigarette. "That is such an astonishingly off-the-mark accusation one scarcely knows where to begin. Why would I conceivably want to get back into that sort of thing?"

"Because you can't escape your antecedents. And because your development business needs a cash infusion. Leslie said y'all been managin' through tight liquidity."

Farkas's eyebrows climb his forehead. "She really does need to go on holiday."

From across the room a voice says, "Perhaps I shall take you up on that, Father."

58

THEY TURN TOWARD THE VOICE. LESLIE STANDS INSIDE THE DOORWAY NEXT
to the bar, pointing a pistol at Jeremiah. Her hair is pinned up under a
baseball cap. A Texas Rangers cap, Jeremiah can't help but notice. She's
wearing dark, loose-fitting sweats, knees smudged white as if she's been
crawling around on all fours.

She says, "As soon as I finish tidying up. Captain Spur, would you be so
kind as to remove your pistol from its holster and hand it to my father?
Use your left hand, please."

As he reaches for his Sig, Jeremiah glances at Farkas. The man looks
shocked. Jeremiah fumbles around, extracts the gun, slides it across the
table, butt first.

Farkas says, "Leslie? Just what is it you think you are doing?"

She says, "It is so painful to watch one's parents grow old, lose those
powers that once made them so like gods, in the words of the Bard, to
their children. In your youth, Father, you never would have let them get
away with killing Jonathon."

Farkas says, "Ah."

"It cannot come as much of a surprise, now, can it, really?"

Farkas is shaking his head. "Leslie, Leslie."

She says to Jeremiah, "Jonathon was such a sweet young man,
Captain Spur. So trusting. One might even say naïve. My mother, made
over."

Jeremiah stubs out his smoke. "I 'spect you take more after your daddy."

She nods. "Indeed. I even had a spot of training with him, a number
of years back. Then we worked together for a time, handling a bit of business involving sales of cocaine to help the Company finance some Central
American adventure of theirs. Father taught me some tradecraft which
has come in rather handy these last few weeks, when it became only too
obvious that certain tasks would fall to me."

*So long as she's talkin', she ain't shootin'. And she come in the back way.
Maybe she didn't see the two cops out front.*

"That whole Dusty-Nelson-done-disappeared-with-our-money story."

"An utter fabrication. But do let's begin at the beginning. I came over to the States last spring, after my brother's untimely death—"

"By drug overdose."

She nods. "I had assumed you had tumbled to that by now. Upon my arrival I told Father we must do the honorable thing. He turned me down, rather sharply at that. Said he had seen enough blood spilt over the years. Hadn't the stomach for more."

Farkas has been sitting with his head hanging. "I never thought you'd act alone."

"Mistake to underestimate me, wouldn't you say? I knew Jonathon was not one to dabble in something like cocaine, not without some exceedingly strong encouragement coming, I suspected, from Little Fuck, who had Jonathon quite under his spell, for reasons I am at a loss to explain. My suspicions grew when I learned that the weekend Jonathon died, they had been together at the same reunion or some such nonsense, down in this ridiculous town where they had attended university."

"College Station?"

"Yes. Perfectly dreadful place. I was able then to ascertain that Little Fuck, either alone or with a friend of his, was in all likelihood the source of the cocaine that killed my brother."

Jeremiah reaches inside his coat. She cocks the hammer on the gun. "Just goin' for my cigarettes," he says.

"Please do make sure that's all you're doing."

He holds up the pack for her to see, lights one. "What makes you figger Dusty for the source of the dope?"

"I did a bit of checking, through acquaintances Father and I had made over the years. Seems there are a number of dealers in the College Station vicinity. Bloody surprising for a place like rural Texas, but"—she shrugs— "I suppose Satan need not confine himself to the city. I shortly learned that our man Little Fuck and a friend of his whose name I would only later learn from Dusty himself—"

"Paul Lipper."

"Yes. That the two of them had been prone, when back in that rather remote corner of the world for games of American football and the like, to patronize a dealer out of Brenham by the name of Lamont Stubbs, whom I ascertained was supplied by certain Houston-based associates of the Cantú drug family. This latter bit thanks to a vigorous search of Mr. Stubbs's abode on the night of his death."

Jeremiah says, "And the point of all that was?"

Farkas lifts his head. "The point was a very Eastern European one, indeed."

Leslie smiles. "Yes, quite. As in, what a Hungarian boy would be duty bound to do were a man to drive his mother—"

"That's enough!" Farkas says. They stare at one another. It's a genuine moment, this one, between father and daughter. Jeremiah wonders if it's the first of the evening.

She looks back at Jeremiah. "The point, then, was to see justice done, by taking the life of those through whose hands passed the poison that killed my little brother."

Jeremiah blows smoke, taps ash. "You must not know much about the Cantús. Either that, or you got a death wish."

"Really? Tell me, Captain Spur, when you came here tonight, who exactly was it you thought had been about the task of bumping off the Cantús' people?"

Jeremiah stubs out his cigarette, says nothing.

Farkas says, "He thought it was Dusty Nelson, working for me."

She says, "Quite so. Frightfully easy to get a story like that going. One need only plant a few rumors to give it legs. This, no doubt, is what the Cantús believe as well."

And with that Jeremiah knows she's lying—and takes him for country stupid into the bargain. *These city folks really don't think we got much by way of minds.* But he's got no choice but to play along, since he's looking down a gun barrel. "Sounds pretty dangerous for your daddy, you ask me."

"Not really. Before long, Little Fuck's body will surface, and word will get around that all this time he was freelancing as it were, trading on the Farkas family reputation to get into the life. The gossip will be that we did not much care for that sort of thing and so he's been dealt with. As has *his* sidekick, Mr. Rashad Fleece. All done so the Cantús would remain, as you Americans like to say, quite firmly on the reservation. Satisfied that we have cleaned up our own mess, so to speak."

Farkas says, "I still can't believe you murdered Dusty Nelson." Jeremiah can hear pain in his voice.

"Just as surely as he murdered Jonathon, Father. One of the advantages, you see, of employing people is the ability to control them. Their time. Their schedules. I merely suggested to Little Fuck one morning that I pick him up at his flat, give him a lift to work, so we could discuss some dodgy idea of his about developing a Web site which could be used by tenants to search for office space for let. Perfectly ridiculous idea, of course, but it gave me an excuse to show him a bit of extra attention without its seeming odd. So I picked him up in my SUV—"

Jeremiah says, "You was by yourself?"

"I had an assistant, actually, lurking in the backseat with a pistol."

"Bruce Snyder."

"Not his real name, of course. And he's older than he looks. Former British SAS. Will do anything for money."

"He sure fooled me with that accent of his."

"He proved to be quite helpful, indeed. Watching you, dropping the odd hint about Little Fuck to keep you going. He's left the country, you know. I shall miss him. Anyway, he and I took Little Fuck to a very out-of-the-way place. We had to get a bit rough with him before he would tell us about the night Jonathon died. But once he opened up, he told us there had been a third person there, the one who made the buy. Can you believe it? The stupid boy actually tried to trade that information for his life." She shakes her head.

Jeremiah says, "He give you Paul Lipper."

She nods. "When we had everything of any conceivable use from Little Fuck, I put a pillow over his face and made short work of him. Bruce disposed of the body."

"Meanwhile, you went looking for Lipper."

"I started at his flat, but he had already left for his job at the gymnasium. I went there, waited for him to appear in the parking garage, but, instead, he did a runner. I lost him utterly, and was in no position to start looking for him myself. Imagine the suspicions. That's when it occurred to me to hire a private investigator. I went to Father, explained that Little Fuck had gone missing with ten millions of our money, which he had not, really. Our money is all still there. I told Father I felt it incumbent upon me to find him. I insisted that, to save ourselves embarrassment, we not involve the authorities, but rather look to someone from the private sector for assistance."

Farkas looks at Jeremiah. "As I have already said, I suggested you."

Leslie says, "At first I had some reservations, since you came from the same county as the soon-to-be-late Mr. Stubbs, but at length I decided no one would make the connection, and, besides, I was in no position to reject Father's advice. In the event, Father had an old friend approach you on our behalf, then I brought you to Dallas on a Saturday, when no one was around the office. Prior to that, I had taken the trouble to set things up a bit—in the office, in Little Fuck's flat—so that even though you thought you were looking for Little Fuck, everything would point you toward Lipper."

"But I never actually found him."

"Ah, but you came close enough. He called the mobile I gave you from a mobile of his own, remember? Your device recorded the incoming number, and Bruce recovered that number from its memory. Now it happens that certain friends of mine and Father's have this bloody brilliant technology that allows one to track a mobile to its location, even if it's switched off, by sending it a special radio signal. One need only load the proper gear on an airplane and fly about in the same vicinity as the mobile one seeks while transmitting at the proper frequency."

Jeremiah says, "I heard tell of this when I was with the Rangers. Wasn't it used in Centra Spike?"

"Centra Spike?"

"The joint CIA–Delta Force operation to catch Pablo Escobar down in Colombia."

"Right you are. In any event, I invited my friends to come to town and to bring their toys with them. We got lucky. Lipper had not run far. We soon had his address. I simply took it from there."

"So you got Lipper and Nelson, plus the dealer and his girlfriend."

"Unfortunate about the girlfriend. All the same, one mustn't leave witnesses."

"Which is why you shot Fleece's cousin."

"Is that who that was? I had no idea. I had been at pains to disguise myself, dressing in this rather unfashionable apparel, when Rashad and I did our little duet, but he told me after the Houston job he had tumbled to the fact I was a woman. 'Bitch' was actually the word he chose. That meant he and his roommate both had to be dealt with."

Jeremiah says, "Which leaves me."

"Quite. The last of the loose ends. The only person who knows the truth and who cannot quite be trusted with it. Please do stand up, Captain Spur. Let's take a bit of a journey, shall we?"

59

TERRI HINOJOSA CAN'T IMAGINE WHAT'S KEEPING JEREMIAH. THE RESTAURANT lights have long since dimmed and the parking lot emptied out. No one has gone inside the place in what seems like hours. She's tempted to go check out the situation. Her cell phone rings. She picks it up. "Hinojosa."

"Terri, it's Brett Wilkerson, down at Homicide."

"Yeah, Brett. What ya got?"

"That APB on Nelson? We've turned him up."

"Yeah? Where?"

"County morgue. Body was found in the Trinity this morning and they just now ID'd him. His mother reported him missin' a week ago. We got a match on the dental."

"What, he drowned?"

"Nope. No water in the lungs. ME's still waitin' for some lab work, but the early betting is the guy was killed somewhere else, then dumped. ME says he's been dead a good two weeks. Guess he's not our shooter, huh?"

"Whoa. Guess not. Thanks, man."

"No problem."

She cuts the connection. She dials Jeremiah Spur's cell phone number, listens to it ring until voice mail picks it up. She presses END, pulls her pistol from its holster.

Leslie says, "I wouldn't answer that if I were you."

Jeremiah holds his hands up so she can see he's going nowhere near his ringing phone. "You want to know what I think?"

"Not particularly."

"I think revenge don't hardly seem a good enough reason to justify all the trouble you've gone to."

"But you are not Hungarian, now, are you?"

"Fourth-generation Texan. So you gon' take your vendetta all the way? Gon' take it to Mexico?"

"How do you mean?"

"You said ever-body what had handled the drugs has to pay. The ones you killed were just workin' for the Cantús. You got to go to Mexico, you want to square accounts with the family itself. They're at the root of it, ain't they?"

Leslie snorts. "Don't be daft. Raul, the old man, rarely leaves his Coahuila redoubt. Tito goes to Mexico City on occasion, but always surrounded by assassins, *sicarios*. It would be madness."

"Okay, then. Let me ask you somethin' else."

"Yes?"

"You pretended to your daddy you needed to hire me to find Nelson when what you really wanted me to do was track down Lipper. What would you have told him if you'd found Lipper when you first went looking for him?"

"About what, pray tell?"

"'Bout Nelson not being around anymore?"

"Simple. That I had grown tired of dealing with him and let him go. It's a family business, Captain Spur. Our employees are ours to hire and fire as we see fit."

"Just like that?" He looks at Farkas. "You wouldn't have been curious?"

Farkas opens his hands. "I have come to rely upon her to run the office since Jonathon died. I prefer to spend my time creating development projects."

Leslie says, "Indeed. Now, let's get going, shall we?"

Jeremiah stands up. Farkas sighs, picks up Jeremiah's Sig, aims it at Leslie. "No. This man has done nothing to us. And his father was for years my benefactor. Please have a seat, Captain Spur."

Jeremiah sits back down.

Leslie glances at Farkas. "Don't be ridiculous, Father. Think of what he knows. He cannot be left alive. I mean, really. Pull yourself together."

Farkas keeps the gun trained on his daughter. "But whom would he tell?"

She drops her left fist to her hip, striking the "warning: female-losing-patience" pose. "How about the Cantús?"

"He cannot get near the Cantús. Have you not forgotten, this is the man who arrested Jorge Cantú, then shot him in prison? The Cantús would kill him on sight."

"Really, this is absurd. Captain Spur, do let's get cracking."

Terri eases to the front door, peers through the glass. She can see some lights on in back, two men sitting at a table. She recognizes one as Spur.

The other looks like a waiter. He's holding a gun, pointed at someone or something she can't see.

She tries the door. It's unlocked. She slips into the entry hall. Now she can hear voices, a man and a woman, apparently having at one another. Staying close to the wall, she eases down the hall to the doorway that leads to the bar and the front room of the restaurant. She peeks around the corner. A female voice says, "Do let's get cracking."

The waiter says, "No! Absolutely not! I forbid it!"

Terri wheels around the corner, aims her gun at the waiter. "Dallas Police. Drop the weapon and back away from the table, sir." The waiter freezes for a split second, then sets the gun down on the table, holds his hands up.

Jeremiah says, "Terri! There's another—"

Movement off to her right. She drops to the ground just ahead of the soft spitting sound of a silenced handgun. Two bullets hiss past. Up ahead something clatters to the floor. She crawls forward on all fours, using the bar for cover. She looks up. The waiter is standing next to the table watching her.

Jeremiah Spur and the gun that was on the table are gone.

As Leslie starts firing, Jeremiah grabs for his Sig, but before he can reach it, Farkas sweeps it off the table. It clatters across the floor. Leslie turns the gun on Jeremiah, then disappears through the doorway behind her.

Jeremiah crosses the room quickly, crawls under a table, fetches his weapon. He picks himself up and starts toward the back of the restaurant.

The next room is another dining area. There are two doors leading out of it. He eases toward the door on the left, peers around it. Still another dining area. Jeremiah surmises the swinging doors on the right lead to the kitchen. He hears footsteps, pivots, gun ready, then lowers it when he sees Terri.

"Where's Clyde?" he whispers.

"Watching the back door."

"Good. Then we got her trapped."

"Who the hell was that?"

"Leslie Whitten. She's the other shooter and apparently Farkas's daughter to boot."

"And the waiter?"

"That was Farkas. Tell you the rest later. Call Clyde. Tell him to keep an eye peeled. And watch them doors while I check back yonder way."

Dining area leads to dining area, and each one seems darker than the last. There's no light other than what comes in through the windows from outside. He moves through them slowly, stepping quickly around corners, gun out, sweeping the room, squinting into dark corners. Gets to the back of the place. No sign of Leslie.

He retraces his steps to where he left Terri. Points to the swinging doors that lead to the kitchen, indicates he'll go through first, then eases through them, moving in a half crouch. Scans the room. At least there are lights on in here. Terri follows him, and they work the room together, checking under tables, in pantries and cupboards.

Jeremiah opens a door leading to a set of basement stairs. Jeremiah opens it, motions at Terri, points down the stairs. He throws a light switch at the top of the stairs, begins walking down slowly. The basement ceiling obscures his view for the first several steps but also gives him some cover. He takes three steps downstairs, stops to listen.

He takes a couple more steps, leans down, tries to see in the darkness, conscious of how exposed he is. The basement stretches away into darkness. A half-dozen rows of shelves, canned goods and whatnot on them, turned perpendicular to the stairs, occupy most of the floor space. Looks like maybe a wine rack along the far wall, but it's too dark back there to be sure.

The light switch is at the bottom of the stairs. He breathes deep, clumps the rest of the way down. Terri follows, covering him. Jeremiah hits the lights. He and Terri move carefully among the shelves. No one there.

Jeremiah says, "Let's give Clyde a call. Find out what he might've seen."

Terri pulls her cell phone out, presses a couple buttons. "Clyde? . . . Yeah, we're still in here. . . . No, no sign of her. What about you? . . . Okay, sit tight." She kills the connection, shakes her head.

Jeremiah reholsters his Sig. "I swear, it's like she up and vanished."

A voice from the bottom of the stairs says, "Actually, Captain Spur, there is a much more rational explanation." Jeremiah and Terri turn, see Farkas standing with his hands clasped in front of him.

"Alright, then. Let's hear it."

Farkas walks to the wine rack that lines the far wall of the basement and pulls on it. It pivots, and part of the wall comes with it. Beyond is a darkened tunnel, about three feet high.

"Sebastian and I designed this restaurant at a time when the INS was being rather hard on the local restaurateurs, occasionally raiding them, hauling away their so-called undocumented workers. Very disruptive for a small businessman. Sebastian wanted a design that would minimize that problem. The tunnel you see here leads under the street to a set of stairs which open into the courtyard of an apartment complex which I also developed. I do so love the real estate business. There are so many outlets for one's creative side."

Terri looks at Jeremiah. "I'm going to go call in an APB on Leslie."

"Bruce Snyder, too, while you're at it. We'll see you upstairs."

Farkas and Jeremiah watch her walk toward the stairs, working her cell phone. Farkas says, "You realize, of course, that you will never catch her. I taught her too well."

"Maybe. But if I was you, I wouldn't be concerned about *us* catching her."

"Really? What would concern you, then?"

"I'd do my worryin' about the Cantús."

Farkas smiles. Makes Jeremiah wonder if the man isn't real proud of his daughter after all. "You heard how she's covered her tracks." He pushes the wine rack gently back into place. "I cannot imagine that the Cantús will bestir themselves given what they've been led to believe. And, I assume, you'll be keeping your distance from them, as we discussed?"

Jeremiah shrugs. "I reckon that's the only healthy thing for me to do. But that don't mean they won't find out. We're both gonna have to go downtown, give the DPD our statements. That sort of thing tends to wind up in the hands of folks like the Cantús."

"Yes, well, the Farkas family version is already on the street, now isn't it? And the facts fit it as well if not better than some alternative version, originating with the DPD, whom the Cantús might reasonably suspect of having their own agenda."

Jeremiah thinks, *That's what I thought you were gonna say.*

"Come," Farkas says, "Let's go speak of your father for a few moments, before we are carted off by the Dallas Police. Surely, you must be curious about him."

"That presupposes you know him."

"Oh, I assure you, I do. Or did. I'm very sorry to say, I haven't spoken to him in many a year."

"Somehow I still ain't convinced."

"Come sit with me for a few minutes, then. Allow me to convince you."

Jeremiah follows the little Hungarian out of the basement, part of his mind already working on how he can get together with the Cantús without being detoured into a coffin.

60

They kept him until dawn in a small interrogation room with a window that looked out upon a mostly empty squad room. Now and again the police would come in and ask their questions, the same questions over and over and over, asked by a succession of police officers, starting with the comely young Hispanic who had been at the restaurant, progressing to two middle-aged Homicide detectives who smoked Marlboros, had bags under their eyes, and stomachs that hid their belt buckles. Whose eventual heart attacks were as certain as a thing could be.

They offered him no food. Nor drink. They gave him no idea how long they would hold him. They let time slip away as though it were theirs in limitless supply. They reduced him to asking for permission to visit the men's room.

The endless, petty torments of the gendarmerie.

And always there in the background, at the edges of this long night, the retired Texas Ranger waited, watching Farkas through the window, smoking unfiltered cigarettes, talking to the black man in the deputy sheriff's uniform.

When they finally told him he could leave, he knew better than to ask for transportation home. He walked into the squad room where Spur sat on a desk, the black deputy in the corresponding desk chair, studying a document. He extended a hand to the deputy. "I don't believe we have been introduced. I'm Benjamin Farkas."

The deputy shook his hand. "Clyde Thomas."

He turned to Spur. "Well, it has been quite the long night, hasn't it?"

The rancher made no reply.

Farkas said, "Indeed. So nice to have met you, Captain Spur. Please do give me a call the next time you're in Dallas. Perhaps we can finally have that meal together." He walked to the elevator, rode it to the ground floor—the one Americans insist on misnaming the first floor. Outside the station he hailed a cab that was prowling the early morning streets. The cabbie was a Russian. The irony registered idly somewhere in his head.

On the ride home his mind went back to the morning this had all begun. That morning in 1984, in the Japanese garden at the Huntington. The last time he saw John.

61

JEREMIAH AND CLYDE WATCH THE LITTLE HUNGARIAN DISAPPEAR BEHIND the elevator doors. Clyde says, "You seen this?" He holds up his reading material.

"What's that?"

"Article, was in the paper last year, 'bout the man yonder. Terri pulled it off the Internet. 'Cordin' to this here, that's a lotta money just went down the elevator."

"Oughta be scared money. Curious to me, he ain't."

Clyde leans back, puts his hands behind his head, his boots up on top of the desk. "What you thinkin', man?"

"That whistlebritches yonder's been pissin' on my leg and tellin' me it's rainin'."

"Yo. You want me to understand that shit, you best be translatin' it into English."

"Way I got it figgered, that whole scene last night was a setup."

The elevator doors open and Terri Hinojosa walks out, heads their direction, hands Jeremiah a file. "Dusty Nelson's autopsy."

"Already?"

"After we got back here, I rousted an assistant ME who's available for the occasional after-hours gig. Looks like Nelson's last few hours were none too pleasant."

Jeremiah opens the file, scans the first couple pages. "Lord have mercy." He hands the file to Clyde. "I knew none of this made a lick of sense. This about cinches it."

Clyde takes the file. "How's that, man?"

"Leslie said she planned to make it look like Nelson had done all this killin' so the cops and the Cantús wouldn't come after her. But this autopsy shows he couldn't've been the shooter 'cause he'd bought it days before. Not only do the police know that, but there ain't no way this report can stay out of the Cantús' hands forever. Once the Cantús find out Nelson died before they started losin' folks, they'll judge her story for a chump play. Farkas is too smart not to know this his own self.

Besides, Leslie has known her cover story was blown since Saturday."

He tells them of finding the note in his hotel room, that he figures it could have only come from the Cantús, and that he showed it to Leslie after dinner Saturday night.

Terri says, "Which leaves you where?"

Jeremiah reaches up, scratches under his Stetson. "I ain't sure. I'm gonna think out loud a minute here. Maybe Leslie started out to make Dusty the fall guy, but then maybe . . . Maybe somethin' went wrong."

Clyde says, "Yeah, man. Like 'stead of keepin' the dude alive until right about now, they got too rough with him. Killed him too early, like by accident, say."

"Right. Then, maybe, she went to the old man, said to him she still aimed to carry out her plan but her cover might not stick. They wouldn't have been nearly as worried about the police as they would've been about the Cantús. So what would Farkas be apt to do in that case?"

Terri says, "Well, the logical thing would be to protect his daughter."

Jeremiah nods. "Exactly. Trade on his relationship with the Cantús from way back, intercede somehow on her behalf, so as to keep them from comin' after her."

"Intercede with what?"

"Money, probably. Man's got God's plenty of it. Give the Cantús enough *dinero* and they would've figured they'd been amply compensated for the loss of their hands."

Clyde says, "Yo, man. Wouldn't Farkas have been riskin' his own lifestyle with an accessory charge?"

"Yep. That's why I'd be willin' to bet him and Leslie made a deal. He agreed to do something to keep the Cantús out of it in exchange for what he got last night, which was that song and dance she put on for me. The only point of it was to try to convince me Farkas had nothin' to do with any of this."

Terri says, "I thought she called you a loose end that needed tying up."

"I wasn't no loose end. I wouldn't've been any the wiser to her bein' the shooter if Farkas had never agreed to meet with me and she'd just disappeared. But sooner or later the police or the Rangers would've started putting all this together, maybe figured Farkas had a hand in it. They would've started makin' trouble for him."

Clyde says, "So, you sayin' Farkas must've figured if they could sell you on her takin' all the blame, him actin' all shocked and shit, then—"

"Then they would run the table—Leslie gets her revenge, Farkas steers her out of the Cantús' cross-hairs, and because she's thrown everybody off his tail, he gets to keep livin' the life of a rich real estate developer.

I figger that's his addiction, see. Ever-body's addicted to somethin'. Might be sex or soap operas or God or whiskey. Cigarettes, in my case." He reaches in his shirt pocket for his Camels even as he says it. "His is bein' rich. That's how come him to go to waitin' tables now and then. When he does that, he's like an alcoholic stayin' away from liquor a couple days to remind himself how much he loves it."

Terri says, "If that's the way it went down, then Farkas is dirty as an accessory to about seven homicides, not to mention the conspiracy charge he could be tagged with. That's a life sentence or two in the kind of accommodations Huntsville is best known for. But how do you prove any of this?"

Jeremiah says, "There ain't but one way, and that's by talkin' to the Cantús. That's just what I aim to do."

Clyde says, "Why don't you just paint a bull's-eye on yo'self, go on out to the firin' range instead?"

Jeremiah holds up a hand. "They ain't necessarily gonna go after me. Not if they're of a mind to pull a good old-fashioned double cross. Whatever protection Farkas arranged for Leslie might not extend to hisself. Maybe if we let them know we're lookin' to get the goods on the old man, they'll take a pass on me. Helpin' us take Farkas down would make 'em feel better 'bout losin' their hands."

Terri says, "I'm sorry, Captain Spur, but all this seems mighty thin to me."

Jeremiah just shrugs.

Clyde says, "Check this out, man. Maybe what Farkas promised 'em is they'd get a shot at you if they let his daughter be. Farkas may have set you up to think you need to go see them motherfuckers to nail his ass, knowin' that's what a man like you would do. Then said to the Cantús, 'Y'all been wantin' to get Spur all these years, here's yo' payback.' He'd be, like, tradin' you for his daughter, see."

Jeremiah shakes his head. "I'm willin' to bet he didn't. And that that's the reason he and Leslie come to me in the first place—because I'm the one person who's most at risk approachin' them folks. He figgers me to be too afraid to try to go get the truth, and that means whatever he's promised them stays between them, and we can't hang that accessory charge on him."

Terri says, "Can't we find someone else to do it? Someone who maybe the Cantús don't have their stinger out for?"

"No. It has to be me."

"But why?"

"Because I'm the one got Paul Lipper killed. It's me that's got to set that right."

Clyde says, "Yo, man. It ain't like you did it on purpose, you know what I'm sayin'? Sounds to me like yo' guilt bone is way overdeveloped."

"Can't help but regret my part in what happened to the man. And I'd feel better about my hand in it if Farkas is dirty and I can pin it on him." Jeremiah stands up. "Y'all got any interest in breakfast?"

"Yeah, man. My ass is starvin'."

Terri shakes her head. "I'm gonna go home and catch a nap." She gives Jeremiah a look he knows he'd be well advised to ignore.

Jeremiah looks at Clyde. "Let's go, then. We can kick this around some more soon as we find ourselves a Waffle House." They walk toward the elevator side by each.

A couple hours later Jeremiah and Clyde are in Trey Beacon's office in downtown Dallas, sitting across the desk from the Ranger as he leans back in his chair, stares at Jeremiah as though his old *compadre* had just announced he's fixing to be named the Emperor of Antarctica. The Ranger's office is thirty floors up in a high-rise. Off toward the Cotton Bowl Jeremiah can see Big Tex, the twenty-foot-tall cartoon cowpoke in red shirt and jeans who presides over the State Fair.

It's so quiet in Trey's office you could hear an ant scratching its butt. The floor is laid with brown carpet, walls painted white, got a few hand-shake photos hanging on them—the last three governors, Clinton, Bush, couple senators. Trey's desktop is stacked with papers and files.

Jeremiah says, "I gather you don't much cotton to the idea."

Trey shakes his head slowly. "You can't be serious."

"Serious as a heart attack."

"You're *loco en la cabeza*."

Clyde says, "That's jus' what I told him, man."

Jeremiah says, "So you gonna help me, or ain't you? On account of if you don't, I'll just have to find a way to contact Cantú my own self."

"I ought to have you committed to the state hospital in Rusk."

"Sounds like I'm on my own then."

Trey holds up a hand. "That's not necessarily my final answer, as they say these days. You want to give me a chance to argue you out of this?"

"I want you to do me the favor I asked."

Trey sighs, leans forward. "There's this guy, works for Enrique Cervantes, the defense minister down yonder. Met him on a multijurisdictional drug task force last spring. Let me talk to him, see if there's some way to set something up. Something safe. How can I reach you?"

"We're hightailin' it back to Brenham soon as we leave here. You can reach me at the ranch. If I ain't in, leave word on the machine."

Trey says, "This may take a day or two."

Jeremiah and Clyde stand to go. Jeremiah says, " 'Preciate it, Trey."

Trey Beacon watches them walk out his office door. Then he picks up his phone, buzzes his secretary, says, "See if you can get Roberto Miranda on the phone for me, please." He leans back in his chair, sticks the end of his ballpoint pen in the corner of his mouth, looks out the window at the Dallas traffic streaming along down below. Wonders just when, at what exact point in time, the legendary Jeremiah Spur started taking leave of his senses.

62

WHAT FOLLOWED THEN WAS A SPAN OF TIME THAT SEEMED PROTRACTED TO Jeremiah, who is under normal circumstances a patient man. But he had been antsy from the moment he'd walked out of Trey's office, in part because of the working over his conscience was giving him about Paul Lipper's shooting, but also because he knew what he had asked of Trey was a lot to ask of a friend whose own conscience was clean and who would just as lief it stayed that way. Which Jeremiah and Trey both knew it wouldn't if Trey helped arrange an opportunity for old man Cantú to kill Jeremiah and that Mexican took it.

The rest of that week and through the weekend, when he was working his cattle, or riding Redbo across his pastures to that spot so high you could see all the way to Gay Hill where he would sit Redbo and smoke, or at home in the evenings when he was trying to compose a note to Martha that was worthy of her, Jeremiah caught himself worrying some that Trey might neglect his request, might engage in a little creative procrastination. Jeremiah would have been tempted himself had he been in the other's boots.

He kept telling himself those doubts did no justice to a man like Trey Beacon. If Trey had changed his mind about setting up the meet, he was big enough to pick up the phone, call Jeremiah, tell him that's how it was going to have to be. So Jeremiah decided to give Trey a full week before he started calling and pestering the man.

It like to took the entire week. He walks into the house the following Tuesday to the sound of a ringing telephone. He picks up the receiver. "Jeremiah Spur."

"Howdy. It's Trey."

"Howdy your own self. How're things in Dallas?"

"Passable. I've done what you asked. It's still against my better judgment."

"I know that."

"You remember a man, name of Jesús Gutiérrez Rebollo?"

Jeremiah reaches up to scratch under his Stetson. "Seems like I should, but I can't quite place—"

"He's a Mexican general, was the head of the INCD, the Mexican DEA."

Jeremiah snaps his fingers. "That's right. For about two months. Then he was arrested for being in the Cantús' pocket for the last ten years. Had them Mexicans walkin' around with so much egg on their faces you could of made omelets for the entire Italian air force."

"Yep. Now he's in a prison near Querétaro. My man in the Defense Ministry talked to him. Gutiérrez is still in communication with the Cantús, as you would expect."

"It bein' a Mexican prison."

"Yeah. So he acted as the go-between. Anyway, the meeting's on. Just three people. You, old man Cantú, and his son."

"Tito?"

"No. His older boy. Vicente."

"Never heard of him. When and where?"

"Sunday afternoon. Three o'clock. Mexico City. In the Catedral Metropolitana."

"A church?"

"They wanted to do it at Cantú's finca, but we said no can do. We insisted on a public place, but told them they could choose which one. Seems Vicente is a priest there. Must be the rebel in the family. The *Federales* are cooperating with the whole thing. They'll set up a metal detector inside the entrance, close off all the other entrances, cordon off the part of the plaza closest to the front door."

"Then we're set, I reckon."

"Except for one thing."

"What's that?"

"They say they need a hostage."

That handkerchief, it ain't nothin' but a prop, the way she twists it in her hands, dabs at her eyes. She's just practicin' now, gonna take this act on the witness stand when the day comes.

Clyde sits in a conference room in his lawyer's office, watching the deposition of Laurice Stubbs. Stephens and Laurice and Gutter Ball sit across the conference room table from him and his lawyer, a white boy Sonya had recommended. Gripes Clyde some how Laurice's lawyer outdresses his. Stephens wears a navy blue three-piece suit with a white shirt and a silver tie, handkerchief tucked in his suit coat pocket, black tassled loafers polished high. Clyde's lawyer looks like he suited up over at the Sears, Roebuck, got a suit on that shines like aluminum foil, unlike his shoes.

The man's shoes look like he's been wearing them to do yard work.

Laurice is saying, "Lamont come home after he done went car shoppin'. Nose all busted up. I said to him, what happened to yo' nose? He say, that nigger cop broke it."

Sears Roebuck says, "What cop? Did he say his name?"

"He say, the one people calls the Judge." Her handkerchief goes up, dabs at her eyes, then shoots out at Clyde. "Was that nigger right yonder."

Sears Roebuck says, "I've objected three times to the use of that word, counsel."

Stephens shrugs, looks at the court reporter sitting at the end of the table, making sure she's getting it all down.

Laurice is working her eyes with that rag again, leaning into it, hitching her shoulders while she cries over her lost brother. Her lawyer leans over, pats her on the back gently. His manicured nails pick up the lights in the ceiling.

Stephens looks at Sears Roebuck. "Would you object to a short recess?"

"Fine with us."

Everybody stands except for Laurice and her lawyer. Clyde walks out of the room, headed for the out of doors, thinking a little fresh air might be in order. On his way out, the receptionist stops him, says, "Deputy Thomas?"

"Yo."

She hands him a message slip. "Mr. Spur called." Gives a phone number. He looks at her. "You got a phone I could use?"

She directs him to a phone closet off the reception area. He steps inside, closes the door, dials the number. Phone on the other end is answered on the first ring.

"Jeremiah Spur."

"Yo, Cap'n, it's Clyde Thomas. How y'all are, man?"

"Tolerable. Listen, I got a favor to ask, if you don't mind."

Clyde listens to Jeremiah tell about the planned meeting with Raul Cantú. "A hostage? What's up with that, man?"

"If they got custody of somebody from our side of the deal, makes 'em more comfortable nothin' will go wrong."

"And if somethin' does go wrong?"

"Then it's adios to the hostage."

"This is what you called me for, man? This is what you want me to do?"

"I know. It's a lot to ask."

"No shit, it's a lot to ask. Alright with you if I think about it?"

"Sure. But I kindly need to get back to Trey today."

"Yeah, man, alright. I hear you. Call you back directly."

He hangs up the phone. There's a soft knock at the door. It opens, Sears Roebuck sticks his head in. "You 'bout ready to get goin' again?"

"Just gimme a minute."

The man nods, pulls the door closed.

Clyde thinks about how his life is getting to be like this phone closet here, the walls closing in around him, all loneliness and isolation. There'd been nothing pass between him and Sonya for days that wasn't business-related. He knew he ought to apologize for calling her a bitch, but he couldn't bring himself to do it somehow, not without her making some kind of move his way. And she hadn't stirred so much as an inch in his direction. Leaving him in his little closet of a world.

This grievance case had everybody in the department steering wide of him, too. Dewey only dragged his punk ass around to whine about how it was hurting his chances of reelection next year, having a police brutality charge brought, written up in the papers, like that. No telling how it's all apt to end, what it'll mean for his career.

Maybe there's some way to settle this sucker, move on outta Shitburg, hire on with the DPS. Sure would help if I was to get me a solid reference from my man Spur.

Through the skinny window in the phone closet door he can see Sears Roebuck lurking outside, glancing at his Casio wristwatch, then at the phone closet. Clyde opens the door, says to the lawyer, "Gimme one more minute, okay, man?"

"Yeah, okay."

Clyde sits down, hits the REDIAL button on the phone.

63

BENITO JUÁREZ INTERNATIONAL AIRPORT, MEXICO CITY. THE TIRES ON THE
Boeing 737 kick up smoke as it lands a little after 11:30 in the morning.
The flight is full of Saturday-night-stays. Jeremiah and Clyde wait in
their seats way in the back while the folks ahead of them collect their belongings and move down the aisle.

Jeremiah stuffs the sports section of the Houston paper in the seat
pocket in front of him. He glances at Clyde, who's reading a paperback.
"What you got there?"

Clyde holds it up for him to see. *Cadillac Jukebox* by James Lee Burke.

Jeremiah says, "What's it about?"

" 'Bout a Cajun detective takin' care of bidness down on the bayou."

"It any good?"

"Yeah, man. The dude can flat write. I figger I got to spend the afternoon with badass Mexicans, might as well have me some decent literature."

Clyde's wearing his day-off attire. Jeans, athletic shoes, short-sleeved
knit shirt, windbreaker. Jeremiah is in sports coat, white shirt, tie, Stetson.
Neither of them carries a bag. They're booked on the 6:30 return this
evening.

Once they deplane, they pass through passport control and customs
into an area where folks are greeting arriving relatives and friends. The
airport has a bustle to it, travelers walking through trailing their bags behind them or pushing them on luggage carts. Faint smell of garlic and
restroom disinfectant in the air. *Federales* walk around in fatigues, toting
automatic weapons, eyeing the crowd.

Jeremiah's instructions are to wait at the curb. Outside they position
themselves for maximum visibility. The air is rank, soot-laden, smells of
smoke.

Clyde says, "You got any idea what to look for?"

"They'll find us, I expect."

Directly a dark green Tahoe rolls to a stop a few yards from where they
stand. The back door opens and out steps a scowling young Mexican who

gestures for Clyde to get in. Through the windshield Jeremiah can see the driver leaning forward, his forearms resting on the steering wheel, pachuco cross tattoo on the back of his right hand. They both got the same look to them. Bored. And dangerous.

Jeremiah turns to Clyde. "I'll meet you right here at five-thirty."

Clyde looks him in the eye. Jeremiah admires the man for not showing him any fear. Clyde holds out a hand. "Five-thirty it is, man."

They shake. Clyde walks down the sidewalk, climbs in the back of the vehicle. The *sicario* at the wheel pulls down on the gearshift. The Tahoe roars away, headed for the airport exit. Jeremiah watches the Tahoe until it's out of sight, then looks around for a taxicab to take him downtown, see if he can scare himself up some lunch.

Clyde gets into the backseat followed by the *sicario*. Clyde's on the hump, got a Mexican on either side. Two more ride up front. They're all dressed like they had escaped from some south-of-the-border road production of *West Side Story*.

Clyde turns to the *sicario* who had let him in. "Where we off to, man?"

The guy doesn't even give him the courtesy of a sideways glance.

"Yo. Any y'all speak English?"

No response.

"Well, then, we in fo' a long fuckin' afternoon, you know what I'm sayin'?"

The driver says a few words in Spanish, and all four of them laugh. The Tahoe merges into the traffic that's exiting the airport.

After Jeremiah finishes his plate of tamales and beans, he still has a half hour to kill. He walks over to the Zócalo, ten cobblestoned acres in the center of Mexico City, one of the largest plazas in the world. There are five- and six-story buildings, offices and apartments, Jeremiah supposes, across the street on the east, south, and west sides. There's a hotel, the Majestic, on the west side with a full view of the Cathedral. The Cathedral dominates the north side.

The scene in the plaza is like something from a medieval trade bazaar, rows of ramshackle stands where carpenters and plumbers and plasterers and bricklayers display their implements and photographed examples of their work. The craftsmen themselves, brown-skinned little men with straight black hair and bad teeth, squat by their displays or sit on lawn chairs and talk to prospective customers in rapid Spanish, gesturing with their hands. Somewhere Jeremiah can hear Mexican music playing. He moves among the stalls, studying the displays.

The Mexican flag flaps at the top of a pole in the plaza's center. Three bars, white between green and red, the Eagle on the Cactus on the Stone in the center. Jeremiah knows the legend from somewhere, about how the Aztec people wandered the earth looking for the place where prophecy said they were meant to live. A place where an eagle perched on a prickly pear cactus growing on a stone. They were said to have found it here.

In recent times an ancient stone carving had been dug up at the National Palace of Mexico, and on it was a similar scene. Only the cactus pears were stylized human hearts and the cactus was itself a mass of hearts erupting from the chest of a human sacrifice. From what Jeremiah knew of Mexican history, the symbol on the stone got it closer to right than the one on the flag. To appease their gods, the Aztec priests performed cardiectomies on live victims, prisoners captured in the wars the various tribes of ancient Mexico fought against one another.

And at the top of the hour, I'll be meeting with a Mexican, got as much blood on his hands as any of them ancient priests. Maybe Trey is right. Maybe I am loco.

In front of the Cathedral there's a market in herbs, crystals, gemstones, ointments. Hand-lettered signs, a few in English, tell of their magical properties, of their power to ward off evil spirits, cure sickness, promote fertility, extend life. Jeremiah wonders if a life extension trinket might not come in handy here in a little while.

A street runs between the vendors and the Cathedral and across the street a path has been roped off, running from the curb to the Cathedral's enormous oak front door. Green-uniformed *Federales* carrying automatic rifles and wearing helmets stand guard. Jeremiah sees an officer standing by the curb. Jeremiah walks up to the man. "Excuse me, sir. I'm Jeremiah Spur."

The officer is young, with a look that says he takes himself too seriously. He nods. "This way, *por favor.*"

The officer leads Jeremiah to the front door and stops and nods and Jeremiah doffs his Stetson and steps inside the Cathedral and through a metal detector. On the other side of the machine a couple of burly Mexicans in business suits are waiting. Each has a squiggly wire running from the back of his suit coat into his ear and a bulge under his coat that must have set the metal detector off like it was a pinball machine.

The Mexican on the left head-jerks at Jeremiah. They walk down the center aisle, Jeremiah following the suit like he was a sidearm-carrying wedding usher. The Cathedral's columns stretch up to fan arches high above. Some illumination comes from the light fixtures hanging from the ceiling and set into the walls, from candles that sputter in alcoves, but mostly the scene is one of darkness and shadow. It is preternaturally quiet, and there is no one else in the place. Jeremiah follows his usher down the aisle, watched by the saints set high into the walls.

He slides the window open, then sits back in the armchair. At his feet, the long flat case he'd used to carry the rifle through the streets to this little room in the Majestic Hotel. A room he selected personally for its clear sightline to the Cathedral's front door, once he heard from his man at the Defense Ministry.

So reliably corrupt, these Mexicans.

He leans forward, shoulders the rifle, the latest snaiperskaya vintovka *from Russia, an SV-98, with a glass-fiber reinforced polyamide stock, a PKS-07 optic scope, a bipod on the front. He rests the bipod on the windowsill, looks through the scope at the man in the Stetson. He lays the crosshairs just under the cowboy hat and keeps them there until it disappears inside the Cathedral. Then he sits back again.*

He doesn't have to wait long. A black Mercedes limo rounds the corner at the south end of the Zócalo and cruises toward the Cathedral, pulling up at the rope line. Two guards get out, flank either side of the rear door on the passenger side. It opens and four men get out, three in business suits, one in a priest's robes.

Benjamin Farkas watches them through the rifle scope as they walk together to the Cathedral door. Two of the men in suits stop outside the Cathedral, position themselves by the front door. The priest and the fourth man disappear inside.

Farkas keeps the rifle trained on the front door of the Cathedral.

Jeremiah watches as a tall priest and a shorter man in a business suit enter the Cathedral, pass through the metal detector, come walking his way, led by Jeremiah's usher. Raul Cantú has black hair with streaks of gray at the temples, a thin mustache, eyes that are a mix of brains and cruelty and purpose. The priest is clean-shaven, has a long chin. Soft, sad eyes.

The usher stops at the row of pews behind Jeremiah's. Cantú and the priest sit down. Puts Jeremiah at a disadvantage, having to lean back over the pew to see the two of them, Cantú to Jeremiah's right, the priest to his left.

Cantú says, "You're a brave man, Spur. Coming to this town. To meet me."

Even here in a church, within arm's reach of a priest, Jeremiah can feel the man's malevolence like an affliction. "Your brother shouldn't have tried to break out of Huntsville. I was just doin' my job."

"I have waited a long time for this opportunity. By rights I ought to take it."

Jeremiah works his jaw, squares around a little more. "Why don't you, then?"

The priest holds up a hand. "Gentlemen, may I remind you—"

"*Basta,* Vicente."

Jeremiah looks at the priest. "You're his son?" The priest nods. "You approve of what your daddy does for a living?"

"I love him as any son would love his father."

Cantú says, "And as any man would love his brother. It is in memory of that love that I agreed to come here. To meet my brother's killer. To square accounts."

Jeremiah says, "With me?"

"That is not today's business. Today's business is with the Wolf. It was he who betrayed my brother to you."

"How you know the Wolf done that?"

"We always suspected someone tipped you off. Jorge was making a lot of trouble for the American CIA and their Nicaraguan *amigos* at the time, so it was natural to suspect the Wolf, who was—how do you say?—quarterbacking that operation. But we were lacking in proof, and to act on a hunch, well—"

Jeremiah says, "Might've started a needless war."

"Exactly. Some time went by, then one of our men disappeared, a man named Pedro Estancia. We soon learned Pedro had been taking money from the Wolf. And Pedro knew just what he would have needed to know to set up Jorge. We went looking for Pedro, to talk to him, shall we say. To find out for sure. We wanted to be very sure.

"It took a long time, but we found him. Living in a new city, under a new name. He had even had his appearance altered. He was running a restaurant financed by the Wolf, in Dallas—"

"Sebastian's."

The man nods. "You have been there? I hear the food is excellent."

"Word is the owner disappeared awhile back."

"We 'disappeared' him. One night, as he was leaving his place. We worked on him until he told us he had given Jorge to the Wolf, so the Wolf could give him to you."

"Surprises me Farkas is still drawin' breath."

Cantú shrugs. "He has paid a price." He holds up a finger. "But we are not here to discuss that. You are said to be looking for certain information only we can provide."

Jeremiah wants to know what price Farkas paid, but thinks better of asking. "There's been some killing, a couple young men in Dallas, some of your people in Houston and the town I hail from."

"Yes. By Farkas's daughter and a man named Fleece, whom she also killed."

"So you know it wasn't Dusty Nelson, then."

"Of course. We knew all along. We left the note in your hotel room. What we could not understand was your role in it."

"They wanted my help finding a man. Didn't find out until it was too late, but they wanted him found so they could kill him."

"I see."

"Farkas is no fool. He knows if his daughter takes out some of your people, she's gonna shorten her own life expectancy considerably. Unless he does somethin' about it."

Raul reaches inside his coat, produces an envelope. "Tell him, Vicente."

"Two Sundays ago, a peasant with a withered left arm gave me this envelope. It was addressed to my brother Tito."

Raul hands the envelope to Jeremiah. Jeremiah slips its contents out. A single sheet of paper, folded in half. He opens it.

BY THE TIME YOU READ THIS, JOSE CALDERON AND HECTOR VILLAREAL WILL BE DEAD. ONE OF THE SHOOTERS WILL ALSO BE DEAD BEFORE THIS WEEK IS OUT. THIS IS RANSOM FOR THE OTHER SHOOTER.

Below that is the name of a bank in Vienna, along with an account number. Jeremiah looks up.

Raul says, "Tito checked the account. It was in my name, and contained fifty million dollars American."

Jeremiah taps the paper. "This is why the man wasn't runnin' scared. He'd bought y'all off any retaliation."

"Fifty million dollars is a lot of compensation for three or four pachucos."

Jeremiah looks at the priest. "You say you got this from a man with a bad arm?"

"Yes."

"Farkas's left arm is withered."

Raul says, "We think it was Farkas who delivered this note."

Jeremiah says to the priest, "Would you be willing to try to identify him from a photograph? And then, if it was Farkas, testify to that?"

The priest nods.

Jeremiah says to Raul, "If I can tie Farkas to this money, I can hang an accessory charge on him."

Raul gestures his indifference.

"I knew it had to be somethin'." Jeremiah holds up the note. "Alright with you if I keep this?"

"By all means. Is there anything further you need from us, Captain Spur?"

"Not that I can think of. I'm gonna want to send a photograph along for the padre here to take a look at."

The priest says, "You can fax it here to the Cathedral." He gives Jeremiah the fax number and Jeremiah writes it down in his notepad.

Raul says, "Adios, then."

The two men stand, turn to leave. Cantú stops, looks back at Jeremiah.

Jeremiah says, "Somethin' on your mind?"

Cantú says, "You took a chance, coming down here. Don't take that chance again." He turns and walks with his son toward the front door of the Cathedral.

Activity around the front door. The men in suits stop talking with each other, straighten their coats, look around. Someone is coming outside.

Farkas works the bolt, snicks off the safety, sights through the scope, his finger inside the trigger guard. Lightly, lightly. It is no more than twenty meters from the Cathedral's front door to where the limo idles at curbside, ground that can be covered in just a few strides. The guards move away from the door.

The moment has come.

The priest and the other man walk out of the Cathedral into the smoky Mexico City afternoon. Farkas takes a deep breath, steadies himself, becomes one with the rifle. Tracks his target. Out of God's house. Into God's arms.

He exhales slowly and squeezes the trigger.

64

THE CANTÚS WALK TOWARD THE LIGHT AT THE FAR END OF THE CATHEDRAL. Jeremiah watches them go, wanting a cigarette like a banker wants collateral. When they're two-thirds of the way to the front door, he gets up to leave. He's still inside the church when he hears a gunshot somewhere outside. The men in suits rush the front door. He breaks into a trot.

Outside the cathedral he stops. In the plaza, chaos. Civilians are screaming and running around. The *Federales* have their weapons shouldered, aimed at the buildings across the street. Men in black suits with handguns drawn are grouped in a rough circle with their backs to a body sprawled on the ground. The priest kneels beside the body.

Jeremiah starts toward the priest. A couple guards level their weapons at him. He stops, holds his hands up, says, *"No arma. No pistola. No arma."* They lower their weapons. He walks quickly to where the priest kneels on the cobblestones.

The body is Cantú's and he is dead. He has an entry wound in his forehead. The back of his head is a mass of blood and brain matter. The cruelty and purpose and everything else are gone from his eyes.

The priest whispers in Spanish, touches Cantú's nostrils, lips, hands, the son administering extreme unction to the father. He moves around Jeremiah, to touch the feet, then remains there, motionless and in prayer. Behind him, Jeremiah hears a man keying a cell phone. That's when he first thinks of Clyde.

Jeremiah says, "Father Vicente. Father Vicente! Please look at me." The priest crosses himself, looks up. Jeremiah says, "This is the Wolf's doings."

"It is the work of the devil."

"Maybe that, too. But there is another man, a friend of mine, being held hostage. He didn't have nothin' to do with this. We need to do somethin', talk to ever-who it is what has him."

The priest shakes his head, holds up a hand. "My brother Tito has him. He will have no choice but to kill him now."

"There's no sense in that."

"I fear Tito will see the sense."

The bodyguard is talking rapidly into the cell phone. The priest looks at the man. Jeremiah says, "Is he talkin' to Tito? Is he tellin' about your daddy?"

The priest looks back at Jeremiah.

Jeremiah says, "Tell him I want to talk to Tito." The priest hesitates. "Father Vicente, please."

The priest stands up, walks over to the bodyguard, starts talking to him. The bodyguard shrugs, hands the cell phone to the priest.

In the distance sounds the high-low sirens of emergency vehicles, drawing nearer. The same people who were running away from the scene three minutes ago now crowd around, gaping at the body on the ground. The *Federales* work them back.

Father Vicente speaks rapidly into the cell phone. At first long, urgent sentences. Then shorter ones, a word or two. *Sí. Sí. No. Sí, por favor. Gracias.* He sighs, walks over to Jeremiah, hands him the cell phone, turns away.

Jeremiah holds the phone to his ear. "This is Jeremiah Spur."

"I am speaking to the man who set my father up to be assassinated by the Wolf, no?" The voice on the other end of the line is trembling. With anger, or with something else? It's hard for Jeremiah to say.

"I did nothin' of the sort."

"You must admit, that is how it appears. Now the hostage must die, and it will be your turn soon enough."

"Wait a minute. Stop. Think on it some. Why on earth would I set your daddy up to be clipped by the Wolf?"

"I'm sure you had your reasons. Money, perhaps."

Jeremiah has long known what men say about him, but he's never stooped to trading on it. He knows now he must. "You must've heard tell of the kind of man I am. That don't sound like somethin' I'd do, does it?"

"But you were working for the Wolf."

The sirens are getting louder now, making it harder for Jeremiah to hear. He stops his other ear with the palm of his free hand. "He tricked me. He used me to get at your daddy. I can see that now, and I ain't proud of bein' used so, but believe me, if I had had any idea that was what he was up to, I never would of come down here. I wanted to meet with your daddy to see if he had evidence I could use to send Farkas to prison. You don't believe me, ask your brother."

Hesitation on the other end of the line. "He has said this to me already."

"There you go, see? And if I did set your daddy up for Farkas to knock off, why would I be here talking to you, trying to get my man back? Instead I'd be hightailing it."

A pause at the end of the line. The emergency vehicles have arrived, a couple police cruisers, an ambulance. Jeremiah moves away from the curb so he can hear better.

The voice on the other end says, "Prove it to me."

"Do what?"

"Prove to me you are not the Wolf's ally."

"I thought I just did."

"Mere words, Captain Spur. Bring me something of value. Bring me the Wolf."

"Did you say, bring you the Wolf?"

"Yes. Alive or dead. Then I will let your friend go."

"But how am I supposed to do that? The man has without a doubt vamoosed. He could be anywhere in—"

Tito cuts him off. "As you said yourself, I know of your reputation. And I know it is *not* that of a man who would do the Wolf's bidding, not, at least, consciously. But it is a fact that my father is dead. And that you played a role in it? Yes, this is also a fact. You are said to be most resourceful. You proved that when you captured my uncle, and again when you killed him. So let us now see you use your resourcefulness to bring Benjamin Farkas to me. By the Day of the Dead. If not, your friend will die."

"But that's only two weeks—"

"By the Day of the Dead, Captain Spur. Adios."

The connection is cut. Jeremiah takes his hands away from his head, looks around. Emergency medical personnel attend to the body of Raul Cantú. *Federales* speak to police in uniform and plainclothes. The padre stands a few feet away, watching him.

Jeremiah walks over, hands the cell phone to the priest, sees the question in the man's eyes. "He wants me to deliver Farkas to him by the Day of the Dead."

The question is replaced by relief. "November 2."

"He says if I don't, my man dies."

"Then you must not fail."

"It's a tall order."

"Nevertheless. Too much depends on success. A man's life. My brother's soul."

Jeremiah's face shows his skepticism. The priest lays a hand on Jeremiah's arm. "My brother is not my father, Captain Spur. If he were, your friend would be dead now and probably you as well. There is hope yet for Tito. My prayer is that a way out will be found for him."

Jeremiah holds out a hand, and they shake. He says, "I'll be in touch."

He walks through the crowd to the street, looking to hail a cab to the airport.

Tito Cantú cuts the connection, walks away from the balcony, back into the living room of the high-rise apartment just off Chapultepec Park, gestures to two leather-jacketed *sicarios*. "Go tie the negro's hands behind his back. Then bring him here."

The *sicarios* leave the room. Tito drops into an armchair, lightly tapping the cell phone on his knee. The sudden loss of his father—it leaves him more numb than sorrowful. It is no surprise his father's life should end like this. So it had been with many of his father's associates. Many others had gone to prison. Tito sighs. *Better a rifle slug through the head than living out one's dotage in a Mexican prison.*

But now is that moment. The one he has wanted to run from all his life. That moment when he is the one in charge, the one others will look to for sound judgment. For clear thinking and decisive action.

What will the others think? Jesus Christ, what will Ray think? What will he think when he hears that I had Spur and let him go?

The thought propels him from his chair. He paces the room. Ray is Tito's cousin and very much Jorge's son. Not yet twenty-five and already a compunctionless killer. Last year he shot three gringos to death in a bar in Cancún, and the family had had to send him to Cannes until he cooled off. Ray had been ten years old when Spur killed his father. That the family had never struck back at Spur was something Ray resents to this day. *I know what he will think when he hears.*

Tito stops, puts his hand on the back of a chair to steady himself. Realizes his heart is racing. *Am I up to this?* He has long wondered. He and everyone else will know soon, so very soon, what with his father's body still lying on the cobblestones of the Zócalo, and already decisions to be made. What to do about the hostage. Whether to believe the Ranger Spur. *Thank God Ray is in France.*

He knows his father would have killed the hostage by now, then dealt with Spur. But he cannot see the harm in it, this snap judgment of his, the challenge to Spur to deliver Farkas. Spur will certainly fail, and then the hostage will die. In the meantime, it will be interesting to see what develops. He drops back in his armchair, tries not to second-guess himself too much. He can hear the hostage now, in the back.

"Yo, man. Get yo' hands off me. Hey, what's up with this?"

Directly his men appear, pushing the black man stumbling ahead of them. The *norteamericano* stops in front of Tito. "You the man 'round here?"

Tito makes no reply. He taps the cell phone on his knee.

"I'm guessin' you is on account of yo' nice suit and all. I'd appreciate you tellin' these motherfuckers to untie me and keep they hands to their own selves."

Tito says, "How well do you know Jeremiah Spur?"

"I know him some. Worked with him now and then."

"Would he set my father up to be assassinated by the Wolf?"

"Say *what?*"

"My father is dead, shot by a sniper after his meeting with your Captain Spur. I probably should have cut your throat by now, but Spur says it was the Wolf who was the killer and that Spur himself was uninvolved, and so, he says to me, you should be spared, as you are his friend and an innocent man. He proved to be very persuasive. So I have said to him, in exchange for his promise to bring me the Wolf, I would let you live until the Day of the Dead."

"The Day of the Dead? When's that, man?"

"The second of November."

"The second of— Look, man. What do you want from me, huh? I didn't know any of this shit was goin' down. I was just tryin' to help the Captain—"

Tito motions the man to be quiet. "Let's go."

The *sicarios* grab the *norteamericano* by the elbows, propel him toward the door of the apartment, Tito bringing up the rear.

Back at the airport, thirty minutes before the 6:30 Continental to Houston is scheduled to board. Jeremiah has spent the last ten minutes wrestling with a lime green Mexican pay phone the size of a small refrigerator, trying to figure out how to work it. All the instructions are in Spanish, which he can't read, and when he picks up the receiver and tries to get an operator, he gets recordings. Again, in Spanish.

The departure lounge is full, a mixture of Mexicans and Americans. One young man, Jeremiah's guessing in his midforties, wearing khaki slacks, black T-shirt, expensive-looking brown sports jacket, a close-cropped salt-and-pepper beard, sits nearby, reading a newspaper, now and then glancing Jeremiah's way.

Jeremiah finally gives up, slams the receiver down on the hook in frustration.

The young man looks up from his newspaper. "Anything I can do to help?"

Jeremiah gestures at the phone mounted on the wall. "I really need to make me a phone call, but that don't seem to be an option around here un-less you know Mexican. You got any idea how this thing might operate?"

"I'm a lot of things, but an expert on Mexican pay phones isn't one of them." He reaches inside his sports coat, produces a cell phone. "Why don't you use this?"

"Ain't that gonna cost you?"

"I got weekend minutes I haven't even thought about using."

Jeremiah walks over, takes the phone. "Much obliged."

"No problem. Just key in the number, press that button there."

Jeremiah walks a ways off so he'll have some space—he's more than happy to borrow the phone, but he doesn't want this young stranger lis-tening in on what he has to say. He connects with information for two-one-four, gets Trey Beacon's home number, keys it.

Trey answers on the first ring. "Hello?"

"Beacon, it's Spur."

"Jeremiah. Y'all done? Everything go okay?"

"Nope, that's why I'm callin'. It went about as not okay as it could've."

He tells Trey what's happened. When he's done, Trey says, "How can you be so sure it was Farkas? I mean, Cantú ran a cotton-pickin' drug car-tel. Guy like that must have more people gunnin' for him than Clinton has girlfriends."

"Okay, I can't say for positive sure Farkas done it. And I'll grant you, when I was talkin' to Tito, I was wingin' it some, tryin' to maintain a measure of control over the situation. But still and all, it's the only thing that makes a lick of sense. Cantú said he had made Farkas pay somehow for tippin' me to his brother. If that's so, and if it was payment big enough— Wait a minute. I just thought of somethin'. Farkas's son. Didn't you say he died of a drug overdose?"

"That's what it said on the Brazos County death certificate."

"Had to have been an autopsy, then. Could you lay your hands on a copy of it?"

"I expect. You think Cantú might've offed Farkas's kid?"

"I'd judge it to be one serious form of payment. And if that's what happened, then Farkas might have decided he needed to respond in kind, and not by knockin' off no two-bit hustlers in Brenham and Houston. He would've been gunnin' for *el jefe* his own self. I think that's what he's gone and done, and he used me as bait to set the man up."

"Could've been his daughter."

"Maybe. Seems a little out of her league. One way to find out for sure."

"Put an APB out on the old man."

"If he's in the wind, we'll know soon enough."

"Where you at now?"

"Mexico City airport. Waitin' to board a plane back to Houston. Figger to go home from there, pack a bag."

"Where you goin'?"

"To look for Farkas."

"Shit, Jeremiah. With his kinda money, he could be anywhere. Where would you even start to look?"

"I don't know. But I damn sure know who does."

"Who the hell would that be?"

"You remember that case we worked, oh, fifteen or so years ago, out in El Paso? CIA boy, from Central America, crossed over and started runnin' guns?"

"Sure."

"There was a CIA feller we worked with by the name of Spencer Tillman."

"I recollect the guy."

"I need you to track him down, today if possible, and tell him everything what's happened. And I need you to get him to a meeting in your office tomorrow afternoon."

"You think he knows where to find Farkas?"

"I doubt it. But he can lead us to the man who does."

"And that would be?"

Jeremiah hesitates, knowing he's fixing to start sounding crazy again. "My daddy. Franklin Spur."

65

JEREMIAH IS UP EARLY THE NEXT MORNING. HE CALLS A PROFESSOR HE knows over at Texas A&M, a prominent lecturer in poultry, asks him to round up a couple students to tend to his livestock. Pays some bills, checks his bank account, which had gotten a shot in the arm awhile back. An oil company had leased the drilling rights to his land for a hundred dollars an acre bonus money plus a quarter royalty. He had used the bonus money to get current on his mortgage and pay what he owed them down at Wilson Feed and Supply, and then he had tucked the rest away. If he has done his sums correctly, he still has close to ten thousand dollars left. He sits at his kitchen table, thinks about how he's fixing to start depleting that.

He calls Sonya Nichols, tells her about yesterday. She says, "You think you can track down this man Farkas?" Anxiety has boarded her voice like it was a streetcar.

"A man can't escape his antecedents, Sonya. The answer is there somewheres."

There's a pause. "What can I do to help?"

"Clyde got any next of kin you know of?"

"His mother. She lives in Dallas. He calls her every Sunday night."

"She will have commenced to worry, then. Maybe you could give her a call, try to 'splain things to her. Tell her not to fret, though. We're gonna get him home."

"Yes, sir. Good luck, and keep me posted."

Jeremiah hangs up, calls the sheriff, goes through the same basic conversation with him. He packs a bag, sits down to write a letter to Martha. While he's working on that, the phone rings. Trey Beacon calling, to tell him he put a call in to Spencer Tillman yesterday, but has yet to hear back from the man. They agree to meet in Trey's office as soon as Jeremiah can get there.

He hangs up, goes back to his struggles with words. Directly the two ag students arrive. He tours them around his place, tells them how he wants things done.

All morning, the clock in his head had been running down the time to the Day of the Dead. It like to made him crazy. By eleven o'clock, he's in Trey Beacon's Impala, headed back to Dallas.

Trey's assistant Edna shows him into a conference room with a table and four chairs, an ashtray, a cup of black, and the Monday edition of the *Dallas Morning News*. "He's just wrapping up a few things," she says. "He'll be in any minute."

He picks up the paper, studies the sports pages until he notices he's read the same paragraph three times and still can't recollect what it says. He tosses the paper aside, lights a Camel, tries to imagine where they got Clyde Thomas, what the man is going through. For the thousandth time he counts the days.

Fifteen left until the Day of the Dead.

One thousand miles to the south, on a Coahuila finca belonging to the estate of Raul Cantú, Clyde Thomas lies on a cot, his hands behind his head, staring at the ceiling. The room, ordinarily a groom's quarters, sits hard by the stables where Tito Cantú keeps his thoroughbreds. There's a whomper-jawed chest of drawers with a washbasin and a water pitcher on top, a bucket in the corner for Clyde to relieve himself in. A bare bulb hangs from the ceiling. There are hooks on the walls for hanging tack, and no windows.

Clyde tried the one door last night but it was locked solid. He tried it again this morning after they brought him a breakfast of beans and tortillas on a tin plate and a cup of bitter coffee. Nothing doing. Through cracks in the door he could see a couple *sicarios* with automatic weapons sitting on stools watching his little prison.

At lunchtime the door opened and two guards carrying submachine guns came in, motioned for him to get up, face into a corner while they replaced the bucket with an empty one. Even though the bucket left, its smell stayed behind. They filled his water pitcher, left him a lunch of beans and tortillas and some kind of stringy meat he suspected of being goat, and a couple of two-month-old *Newsweek* magazines. He washed up and ate, chewing the meat guardedly.

He finished up, moved over to peek through the door at the *sicarios* sitting on their stools, then took the *Newsweek*s back to his cot and lay there, scratching at the stubble on his face and head, reading articles about the New Economy and the Internet.

Directly he tires of reading stale news and tosses the magazines on the floor. He lies there, hands behind his head, staring at the rough board ceiling, listening to the horses stirring next door, trying to summon up mental images of his mama. Of Sonya. Counting down the days to the Day of the Dead. Knowing they're all going to be pretty much identical to this one.

Wondering if Jeremiah Spur is as good as his reputation says.

He reaches down, picks his Burke novel up off the ground. He'd finished it yesterday. He sighs, opens it to page one.

Trey Beacon walks into the conference room carrying a file in one hand and a cup of coffee in the other. He howdies Jeremiah and drops into a chair on the other side of the table. "Farkas is in the wind alright. I went by his house last night. You oughta see that place. Must have cost the gross domestic product of Ecuador. Nobody but servants home. They said Farkas packed some books and clothes and left out of there a few days ago."

"What kind of books?"

"Don't know for sure. Seems he's some kind of collector. The servants said what he packed came from his collection. After I finished at his house, I went to his office, not expecting to find anything, but there was a guy named Scurlock there."

"What was he doin' there on a Sunday evenin'?"

"Working on some kind of real estate project, I expect. Said he was gettin' ready for a conference call with some folks in Tokyo, since it was fixin' to be Monday morning over yonder. He let me in, gave me a few minutes of his time. I asked after Farkas. He told me the man had retired, had sold his business to his EVPs—"

"Eee vee pees?"

"Executive vice presidents. His senior officers. Farkas called them in awhile back, said he was gonna hang 'em up, sell out to them, soon as the financing was set. So, according to this Scurlock, he went to the banks, leveraged up his real estate portfolio—"

"What's that mean?"

"Means he put debt on it. That reduced the amount of equity the EVPs had to come up with. The EVPs pooled their capital to finance their share of the purchase price. Transaction closed Tuesday of last week. Farkas walked away with almost two billion dollars, wire transferred to a bank in New York. We checked with them first thing this morning and they had transferred the money to a half dozen other banks, in London, Frankfurt, Zurich, and Vienna.

"Meanwhile, I got the tail number of Farkas's jet, tracked it through the FAA and the Mexican Department of Civil Aviation. He left out of here the day after the closing, filed a flight plan to Cabo San Lucas. He was down yonder until Sunday morning, when he flew to Toluca Airport, the corporate airport north of Mexico City."

"So it *was* him shot Cantú. Must've paid somebody for the information 'bout the meeting."

"Probably. The Mexicans say he landed at ten in the morning. They found the rifle, by the way. Some kind of Russian-made job. New model. No prints. Farkas's jet was wheels up again at five o'clock, flew to Halifax, Nova Scotia, spent thirty minutes on the ground refueling at"—Trey checks his notes—"Atlantic Sky Services, then flew on to Farnborough, outside London. I talked to Scotland Yard this mornin', got them to give us a hand. They checked the airport and the plane's still there. They talked to the flight base operations people, found out that Farkas and a tall blonde—"

"Bet that was Leslie."

Trey nods. "Matched her description. They were picked up by limo. Took awhile for Scotland Yard to track down the limo driver. He said he dropped his passengers off at a train station in London sometime around noon, which would be six in the morning here."

"A train station. They must still be in England then."

"Not necessarily. The station was Waterloo International. The Eurostar operates out of there, to the rest of Europe through the Channel Tunnel. I'm guessin' they caught the train to Paris or Brussels."

Jeremiah reaches into his pocket for his Camels. "He done give us the slip, then."

"Looks that way." Trey leans over, opens the file, pulls out a set of papers, hands it to Jeremiah. "Here's the autopsy report on Jonathon Farkas."

Jeremiah squares it up on the table, looks it over while he lights up a smoke. In the "Summary Conclusion" box, the ME had written: "Death by combination of brain hemorrhage, cardiac arrest, and pulmonary edema caused by drug overdose: cocaine inhalation." Jeremiah flips through the pages, scans the ME's description of the body, the notes of his external and internal examination. He stops. "What's mediastinal widening?"

"The medical guys say that's a widening of the space between the lungs."

"That generally go with drug overdose?"

"They say it's a little peculiar."

Jeremiah flips through the report some more. "The lab data ain't in the back here, where it's supposed to be."

"Let me see that." Trey takes the report back. "You're exactly right. I'm sorry, I should've noticed that. I'll call down to Brazos County, get 'em to fax the rest of it up."

Jeremiah takes a drag, taps ash. "You want to know what I think?"

"What?"

"I think Jonathon Farkas was murdered. I think it was payback for Farkas rattin' out Jorge Cantú. I think Farkas found out, and went after the old man."

Jeremiah leans back, front two legs of his chair off the floor, sticks the smoke between his lips, his hands in his pockets, stares at the tabletop for a while. He says, "He planned it this way all along. Wanted me to lead him to Cantú, and I done it, pretty as you please. Farkas knew my every move before I knew it myself."

"That scene between him and his daughter in the restaurant—"

"Set me up to go track down Cantú, to try to link Farkas to the killings."

"So he could waste Cantú, even the score."

"I was countin' on him not thinkin' I would do it. And he knew that. See, he figgered I'd figger he'd rule it out on account of my history with the Cantús. God O-Mighty." He lets the chair back down, taps ash, looks at Trey. "When's Spencer Tillman get here?"

Instant hesitation. Trey leans forward, elbows on the table, hands folded. "Jeremiah, we've known each other a long time—"

Jeremiah crosses his arms. "When a man sets out to tell me how long he's known me, that's usually because he's fixin' to say somethin' I won't care to hear."

"Look, the world is a mighty big place."

"Rich people are like snails. They always leave a trail."

"But you got to know where to start looking."

"That's why I need to speak to Tillman."

"Why not let us turn it over to Interpol?"

"I don't need him arrested. I need him to help me get my man away from Cantú."

Trey leans back. "But even if you found Farkas, what would you say to him? 'Come with me; I need you to get yourself killed so I can get a man home?'"

"I'm workin' on some ideas how to handle it."

"Care to share them?"

Jeremiah leans forward, crushes the butt. "Not just yet."

"Let me give you a different idea to cogitate on. Suppose we work with the *Federales,* find out where they got Thomas locked down, raid the place. Wouldn't take but two or three Rangers, couple dozen Mexicans."

"The way them Mexicans spring leaks? Clyde would be dead faster than a sheep can twitch its ass."

"It's worth thinking about, though."

Jeremiah nods. "You're right about that. But for a whole other reason."

"Do what?"

Jeremiah leans forward. "Look, I got me two weeks until the Day of the Dead. I got to at least try. Maybe I don't find Farkas, or maybe I do and he ain't willin' to cooperate. Then we can do it your way."

"We need to start looking for Thomas in the meantime, try to figger out where they got him."

"Okay, but be quiet about it."

"Fair enough."

"Tillman ain't comin', is he?"

"He said he didn't want to get within a country mile of this thing."

Jeremiah works his jaw. "Can Edna get him on the phone?"

"I expect."

"Then I need her to do that for me."

Trey pauses, shrugs, stands. "Let's go to my office."

They wait there while Edna does her dialing, Jeremiah sitting at Trey's desk, Trey at the window taking in the view of the traffic down below. Jeremiah says, "You been able to find out anything about Tito Cantú?"

"Rumors, mostly. What his brother, the padre, said about Tito not being like the old man? The way we hear it, there's somethin' to that. He loves the money plenty, but would just as soon be spared the headaches of running a big drug operation, always having to watch his own six, stay ahead of what passes for law down yonder. The guy's said to be more dilettante than drug lord."

Edna squawks in. "Captain Spur, I've got Mr. Tillman on line two."

Jeremiah picks up the handset, punches a blinking red button. "This is Spur."

"Been a long time, Captain Spur," a vaguely familiar voice on the other end says.

"Yep. You probably figgered you was shed of me. But now I got my ass in a sling and I need your help."

"Trey told me. You understand, I can't possibly be a party to this."

"I don't understand nothin' of the sort."

"The Agency has very strict—"

Jeremiah hardens his voice. "I don't give the remotest shit what the Agency is strict about. Now you be still and listen while I tell you how it's gonna be. There's a Mexican drug lord holdin' a man who didn't do nothin' but pay me a kindness, and I aim to get him back. That means I got to find Benjamin Farkas and the best way I know to do that is to talk to the man who ran him for y'all for twenty-five years."

"Captain Spur, that is just so beyond impossible—"

"You ain't lettin' me finish. There's an 'or else' you need to hear."

"Fine. Let's hear it."

"The 'or else' is this. You don't let me talk to that feller, my next phone call is to the newspapers, startin' with that one out in San Jose, California, run that story a few years back, 'bout you all helpin' the Nicaraguans sell crack to inner-city folks—"

"Hold it right there! We denied that story six ways from Sunday, had an internal investigation—"

"Sure you did. But I can give 'em details they didn't have, see. I can put 'em on to Farkas and his daughter and the whole shootin' match. Don't think I won't, neither. Then you're gonna have yourself a first-class shit storm, especially when I round it out with the fact that the Farkases been runnin' around Texas on a killin' spree. When I'm done with 'em, they'll stake you all out on a media ant hill."

Silence on the other end of the line. Then, "You're bluffing."

"Call it then."

More silence. Then a sigh. "This is above my pay grade."

"Then kick it upstairs."

"It's gonna take a little while."

Jeremiah looks at his watch. "You got two hours."

"That's absurd! There's no way—"

"You can reach me in Trey Beacon's office."

Jeremiah slams the phone into the cradle, looks up at Trey, who's looking at him like he's suddenly turned into a space alien. Jeremiah says, "He'll call back."

"You think you can get what you want by threatening those folks?"

"I expect it's the only way I'm gonna get what I want."

Trey drops into a chair across the desk. "Just exactly when did you decide it was okay to stop playing by the rules?"

Jeremiah jerks a thumb at the phone. "When their boy put a bullet in Cantú and hung my man out to dry."

Trey shakes his head. "I don't think it's gonna work, Jeremiah."

"Hide and watch."

It takes less than forty-five minutes for Tillman to call back and prove Jeremiah right.

66

Tuesday morning and the Kärntnerstrasse has just begun to stir. Men in aprons stand in front of shops hosing down the cobblestones. A refuse truck stops next to a trash receptacle, air brakes hissing. The chairs are still up on the tables at the outdoor cafés. A couple of joggers lumber by talking about some business deal in American-accented English.

He walks slowly, sipping coffee from a Styrofoam cup, admiring the early morning beauty of the Innere Stadt, window-shopping, working the long trip out of his system. Jet lag had him up at four this morning. He had read all the papers before dawn.

Some Pavlovian impulse turns him down a wide street just before he reaches St. Stephan's black spire, toward the Café Central even though it will not open for another hour. He glances at the shops on the left. He stops. The Styrofoam cup slips from his fingers. Coffee splashes on his shoes, on the cuffs of his Armani slacks.

He walks to the fourth shop in from the Kärntnerstrasse, the one that was once a milliner's, but that today is a travel agency. Next to the front door, a metal plaque with the street address in raised numerals. On the wall, beside the plaque, a sign from long ago. Meant specifically for him. He lifts his hand to touch the red chalk mark.

The Gloriette dead drop needs servicing.

At just past eleven he catches the U4 line to Schloss Schönbrunn. The train is packed with jabbering day-trippers wearing backpacks and pushing strollers, on their way to visit the Habsburgs' summer palace, the one built in the early eighteenth century to replace the château de plaisance that the Turks destroyed when they besieged Vienna in 1683. The place where Marie Antoinette spent her summers as a child.

At the Schönbrunn stop he exits the train, trails along behind the day-trippers. They head for the palace's front door. He veers to the right, to the gardens in the back, climbs the hill toward the Gloriette, literally the crowning glory of the gardens. It dates to 1775, has a central section that today serves as a restaurant and in Mozart's day was used by its royal owners as a dining room. Two lateral wings open onto a colonnade of eleven arches between Doric columns. Atop the central section, a massive eagle rests on a globe.

He pauses at the top of the hill to catch his breath, take in the view of the city. It must have been from such a place that Satan offered the world to Christ. He walks around the east wing and up the front steps to the restaurant. The waiter seats him at a window table looking out on the palace below and the city beyond. He orders a still water and a plate of sausages, then gets up, drops his napkin in his chair, takes the interior stairs down one level to the WC. He goes inside, shuts and locks the door.

Inside the first stall, he reaches behind the toilet. The envelope is there, just where he had always found it in the past.

Farkas folds the envelope in half, sticks it in his pocket. He goes to the sink, washes his hands, looks at himself in the mirror. There is only one person in the world who would choose to communicate with me in this fashion.

67

HE DRIVES HIS MERECEDES THROUGH THE STREETS OF SAN MARINO, California, and into the employee parking lot a little before 8:00 and gets out. He wears a blue jumpsuit with "Huntington Gardens" stitched in white lettering above the breast pocket, old sneakers, a floppy straw hat.

At the toolshed he nods at the other staff standing around, drinking coffee, laughing, smoking. Hispanics mostly, a black man or two. He punches in, chucks some tools in the back of an electric golf cart, drives off toward the Japanese garden.

It's too early for the sun to have climbed the mountainsides to the east and hit the low spots where the mist lingers, a wispy remnant of the night. He worships the silence and the solitude like a primitive praying to some distant god. He doubts that he will be driving this gravel path tomorrow morning and is all the more worshipful for it.

He parks the golf contraption behind the Japanese teahouse and walks with his tools into the low-walled sanctuary of the bonsai garden. He ties his hair back in a ponytail to keep it out of his face, puts his hat back on. He starts on the left, just inside the gate, leaning down to tend to the little gnarled forms, stopping now and again to stretch and straighten his back.

He is a third of the way through the morning routine when he hears the footsteps. One person, a heavy tread, a booted foot, stopping just inside the wall. He tends to the little tree named "Kingsville."

A voice says, "You Franklin Spur?"

He does not respond. He tends the tree. He asks himself what he feels. The answer is this: He doesn't feel a thing. He straightens, turns to look at the man in cowboy boots, Stetson, sports coat. "They warned me you would come."

"Did they warn you why?"

He nods. "Rather odd circumstances for a family reunion, I'd have to say."

"We wasn't ever a family, so that can't be what this is. I need to find Benjamin Farkas. He's run off to Europe. I need you to tell me where you think he might be."

He watches his son light a cigarette. "I saved the world, Jeremiah. I and guys like me. That sort of thing comes at a price."

"Your wife was the price."

"And you. But it was a price that had to be paid."

"It's not a trade I would've made. Leastwise where Mama was concerned."

"I didn't feel like I had a choice."

"A thing can only be what it is. I need you to tell me where to look for Farkas."

"He could be anywhere."

"But he ain't anywhere. He's in one place at any given time. I'm guessin' someplace special to him. I'm also guessin' you got a feel for where that place is."

"Okay. Try Paris or Vienna."

"Make a choice. I ain't got time but for one town."

The gardener thinks a minute. "Vienna, then."

"Why?"

"Partly because he was betrayed once in Paris and it left him feeling differently about the place. But mostly because Vienna was where he first felt freedom, and he once told me if he ever left America he would go back there. You know the city?"

"Ain't never set foot in Europe."

"You will want to check the five-star hotels. The museums. The Café Central, the other coffee shops in the Innere Stadt."

"Alright then. Let me ask you this. If you had to sum the man up, everything you know about him in the fewest possible words, what would you say?"

The gardener looks off into the distance. "Benjamin lost his parents when he was young, in tragic circumstances. He had to figure out how to fend for himself, and in Budapest, in the late fifties, that wasn't easy. He did what he had to do to get out and make a life for himself, and a lot of it wasn't pretty. But really and truly? All he ever wanted was to be left in peace. And until these last few years his life never gave him that option." He pauses. "I'm a big part of the reason why he never had that option."

The Ranger nods. "You can't escape your antecedents." He takes one last draw on his cigarette, stubs it out on the garden wall. " 'Preciate it." He turns to go.

"Jeremiah?"

The Ranger turns back.

"You just need to know, if you show up in Vienna looking like that, I mean, with the hat and the boots, you're—well, you're going to stand out."

"I'm sorta countin' on that. Adios."

The gardener listens as the Ranger's boots crunch away. When the sound has disappeared, he turns back to his little tree. In his heart, where nothing had been five minutes ago, there is instead, now, something. Regret has moved in. It feels to him like it might be here to stay.

He glances at his wristwatch. *Ten minutes time to walk to the front gate. Five minutes by cart.* He starts gathering up his tools.

Jeremiah is almost at the front gate when he hears someone say, "Jeremiah. Jeremiah!"

He turns around, sees his daddy stepping out of a golf cart. It had surprised him some to see how fit the man seems to be, even though he's got to be a good seventy-five years old. He also hadn't imagined the man would have such long hair and a beard to go with it. Franklin Spur walks toward him showing no sign of the stiffness, the aches and pains you would expect a man of his years to feel.

Jeremiah says, "You think of somethin' else?"

Franklin walks right up to him. "Yes. I want to go with you."

"Do what?"

"Yes, they told me you were coming and, yes, they told me why. I want to help you find Benjamin. I know this is very important to you."

Jeremiah shakes his head. "Mister, I ain't got time to be joked with. We'll be seein' you." He starts to turn away. Franklin grabs his elbow.

"I'm serious. I know Vienna and I know Benjamin. Maybe better than anyone else in the world. If I go with you, your chances of finding him are greatly enhanced."

"You're an old man."

"But well preserved. I've been a vegetarian for nearly fifteen years, and I've stayed in shape. I can keep up."

"'Preciate the offer." Jeremiah turns to leave again.

As he walks off, his daddy says after him, "To catch Benjamin, you have to know how he thinks. You do not, but I do. His number-one priority now will be protecting his daughter. From the Cantús, from the police. She's in a precarious position. And he's got to do something about that. Something will happen in Vienna, to his daughter, and that will be the key to finding him. But you have to know where to look for that key. You have to know how."

Jeremiah stops, turns around. "How you figger this?"

"Because I know Benjamin," Franklin says. "And I know Vienna."

Jeremiah can see the sense of what the man is saying. Still he hesitates.

Franklin says, "Come on. You need my help. Don't let your anger at me stop you from accepting it. It's the best chance you have to save your friend."

Jeremiah reaches for his Camels, lights one. "I reckon. But look, there's somethin' else. I'm takin' care of this out of my own pocket. And since I ain't nothin' but a rancher now, it ain't like—"

His father smiles. "You're worried about my travel costs?"

"Hell, I'm worried 'bout my own."

"No problem, my boy. I've put some money away over the years, and the government pension is very generous indeed. I can take care of myself." He smiles again. "I'll simply be spending your inheritance, after all."

That afternoon they meet at LAX. Jeremiah is waiting just inside the terminal when the taxi pulls up to drop off his daddy. He watches as the old man gets out the cab with his bag, comes through the sliding glass doors. He's wearing a blue blazer, gray slacks, a blue shirt, and carrying an expensive-looking leather grip.

They nod at one another, walk together to the ticket counter. Jeremiah winces a little when he hands his credit card over. The amount he is spending on this Lufthansa nonstop to Vienna—no advance purchase, open return—would have gone a long way toward paying for a vacation for Martha and him when she got home from treatment. They could have gone over to San Antonio, stayed in the best hotel on the Riverwalk for a week, eaten out every single night, gone to the picture show, you name it. Still had money left over for a new dress for his bride. Instead, his money is disappearing into the pockets of a German airline.

They wait in silence in the departure lounge until the gate agent invites the first-class section to preboard. Franklin picks up his bag, heads for the jetway.

Jeremiah looks up from the newspaper he's reading. "You tellin' me you bought a first-class ticket?"

"You're telling me you didn't?"

Jeremiah watches his daddy disappear down the jetway.

When they call his row number, Jeremiah makes his way to the seat he's been assigned, places his grip and his Stetson in the overhead bin, tries to figure out how they expect him to fit in this space that seems to have been designed for a midget with retractable limbs. He reconciles himself to riding with his right leg stuck a little ways into the aisle, pulling it back whenever it's in danger of being ran over by the drink cart, his left leg pinned up under the seat in front of him.

A young lady sits to his left. Says she's going to Vienna to join her fiancé, who works for an American investment bank there. Then she slips on headphones, puts a pillow under her head, closes her eyes. She's about the age Elizabeth would have been if she'd lived, and the memory of his lost daughter is like an ulcer in his heart.

Soon they're flying through the air, the flight attendants in their blue and yellow uniforms working the aisle with the food and beverages, and Jeremiah is faced with having to choose between thinking about how he feels now that he's met and hooked up with his daddy after all these years and reading the guidebook about Vienna that he has stashed in the seatback pocket.

He starts to reach for the guidebook, then sits back in his chair, drums his fingers on the armrest, his mind going back to this morning's events. Over the years he had imagined his daddy a lot of different ways. Living with some other family. Retired up in the mountains somewhere. Dead, even. He never would have imagined him in coveralls, tending to little trees in a Japanese garden in Southern California. Maybe he's got a wife or girlfriend at home. Maybe an entire second family.

Makes me no never mind either way. The man is as much a stranger to me as the German flying this aircraft. Jeremiah wouldn't have even troubled to look for him if he hadn't had to, as his only plausible way of tracking down Farkas.

But then he catches himself wondering about his daddy, his past, the life he's made for himself. *Might not hurt to know somethin' about that. Maybe while we're off in Europe together, I oughta sit down, visit with the man some, see what he's like, what kind of life he lived.*

But just at the moment, he's got a job to do. He reaches for the guidebook, settles back, tries to get used to the notion he's stuck in this seat for the next twelve hours and won't be smoking a cigarette until his boots hit Austrian soil.

Filing off the Airbus. Waiting in line to get through passport control and customs, feeling that hot, miserable feeling you get when you're operating on three hours sleep. *Nothin' particularly easy about this.* That thought sticks in Jeremiah's head and he thinks it over and over and over again as though it were beyond wise, an observation that transcends all human knowledge, some kind of eternal truth.

He catches up with his daddy at the foreign exchange desk. His old man looks rested, clothes still neat looking. Jeremiah had caught a glimpse of himself in the restroom mirror just before they landed. He knows he looks like he collided with his apparel, and his eyes are bagged up.

Franklin says, "Get any sleep on the way over?"

"You're kiddin', right?"

"Not at all. I took a sleeping pill. Must have slept six hours."

They trade greenbacks for the local funny money, then walk out of the airport. Stand in the taxi line. Jeremiah feels better just getting shed of the airport and its attendant hassle. He looks around. "She's a beauty of a fall mornin', ain't she?"

"Autumn."

"Do what?"

"The Europeans never say 'fall.' They refer to the season as 'autumn.'"

"Seems like the same difference, you ask me." *He's lettin' me know we're on his turf now. Let's see if he does it again.* Jeremiah holds out his guidebook. "I been lookin' at the hotels. This'un looks respectable and it's priced the right way."

His old man peers at the guidebook, hands it back. "One star. A vermin-infested firetrap." He actually sniffs.

Jeremiah stuffs the guidebook back in his bag. He reaches for his cigarettes, sets fire to one.

His daddy eyes it. "That is a particularly noisome and unhealthy habit."

Jeremiah blows smoke. "Maybe if I'd had me a clean-livin' role model when I was growin' up, I wouldn't have fallen victim to it."

"I smoked myself, up until fifteen years ago. Had to give it up. Doctor's orders."

They get to the head of the taxi line, throw their gear in the trunk, climb in the backseat. His daddy says something to the driver in German, then leans back.

Jeremiah says, "Where's he takin' us?"

"The Kaiserhof. I've known the manager for years. He owes me a few favors."

Jeremiah turns to stare out the window at the Austrian morning. *Nothin' particularly easy about this.*

After they check into their hotel, they part company. Franklin said he wanted to go over to the Café Central for a cup of coffee and to read the local newspapers. Said that was the best way to get oriented in Vienna.

Jeremiah wanted to walk around, get his bearings. They agreed to meet back in the lobby at six o'clock, get dinner together.

Franklin watches the street through the window of his hotel room until he sees his son leaving through the front door wearing the only Stetson Franklin has ever seen in Vienna, headed in the direction of the Ringstrasse. He drops the sheer curtain from his hand, picks his coat up off the bed, shrugs it on. Outside the hotel he turns right on the Kärntnerstrasse toward St. Stephan's. He turns left just this side of the cathedral, looks at the wall next to the fourth shop on the left. Smiles when he sees the white chalk mark.

He walks along admiring how neat and tidy and compact and clean, how very *civilized,* this city is. He remembers how it looked when he first saw it, right after the war—its Old World elegance smashed by the Allied bombers. Wrecked buildings, charred vehicles, bomb craters at every turn, the city itself divided among the four powers.

This morning well-dressed young mothers push their children in carriages. At the outdoor cafés people sip coffee, eat pastries, read newspapers, chat. Lovers stroll and laugh and hang on one another. Mimes mime and jugglers juggle. Here and there a beggar or two. *What a glorious city.*

At the Café Central he takes a seat on a bench in the nonsmoking section, looks up at the vaulted ceiling. An ancient waiter sees him, selects a newspaper on a wooden dowel from the rack, approaches his table, sets the paper down before him. It's the *Wiener Zeitung.* "Nice to see you again, sir."

Franklin reaches up, shakes the man's hand. "How have you been, Kraus?"

The waiter shrugs. "As always, sir. Just a bit older."

"Have you seen him?"

"Only yesterday."

"Good. I'll have coffee, please."

"Certainly, sir." He shuffles off. Franklin picks up the newspaper.

Jeremiah spends the day walking the city, drawing stares from the Viennese, what with his Stetson and boots and guidebook map. He walks through the old city, past St. Stephan's Cathedral, connects with the Ringstrasse, follows it around almost the entire way. He marks the places his daddy had mentioned and other landmarks besides.

Toward dusk the wind picks up, blowing trash along the cobblestones like a city version of tumbleweeds. The chill sends him back to his hotel room to fetch his jacket.

He shows up in the lobby at six o'clock. Franklin is already there. His daddy stands up, buttons his sports coat, says, "We have a table at the Hotel Bristol. They may very well have the best wine list in town."

Jeremiah starts to say something. Franklin holds up his hand, cuts him off. "Not to worry. I'm buying."

"Fair enough."

They walk out the front door of the hotel side by each.

68

FRANKLIN SPUR HANDS THE WINE LIST TO THE SOMMELIER. "THE GAJA IT IS, then." He rubs his hands together, grins at Jeremiah.

The sommelier bows. "Very good, sir."

Jeremiah watches the man walk away. The restaurant is done in pale pinks and yellows and lit by long candles and dimmed chandeliers. The silverware is as heavy and the china as thin as Jeremiah has ever seen. Cut flowers are everywhere.

Franklin takes a sip of water from a stemmed glass. "Ah, yes. Gaja. You are in for a treat tonight."

"I ought to tell you, I ain't much of a red wine drinker."

"I'll bet you like this. It's one of the finest Italian barbarescoes. Made entirely from the nebbiolo grape. A wee bit on the expensive side, but worth it if any bottle of wine ever is. At the rate we're going, we'll have your inheritance spent in no time."

Jeremiah works his jaw. "That's the second time you've brung that up, so you might as well know this, too. I don't want nothin' from you. Not so much as a dime."

"What would you have me do with it then, modest though it may be?"

"*No le hace.* Leave it to charity. Leave it to someone takes care of orphan kids."

The sommelier arrives with the wine. Carefully decants it. Walks away.

Franklin sighs, leans forward. "Let's go ahead and get this out of the way. Three years after I came back from the war, a man named Bill Donovan—"

"I know who Bill Donovan was."

"Okay. He called me because he was helping the government assemble what was eventually to become the CIA, relying a lot on former OSS personnel. I served with the OSS during my last six months in Europe and met Bill several times. When he called, he said Uncle Sam needed my help to fight communism, which we all saw as a menace to freedom every bit as great as Nazism. It was just a matter of time before the Soviets got the bomb, and then the world would be on the very brink of total disaster.

Total. Disaster. I had no choice but to answer our country's call as I did. No choice. Not even when your mother told me to choose between her and what I had been asked to do."

"Even though it meant leaving her to raise me alone."

"That's right. Seems to me she did a pretty good job of it, too."

Jeremiah reaches for his Camels, lights one up.

Franklin says, "Look, Jeremiah. I'm sorry about how it turned out with her. I loved Fiona, and it broke my heart to leave. I never remarried, never even dated much, because I knew no one could take her place in my life. Then, when I heard she'd died—"

He stops, stares off across the room. Shakes his head. "What's really ironic is, in all these many years, from that awful day your mother and I decided to call it quits up until the present, my only personal relationship, the only one you might call at all close, was with none other than Benjamin Farkas. He and I worked together so well for so long, we became almost like family. Just as he had lost a father, I had lost a son, and so it was only natural that . . ."

He stops again. Shrugs. "Draw your own conclusions about what I did and why I did it. If I had it to do all over again, I would make the same choice. The good news is, the world turned out okay. At least from a geopolitical perspective."

Jeremiah taps ash, watches as the sommelier returns, pours a dribble of wine into Franklin's glass. Franklin sips it, nods. The sommelier pours wine for both of them.

Franklin raises his glass, looks at Jeremiah. "To you, then. Thanks for reaching out to me, and also for letting me help you. It has done an old man's heart good despite the fact that you only sought me out when you really needed me."

They touch glasses. Jeremiah takes a sip, sets his glass down. "That's mighty tasty alright."

"You should try it without cigarette smoke fouling your palate."

But Jeremiah's not listening to his daddy's nagging. He's thinking instead about where Clyde Thomas might be right now, what he might be going through, while Jeremiah's enjoying the fine cuisine and culture of Vienna.

About then a black Jaguar convertible with the top down slides to a stop in front of the gate at the Cantú finca in Coahuila. One of the two *sicarios* standing guard gets up from his chair, slings his automatic weapon over his shoulder, goes to talk to the driver.

"What do you want?" the *sicario* says.

The driver is a young man, in his twenties, with fair skin and dark hair and longish sideburns. "I am here to see my fucking cousin."

The *sicario* looks more closely at the driver. "Ray? Is that you?"

"Open the fucking gate."

"I did not know you were back in the country."

"Open the fucking gate."

The *sicario* looks over at the call box. "Don Tito requires that we announce—"

The driver produces a revolver and points it at the man's head.

The *sicario* holds up his hands. "Okay, okay," he says. He nods at the other guard, who presses a button. The gate swings open, and as the Jaguar roars through it, the first *sicario* walks to the call box and lifts the handset.

When Ray Cantú pulls up to park in front of the hacienda, Tito is already outside waiting for him. Ray kills the engine and takes the revolver in his right hand and opens the door with his left and gets out and looks at his cousin.

Tito says, "Welcome back."

Ray raises his hands and drops them again and shakes his head. "You had Spur. You fucking had Spur and you let him go. You fucking let him go."

"I let him go so he would bring me the man who killed my father."

"But Spur killed *my* father!"

"I know this."

"And not only that. They say you took a hostage and he is still alive. Alive!"

"He is nothing. I'm using him as bait. That's all. Bait for Spur. And for Farkas."

"You are making us look like fools!"

"Maybe you should come inside and calm down."

"Fuck that."

"Come on, Ray."

"Where's the hostage? Where are you keeping him? In the old groom's quarters?"

Ray walks past Tito toward the back of the hacienda, talking as he goes. "If you don't have the *huevos* to do the simplest thing then I'll do it. Fucking left the hostage alive. Jesus Christ!"

Tito follows him. "Ray. Listen to what I am saying to you. He is bait, nothing more. He is what we need for another chance at Spur and Farkas. Without that, neither one of them will return."

They argue all the way to the stables. Ray walks past the two guards holding automatic weapons and up to the door of the groom's quarters and sees it's locked. He turns on Tito. "Unlock this fucking door."

Tito says, "Ray, think about what I'm saying to—"

Ray points the pistol between Tito's eyes.

The two guards point their guns at Ray and work the action.

Without taking his eyes off Ray, Tito says, "Do as he says."

Ray lowers the revolver as one of the guards slings his weapon over his shoulder and walks to the door fumbling with a ring of keys. He throws the deadbolt and opens the door and steps back. Ray goes through the door into the quarters. Tito follows right behind.

The hostage is sitting up on a cot blinking at the sudden light from the outside. He says, "Yo, man. What th' fuck—"

Ray walks over to the hostage and pulls the black man off the cot by the front of his filthy shirt and slams him against the wall and sticks the revolver under his chin and cocks the hammer and says, "Now you are going to die, my friend."

Tito walks up to Ray from behind and puts his hand on Ray's shoulder and says softly, "If you pull that trigger, you will never have another chance to kill Spur. He will not come back except to rescue this man."

Ray doesn't take his eyes off the hostage. "You told him to return with Farkas. He will never find the Wolf and bring him here. So this man dies anyway."

"Nothing is lost by waiting until the Day of the Dead. That is Spur's deadline. In the meantime this man will suffer the uncertainty of not knowing when we will come to get him and finish him."

The hostage's eyes shift between them as he tries to follow their Spanish. He does look to Ray like a man who has already decided that he is going to die, and very soon. In the black man's eyes he sees no fear. Only a strange calm curiosity.

Tito says, "You should give Spur a chance to succeed. Think how it would feel if you had your gun under his chin instead. Think how many years you have waited for that chance. Think, Ray."

Ray stares at the hostage. Slowly he lets the revolver's hammer down and backs away from the man. Then he takes a quick step forward and raises his arm and brings the pistol butt down on the hostage's temple as hard as he can. Once, twice. He steps back again and watches the hostage slump to the floor.

Ray spits on the ground beside the hostage and wipes his mouth with his sleeve and glares at Tito and walks away.

———

At the end of the evening, Jeremiah and Franklin part company in the hotel lobby. Jeremiah explains that his plan for tomorrow is to make the rounds, showing Farkas's picture to everybody he comes across. See if anyone might have seen the man.

Franklin says, "Why don't we meet for lunch at noon? At the Café Central."

"Fair enough."

They shake hands and say good night.

Jeremiah wakes up the next morning at three o'clock, lies in the dark, the digital clock glowing on his bedside table making the room look strange. He thinks about last night's dinner, his first meal in a half century with his daddy. Wonders if maybe he ought to try to find some forgiveness in his heart for the old man. Knows he himself had many a time put his Rangering ahead of what he owed Martha as her husband. But he also knows he never would have left Martha to keep his job.

He turns over, closes his eyes, tries to get back to sleep. His eyes fly open. He sits up, turns on the light. Last night's conversation. It had given him the answer. How to convince Farkas to do what he needed him to do. If only he could find Farkas.

He gets out of bed. He knows he won't be going back to sleep this morning.

Seven time zones to the west, Clyde lies on his cot and listens to the unceasing small cries of tortured wood as a rainstorm rakes his little prison cell and he stares vacantly into the darkness and tries not to get too used to the notion that he's still alive since that condition doesn't promise to be of much duration. He can still feel the pressure of that gun barrel under his chin even though that was hours ago, and his ears are yet ringing from the pistol-whipping he took, and his head pounds. He reaches up and touches his temple and the blood that has dried there. He is ill-fed and lonely and about ready for all this to be over, no matter which way it goes. He sighs and turns on his side to get as comfortable as his body will let him and closes his eyes and tries his level best not to think at all.

69

AT NOON JEREMIAH WALKS INTO THE CAFÉ CENTRAL, NOTHING TO SHOW FOR his morning on the streets asking after Farkas but thinner soles on his Tony Lama's and a larger credit-card payable. His daddy is sitting at a table reading a newspaper and sipping from a cup. Jeremiah takes a chair that lets him see the rest of the place and through the plateglass window out onto the street.

His daddy closes his newspaper. "Any luck?"

"Not a speck. What you been doin'?"

"Sitting here. Reading the papers. Drinking coffee."

Jeremiah feels irritation's mild jolt. "Sittin' all mornin' in this one place?"

Franklin sets the cup down, dabs at his mouth with a napkin. He signals across the room to an ancient waiter. The waiter disappears behind a door. Franklin says, "This café is the epicenter of Vienna. If it happens in this town, these waiters, the people in here, will know it. A man need only sit here and let what he seeks find him."

"Way I was trained, it's the other way 'round. You got to go git it. Got to work at cullin' the blackfeet from the whitefeet."

"Yes. But this is Europe. Not Texas. For example, this morning I happened to run into an old friend of mine here. Retired Interpol. He sat right where you are sitting now and told me that certain former colleagues of his are saying someone has offered a sizable amount of money for the killing of Benjamin Farkas and Leslie Whitten."

"Cantú, I reckon."

"More than likely, yes."

"That'll just drive the two of them deeper underground."

"Perhaps. But they do enjoy a reputation for being exceedingly tricky to target, and a dangerous assignment, indeed. It is not at all clear that anyone in the world would be bold enough to make an attempt on them."

The ancient waiter reappears, shuffles their way. Jeremiah watches him. He's got to be every bit of seventy years old. He arrives at last at their table, sets a menu in front of Jeremiah. "The soup today is lentil."

Jeremiah starts to reach for the menu, stops when something catches his eye through the window. A young woman jogging past. A halo of yellow hair crowned by a Texas Rangers baseball cap.

"Dammit," he says. He pushes the table away from his knees, runs to the front door, dodging waiters carrying trays and heavyset women hauling umbrellas and shopping bags.

He reaches the street. The jogger is just disappearing around the corner of the Lipizzaner Museum. Jeremiah sprints after her. Past the museum now, he catches sight of her again, crossing the road, running along the sidewalk in front of the Opera House. He runs as hard as he can, gulping air, feeling the burden on his lungs from his years of smoking. *I got to give them damn things up.* People on the sidewalks stop to stare as he wheezes past them in his strange getup.

He had spent considerable time in this part of town yesterday when he was getting his bearings. Just beyond the Opera House, the city opens up. There the Kärntnerstrasse, the Innere Stadt's main shopping street, intersects with the Ringstrasse, the road that, as its name suggests, makes a rough circle around the Innere Stadt. A little farther down to the left, the Hotel Bristol and the Hotel Imperial face each other across the Ringstrasse like two aging gunfighters.

The logical thing for the runner to do would be to continue on the Ringstrasse, either left toward the two hotels or back to the right, toward City Hall. Since he's just a few seconds behind her, Jeremiah figures to know which option she's chosen as soon as he gains the corner of the Opera House.

He hauls around the corner as fast as his body will take him. He looks both directions down the Ringstrasse. He can see for hundreds of yards both ways. He stops.

No blond jogger anywhere.

He turns to his right, looks at the Opera House. Nothing. It's as though she had vanished into thin air. Jeremiah leans forward, hands on his knees, tries to catch his breath. Wipes his brow with his sleeve. Straightens up, looks all around again.

"Damn. That's the second time she's pulled a danged disappearin' act on me."

He starts to turn around, head back to the café. Then he notices a kiosk, not twenty yards away. Has posters plastered on it. Racy advertisements for women's underwear, staid notices of Mozart concerts, cigarette ads. He thinks about something he read in his guidebook. He walks to the kiosk, sees a door, tries the handle.

It opens. Behind it, a set of stairs, leading downward into the darkness.

Franklin and Kraus watch Jeremiah run through the restaurant, followed by shocked looks from the Viennese. Once he's out the door, Kraus turns to Franklin. "Your son?"

Franklin nods.

"He is very energetic. He looks like a cowboy."

"I suppose he is. He owns a ranch in Texas. I had better go find him. Check, please, Herr Kraus."

"Right away, sir."

Kraus returns, sets the black folio on the table. Franklin opens it. Inside, a note:

"It is set to happen in three days' time."

At dusk Jeremiah goes back to his room, tosses his Stetson on the bed, checks his watch. Late morning back in Texas. He goes to the telephone, dials up Trey Beacon to see if there's anything new.

"Yeah," Trey says. "There's something new alright. We got the missing page from the Jonathon Farkas autopsy. The lab data. Wasn't easy to find, either. Somebody had gone through the county's files, pulled all the reports, taken that page off every single one. But we were able to get the data finally, turn it over to our medical guys."

"Anything interesting?"

"What our guys called a 'positive bacterial/viral.' An antibody that ordinarily wouldn't be there."

"You mean he'd took sick?"

"Or been poisoned."

"With what?"

"Pure guesswork based on what we got here, autopsy done by a country doctor and what have you, but our guys would be willing to bet ricin or something like it."

"How would the kid get tangled up with ricin?"

"Could have been laced into the coke. Once the kid sniffed it, it would have pretty much gone straight into his bloodstream, and assuming it was there in enough quantity, he would have been dead in no time."

"How hard is it to produce ricin in a powdered form?"

"According to our guys, not very."

"And the doc down in Brazos missed this?"

"We asked him about that. He said he thought that antibody was curious, alright, but the rest of the data strongly indicated coke overdose, so he didn't feel like he needed to look for anything exotic. Made some reference to zebras I didn't quite follow. Anyway, he just kind of shrugged it off."

"God O-mighty. So the kid might've been murdered after all."

"Just like you had hunched it out."

Jeremiah thinks a minute. "If the lab data had been pulled off all the reports, where did you all get it?"

"From the ME himself. He kept copies of the raw lab reports in his personal files. Knew right where to go looking for them, too. Said we were the second folks to ask him for this stuff in the last couple months."

Jeremiah works his jaw. "Farkas."

"His daughter. The ME said a tall, good-lookin' blonde, sister of the deceased, was nosing around down yonder a few months back."

"So Cantú *was* payback."

"Looks that way. Any luck on your end?"

"I think I saw Leslie today."

"You're kiddin'."

"Not a bit. I was sittin' down to lunch with my old man and this blonde just happened to go joggin' past the café where we were sittin'. Runnin' down the street in broad daylight as if she weren't wanted for murder in Texas."

"You sure it was her?"

"Pretty sure. I ran after her but I lost her. I think she went down into the sewer system."

"Do what?"

"They got an underground sewer system here, runs all over the city, with sidewalks along it. Folks used to hide out there during the war, to get away from the bombin'. I lost her in a big square, where she should have been in plain sight, and the only thing I can figger is she took a staircase belowground. She had such a head start on me, wasn't no way I was gonna catch her down there."

"Better luck next time."

"Yeah, I reckon."

"Your daddy been any help?"

"Hell, no. He just sits around a café drinkin' coffee and readin' the papers. But somehow he knew Farkas and his daughter would be in Vienna."

"You think he might be in touch with 'em?"

"Maybe. Wouldn't put it past him, I'll tell you that for sure."

"Don't forget, your daddy goes way back with Farkas. He knows Farkas better than he knows you, even though y'all are blood kin."

Jeremiah grunts. "Yep. He said as much to me hisself just last night. Don't worry, I'll be careful 'bout trustin' him too far. Listen, I got a favor to ask."

"Go ahead on."

"Tomorrow night, Martha's comin' into Houston Intercontinental from a . . . trip out of town. I wanted to be there myself to pick her up, but it don't look like—"

"I'll get Doug Christie from Company A to meet her, carry her up to your place."

" 'Preciate that. Ask him to tell her I'll call once she gets home."

"Fair enough. You watch yourself, hear?"

"Yeah. Adios."

Jeremiah hangs up the phone. Twelve days to go.

70

ON THE AFTERNOON OF HIS THIRD FULL DAY IN VIENNA, HE GETS HIS NEXT solid indication Farkas might be here.

His routine is the same every day. Each morning before he leaves his room he stores his grip on the closet shelf, jammed against the far wall, a scrap of paper pressed between bag and wall. Then he walks the city, visits shops, restaurants, hotels, coffeehouses, museums, wanders the alleys and public gardens, talks to clerks, waiters, cabbies, bellhops, shows them Farkas's picture. "Any chance you've seen this feller?"

They cock their heads at his funny manner of speech and unusual apparel, then stare at the picture he's showing them. *"Nein, mein Herr."* "Sorry, no." "Never seen him before." Sometimes just a shake of the head, an indifferent shrug.

He makes himself noticeable. He wears his hat and boots. He sits at open-air cafés, smoking, drinking coffee, coat off, so anyone can see he isn't carrying.

So intent is he on his search that he loses interest in what his daddy is up to. They take their meals together, but they can't find much in common to discuss. His daddy was sworn to secrecy about his career. And Jeremiah isn't one to dwell on his own life for the benefit of someone who still feels like a stranger to him. He's never been able to understand how television talk show guests can talk about the particulars of their lives in front of untold numbers of people. Strikes him as psychotic behavior.

Once his daddy tried talking politics, mentioned he's a Democrat who can't stand Clinton but hates the Republicans worse. Jeremiah allowed as how he never has had an opinion about politicians. He'd seen too many crooked ones in Texas. Another conversation died aborning.

One time his daddy asked whether he and Martha had children. Jeremiah had said, "Had a daughter named Elizabeth. Lost her to cancer last spring."

That one left them both staring in their soup bowls for awhile.

Each time he gets back to his room, he checks to see if the paper scrap is where he'd left it. At the end of the third day, he finds it on the shelf, evidence his bag had been moved, his room searched. He judges it a good sign.

That evening he calls Trey Beacon. Trey says, "We got a fix on where Thomas is. Cantú's got him locked-down in a stable hand's quarters on his ranch in Coahuila."

"Good. Y'all get a visual?"

"Not of him. They got it guarded round the clock. They don't even let him come outside to go to the bathroom."

"Any chance he could make a break for it?"

"I don't see how, not based on what I've heard. But that would depend a lot on what kind of man he is in the first place. You know him well at all?"

"Well enough. He's a pretty good hand. Would be even better if somebody took the time to plow some couth into him."

"Bear in mind, we got the option of trying to go in there and get him."

"No. Not yet. I still think I got a shot at Farkas."

"There's one other thing."

"Okay."

"Ray Cantú's back in Mexico. He's been seen at the finca with Tito."

"That's Jorge's boy, ain't it?"

"Yeah. The kid's a psycho. If he sees you, he'll kill you for sure. You need to think about letting us try to go in and get Thomas."

Jeremiah hesitates. "Let's wait a little longer. See how it plays out."

"Alright. You watch yourself."

Jeremiah hangs up the phone. He pauses a minute, takes a deep breath. Picks up the phone and dials his home number.

Steels himself for his daily talk with Martha about why he isn't back home with her where he belongs.

Twenty-four hours later, nothing has changed. Jeremiah is sitting in the lobby of the Kaiserhof after only a half day of working the streets. He had spent most of this morning in his bathroom. Maybe it was something he ate—his daddy favors restaurants that serve victuals a lot richer than a Washington County rancher ever sees—or the jet lag that had turned his lower intestines into a six-lane highway. Whatever it was, it had him going for the silver buckle in the Toilet Seat Rodeo. He didn't feel well enough to go outside until almost lunchtime.

Now it's six o'clock in the evening. The elevator doors open, out steps his father, as well turned out as ever. Gray slacks, blue blazer, dark turtleneck. He seems to have an endless supply of fashionable duds packed away somewhere.

For Jeremiah's part, he's got two pairs of khakis and three white shirts he's been rotating. He's about to have to give up, send some of his stuff to the hotel laundry. Jeremiah rises to meet his daddy.

Franklin says, "I thought we might give the bar at the Hotel Imperial a spin. They serve a very sturdy martini."

"Fair enough."

They walk outside. Franklin says, "Any luck today?"

"Not enough so's you could tell it."

"Patience. This is a game that requires the utmost patience."

Jeremiah sets fire to a cigarette. "My patience is fixin' to give out. I'm down to a nine-day supply."

They turn left at the Kärntnerstrasse, toward the Ringstrasse. Ahead, emergency lights flash, some kind of commotion up at the intersection. Police cars, an ambulance. Jeremiah had heard sirens nearby while he was waiting in the lobby.

Franklin says, "Can you see what's happening?"

"Looks like maybe some kind of accident."

They're close enough now to see that the police have part of the Ringstrasse blocked off. A crowd has gathered.

Franklin says, "Think I'll go see what it's about." He walks over to a Viennese cop, starts talking to him in German.

Jeremiah works his way around the perimeter of the crowd. Sees a body on the ground, its arms spread wide, feet close together, covered head-to-toe by a bloody sheet. Looks like something's lying next to it. He stands on tiptoe, tries to get a better look.

The object on the ground is a Texas Rangers baseball cap.

His daddy walks over, says, "Looks like a hit-and-run. Female jogger."

"Yeah. Just waitin' for us to trip over it on our way to get you your martini." Jeremiah takes a long drag on his cigarette. Blows smoke. "Imagine that."

The next morning Jeremiah is up early. He's making his way across his tiny room to wash up when he sees an envelope on the floor, just inside his door. He picks it up, tears it open. Inside, a fax from Trey, dated sometime early this morning Vienna time.

"Jeremiah—I called the Vienna police like you asked. Officer named Kurtz confirmed that Leslie Whitten was killed last night in a hit-and-run. No suspects and no witnesses. A man who said he was her father identified her body and had it claimed from the morgue by a funeral home before midnight. Call me later today."

No witnesses? They ain't got a witness to something what happened in the busiest danged intersection in Vienna at six o'clock of a Saturday evening? Come on.

Thirty minutes later he walks into the breakfast area downstairs. Gives the girl at the lecturn his room number, asks to be seated with the distinguished-looking elderly gentleman with the long hair, eating fruit and reading a newspaper over by the window.

Jeremiah takes his seat. "Mornin'."

Franklin folds the newspaper, hands it across the table. "Good morning."

Jeremiah looks at the paper. It's the *Wiener Zeitung,* inside front page. A picture of Leslie Whitten. The text is in German.

Franklin says, "The paper identifies her as the daughter of Benjamin Farkas, a wealthy American ex-pat now living in Vienna. It says she was wanted for questioning in connection with multiple homicides in Texas."

"Yep."

"The funeral is tomorrow afternoon at three o'clock. Burial immediately to follow, in the Central Cemetery."

Jeremiah lays the newspaper to one side, looks out at the Vienna streets, the false peace of Sunday morning laid over everything. Pulls out his Camels. "And we're goin' to it." Fires up a smoke.

Tomorrow is October 25. A little more than a week from the Day of the Dead.

71

They stand in the obliging rain, watching the coffin being lowered into the ground, listening to the minister speak a few final words. Around them, headstones, monuments, crosses. The wind moves the branches of the old hardwood trees, the only constant life there is in this place. Mozart's "Requiem" plays in his head.

Softly John says, "Let me say again, I'm very sorry for your loss."

He makes no reply.

John shifts his umbrella to his other hand, looks around. "This cemetery has been here many a year, and she is being laid to rest among more than a few notables. Harry Lime, for example. Tell me, do you have any idea where he is buried?"

He has been standing out here too long, and the cold and the rain and the funeral music in his head have begun to make him feel out of sorts. But John's question prompts a smile. He turns partway, points over to where a man in a Stetson is standing under an oak tree that has shed all its leaves. "I think somewhere beyond where that cowboy is."

"He is thoroughly well intentioned, Benjamin."

Benjamin looks at John. "I have observed this, and that's exactly what bothers me. How can it be that you are his father? Does the moral ambiguity gene skip a generation? Even if one doesn't come by it genetically, one is expected to acquire some ambiguity merely through the process of living. Every ship has its barnacles."

"He's an anachronism. Accustomed to seeing the world as a place divided between blackfeet and whitefeet."

"Which would make us grayfeet. The third color, and dominant by far."

John smiles. "Very good. But I'm not joking. He actually puts it that way, you know. Blackfeet versus whitefeet. Nothing wrong with that, really."

"If one doesn't mind being predictable."

"Yes. You will see him, then?"

"I will see him, but not today. I am too grief-stricken. Tell him I said that, and that we will meet tomorrow morning, inside the hedges at Schloss Belvedere. Nine o'clock. He is to be alone. I will be there. He has my word."

"I appreciate it, Benjamin. I surely do."

Farkas turns back to face the grave, watches as they fill it with dirt. "It's ironic."

"*What's ironic?*"

He glances at John. "*The third man turns out to have been a woman.*"

Jeremiah watches Franklin walk up the hill in his direction. Thinks, *I sure would like to get me a look inside that coffin.*

His daddy walks up to him. "You and he will meet tomorrow morning inside the hedges at the Schloss Belvedere. You know where that is?"

"Yep. You really think he'll show?"

"Of course. You have his word that he will."

"I'd rather go talk to him now, so he don't have a chance to lam on me again."

Franklin shakes his head. "He said no. Now is not a terribly conducive time, under the circumstances."

They turn and stare at the grave, almost filled now with dirt. The minister is talking to Farkas. Jeremiah sets fire to a cigarette. "You're sure he'll show."

"He is and always has been a man of his word, Jeremiah. I wouldn't worry about it if I were you."

"Peculiar set of scruples the man's got. Tomorrow morning it is, then, I reckon."

Sure would like to get me a look inside that coffin.

72

A LITTLE BEFORE SEVEN O'CLOCK THE NEXT MORNING. JEREMIAH WALKS OUT of the elevator into the hotel lobby, sees his father standing at the reception desk, his bag at his feet. Jeremiah walks up to him. "You're leaving?"

Franklin nods. "I must return to my garden. Besides, I have done all I can here."

"Maybe you ought to tell me exactly what it is you done. I ain't sure myself."

Franklin smiles. "And yet I perform wonders." He lifts his bag to his shoulder. "It's been nice spending some time together. I'd like to do more of it. You and your wife—what's her name again?"

"Martha."

"Ah, yes. Martha. You must come out to Southern California sometime."

"We'll see."

"So long, then. Tell Benjamin I said farewell. And stay in touch."

"Adios."

Jeremiah watches his daddy disappear into a cab the doorman has waiting for him. Then he leaves his room key with the front desk, walks outside, zipping up his jacket against the north wind. The rain has stopped, but the sky still carries a low overcast and the early morning darkness fairly imitates the night and the streetlights glow yellow. The pavement glistens from last night's rain. Traffic hisses as it passes by. It strikes Jeremiah again how alien the traffic is. Peculiar-looking buses with strange graphics and foreign lettering. Tiny cars, abbreviated two-seaters, that look like dogies from a herd of amusement park rides. Traffic entirely bereft of pickups.

Jeremiah walks along the Ringstrasse to a wide boulevard that shoots off to the northwest, continues down it past a sizable fountain, parabolic water arcs lit in constantly changing colors. Soon he's through the front gates of Belvedere Palace and on to the grounds. The wet lawn is soft under his boots.

The hedges at Schloss Belvedere stand just inside the main entrance, four rows of ten-foot tall fir trees growing so close together you can't see through their branches, forming a box with open corners. He walks to a corner, looks inside the box, sees four benches, one set in front of each fir tree wall.

Beyond the hedges the land rises in precise terraces laid out with water fountains and statuary. Wide marble staircases run up each side. The land levels off at the top of the hill where the rococo palace sits, built, according to his guidebook, by the Baroque architect J. L. Hildebrandt for some general named Prince Eugene of Savoy. Jeremiah climbs the staircase on the left to the top, looks down on the hedges, then out across the lights of the Innere Stadt sparkling in the wet dawn. Like the city is still trying to wash the sleep from its eyes. In the distance, the dark outline of the steeple at St. Stephan's punctures the horizon.

From his coign of vantage, Jeremiah can see the front gate. He takes out a cigarette, cups his hand against the wind, lights it. He settles in to wait.

At straight-up nine o'clock a figure walks through the gates below and disappears inside the fir tree box. Jeremiah takes a last drag on his cigarette, flicks the butt on the ground with the others coveyed there, adjusts his Stetson, walks back down the mable staircase. At the bottom he steps through the nearest open corner into the fir tree box.

Farkas is sitting on the bench opposite. The little Hungarian has on slacks and a turtleneck under a sports coat and over it all a trench coat. Every stitch and button is black. The clothes fit him well, but not so well he couldn't be carrying. He is bareheaded, his thinning gray hair combed straight back. He is not smiling. He says, "I should think the word best describing you, Captain Spur, is 'dogged.' Leslie told me not to reveal myself to you, of course. Before she died."

"Sorry you lost your daughter."

Farkas looks away, shakes his head. "I taught her everything she needed to know to live a spectacular life. A long life. Except, it seems, that one must look both ways before crossing the street."

"Hardest part 'bout bein' a parent, I reckon. You want to look after your kids every minute of the day, even after they're grown, so as to keep 'em safe, but there just ain't no way. Got to let 'em live their own lives."

Farkas leans back, puts his hands on either side of him on the bench. "So, now, here we are. I doubt I would have agreed to see you were Leslie still alive. Or if your father, whom I love as though he were my own, had not interceded on your behalf. But now"—he shrugs—"there is little reason not to hear you out. Besides, I can't have you wandering around my new hometown asking for me at every turn. Really, it has become quite annoying."

"I'm a little annoyed my own self."

"Why should that be?"

"Because you used me to flush out Raul Cantú. Then you killed him."

"He killed my son, Captain Spur."

"You should have been more careful, had Jonathon under guard or somethin'. Should've known Cantú was comin' after you, once Pedro, or Sebastian, or ever-what his name was, disappeared."

Farkas sighs. "As you yourself said not two minutes ago, once cannot watch one's grown children constantly. Besides, Sebastian was a drunk Mexican paranoid. Natural selection never produced more unstable DNA. He would disappear for months without a trace. He once went missing for an entire year, and when he came back, he told me he had spent nine months in New York City, riding the subways, to make sure he wasn't being followed by men in lowriders. He always came back, though. I had no reason to think this time was different."

"But when Jonathon died—"

Farkas cuts him off with a wave. "What they did to Jonathon? It was brilliantly done. You must understand this. The key was to make me believe he died from a drug overdose. That way, you see, I would suffer loss, as had Cantú, but even more, I would suffer the guilt of the overindulgent parent who lives to see his overindulgence destroy what he most loves."

Farkas holds up a finger. "And I was not just an overindulgent father, but one who also was once involved in the narcotics trade. As much as I would like to forget that, it has left a stain that will not wash away, a damned spot that cannot be commanded out. Cantú knew these things, and he wanted his revenge to hurt more than mere death. He sought to turn me against myself. It was so deftly done—I really had no clue—that for months after Jonathon died, Cantú's plan actually worked. I walked around barely alive, lost to myself—"

"I lost a daughter once. I know how that feels."

"You do not know how this feels. To hate one's own life. To be certain one has all but killed his own son." He shakes his head. "No. You cannot imagine how that feels. Eventually, Leslie—" He stops. He swallows hard a couple times. He takes a handkerchief from his pocket, wipes his eyes, blows his nose, puts it away.

Jeremiah watches him. If it's a performance, the man has tricks in him he could teach professionals. Jeremiah tries to think of a delicate way to challenge the man, ask if his daughter is really dead. Decides there isn't one. Decides to leave the subject be, not risk saying something he would end up regretting. *Makes me no real never mind, long as he'll do like I ask him to.*

Farkas says, "She became concerned about my mental health, came to be with me from Europe. She effected my salvation. A salvation by works, not by grace. By her works we uncovered the truth of Jonathon's death. She became suspicious, began checking about, looking into matters, found information that had been hidden from us—"

"The lab data from the autopsy."

Farkas looks surprised, then nods. "We had specialists examine it. They said there could be an alternate explanation for Jonathon's death, involving a very deadly powdered substance. That's when we began to suspect he had been murdered."

"When exactly was that?"

"About three months ago. By then Leslie had learned that Jonathon had been with Dusty Nelson and Paul Lipper at their college reunion. She checked into Dusty's phone records, saw calls to Mexico City. From this we surmised that Dusty had in all likelihood betrayed Jonathon to Cantú. Which he confirmed under her rather aggressive interrogation."

"Why would he do such a thing to a friend?"

"One cannot be completely sure, but we guessed it was for money. He told her the Cantús had promised him a substantial sum, but only if he remained in my employ at least until year-end."

"How come?"

"Because for Cantú to 'exfiltrate' him, as it were, too soon after Jonathon died, might have led us to suspect that his death was from something other than a cocaine overdose. Especially were we to learn that Jonathon and Dusty were together the night Jonathaon died. Any suggestion of murder could—indeed, did—lead back to Cantú, and it was something Cantú obviously took pains to avoid. In the event, once we had confirmation that Cantú had Jonathon killed, we had the problem of how one gets to Don Raul, surrounded as he was by *sicarios* in his Coahuila bunker."

"And that's where I come in."

Farkas lights a smoke. "I did a variation on a method we called 'walking back the cat.' I asked, how do we draw Don Raul, the famous kingpin recluse, into the open? What would be irresistible to a man like that? The answer was provided, ironically enough, by a small but important fact about Jonathon's death. The cocaine that was used to convey the poison into my son's body was bought from a small-time dealer in Brenham, Texas."

"Lamont Stubbs."

"Yes. When we learned this, it brought to mind the fact that you lived in that vicinity. I had seen reports earlier this year—a story about the bombing of your courthouse and your tangential involvement in that matter—and I remembered, of course, that it was you who arrested and eventually killed Jorge Cantú, thanks to the information I had slipped you at the suggestion of your father. I thought it possible—not likely, but possible—that Cantú would surface to meet his brother's killer, if at the same time he could bring me down."

"But not if Cantú thought you knew he'd killed Jonathon."

"Precisely. So Leslie and I behaved as though we sought retribution against only those who would have been implicated had he merely over-dosed, thus indirectly signaling to Don Raul that his ruse had succeeded. We hired you to help find Paul Lipper, who had, after all, genuinely gone missing. Then we created the impression with both you and Cantú that I was working behind the scenes, helping Leslie, yet hiding behind her."

"So I would go to Cantú for confirmation, and he would oblige me as a way of gettin' at you."

"The two of you practically ran into each other's arms. Thanks to the sievelike quality of the Mexican security forces, learning the time and place of your meeting was child's play, as was the rest of it."

"You left a loose end."

Farkas takes a drag. "I'm sorry. I don't believe I did."

"I got a man down there. Cantú's son is holdin' him."

"That, Captain Spur, is your loose end. Not mine."

"I told Tito Cantú I'd bring you back."

"I think I shall give that a miss."

"Tito will keep my man alive until I do, but he only gave me until November 2."

Farkas smiles. "Tell me, Captain Spur. Have you read much Ambrose Bierce?"

"Can't say as I have. Leslie told me you collect his stuff."

"Yes, indeed. Quite an underappreciated writer. He disappeared in Mexico in 1914, at the end of his life. Went down there, he said, in search of 'the good, kind darkness.' He went there, in short, to die."

"You think that's what I'm askin' you to do."

"Go home, Captain Spur. You have wasted your money and your time. Worse, you are at the moment wasting my time. I have no intention of returning to Mexico only to be killed by that ridiculous dilettante Tito Cantú. Even Bierce did not covet death so much." Farkas stands to leave.

Jeremiah lights a Camel. "Let me ask you somethin'. How much are you worth?"

"Bit of a forward question, don't you think? Rather like me asking you how many cattle you run."

"Last list of rich folks I saw had it between a billion and a billion and half."

"And if one of my people got a number that important that wrong, he would surely be seeking new employment the very next day."

"What's a man need that much money for?"

"No man needs that much money. And having it is not the thing. Making it is the thing. As someone else once said, it's a way of keeping score."

"Whatever game you're playin', you must feel like you won. You've scored a touchdown on every play, and a guy like me, heck, I ain't even gotten my hands on the ball."

Farkas shrugs, leans down, crushes his cigarette on the bench. "Have a nice trip home." He starts walking away.

"Hang on a second. You ever think 'bout doin' some good with your money? Maybe usin' it to make the world a better place?"

Farkas stops, turns around. "Silly though the notion is, it has crossed my mind. That is, after all, what people of means are wont to do."

Jeremiah taps ash on the ground. "Sit back down for just another minute or two. Let me run an idea past you. A way you can use your money, do one last service for your adopted country, also provide kind of a memorial, maybe, is the way to think of it, to your boy. You don't like my idea, then you can walk on out of here. Go back to worrying about when and where Tito Cantú's going to reach you."

Farkas retraces his steps, sits down on the bench. "I'm listening."

Jeremiah sketches out his idea. Halfway through, Farkas leans forward, elbows on knees. When Jeremiah's done, he leans back, says, "What if he refuses?"

"I'm willin' to bet he won't."

"Pardon me, Captain Spur, but that's rather easy for you to say. You are not the one that would get killed."

"I might be."

"Meaning what?"

"Meaning I aim to be right there with you. And we hear Jorge Cantú's son Ray has joined the party in Coahuila. If there's anybody on the planet that would like to see me dead, it's him."

"I don't know. It's a lot of money."

"You'd still have plenty left."

"But to use so much of it like *that*—"

"Better than spendin' the rest of your life lookin' over your shoulder."

Farkas falls silent. Then he stands up. "Give me awhile to think about it."

"I'm runnin' out of time."

"I know this. Where can I reach you?"

"You know where. If I'm not at the Kaiserhof, I'll be at the Café Central."

As they walk out from between the hedges together, Farkas says, "When he lived in Vienna, Lenin often took his coffee at the Café Central. Your father told me that."

Jeremiah takes the last drag on his cigarette, flicks the butt on the ground. "You can't escape your antecedents."

73

IT'S GOING ON NOON THE LAST DAY OF OCTOBER AND TREY BEACON IS
shrugging on his sports jacket, fixing to leave the office for lunch, when
Edna buzzes him. "Captain Spur for you, Trey." He sits back down, picks
up the handset. "Jeremiah."

"Mornin'."

"Look, I'm glad you called. If we're gonna try to bust Clyde Thomas
out, we need to get started with the planning."

"Farkas is comin' to see Tito, Trey. And I'm comin' with him."

Trey leans back in his chair. "Holy shit. You did it."

"Try not to sound so danged surprised. His jet is pickin' us up tomorrow mornin'. I expect we'll be landing at Toluca Airport in Mexico City
by mid to late afternoon. Can you get Cantú to have his people meet us
there?"

"Sure. No problem."

"I also need you to let Cantú know, Farkas is comin' to make him an
offer, and he needs to hear the man out."

"What kind of offer?"

"A business deal. A documented business deal, so Cantú's gonna need to
have a lawyer who can read English handy and one of his bankers standin'
by on the phone. And he's going to need to control that loco cousin of
his."

"A business deal."

"Yep. One I think Cantú will like, but in case he don't, I aim to
sweeten the pot."

Trey listens while Jeremiah tells him what's he's got planned, then says,
"I take it Farkas isn't wise to this."

"Nor is he gonna be until I spring it on him."

"What about the metal detector at the airport?"

"You ain't got to go through a metal detector to fly general aviation."

"Oh. Right."

"Remember. Tell them Mexicans, when they're pattin' us down, stay
away from my right coat pocket. And Tito's gotta agree to sit on Ray."

"Alright then."

"Can you arrange the rest of it?"

"I'll sic a couple guys from Company D on it."

"Can they get there in time?"

"They can if they start this afternoon."

"Tell 'em to get high and behind it."

With that the line goes dead. Trey hangs up, buzzes Edna. "Get me Frank Cade."

That night Clyde wakens to the sound of someone unlocking the door to his room. He rolls over and sits up slowly and watches as the young Mexican who'd pistol-whipped him walks in with a couple guards toting automatic weapons. The Mexican pulls the string that turns on the ceiling light. Clyde shields his eyes from it.

He thinks, *This is it.*

The Mexican says, "Smells like shit in here, bro."

Clyde says, "It's the maid's day off."

"Very funny, bro. That's how I will always remember you. I will tell people that was one funny nigger. But he stunk so bad we had to shoot him."

Clyde blinks, drops his hand now that his eyes have commenced to adjust. "You know what, man? I think maybe you got some issues need dealin' with. Maybe you ought to go see a mental physician, have yo' head looked at, you know what I'm sayin'?"

"You know what tomorrow is?"

"The Day of the Dead?"

"The day before. And guess what. We are expecting company."

Clyde tries to read the man's face.

"That's right," the Mexican says. "Your friend the Ranger. He claims he's bringing the Wolf."

For the first time since they threw him in here, Clyde can feel a little hope begin to grow. But it doesn't last long.

The Mexican says, "And I just wanted you to know that when you hear the automatic weapons fire coming from the hacienda, you'll know that you are next."

He clicks off the light and walks out of the room.

The next morning a black Mercedes sedan is waiting for Jeremiah at the curb in front of the Kaiserhof. The driver rushes forward as Jeremiah walks out the door, offers up a *"Guten Morgen,"* takes his grip, holds the car door open for him. Jeremiah hears the trunk lid slam, watches the man scurry around the vehicle, get behind the wheel.

"Flughafen, ja?"

"Yep."

They're wheels-up by seven o'clock, the red-on-white jet taking to the sky with a roar, pushing Jeremiah back into his seat on the right-hand side of the cabin. Farkas sits across the aisle, wearing a blue jogging suit, reading the *Financial Times*. Jeremiah watches Austria disappear behind the clouds.

When they're level at thirty-five thousand feet, the pilot comes back to tell them the flight plan—refueling stops in the Azores and Bermuda and then on to Toluca Airport. It doesn't escape Jeremiah that the routing avoids the States. ETA Toluca three o'clock Central Time. The man hustles around the cabin, getting them coffee and juice and water, working on their breakfast, omelets and bacon catered in Vienna that he warms in a microwave, then lays out for them on mahogany tables that fold out from pockets in the cabin wall.

While they eat, Jeremiah listens to Farkas speak of Franklin, their years of working together, the kindnesses the man had done him, how he'd always been as good as his word. The debts Farkas owes the man always known to him as "John." Debts beyond repayment. Farkas says, "Has it occurred to you, how like brothers we are?"

Jeremiah's head snaps around. "Do *what?*"

"Really. I'm quite serious. The same man fathered you, literally, and fathered me, figuratively. He was my teacher, mentor, benefactor, protector, best friend. For that reason, I really cannot help but feel a strong and very genuine sense of kinship toward you. It was that sense of kinship, to be honest, that tipped the balance. It's why I met with you in Vienna—that, along with the fact that the man I think of as my second father asked me to. I could have stayed entirely hidden, you know, or relocated to some other city. But you were working so hard to find me and, really, agreeing to meet with you, well, it seemed"—he smiles—"the brotherly thing to do."

Jeremiah goes back to work on his omelet. "We ain't kin. Kin wouldn't city-slick one another like you city-slicked me."

Farkas's smile grows. "You do harbor some quaint notions, Captain Spur."

"A thing can only be what it is."

"And you are fond of that expression, I've noticed. Leslie even remarked on that. She said she explained to you that it is patently at odds with the duality of the universe." He sets his fork down, looks at Jeremiah. "When one thinks about it, she was a bit of an argument for duality herself, or how else could she have fooled you so completely?"

Jeremiah works his jaw. "Yeah. She give me that high talk about waves and particles and what have you. But, with respect, her havin' passed on and all, here's somethin' I know that don't require a lot of fancy math in the provin'. There's one place in the universe where there ain't no duality, and that's inside a trigger guard. You put your finger inside one, squeeze the piece of metal you find there, intendin' to end somebody else's life, that makes you one thing and one thing only. A thing that can only be what it is."

Farkas makes no reply. Jeremiah reaches for his Camels, thankful that at least his host is a smoker, makes up some for the man's cracked views.

Directly the pilot comes back to clear the breakfast dishes, fold their tables back into the wall. Jeremiah stares out the window. Farkas leans his chair back and goes to sleep. The plane thunders westward, followed by the sun, adding hours like lead weights to Jeremiah's day, until mercifully they descend into the Mexico City smog.

The eve of the Day of the Dead. A Ford Excursion pulls through the front gate of the Cantú finca and climbs the long asphalt road to the main hacienda, the trunks of the oak trees on either side of the lane flashing in the headlights, then disappearing as they drive past. The Ford pulls to a stop in front of a sprawling adobe house with a red tile roof. All four of the vehicle's doors open.

Farkas gets out of the backseat, followed by Jeremiah. Before they landed, Farkas had changed out of his jogging suit into a chocolate brown business suit, pale blue shirt, matching tie. He carries a thin black folio under his arm.

Jeremiah puts on his Stetson, follows Farkas into the hacienda. *Sicarios* toting automatic weapons form an escort square, two in front, two behind, two on each side. Cantú's men lead them down a long hallway to a great room with a twenty-foot-high ceiling, an enormous fireplace at one end, floor-to-ceiling windows along the entire back wall, a chandelier made of elk horns. Oriental rugs are visible through clear plastic drop cloths spread over the floor.

Three men sit in armchairs facing the doorway. The man on the far left is the youngest, in his twenties, with long sideburns and fair skin. The man in the middle is in his late thirties, with longish black hair parted in the middle, a thin mustache. The third man has white hair and a drooping mustache, wears a rumpled business suit, briefcase resting at his feet. Between the two men on the right is a table that has two items on it—a lamp and a revolver.

As Farkas and Jeremiah walk into the room, the *sicarios* fan out to either side and behind them. The drop cloths on the floor make a crunching sound as the men walk. The three men across the room stand, and the one in the middle—Jeremiah figures him to be Tito Cantú—picks up the gun. Jeremiah makes the man on the left to be Ray.

A *sicario* crosses the room. *Crunch, crunch, crunch.* He opens the passports he had taken from Jeremiah and Farkas when they were frisked after they deplaned, hands them to Tito, stands off to one side.

Tito looks at them, nods, looks at Farkas. "The Wolf. At last." He hands the passports back to his man, who walks back to join the *sicario* chorus line.

"*Buenas noches,* Señor Cantú."

Cantú lifts the revolver, points it at Farkas. "You have come to Mexico to die. Unbelievable."

Farkas smiles thinly. "As Ambrose Bierce once wrote, 'To be a Gringo in Mexico—ah, that is euthanasia!' "

Cantú nods. "As they say, attitude is everything, *pendejo.*" He cocks the hammer.

Toluca Airport, Mexico City. A black Suburban with tinted windows pulls up to the gate at Aerolíneas Ejecutivas. The driver slides the window down, punches the call button on the squawk box. The box erupts with static. A male voice says, "*Sí?*"

"I'm here for a pickup, from Whiskey Kilo seven-niner-five-zed."

"Zed?"

"Zed. Zero."

"Ah. *Sí.*" The gate rolls back to let the vehicle on the tarmac. The driver pulls up next to the Falcon 50, gets out, tucks her blond hair under a Texas Rangers baseball cap. The pilot walks down the jet's steps, gives her a little salute, walks back to the cargo hold, starts setting cardboard boxes on the ground.

Farkas holds up a hand, says, "I understand, you very much want to take my life." He speaks quietly, calmly, no outward sign of stress save for a vein in his temple Jeremiah can see throbbing.

"As you took my father's."

"And as he took my son's."

"You began the cycle. With Uncle Jorge."

Farkas drops his hand. "I merely betrayed him to Captain Spur here. I was not involved in his death."

"You set in motion the events that led to his death. You set in motion this cycle. And now the cycle will end."

Ray speaks for the first time. "Both of you will die."

Farkas says to Tito, "I came here, at Captain Spur's request, to offer you something in return for ending the cycle in a different way."

Tito's eyes flick to Jeremiah, then back to Farkas. "There is only one way to end this cycle."

"Please. Hear me out." Farkas indicates the older man. "This is your lawyer?"

"Yes."

Farkas holds up the black folio. "May I?"

Tito nods. Farkas extracts a document, indicates that the lawyer should take it. At another nod from Tito, the lawyer crunches across the room, takes the document, returns to his chair, commences reading.

Farkas says, "That is legal documentation establishing an irrevocable trust giving the beneficiary exclusive power over that portion of its corpus that has been released from escrow, so long as its conditions are satisfied. Its sole beneficiary is Tito Cantú, and its corpus is one thousand million American dollars, which were transferred this morning into an escow account at a Swiss bank established for the benefit of the trust. The corpus will be released from escrow annually, over ten years, at the rate of one hundred million dollars per year, beginning sixty days from today, so long as, on each release date, its conditions are satisfied."

Tito glances at his lawyer. "Well?" His lawyer looks up. Nods.

Tito looks back at Farkas. "What are these conditions of which you speak?"

"They are quite simple. Before the first release from escrow you must cease distributing narcotics and disband your operation—"

"That is absurd!"

Farkas holds up his hand again. "I assure you. There is nothing absurd about one billion dollars. This is the magic number to end all magic numbers, the ten digits around which every young man's dreams revolve. One need look no further than Silicon Valley, at the brains being taxed and capital being risked there, to know this is true. Believe me, Señor Cantú, I am quite expert as to the economics of your operation, and while they are very lucrative indeed, on a risk-adjusted basis, they are as nothing compared to one billion dollars freely given. This is money for which you need not create, nor work, nor run risks. You need only decide how best to enjoy it. Having had such money myself, I can assure you, there are many pleasant ways to enjoy it."

The lawyer says, "If I am reading this correctly, Don Tito can demonstrate compliance with this condition by filing an affidavit with a bank officer in Zurich."

Farkas says, "Along with affidavits from the American DEA and its Mexican counterpart. Both agencies must be given full access to all real estate owned and records maintained by the Cantú family."

The lawyer looks at Tito. "It can be done. But there are other conditions."

Tito says, "What are they?"

Farkas says, "Captain Spur, his friend, and I must all leave here alive. In addition, both I and all my descendants must be alive on each escrow release date. Or, if not, then the appropriate authorities must have certified to the bank that the decedent's death was due to natural causes."

Ray says, "This is bullshit." He reaches around behind his back but freezes at the sound of the action on half a dozen automatic weapons being worked and at the sight of them being aimed his way.

Tito says, "Drop it, Ray."

Ray stares at Tito. "You are not fucking saying—"

Tito shrugs. "A billion dollars, cousin. That's a lot of money." He nods at a couple *sicarios* who break ranks, walk over to Ray. One of the guards takes a pistol out of Ray's hand and they grab him by the arms and start walking him from the room.

Ray stops in front of Tito, says, "You son of a bitch. You son of a *bitch!*"

Tito looks at the two *sicarios.* "Take him for a long ride. He can walk back."

The *sicarios* hustle Ray out of the room and he curses them all the way.

Once he's out the door, Tito turns to Farkas, says, "I don't understand why the condition covers your descendants. Two of your children have already died."

"Obviously, the condition does not apply to a child who has already passed away."

Cantú looks at his lawyer. His lawyer nods.

Farkas says, "Perhaps I shall remarry, start a second family someday. I would not want my children to become targets. To fall victim to a hit-and-run accident, for instance."

Cantú frowns. "We had nothing to do with that."

"I'm very glad to hear it."

"How can I know this is not a trick? How can I know the money is truly there?"

"Despite the hour," Farkas glances at his wristwatch, "my banker in Zurich awaits a call from your banker. I feel certain your banker will find the proof he will be provided to be quite adequate. Your lawyer will find the number to call in Zurich written on the back of the Declaration of Trust."

Cantú lowers the gun, nods again to his lawyer, who produces a cell phone from his briefcase, keys in a few numbers, begins speaking in Spanish. Then he says, "Adios," sets the cell phone on the table next to him. "He will call back shortly."

Farkas says, "Would you care if we smoke?"

Cantú motions "go ahead." As Jeremiah and Farkas reach for their cigarettes, Cantú says, "I do not understand why you would do this. Why you come here, put your life at risk, offer me one billion dollars to abandon my business."

Farkas lights his cigarette, tosses the spent match on the plastic sheeting. Takes a drag. "I must be honest. I have Captain Spur to thank for the idea. At first, it sounded—well, the word you used was 'absurd.' But as I thought about it, I began to see it as a fitting way to bring peace between our families and yet honor the memory of my son, whom, after all, your father did poison with cocaine. If you were to abandon this activity, the distribution of these drugs to America would be substantially curtailed. Many young lives would be spared ruination." He puffs on his cigarette, gestures. "Rarely does one have the chance to put one's money to such splendid use. It would mean my son's life was not needlessly sacrificed. And it would mean an end to the war between us."

"Perhaps I see your point. But one billion dollars?"

"As I have said, it is the magic number. And the offer had to be compelling. I assure you, I still have plenty left."

They fall silent, the minutes drag by. Finally, the cell phone on the table chirps. The lawyer snatches it. *"Bueno."* He listens, then hands the phone to Cantú. Cantú takes the phone, listens, grunts. Cuts the connection. Looks at Farkas. "It is as you say."

"I take it, then, we have a deal?"

Cantú looks at Jeremiah. "It is said you can sweeten the offer."

As Farkas turns to look his way, Jeremiah moves toward Farkas. Farkas starts to back up, then stops when he sees the *sicarios'* weapons pointed at him. Jeremiah grabs Farkas's good arm just below the elbow. Jeremiah reaches in his coat pocket, pulls out a pair of handcuffs, snaps them first on that wrist, then on the man's damaged left wrist.

Farkas says, "What do you think you're doing?"

"I'm takin' you into custody. I thought Señor Cantú here might like the deal better if he knew you was gonna spend the rest of your life in Huntsville."

Farkas tries to jerk away, but Jeremiah is bigger and stronger, and the weaponry trained on him argues powerfully against resistance.

Farkas says, "You are arresting me? After I took this risk for you? Risked my very life, not to mention one billion dollars, to help you get your friend back?"

"That don't excuse all the killin' you been an accessory to back home. Besides, you said money was just your way of keepin' score. Well, this is how I keep score."

"This is truly unbelievable. I thought we were like brothers."

"That's your peculiar notion. I don't hold with it."

Cantú looks at his lawyer. "Is there anything in those papers that would void the trust if Farkas is arrested?"

"No, Don Tito."

Cantú turns to Farkas. "I'm sure you see the symmetry, Señor Wolf. My father for your son. You for my uncle. Two dead on each side. Two in prison. Nice even numbers. That is the proper balance. Wouldn't you agree?"

Farkas shouts. "I should have thought one billion dollars brought a lot of balance!"

"Alas, no."

Farkas looks at Jeremiah. "You cannot be serious."

"There are two Texas Rangers waitin' just outside the gate to this place. They're here to give you a ride north."

Farkas sputters. "You have no authority here. This is kidnapping."

"Call it ever-what you want." Jeremiah looks at Cantú. "We about done here?"

Cantú smiles, lets the hammer down on the revolver dangling at his side, sits back down in his armchair, crosses his legs.

Jeremiah says, "Once I've turned Farkas over to the Rangers, I'm comin' back to get my man."

Cantú looks at Farkas. "Adios, Señor Wolf. Thanks so much for coming."

He's still smiling when Jeremiah leaves the room, pushing Farkas ahead of him.

A couple of *sicarios* carry Jeremiah and Farkas in the Excursion to the front gate of the finca, park the vehicle while Jeremiah wrestles his prisoner out into the night. The finca gates swing open. A sedan with Texas tags idles with its headlights on just outside the gate. Jeremiah marches Farkas to the rear door, sets him inside, careful to keep his head from banging against the door frame.

Farkas works his way over to the middle of the seat, looks out the door at Jeremiah. "Were your father here, he would tell you two things. First, that he is proud of you."

"Makes me no never mind if he would be proud or not. What's the other thing?"

"That no prison, no jail, anywhere, certainly not in Texas, can hold me for long."

"Yeah. Well. We'll see about that."

"I suppose we shall."

"Adios, Farkas."

Jeremiah closes the door, looks in at the two men in front. He recognizes one, a young Ranger named Dexter Cooley. The other man is a stranger. Both are in plainclothes. Jeremiah sticks his hand through the window. "Jeremiah Spur," he says.

The stranger takes it. "Dan Franshaw."

"Don't believe I've heard tell of you. You a Ranger?"

"No, sir. Highway Patrol."

Jeremiah looks past the man at Dexter, the question showing on his face. Dexter says, "We're workin' a whole mess of bank robberies in Bexar County. Captain Cade couldn't free up two men."

Jeremiah works his jaw. "Well, y'all be careful. This man you got here, he's apt to be dangerous. Drive straight back and stop as little as you can."

"Yes, sir, Captain."

"Alright, then." Jeremiah stands up, watches as the vehicle drives off into the Mexican night. Then he turns back to where the *sicarios* are waiting in the Ford.

The closer it had gotten to the Day of the Dead, the harder it had been for Clyde to sleep. Every night, when darkness would come, he'd lie on the cot and fret. Fret about whether he was going to get out of here alive. About what would happen to his mama if he didn't. About the parasites that had taken up residence on his person, that kept him scratching morning, noon, and night, so he couldn't ever get comfortable. About the diseases they might be passing on to him, even if he were to survive this ordeal.

After the visit from that Mexican last night, he hadn't been able to sleep at all, but not because he was fretting. His fretting has stopped. Now he knows how this is going to end.

Tonight he has been lying on his cot, scratching away, trying to reconcile himself to the fact, tonight is probably his last night on this earth. Later on, or tomorrow morning, a bullet in the head, then a burial out in some field somewhere. No chance to tell nobody good-bye, to make out a will, nothing like that. They'd probably never even find his corpse, get it back to Texas where his mama could visit the grave. He wonders if Sonya will miss him even the least little bit.

He hears voices coming his way. *Okay, I didn't hear no gunfire like that motherfucker said I would, but I guess it don't matter a shit. This has gotta be it right here. Now I got to try to die as best I can.* He swings his feet to the floor, sits there holding his head. The sudden movement has made him dizzy. He rubs his temples, tries to get his head to stop swimming. Tries to find a prayer somewhere in him but comes up short.

Sounds at the door. A lock being turned, chains unhitched. The door swings open. A big man stands there, wearing a Stetson, backlit by flashlights.

The man says, "You ready to go home?"

74

He spends much of the night leaning against the door, dozing. They stop for gas once, and he awakens for that. The one that said he was DPS pumps the fuel, while the Texas Ranger holds a semiautomatic on him. He twists in his seat, tries to get some feeling back in his hands.

"I don't suppose I could persuade you to loosen these handcuffs?"

The Ranger just grins.

When they pull away from the pumps, he goes back to sleep until daybreak. He sits up, blinks at the light coming into the world. The sun rises slowly above a howling desert empty save for cactus, sage, mesquite. He squints at the barren land and wonders how far north they have come. There are no other vehicles on this black strip of highway.

About a half hour after sunrise, the DPS man says, "That a vehicle up yonder?"

"I do believe."

"Looks like it's broke down."

He looks out the windshield. Way up the road, a speck over on the shoulder. As they get closer, he sees it's a Suburban, with the hood up. Someone is leaning inside, looking at the engine. The person under the hood steps back, straightens up, starts waving at them. A young woman wearing blue jeans and a denim shirt with the tail out, Texas Rangers baseball cap on her head.

"Guess we better see what's up," the driver says.

He passes the Suburban, pulls the sedan to the side of the road, watches in the rearview while the young woman walks his way. Slides his window down. She stops right beside the car.

"Got a problem, ma'am?" the Ranger says.

"Engine overheated. Looks like a belt broke. I don't suppose I could get y'all to give me a ride to the next town."

"Sorry, ma'am. We're law enforcement, carrying a prisoner back to Texas. We ain't allowed to do that. We could send a tow truck back for you."

The young woman's fists go to her hips. "That's just swell. In the meantime I sit out here in the middle of nowhere, with a load of rare books I'm supposed to be delivering to my employer, waiting to be set upon by desperadoes or wild animals."

"What kind of rare books, ma'am?"

"First edition Graham Greene and Ambrose Bierce. Ironic, really. Bierce disappeared in Mexico."

"News to me, ma'am. If you want to tell us what he looks like, we'd be happy to keep an eye out for him."

"Who?"

"That man you said disappeared down this way."

She sighs. "That was eighty-five years ago."

"Oh. Sorry."

"Well, thanks for stopping anyway. Send back a tow truck, okay?" She turns, walks back to her vehicle.

The Ranger says, "Damn. She's nice-lookin'."

"Man, I mean."

"What kind of accent you reckon that was?"

"Beats the heck out of me. Sounded sort of Texan and sort of not."

The Texas Ranger looks in the rearview mirror. "Maybe we ought to go have a look at her vehicle. Might be somethin' simple we could fix."

The DPS man looks over the backseat at their prisoner. "You sure it'd be okay?"

"Hell, he ain't goin' nowheres. What harm could it do?"

"But ain't he supposed to have a daughter that's a trained killer?"

"Died in a car wreck in Europe last month." The Ranger kills the engine, pockets the keys. The two cops get out of the car, walk back to where the Suburban is parked.

A minute or so later, voices, the sound of shouted commands.

Farkas turns to look out the back glass of the sedan. The doors of the Suburban are open and three men are standing beside them, holding automatic weapons, pointed at the two Texas lawmen. The two cops have their hands in the air and the woman is disarming them.

The woman turns, walks toward the sedan. Opens the back door, looks in. "Would you mind, terribly, Father? I do need to get those handcuffs from you."

75

SEVERAL DAYS LATER, IN A FIVE-STAR HOTEL IN MEXICO CITY, TWO MEN dressed in business suits walk down a hallway and stop in front of a guest-room door. The larger of the two, a broad-shouldered man with a squiggly wire running from his ear down the back of his coat, steps to one side and plants himself with his arms across his chest. The smaller man goes to the door and knocks.

"Hello? Señor? Are you in there?"

He stops to listen. He looks at the larger man who says nothing.

The smaller man knocks again. "Señor? It is the assistant manager of the hotel. Would you let me in please?"

Again he stops and waits for a few moments. He steps back as the larger man takes his place at the door and produces a key and inserts it in the lock. He opens the door and walks into the room followed by the smaller man. They turn the corner around a short wall and catch sight of the room.

The smaller man gasps, crosses himself. "Mother of God."

76

THE SUNDAY AFTER HE GOT BACK FROM MEXICO, JEREMIAH SPUR IS SITTING on his back porch, resting up from his globe-trotting and from all the work he had done, catching up around the ranch the last couple days. He'd promised Martha he'd lay off cigarettes starting tomorrow, so this afternoon he's enjoying one of his last smokes, sitting in his rocker, looking out at his dog Duke's grave and past that to his pastures.

He thinks about the package that came with yesterday's mail. A plain brown envelope, addressed to him, no return address. California postmark. In it a videotape, a movie called *The Third Man,* and nothing else. The cover box said it was the fiftieth-anniversary edition.

He and Martha watched the movie last night. It was about a man, a criminal, who faked his own death in a car accident so as to throw the police off his trail. In Vienna, Austria. It was based on a story by Graham Greene.

His old man's way of explaining himself, he reckons. *And yet I perform wonders.*

He figures his daddy must have somehow been in contact with Farkas even before Jeremiah went out to see Franklin. Franklin said he had been told to expect Jeremiah's visit. Would have given Franklin a chance to tap his old network, find out where Farkas went to ground, if he didn't know already.

Between the two of them they worked to make it look like Leslie had been killed, with Jeremiah handy to vouch for it. His glimpse of Leslie jogging by, her disappearance down the stairs into the sewer. That had to have been staged purely for his benefit.

Then her faked death and burial. Farkas had all the money a man would need to pull off a stunt like that, probably hired some guys, dressed them in police uniforms, had them stand around the so-called accident scene to make it look like the real deal.

Leslie "died" for the same reason Harry Lime died in the movie. It's the ultimate getaway. The authorities and vengeful rivals don't chase folks into the grave.

She died for Farkas's sins, not to mention her own.

Their plan wouldn't have stood up to all that much scrutiny, but it wouldn't have had to, if Jeremiah hadn't made his play for Farkas. Leslie would have stayed dead and out of danger, and no one would have been the wiser or thought to ask awkward questions. But when Jeremiah took Farkas into custody, that smoked her out into the open, forced her "resurrection," so as to be her daddy's savior.

Jeremiah crushes his cigarette butt. Odds are, she wouldn't have been able to get the drop on Cooley and Franshaw, ambush those two, if they hadn't thought she was dead. That's another way her "death" worked to the Farkases' advantage. It served to protect her from the police and the Cantús as well as to provide a hedge against Jeremiah pulling a fast one of his own.

Jeremiah doesn't fault Cooley and Franshaw. Folks thought to be dead commonly stay that way.

He wonders how much of this his daddy had thought through. Jeremiah is convinced Farkas had it thought through from one end to the other, adjusting his plans as need be to account for Jeremiah's ideas about how they could go about ransoming Clyde out. *Which Farkas didn't know of 'til after he "buried" Leslie, of course.*

Trey Beacon had called the Vienna police, tried to speak to the Officer Kurtz who had told him Leslie was dead. The Viennese cops told him there was no Officer Kurtz working for them. That had pissed Trey off no end, and he had sworn he would get to the bottom of that bit of business.

Jeremiah sets fire to a new cigarette. Even though Trey had been hard at it all week, the affair of the hit-and-run still remains to be resolved to his satisfaction. The Vienna police insisted there had been a fatal accident at that location on the Ringstrasse, called in by some anonymous citizen that Saturday night, but when asked to produce the official report, they admitted the accident report had been filed by the nonexistent Officer Kurtz. Next week, the authorities will disinter the body that Farkas had pretended was his daughter.

He thinks about his daddy, Farkas, himself. The complicated way the three of them relate to one another. Wonders how much Farkas may have been motivated, honest to goodness, by the debts he said he owed Jeremiah's old man. And how much Franklin may have been motivated by the guilt he felt over having abandoned his family long ago. *Was that the mixture that was behind them bein' willin' to help me get Clyde out of that scrape I got him into—gratitude and guilt?*

On the other hand, I reckon those same two things was drivin' me, too.

Or maybe none of that mattered to them at all. Maybe they was just doin' what they love to do anyway. Play them little games they been playin' all these years. A little sleight of hand for old time's sake.

There's no denying, by going to Mexico and making Cantú that offer, Farkas saved Clyde's life and saved Jeremiah carrying a heavy burden the rest of his. So everybody was busy saving everybody else, for their own obscure purposes, maybe even hoping to earn some form of salvation of their own. *Salvation by works, not by grace.*

Got no problem with salvation, so far as it goes. It ain't a substitute for justice, though. Salvation don't do a thing for Dusty Nelson, Paul Lipper, Diedre Brown, or for their families, neither. Them's the kinds of folks I've acted for all my life.

And that's why, even though he got Clyde back home safe, he can't be very satisfied with the way it all turned out in the end.

He listens to the cars passing out on the state highway east of his place. Notices one of them has a familiar-sounding engine. And that it's getting closer.

Directly Trey Beacon's Impala pulls around his house into the backyard. He pushes himself out of his rocker, steps down off the porch, just as Clyde Thomas stands up out of the car. Jeremiah leans against the top rail of his fence.

Clyde holds his arms out. "What d'ya think, man?"

"So you went and did it."

"Yeah, man. Promised myself I would, if I ever got out that hole that Mexican had me in."

Jeremiah shakes his head. "Washington County roads ain't gon' be safe no more. How's your headache?"

"Gettin' better. Doc says that Mexican gave me a concussion but I ought to be fine as can be 'fore long."

"I can't seem to think of nothin' to say that don't include the phrase 'hardheaded.'"

Clyde grins, walks around the car so it won't be between him and Jeremiah, leans up against it. "You heard about Cooley and Franshaw?"

"Heard they walked into a police station in Matamoros on Friday."

"Farkas's people cut 'em loose, huh?"

"Yep. Once they got back to San Antonio, they ID'd Leslie Whitten from a photograph. I also heard Tito Cantú's gone missin'."

"Fuck him, man. Motherfucker deserves whatever he gets. Keepin' me in that fuckin' stable for two weeks." Clyde stands up off the car. "Listen, man, I been thinkin' how best I could say thanks to you for comin' and savin' my ass."

Jeremiah holds up a hand. "There's no need—"

Clyde turns, opens the back door of the Impala. "Too late, man. Already done it." He reaches inside, turns around. He's holding a two-month-old black Lab puppy in his arms. "Thought you might like a replacement for that dog of yours, got hisself killed."

Clyde sees Jeremiah's expression. "Whatsa matter, man? You alright?"

EPILOGUE

CLYDE THOMAS LOOKS AROUND HIS DESK, TRYING TO MAKE SURE HE HASN'T missed anything. The sheriff had collected his badge and gun when he came in this morning. Then Dewey had mumbled something about some meeting he needed to go to out on the bypass. He gave Clyde a quick handshake and waddled out the door.

Clyde says, "Seems like a man ought to have more to show fo' six years uh hard work than what he can fit in a filin' box."

Deputy Bobby Crowner watches him from the next desk over. He shakes his head. "I still can't believe they done you this way."

"Yeah, well, believe it, man. You know what I'm sayin'? They done throwed my ass to the wolves."

"I reckon was the newspaper coverage done the trick, huh?"

Clyde leans back, puts his hands behind his head. "Yeah, man. Once the big city papers started runnin' that bullshit 'bout Washington County havin' themselves another police brutality scandal, all Sonya and Dewey wanted was to settle out with Lamont's sister and that asshole Gutter Ball. Wasn't interested in fightin' to save the likes of me. Next thing I know, they tells me I got to resign so the other side will do the deal. Threatened to run me off if I didn't. It's some racist shit, you know what I'm sayin'?"

"Ain't gon' be the same without you 'round here."

Clyde stands up, sticks his hand out. Bobby grips it. "'Preciate that, man. Been nice workin' with you and all." Clyde picks up his box of stuff, heads for the door.

Bobby says, "Hey, Clyde. What you gon' do now, anyway?"

Clyde turns back, shrugs. "Don't know. Maybe go home, see my mama. Try to sort some shit out."

"Good luck, alright?"

"Yo. Same to you."

Clyde steps into the hallway outside the office, walks to the elevator, stops. Thinks maybe he ought to go up one floor to the District Attorney's offices, adios Sonya. *Shit. I ain't got nothin' to say to her.* He hits the down button, shifts his box from one arm to the other.

He walks out the front door of the bank building, sees Jeremiah Spur leaning up against the door of his pickup. Jeremiah straightens up, walks his way. "I heard this was your last day."

"Yeah, man."

"I come by to see what you're plannin' to do next."

"Ain't figgered it out my own self."

The Ranger pops a piece of nicotine gum in his mouth.

Clyde says, "Tryin' to give up the cigs again, huh?"

"Yeah. Gonna get me that patch this time. Plus Martha, she's ridin' my tail about it."

"Uh-huh. Hey, I heard they dug up that body in Vienna."

"Yep. Was a young lady who had been in a car wreck on the autobahn, south of Munich, earlier that week. She was supposed to of been cremated. Somehow the Farkases got their hands on the body, used it to fake the hit-and-run. May have just dropped her in the street, for all anybody knows. Vienna cops been chowing down on crow barbecue over it. You hear about Tito Cantú?"

"Heard he got dead."

"Yep. Throat was cut in a hotel room in Mexico City. No suspects."

"Uh-huh. Bet we know who done it, though."

"Could've been either Farkas or Ray Cantú, I reckon. Both of 'em had motive aplenty. Not sure how much it matters."

"Wonder what happens to all that money now."

"That trust Farkas set up for Cantú had some kind of clause in it. Said if Cantú was to die before he got the money, it was all to go to the Gitch Foundation."

"What's that, man?"

"Some kind of international organization for the education and support of orphans. It's not all bad news, though. With both Raul and Tito dead, sounds like their drug operation is in a world of hurt. Trey Beacon says the folks what's left are too busy fightin' Ray Cantú for control to get much product shipped across the border. The whole shootin' match is somewhat comin' apart at the seams. Thanks to the Wolf, I reckon."

"Motherfucker planned it that way all along, huh?"

"Could be."

Clyde sticks his hand out. "Look, man, I want you to know, I appreciate—"

Jeremiah takes his hand, says, "You done thanked me already. If you don't remember, you can go have a look at your thanks. He's sittin' in the front seat of my pickup."

"Yeah, well. Glad you like yo' dog, man." Clyde turns, heads toward his car.

"Hang on a second."

Clyde turns around.

Jeremiah says, "I got a call from the governor yesterday. Even with the drop in the narcotics traffic, he's still madder'n hell about the way all this turned out. He's runnin' for president next year, and he says it makes him look bad to have all these killin's happenin' in his own state, nobody goin' to jail over it. He asked me, would I accept a commission as a Special Ranger, then maybe see what I could do to fix things some."

"You mean go after Farkas?"

Jeremiah shrugs.

"But ain't Farkas in Mexico, man?"

"More'n likely."

"So you gonna do it? Become a—what'd you call it?"

"A Special Ranger. Legislature created the office, back in the 1980s. It's just like being a Texas Ranger: You get the badge, carry a weapon, got the power to enforce the law. Open to all retired Texas Rangers and three hundred others selected by the governor."

"So you thinkin' 'bout maybe chasin' that Hungarian all the way to Mexico?"

"I told the governor I would consider it if I could have my choice of partner."

"Who would that be, man?"

"I'm lookin' at him."

"Say what?"

"I said to the governor if I did it, I would want you to give me a hand, and I'd need him to make you a Special Ranger, too. He said he'd do it if that's what it took to get me."

"You're shittin' me, right?"

"Not for a minute. I told the governor we'd need to be paid, too. He said he'd authorize two hundred fifty dollars a day for us each."

"Damn, man. When do we start?"

Jeremiah turns, walks to his pickup, reaches inside. Jake's sitting in there, watching him, tail a-going ninety to nothing. He gives Jake a head scratching, takes a file folder off the dashboard. He comes back, hands Clyde a document and a ballpoint pen. "Just as soon as you accept the commission."

Clyde sets his box on the ground, takes the file, looks at the document inside. It says the Governor of the State of Texas commissions C. Livermore Thomas as a Special Texas Ranger. It's dated yesterday, has the governor's scrawl on the bottom.

Clyde sets the document on the hood of a car and signs his name. Hands the pen and the file back to Jeremiah. The Ranger takes them in his left hand, hands Clyde a Texas Ranger's badge with his right hand. Clyde accepts it like it's a holy relic.

Jeremiah says, "Welcome to the Texas Rangers."

"Thanks, man."

They shake. "I'm lookin' forward to workin' with you, podna."

"Yeah, man. Me, too."

When he gets to his Impala, Clyde sets his box in the backseat, climbs behind the wheel, sits staring at the badge he holds in his hand, the five-pointed Lone Star inside a silver circle, stamped out of a silver Mexican coin. *Wish my mama could see this shit right here.*

He cranks the engine, then looks up at a rapping noise. A kid is standing just outside the passenger's-side window. Takes Clyde a minute before he realizes it's that kid with the mouth on him, Rocket. Clyde slides the window down. The kid has streaks on his face.

"Yo. Why ain't you in school?"

"I done run off from home, Judge."

"Say what?"

"That motherfucker my mama lets in the house, he done beat me fo' the last time."

"He beat you?"

"Took a belt to me, 'cross the back and shoulders." A tear breaks loose. He swipes at it.

"How'd you get all the way downtown?"

"Bicycle." Rocket sniffs, wipes his nose with his sleeve. "This a sweet ride you got here, Judge."

"You bet it's sweet. You wanna ride around in it some, maybe talk 'bout what's goin' down back at the house?"

"Sho'."

Clyde leans over, pushes the door open. "Get on in here then."

"What about my bike?"

"I'll set it in the trunk."

Jeremiah watches Clyde put the bicycle in his trunk, get in the car with the kid he'd been talking to, drive off. He shoos Jake away from the driver's side of his pickup, gets in, gives his dog a head scratching, a good one, behind the ears and everything. He ignitions the vehicle, slips it into gear, pulls away from the curb.

He can feel it stirring his blood now, that old chase feeling he used to get. He knows that by rights he ought to have said no to the governor, but he's never said no to this governor or any of his predecessors when they'd called and asked something of him.

His only real hesitation had been Martha. She had come back from treatment to find an empty house, and that hadn't been the way either of them had planned it. He had gone home with nothing in mind other than to do his level best to make it up to her, he had pretty much stuck to that intention.

Then the phone had rung yesterday and it had been the governor on the other end of the line and Jeremiah was back in that old quandary of his again. He told the governor, before he could give him an answer, he'd need to speak with his wife. She had been in the same room, right there in the kitchen with him, listening to his side of the conversation. He had hung up the phone, looked at Martha.

She said, "He wants you to chase after Farkas."

"He thinks I'm the best man for it. What with the time I've already spent around the man and all."

She poured herself a cup of coffee, went to sit at the kitchen table. He followed suit, sat beside her. They stared out the back window, across the fields to where the cattle grazed. In another week it would be Thanksgiving, the first one to come around since Elizabeth died. The thought of the holidays made Jeremiah wish he could saddle Redbo up, ride him out to the far pasture, sit him there until January.

Martha set her coffee cup down. "In treatment, they talked a lot about the need to come to grips with the damage we've done as alcoholics to ourselves and others. How important that is to recovering."

"I reckon."

She looked at him. "Sorting that out is going to take me some time."

"Can they help you with that in your meetings?"

"A little, I suppose. But, mostly, it has to be me."

"Maybe I ought to tell the governor to find—"

She cut him off with a wave. "Jeremiah, Jeremiah. A thing can only be what it is."

He looked out the window, stared at his pasture for a spell, thought about all the times they'd sat at this table and had one version of this conversation or another. How he'd never been equal to the task of speaking what was in his heart to her. He decided, for once, not to be a failure at it.

He looked at her. "And you're what makes it possible for me to be the thing I am."

She smiled, and in that smile he could see all the reasons he loved her. She said, "Go call the governor back and tell him you'll do it."

He's out on Highway 36 now, headed for his ranch, his blood like thunder in his head. Jake tries to crawl up in his lap. Jeremiah gently pushes him back toward his side of the seat. "Listen here, podna. You need to learn to ride over yonder, leave me to my drivin'." He reaches out a weathered hand, scratches Jake behind the ears.

No, there wasn't a way in the world he was gonna turn the governor down, or that Martha was gonna ask him to.

You can't escape your antecedents.

ACKNOWLEDGMENTS

I just want to say thank you . . .

To those who helped: Tom Bacon, Marian Brown, John Clutterbuck, Scott Doyle of www.firearmsid.com, Dan Dubrowski, Paul Erhardt, Tom Falus, Sharon Fiffer, Anita Groves, Karl Hime, Chris Hughes, Hasty Johnson, George Lancaster, Dan MacEachron, Carl Mertz, Dr. Karl Petrokovics, Michael Skelton, Randy Smart, Mike Toellner, and Andrew Weber and to the people of Hines for your indulgence and support.

To those who labor: my original Web site designer, Ann Kifer, and her buddies at the Hill Group; my publicist and Web maven, Maggie Griffin; my editor, Kelley Ragland, and her assistant, Carly Einstein; my agent, Philip Spitzer, and his assistant, Lukas Ortiz; and all the bookstore owners who have made me feel welcome in their shops and who have been kind enough to speak well of a book of mine.

To three really special people: Brenda de Graffenried, Debbie Emory, and Debbie Goodykoontz, who get me from place to place and handle a lot of stuff behind the scenes and always do it with a smile.

And to that lady who is in fact essential, my *sine qua non,* Paulette Toellner Hime.

In fairness I should also mention that there is a Prince de Condé Hotel on the Rue de Seine, which, so far as I know, has never suffered from an act of arson.